THE DEMI-MONDE

by Rod Rees

Books in the Demi-Monde Saga

The Demi-Monde
The Shadow Wars

THE DEMI-MONDE

ROD REES

wm

WILLIAM MORROW
An Imprint of HarperCollinsPublishers

THE DEMI-MONDE. Copyright © 2010, 2012 by Rod Rees. All rights reserved. Printed in the United States of America. No part of this book may be used or reproduced in any manner whatsoever without written permission except in the case of brief quotations embodied in critical articles and reviews. For information address HarperCollins Publishers, 10 East 53rd Street, New York, NY 10022.

HarperCollins books may be purchased for educational, business, or sales promotional use. For information please write: Special Markets Department, HarperCollins Publishers, 10 East 53rd Street, New York, NY 10022.

This book was first published under the title *The Demi-Monde: Winter* in Great Britain in 2010 by Quercus Books, London, and in 2012 by William Morrow, an imprint of HarperCollins Publishers.

FIRST WILLIAM MORROW PAPERBACK EDITION PUBLISHED 2012.

The Library of Congress has cataloged the hardcover edition as follows:

Rees, Rod.
    The demi-monde : winter / Rod Rees. — 1st U.S. ed.
        p. cm.
ISBN 978-0-06-207034-0
1. Virtual reality—Fiction. I. Title.
    PR6118.E57D46 2011
    823'.92—dc22

2011005754

ISBN 978-0-06-221081-4 (pbk.)

12 13 14 15 16 OV/RRD 10 9 8 7 6 5 4 3 2 1

CONTENTS

Map of the Demi-Monde / vii

The Demi-Monde
THE NOVEL

Prologue / 1

**Part One
Auditioning / 15**

**Part Two
Entrance / 103**

**Part Three
Warsaw / 275**

**Part Four
Spring Eve / 453**

Epilogue / 504

The Demi-Monde
Glossary of Terms and Slang / 506

Demi-Monde (noun):
1. a subclass of society whose members embrace a decadent lifestyle and evince loose morals;
2. a shadow world where the norms of civilized behavior have been abandoned;
3. an MMP simulation platformed on the ABBA quantum computer and utilizing ParaDigm Cyber-Research's Total Reality User Envelopment technology to re-create in a wholly realistic cyber-milieu the threat-ambiance and no-warning aspects of a high-intensity, deep-density, urban Asymmetric Warfare Environment;
4. hell.

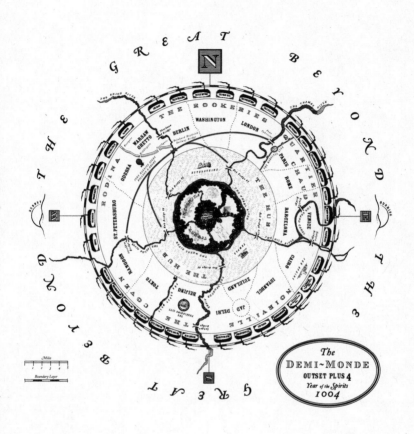

THE DEMI-MONDE

PROLOGUE

The Demi-Monde:
37th Day
of Winter, 1004

Norma ran. Picked up her skirts and ran as she had never run in her life. Ran as though the hounds of hell were at her heels.

Fuck it . . . the hounds of hell are at my heels.

And as she ran she heard a crackle of gunfire behind her, the sound of the shots ricocheting through the night-silent streets of London. The gunfire told her that Mata Hari and her Suffer-O-Gettes had kept their word. They had tried to delay those SS bastards for as long as they could. Suffer-O-Gettes died hard.

Run, Norma, run! Mata Hari had screamed at her as Clement's SS–Ordo Templi Aryanis thugs had smashed down the pub's door. And she *had* run. She couldn't—wouldn't—let the SS catch her.

Mad, evil bastards.

But she was running blind.

Snow-blind.

The snow was so thick that she could barely see a dozen strides in front of her, snow that the icy wind was whipping into her eyes, making them water with pain.

Angrily Norma shook her head, ordering herself to ignore the pain, ignore the cold, ignore the frosted numbness crawling along her fingers and her toes, ignore the protests of her mutinous body. Ordered herself to ignore everything but the need to put as much distance between herself and the animals chasing her as was humanly possible.

She had to forget everything but the need to run. Forget that duplicitous, scheming, treacherous, underhanded, slimy son of a bitch Burlesque Bandstand.

Bastard.

She ran until her heart pounded in her chest, until her legs throbbed with pain, until her lungs felt as though they were on fire. She ran hard, keeping, as best she could, to the ruts in the road left by the rubber-covered wheels of a steamer, desperately trying not to leave tracks in the freshly fallen snow. Tracks they could follow.

The sound of a hunting horn echoed behind her ... maybe only a few streets behind her. The SS had shaken off the Suffer-O-Gettes. Now the Daemon Hunt was on in earnest.

Run, Norma, run!

Yes, now she was sure she could hear them. She could hear the smash of the gang's hobnailed boots snapping through the tight streets and along the narrow alleys that made up the Rookeries. She could hear the bellowed shouts of that hideous, hideous man— boy, rather—Archie Clement and the screams of his pack of Blood Hounders as he flogged them in pursuit.

The leather soles of her boots skidded on cobbles patinaed by a slick coating of snow, sending her tumbling into the fetid gutter, sending her sliding on her knees and on her outspread hands. The pain as the stones ripped through her skin was excruciating, but driven by adrenaline and the knowledge of the fate that awaited her if she was captured, without even pausing to inspect the damage to her body she rose to her feet and began to hobble on, sobbing with pain, desperation and terror.

Get a grip, Norma.

This was no time for weakness. Not now that she was cut. Cuts seeped blood. The Hounders would just love that. It'd drive them crazy . . . blood-crazy. Now they'd have her spoor for sure.

As though in reply she heard the mournful howl of a Hounder as it picked up the scent of her blood.

Run. Don't give up.

Maybe the snow would cover her tracks . . . cover her blood trail.

Please, please, snow harder.

She slowed at the corner of the street, trying to get her bearings, trying to catch her breath. For a gasping instant she looked around to check the street signs. So near: she was only three blocks away from the Thames . . . from freedom. Just another couple of hundred yards along the backstreets shadowing Regent Street and she'd be out of the Rookeries. Just three more blocks and she'd be able to see the Awful Tower.

Her breath was shorter now, her body rippling, trembling uncontrollably with cold and exhaustion. There was another eddy of wind and she felt the sleet cut across her face, felt the cold scythe through the thin cotton of her blouse. She had never been so cold in all her life. When she had made her escape from the Prancing Pig there hadn't been time to search for a coat or a hat or a pair of gloves.

There had just been time to run.

If she didn't get out of the snow soon she'd be finished. Frozen to death.

Concentrate.

This wasn't a computer game. Not anymore. She wasn't just a player. Not anymore. Now she was one of the Kept. Now she was a Demi-Mondian.

Damn it all, concentrate, Norma. Die in the Demi-Monde and you die in the Real World.

Another plaintive howl from a Hounder. They were getting closer.

She pushed herself forward, slipped on the icy cobbles and caromed painfully against a wall, tearing the shoulder of her blouse and scraping skin from her arm.

Ignore it.

But she couldn't. The pain and the cold and the tiredness overcame her desperation. She did her best to keep moving but she was spent.

Now all she had the strength to do was limp as fast as she was able toward the sanctuary of the French Sector. Just get to the Pons Fabricius . . . once across the Thames she'd be in Paris, only minutes away from the Portal.

Please, God . . .

She could smell the river, that sweet, sickly stew of ships, slaves and sewage. So close. And it was snowing even harder now. Wonderful, glorious snow, snow that would cover her tracks.

Still the thought nagged at her that this was all nonsense. This couldn't—shouldn't—be happening. It seemed impossible for her to have been caught up in such a terrifying surreality . . . in such a terrifying *reality*. Yeah, the Demi-Monde was real all right. Too fucking real. The pain she was feeling was real. The cold was real. The fear was real.

As she stumbled along she threw a glance over her shoulder, peering into the dark, snow-shrouded streets of the Rookeries. She couldn't hear her pursuers anymore. Maybe she'd lost them? Maybe they'd abandoned the chase? Maybe her young legs had outrun theirs?

Fat chance.

They never gave up. No one wanted to go back to Crowley and

tell him they'd failed. Even Clement was scared of Crowley. No, they would hunt her down like the pack of rabid dogs they were. And she knew she wouldn't be able to go much further. She was finished, defeated by the cold. She had to find somewhere to hide.

Looking around she saw, ten feet on from where she was standing, the entrance to a narrow alleyway, an alleyway without streetlights, its darkness so complete that no one, not even Clement, would be able to find her in there. Maybe he wouldn't even *want* to follow her in there. No one knew what was hidden in the shadows of the Demi-Monde, the shadows hiding the horrible things that crept out of the Hub.

Terrific.

Norma limped painfully toward the beckoning darkness and dodged down the black, rancid alley. Skirting along the twisted tenement walls that crowded in on her—trying to ignore the unspeakable things that scuttled about in the shadows—Norma found a dark doorway that offered a semblance of safety.

Hidden there, she stood for a moment bent over, hands on knees, trying to catch her breath, trying to pant new energy into her cold, aching body, all the time trying to still her sobbing, trying to stay quiet. She had to remain quiet.

Please don't let them hear me.

Norma shook her head, trying to clear it. This was wrong . . . what she was feeling . . . what she was enduring . . . wrong. She was an eighteen-year-old girl and this, she kept reminding herself, was just a computer simulation. Eighteen-year-old girls didn't get hurt or feel pain and panic in make-believe worlds. Even make-believe worlds as made-believable as the Demi-Monde.

You didn't feel fear playing a computer game, not horrible gut-wrenching, stomach-churning fear like this. It was wrong. Totally, totally wrong. If what they—they?—were putting her through was deliberate, it was sadistic.

Bastards.

She looked around. It was pitch-dark, the only illumination provided by the light seeping out from behind a half-open door at the end of the cobbled alley, the light spilling onto the facing wall to show the graffiti crawling over the scarred brickwork.

The Only Good Nuju is a Dead Nuju

Welcome to the Demi-Monde.

She tried to relax. The alley was a good place to hide. Except . . . except that it was a dead end. She was trapped. She felt the bilious taste of panic rising up in her throat. Her head swam and she thought she would faint from cold, exhaustion and sheer unadulterated terror. Maybe she was ill. What did the prof call it . . . ill-ucinating?

Ill-ucinating.

A condition caused by the confusion of Realities, often experienced by inveterate players of hyper-realistic computer simulations such as the Demi-Monde. The prof had a lot to answer for.

Bastard.

When she told her father what she'd been through there'd be hell to pay. He'd go ballistic. The cyber-torturing of his daughter wasn't something the president of the United States would be big on. The things she'd tell her father when she got back.

If she got back.

She heard the scrape of boot heels on cobbles. She pressed back into the darkness, hardly daring to breathe, motionless apart from the shivers of cold rippling over her flesh. She clenched her jaw tight shut, trying to stop her teeth chattering.

A shout, the voice hard and merciless but at the same time childish . . . Clement's voice. She should have known Clement would be the one leading the hunt. Lunatic he might be but he was smarter than all of them. It would be his Hounders who had followed the bloody tracks she'd left in her wake.

Hounders: horrible, horrible things.

She could hear orders being shouted, could hear the snapped replies from Clement's SS troopers. She hated the SS. The SS were the most fanatical of the fanatical. They never questioned orders. They were the true believers. They were the ones charged with the protection of the ForthRight's black soul and with enforcing the perverted creed of UnFunDaMentalism. They were the ones responsible for safeguarding the Demi-Monde from Daemons . . . Daemons like Norma.

She heard an urgent and heated conversation coming to her from around the corner of the alleyway. Maybe they'd lost her? Maybe the snow had come in the nick of time? She edged her head out of her doorway, trying to make out what was being said. The conversation stopped, only the whimpering of a Hounder signaling that Clement's hunting party was still nearby. The silence seemed oppressive . . . threatening. Her body was taut with panic: she was ready to run again. Run for her life.

Run where?

The pain as the cane lashed across her knee was indescribable; it smashed up through her body, paralyzing her in shock.

Norma had never imagined that the human body could have so much suffering inflicted upon it. The pain was so bad that she didn't even scream or cry out: she was stunned into a gagging silence, her eyes bleeding tears of agony, her right leg twitching in numbed torment. Her ruined knee buckled and she sank to the cobbles.

She must have blacked out. When she came to, she found herself lying in a pool of icy water. A dozen or so men moved to circle her, their shadowed faces peering down. She felt all hope drain out of her: even in the Demi-Monde the two men who stood at the front of the pack were known as the hardest and the cruelest of them all.

Singularities.

They were men without pity, without conscience and without remorse. Men who could laugh even as they slaughtered the innocent and the helpless: psychopaths.

Bastards.

Evil, evil bastards.

Norma knew the two men who stood over her. Su Xiaoxiao had warned her about them when she had first entered the Demi-Monde. Told her to avoid them. Told her they represented the more dangerous of the Dupes that populated this cyber-world, warned her that Matthew Hopkins was Clement's creature and Clement was, in turn, the unthinking disciple of His Holiness Comrade Crowley.

Automatically, instinctively, the would-be politician cowering inside Norma's bruised and bloodied body studied the two men. She'd always been fascinated by psychopaths, the most fatally flawed of men, whose souls were blistered and hardened by hatred and wickedness, and it was this fascination that Crowley had used as bait to lure her into the Demi-Monde. But it was one thing to read textbooks and write papers on the genesis, on the diagnosis and on the treatment of psychotics; it was quite another to look such evil full in the face. Their eyes were empty, crystal-cold and shark-black. They were eyes that contained no humanity and no forgiveness.

Doll's eyes.

Suddenly one of the Blood Hounders sprang at Norma, the beast obviously incensed by the smell of blood coming from her tattered knees. Clement beat at the creature with the leather switch he carried. "Back, damn your eyes, you spawn of Loki," he snarled, thrashing the Hounder until the pain of the whipping exceeded the creature's bloodlust and it cowered back. "You," he growled at the Hounder's handler, "hold the thing fast or by ABBA ah'll knout you to ribbons and rip out your eyes."

Terrified by the venom in the boy's voice, the handler hauled on the rope tethered to the Hounder's collar and pulled the hideous creature away from Norma. She hated Hounders. Half-man, half-animal, they were the obscene creation of Archie Clement, who had abducted perfumiers from the Quartier Chaud, and by blinding and deafening them, by ripping out their tongues and chopping off their fingers, he had removed all their senses but one: their sense of smell. Then he had stoked their bloodlust to a frenzy. The result was that these monsters could smell a single drop of blood at a hundred yards. Clement used Hounders to track Daemons. Daemons like Norma.

Clement stepped forward to stand over her as she lay shivering on the cobbles.

Little Archie Clement, who in the Real World had ridden for the Confederacy under Bloody Bill Anderson, who had fallen into the habit of scalping all the men, women and children he murdered as he rampaged through the South, and who was friend and partner in crime to Jesse James.

Even if she hadn't been forewarned by Su Xiaoxiao that his boyishness and his wide-eyed innocence masked a spirit so twisted and bent that he could hardly be called human, she would have known to avoid him. Yes . . . though small, almost frail-looking, Clement had such a hateful aura about him that even the ferocious Beria was careful in his presence.

Clement took off his peaked cap and wiped his brow with his sleeve. It still shocked Norma how real Demi-Mondians were, how flawlessly these Dupes had been rendered. No, that wasn't right: it was the very fact that they *weren't* flawless that made them so perfect. Little things . . . like the mud-flecked slush that splattered the black of the boy's uniform; how down-at-heel his boots were; how spittle sprayed from his mouth whenever he spoke; and how wonderfully contrived was his sweet, noxious body odor that perfumed the still air of the Demi-Monde, an odor that reeked of Solution, tobacco and a negligent attitude to washing.

The perverted genius of the Demi-Monde was in the detail. Loki was in the detail. ABBA was in the detail.

And ABBA was God in the Demi-Monde.

Clement smiled down at Norma, a smile that displayed his tobacco-blackened teeth and sucked all the hope out of her soul. He gave her an exploratory prod with the toe of his boot. "You best examine the wench real careful, Witchfinder," he ordered in his piping, adolescent voice. "Ah need to be certain sure that she is who we think she is. Far as ah can see she ain't sporting horns or a tail, like ah'm told Daemons are wont to do. So test her close, Witchfinder; ah'll have no mistakes on mah watch."

Matthew Hopkins—the Witchfinder—used his cane to point to the Celtic cross Norma had tattooed on her shoulder. "See, Comrade Colonel, she wears Loki's Mark and that is as sure a sign as any that she be a witch. And note how she has colored her hair black and made many strange and unholy perforations in her face. Only those in thrall to Loki mutilate themselves in such a Lilithian way." He stooped down beside Norma and taking her chin roughly in his callused fingers turned her face toward the light.

"And look you too, Comrade Colonel, sir, she openly flaunts her otherworldliness with the profane baubles she wears." The Witchfinder wrenched off the "I ♥ Blood" necklace Norma was wearing, sending the glass beads skittering over the frost-hard cobbles.

The Witchfinder chuckled. "Indeed . . . 'tis the Daemon, Comrade Colonel; that I can say with all assurance. The Daemon disports itself in the form of the wench I saw in the Prancing Pig not yet an hour ago when she did dance in a most lewd and lascivious manner, in flagrant disregard of the teachings of UnFunDaMentalism." He ran a hand through Norma's hair, his thick, filthy fingers fondling her scalp in a truly repulsive manner. "You're right though, Comrade Colonel Clement, sir: the Daemon has no horns. But that don't signify, these Daemons being masters and mistresses of deceit." He moved his hand down to her knee and began to slide her skirt up over her legs. He looked up at Clement and licked his lips. "Shall I examine this creature of Loki to see if it possesses a tail, Comrade Colonel?"

Please, God, don't let him touch me.

Clement gave an embarrassed laugh. Like many men in the ForthRight he was awkward around women: UnFunDaMentalism wasn't big on promoting caring, loving relationships between men and women. "Ah think you oughtta give that a go-by, Witchfinder. You start delving under them calicos there's no telling what you might find snapping at your fingers."

"As you will, Comrade Colonel, but see she seeps blood from the wounds on her knees. Only Daemons from the blackest depths of Hel can do that."

Clement studied the cuts for a moment then slowly raised his gaze until his mad eyes were staring straight into Norma's. "Got you, ain't we, Daemon? You led me and mah crew a merry dance, so you did." He gave her another kick. "But Daemon though you be, you couldn't bamboozle Colonel Archie Clement."

Norma glared courageously back. Weakness and fearfulness were not virtues celebrated in the Demi-Monde: here strength, courage and viciousness were vital talents in the everyday task of surviving. But her playacting had little effect on Clement: all she saw staring back at her was insanity. The man was certifiably nuts.

"See there, Comrade Colonel," observed the Witchfinder, "how this Daemon declines to lower her gaze as a respectable female should. And see how she openly flaunts her charms and her female allure. She seeks to beguile us, to lead our thoughts to the carnal and to the unholy. Is it not so, Comrade Colonel?"

"Sure is, Witchfinder, sure is. Church tells us that these here Daemons are real mischievous, them being sent to the Demi-Monde by Loki to torment and tempt us poor souls who labor to do

ABBA's work." Clement pointed to Norma's ruined knees. "Know this, Daemon, despite your cunning form and your saucy smile, your body betrays you. Ah knows you for the trickster you is, a lickspittle to that most insidious of masters, Loki." He paused to spit a wad of tobacco into the gutter. "But even with your devilish arts and your seductive wiles, you couldn't outsmart Archie Clement. No, sirree; battling the forces of Loki is the sacred responsibility of me and mah boys in the SS, the Soldiers of Spiritualism. You should know ABBA has commanded us to use all our strength to uproot from the Demi-Monde the pernicious arts of sorcery and malefice invented by Loki and propagated by Daemons such as you."

The Witchfinder came to stand beside Clement. Hopkins had obviously enjoyed the hunt; his tight black SS uniform was stained with sweat and excitement. "I trust you will remember my assistance in the capturing of the Daemon, Colonel Clement, sir, when you speak with His Holiness Comrade Crowley. 'Twas my agent, Burlesque Bandstand, who sent us word of her manifestation."

"Sure will, Witchfinder, this was a mighty smart piece of work." Clement took a swig from a silver flask he conjured from a pocket in his coat. "And ah don't doubt that you'll be rewarded mighty well. His Holiness ain't one to be miserly when it comes to paying for a job well done." He offered the flask to the Witchfinder. "Here, try a shot of Solution to put some warmth back in your bones."

The Witchfinder took a long pull on the flask. "My reward shall be the destruction of the Daemons who torment the ForthRight, and those foul and HerEtical Sisters of Suffer-O-Gettism who serve the witch Jeanne Dark." He made the sign of the Valknut—the sign of the three interlocked triangles that was the symbol of the Party, of the ForthRight and of UnFunDaMentalism—across his chest to ward off the evil evoked by pronouncing Dark's name. "That and the destruction of those conniving vermin, the nuJus and the damnable Shade zadniks who call themselves Blood Brothers."

Norma shivered, but not through cold. There was something fanatical in the way Hopkins talked. His hatred of anybody he did not perceive to be white or male bordered on mania. No wonder the racist, sexist son of a bitch had risen so far and so fast in the Party.

UnFunDaMentalism celebrated hatred.

Clement pulled his cloak tight around his slim shoulders; he was obviously beginning to feel the cold. "Well, enough of this jawing, Witchfinder, let's be away with this Daemon before any of her ilk come a-galloping to her rescue. The Red Gold pumping in her veins is worth a wonderment of Blood Money. She'd make a grand prize for the Zulus or the Chinks."

"It might be better to finish her now," said the Witchfinder quietly.

Once again Archie Clement hawked and spat into the gutter. "No, Witchfinder, ah have been ordered by His Holiness Comrade Crowley to return with the Daemon alive, so best we be away before the crows start to circle. Chances are that witch Mata Hari will be all of a lather to rescue the Daemon."

The Witchfinder saluted. "As you will, Comrade Colonel, sir." He turned and stabbed a grimy finger toward two of his men. "You there, take up the Daemon, and be sharp about it. And shut your ears to her blabbing. This one is a temptress, adept in the Lilithian skills that ensnare the hearts and minds of the unwary and of the weak." The Witchfinder paused as though struck by a thought. "Indeed, it may be best if the Daemon was rendered dumb." He stepped forward; Norma saw him twirl his cane in the air and slam the knobbled handle hard against the side of her head. She felt a searing pain, then everything went black.

Part I
AUDITIONING

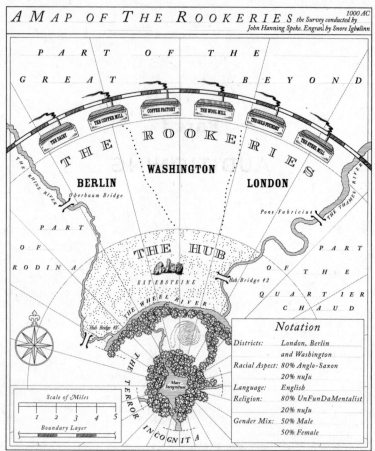

A MAP OF THE ROOKERIES — *the Survey conducted by John Hanning Speke. Engrav'd by Snore Igbolinn.* 1000 AC

PART OF THE
GREAT BEYOND

THE ROOKERIES

THE DAIRY · THE COPPER MILL · COFFEE FACTORY · THE WOOL MILL · THE GOLD FOUNDRY · THE STEEL MILL

WASHINGTON

BERLIN

LONDON

THE RHINE RIVER

Oberbaum Bridge

Pons Fabricius

THE THAMES RIVER

PART OF RODINA

THE HUB

EXTERSTEINE

PART OF THE QUARTIER CHAUD

Hub Bridge #2

THE WHEEL RIVER

Hub Bridge #3

Mare Incognitum

THE TERROR INCOGNITA

Notation

Districts:	London, Berlin and Washington
Racial Aspect:	80% Anglo-Saxon 20% nuJu
Language:	English
Religion:	80% UnFunDaMentalist 20% nuJu
Gender Mix:	50% Male 50% Female

Scale of Miles
1 2 3 4 5
Boundary Layer

Reproduced by kind permission of Snore Igbolinn, Cartographer-General to the Court of His HimPerial Majesty, Shaka Zulu

MAP OF THE ROOKERIES.

PLATE 1

The Real World:
June 12, 2018

The Demi-Monde® is the first simulation product ever to be platformed on and operated by the ABBA quantum computer. ABBA is a Quanputer-based system developed and operated by ParaDigm CyberResearch Limited. ABBA, by utilizing an Invent-TenN® Gravitational Condenser incorporating an Etirovac Field Suppressor®, is the only computer to achieve a full SupaUnPositioned/DisEntangled Cyber Ambiance. As a consequence ABBA is capable of prodigiously rapid analysis (a fully tethered 30 yottaQuFlops) to give the bioNeural-kinetic engineers at ParaDigm access to almost unlimited processing power.

—The Demi-Monde® Product Description Manual: June 14, 2013

Tap, tap, tap, went the general's pencil.

Jeez, that's a habit that could get right up your ass.

The guy was obviously mega-tense, which was odd because it was Ella who was being interviewed for the gig. It was Ella who had exactly twelve dollars in her pocket and rent of fifty dollars due tomorrow. It was Ella who would be living on air pie for the rest of the week.

And more to the point it was the general who was asking all the questions. But oddly he was the one who was uptight. So uptight that by Ella's reckoning if she shoved coal up his ass, a week later the guy would be shitting diamonds.

Tap, tap, tap.

The oracle spoke. "You sing, Miss Thomas . . . ?"

Dumb Question #1.

It was a weird thing to ask, decided Ella, especially as singing was all she had been doing for the last week. That and being tested all ways and sideways. Tested physically and tested mentally. She had had blood tests, genetic tests, sight tests, hearing tests, initiative tests, aptitude tests, fitness tests, Rorschach tests, IQ tests, MBTI tests and that test the doctor had done with the endoscope that she didn't really wanna think about. Most of all she had had her patience tested.

But she'd made it through to this, the last interview. She was so close to success she could smell it. Ella Thomas took a long steadying breath; now was not the time to freak or to make waves.

Gotta stay cool.

This might have been the weirdest audition she'd ever been through and it sure as hell had been the most frustrating, but she needed the gig.

Boy, she really, really needed the gig.

The rent was due tomorrow.

She gave the general her sweetest smile and batted her big brown eyes. "Yeah, I sing, General. The captain over there has been listening to me doing that all week."

All week . . .

They'd warned her that the army's recruiting procedures, in the wake of 9/11 and 12/12 and all the other terrorist outrages, were protracted and rigorous but this was ridiculous. If they hadn't been paying her to undergo the battery of auditions and the multitude of other checks she'd have cut bait a long time ago.

Tap, tap, tap.

Ella gave the general an impish grin. "Would you like to hear me?"

The general shook his head. As he did so his perfectly coiffed gray hair didn't move. He had probably ordered it not to move; the general looked like the sort of guy who when he ordered something done expected it to be done. "That won't be necessary, Miss Thomas. Captain Sanderson is the U.S. Army's expert on all things musical."

The general's eyes drifted back to the report positioned exactly square in the middle of his immaculate desk.

"Do you sing jazz, Miss Thomas?" he asked.

Dumb Question #2.

Of course I sing jazz.

It was just that nobody wanted her to sing jazz. Not anymore. Jazz was old-school. Jazz was so unhip it had a limp. Maybe, Ella wondered, this general character dug all the old stuff? He sure looked antique enough but somehow he seemed a mite too uptight and buttoned-down to be a jazzer.

Nah . . .

Ella couldn't see him in a beret and bebop glasses ready to fall in and dig the happenings.

"Yeah, I sing jazz. Jazz is my first love. My dad was a really neat horn player so he taught me everything there is to know about jazz. So yeah, General, I sing jazz, but mainly in the shower. There ain't a lot of interest."

Captain Sanderson intervened. "Miss Thomas has a wonderful voice, sir, with a good range and an interesting timbre. Her timing is excellent. I think Miss Thomas will make a fine jazz singer."

Ella preened and shot the captain a smile. She liked compliments; she liked good-looking guys like the captain telling her she had a keen voice. And now that she thought about it she realized that the captain *was* cute, albeit in a tightly wrapped, cramped and stamped kinda way. She wasn't big on crew cuts.

The general nodded his understanding, then went back to the silent perusal of Ella's file. "The health checks seem satisfactory," he mused to no one in particular. He looked up and studied her for several silent seconds. "And she's certainly pretty enough."

It might have been a compliment but the way he said it made her feel like a cow at market. People didn't talk about other people in such an offhand way. It wasn't polite. Anyway, she wasn't "pretty," she was more than just "pretty"; she was tall and slim and beautiful. Eat your heart out, Halle Berry.

"And she *is* an African-American," observed the general absentmindedly.

What does that have to do with the price of beans? Haven't these guys heard of racial discrimination?

"Miss Thomas is in first-class physical condition and, as you rightly observe, she has the correct racial antecedents," agreed the captain, who made it sound as though they were discussing a secondhand car. "The rigors of the Demi-Monde shouldn't pose her any problems."

Demi-Monde? wondered Ella. *Weird name for a club.*

"Psychological assessment?"

"Excellent," confirmed the captain. "Her profile is an almost perfect match for the psychological template developed by PsychOps. She has a robust psyche, is flexible minded and quite pragmatic. Phlegmatic, I suppose the word is. Phlegmatic with just a dash of rebelliousness."

Phlegmatic?

Now there was a word Ella didn't hear every day. That was a ten-dollar word and she went to a two-bit school. To the guys she hung with "phlegmatic" was what you did when you spat on the sidewalk. She flicked through her synonyms. Phlegmatic, a.k.a. cool.

Yeah, she was cool. So cool she was straight from the freezer, man.

"Miss Thomas has almost optimum levels of both serotonin receptors and p-eleven . . . she should have no difficulty in coping with the stress levels extant in the Demi-Monde. She also scored very highly in both the leadership and the initiative tests . . . very highly."

Yeah, if the army ever wanted someone to organize the building of a raft from a couple of old oil drums, some driftwood and a length of rope and use it to float across a river then Ella was their girl.

The things they'd made her do over the past week.

Ella looked to check out the two men who were discussing her in such an impersonal way but neither of them met her gaze. She had the distinct impression that they had started to talk around her, as though she wasn't there with them in the room. It took an effort to still a feeling of irritation. She took another deep breath, reminding herself as she did of how much she needed the gig.

The rent was due tomorrow.

"She also scored well in the IQ tests," added the captain encouragingly. "*Very* well. At the upper end of the top quartile."

The general looked up from the report and spent several long seconds silently examining Ella. He didn't say a word; it was as though he was reluctant to speak. Finally he let out a long, doleful sigh and turned to the captain. "Miss Thomas is your preferred candidate? She is *very* young, only eighteen last birthday."

"Miss Thomas is old beyond her years, sir. She's by far the most impressive of all the candidates, and her resemblance to Professor Bole's Dupe is uncanny."

She'd gotten the gig!

Though this Dupe shit wasn't strumming her strings.

The captain noted her confusion. "A Dupe is our term for a cyber-duplicate of a real person." The general looked across the desk toward Ella, his expression hugely serious; the shadows under his eyes seemed suddenly to have gotten deeper and darker.

There was another long silence. Finally, reluctantly, he spoke. "Miss Thomas . . . how would you like to earn a million dollars?"

2

The Demi-Monde: 40th Day of Winter, 1004

UnFunDaMentalism *is an array of political, racial, metaPhysical, sexual and social ideas and philosophies relating to the purification of the Demi-Mondian race, the triumph of the Aryan people and the rehabilitation of the semi-mythological Pre-Folk. Adopted as the state religion of the ForthRight, the ultimate aim of UnFunDaMentalism is, by a process of selective breeding and measured culling, to eliminate the contamination of the UnderMentionable races from the Demi-Monde's Aryan stock (Aryans are generally considered to be the Anglo-Slavic races) and by doing so to return the Aryan people to the racial perfection they possessed before their ancestors—the Pre-Folk—fell from ABBA's Grace.*

—RELIGIONS OF THE DEMI-MONDE, OTTO WEININGER,

UNIVERSITY OF BERLIN PUBLICATIONS

Comrade Commissar Dashwood made a point of arriving at his ministry before seven. He knew that only by working fourteen hours a day would he be able to ensure that the deadline for the building of the new railway lines would be met. And as Comrade Leader Heydrich had decreed that the railway lines were vital to the success of the ForthRight's imminent invasion of the Coven, missing the deadline would make it very much a *dead* line: Comrade Leader Heydrich rewarded failure in a very uncompromising fashion.

But even as the slave driver brought his steamer to a wheezing halt in front of the Ministry building, Dashwood knew that there was something unexpected taking place at the Ministry of Transport, that today wasn't going to be a normal day. He had an unmistakable feeling in his water that signaled him to be extra-careful.

It might have been that the Militia officers patrolling the top of the steps leading to the Ministry's great double doors were decidedly less sleepy than they usually were at this time of the morning. It might have been that their salute was a trifle crisper and more enthusiastic than he was used to. Tiny things but important— important to notice, that is, if you wanted to stay alive in the internecine bedlam that was the ForthRight.

Oh, please don't let it be another purge. Surely enough of us have died already?

As Dashwood strode imperiously across the great marble floor of the Ministry he tried to distract himself from these disturbing thoughts by adding up all those who had died in the Cleansing.

A hundred thousand? Two hundred thousand?

No . . . the Party had arrested and executed nearly a quarter of a million persons after the Troubles, accusing them of being Royalists, Counter-Revolutionaries and Enemies of the People and sending them (Dashwood was disgusted that it had been he who had cravenly signed the transportation dockets) to the Warsaw Ghetto and to the death camps in the Hub. Overnight—and the arrests had always been made at night or when thick smog had enveloped the Rookeries—Dashwood had seen many of his friends, his relatives and members of the Court disappear into the Checkya's black-painted steamers, never to be seen again.

And he had been complicit in their destruction.

That had been the price the Party had demanded for his survival and that of his family: complicity in mass murder. Maybe now it was his turn to be purged? As he walked through the Ministry he racked his mind, trying to identify what infraction he might have committed that would have persuaded Beria—the head of the ForthRight's dreaded secret police, the Checkya—to sign his death warrant. He had been so very careful.

He stopped for an instant.

Maybe Trixiebell . . .

Oh please, not Trixiebell. Not my precious little Trixie.

For a second he was tempted to turn on his heel and scuttle off home, collect Trixie, jump on a barge heading for the Hub and seek exile in . . . in where exactly? The sad truth was that there was nowhere to run to in the Demi-Monde.

The Checkya had a long reach, and, from what he had heard yesterday at the PolitBuro meeting, by the Summer the ForthRight Army would have conquered the Coven and would, in all probability, be turning its malignant attention toward the Quartier Chaud. Maybe he and Trixie should try NoirVille? Somehow though he didn't think Trixie was cut out for a life in purdah. HimPerialism was a harsh regime and very antagonistic toward women, especially independently minded women like Trixie. No, there was nowhere to run to, and, anyway, he had other things to do, other things to organize.

Dashwood stopped before the great oak door of his office and took a moment to brush a few errant steamer cinders from his immaculate suit. He doffed his top hat, took the door's handle in a firm grasp and entered. When he saw the man who was sitting behind his desk, idly smoking a cigarette and very systematically scanning his correspondence, all his worst fears were realized.

"Ah, Comrade Commissar Dashwood . . . at last. I am *royally* blessed."

Dashwood fidgeted uncomfortably under Beria's scrutiny. The

rather feeble joke Beria had made—a reference to Dashwood's aristocratic lineage; he had once been *Baron* Dashwood—was one he would do well to mark. Beria's purge of the aristocracy after the Troubles had condemned almost all of those with any hint of a royal pedigree—like Dashwood—to a painful death.

Desperately he tried to compose himself. Automatically he raised his forearm to give the Party salute. "Two Sectors Forged as One," he intoned.

Beria flipped an arm casually in response and then made a great show of checking his watch. "Your secretary informed me you would be at your office at seven. It is now three minutes past: I trust, Comrade Commissar, this is not a demonstration of the laxity with which you order the rest of the workings of your Ministry."

"No, Vice-Leader, Comrade Beria."

Vice-Leader: had there ever been a more appropriate title?

With a bleak smile Beria nodded him toward the guest chair stationed in front of the desk. As he sat down, Dashwood was suddenly aware of a presence behind him. He twisted around and saw the tall, saturnine figure of an army officer lurking in the corner.

"This is Captain Jan Dabrowski, a member of the Checkya," advised Beria idly.

The captain offered no salute; he just stood, cold and implacable, staring at Dashwood's neck. Dabrowski certainly looked the part of a secret policeman and Dashwood had absolutely no doubt that this Polish bastard—he was instantly identifiable as a Pole by his lapel flashes—would do whatever it was his master commanded, murder included.

"I had not been aware, Comrade Commissar," began Beria as he arranged Dashwood's desk stationery in a more precise fashion, "that you worked to such an undemanding schedule. A seven o'clock start—even on a Sunday—is decidedly remiss. We are, as you know, about to embark on the divinely ordained crusade to cleanse the

Demi-Monde of UnderMentionables, of the nuJu and Shade scum which contaminate our world, and to be successful Operation Barbarossa will require diligence and sacrifice by all Party members. The Party *demands* sacrifice and it behooves us, the upper echelon, to set an example. I myself am never at my office later than five in the morning; I would suggest you imitate my example."

"Yes, Vice-Leader."

Get on with it, you bastard.

"You are, after all, Comrade Commissar, one of the few survivors of the Court of that Arch-Imperialist and Oppressor of the People Henry Tudor. Anything less than total dedication to the Party and to Comrade Leader Heydrich could be interpreted as your having recidivist tendencies."

"Comrade Leader Heydrich should have no doubts as to my total and undying loyalty to the ForthRight and to the Party."

Beria slowly drew a handkerchief out of his sleeve, used it to shine his tiny spectacles and then dabbed it to his moist lips. "I am sure the Leader will be delighted to hear of your declaration of fealty, especially as I am here to present you with an opportunity to perform a great service to the Party and to the ForthRight."

Dashwood almost cried with relief; he wasn't going to be purged. Not today, anyway. "I am ready to perform any task that might be of service to our Leader."

"The Leader was impressed with you when you attended the PolitBuro meeting yesterday. You are held in high esteem by the Great Leader. Your expertise in logistics is second to none."

Which is probably why I haven't been purged, mused Dashwood. *Yet.*

Beria leaned back in his chair and gazed up at the ceiling as though in search of higher inspiration. "But unfortunately I cannot say the same thing about *all* your family. I had Captain Dabrowski attend a social given by Mrs. Albemarle two days ago with the express intention of making an evaluation of your daughter."

Dashwood stiffened in his chair and he felt a shiver run down his spine: in the ForthRight the word "evaluate" was replete with many meanings, none of them good.

"My daughter?" he asked as casually as he was able.

Beria didn't answer immediately. Instead he pulled a buff-colored file toward him, opened it and began slowly to turn each of the pages, studying them with theatrical exactitude. "For one so young, your daughter has amassed a commendably . . . or should that be *censurably* thick file." He shook his head in mock astonishment. "From what I can glean, the received wisdom is that your daughter has all the hallmarks of a future troublemaker, a girl with potentially disruptive HerEtical tendencies. It takes real counterrevolutionary zeal to be Censured before the age of sixteen."

"Trixiebell was very upset by the death of her mother . . ."

"But to have publicly lambasted her UnFunDaMentalist Ideology Tutor for teaching, and I quote here, 'twaddle' . . . Tut, tut, tut . . . this is not something one expects from the daughter of a high-ranking Party official. She also seems to have made a protest to the principal of her academy regarding the removal of references to a nonNix . . . an unperson."

Dashwood did his best to defend his daughter. "Trixiebell *was* chastised and attended a two-week Political Re-Education Camp last summer. I am sure she is now totally realigned both politically and ideologically."

"I wish I could share your confidence, Comrade Commissar. Young people today are such a trial. Unfortunately, the report of the captain here suggests that your daughter is still possessed of subversive inclinations."

Dashwood surreptitiously unclipped the holster that held his Colt revolver. If there was one thing he was certain of it was that he wouldn't let Trixie fall into the hands of this degenerate. He'd kill Beria first.

Beria picked up a likeness of Trixie from the file and studied it.

"Your daughter is very beautiful, Comrade Commissar." He licked his lips. "So slim, so blond, so athletic, but, unfortunately, so willful. It would be a tragedy, would it not, to lose such a perfect example of Aryan womanhood to the pernicious cant of HerEticalism? The captain has suspicions that your daughter could be a proto-RaTionalist . . . perhaps even a Suffer-O-Gette."

"Never."

"Perhaps that is a *little* excessive. But I must warn you, Comrade Commissar, that your daughter is on the slippery slope that leads to destruction. However, your daughter's teachers report that she is remarkably intelligent and a gifted debater." He took a pull on his cigarette, then blew a nimbus of smoke up to the ceiling. "I have a task that requires the services of a young girl . . . an intelligent young girl. It is a task that, if performed with diligence, will result in the rather compromising contents of this file"—here he closed the file and tossed it disdainfully into the wastebasket—"being consigned to oblivion."

"And what is this task?" asked Dashwood.

3

The Real World:
June 12, 2018

The Demi-Monde® remedies all of the shortcomings identified in previous-generation Asymmetrical Warfare Virtual Training Programs and achieves a fundamental upshifting of the Realism Quotient, of Inter-Sectorial/Inter-Personal DisHarmonic Measures, of Emotional and Psychological Impact Motifs, and of Battle Performance Indices (all of which dramatically and comprehensively exceed those specified in the Tender Document). In short the Demi-Monde® provides the perfect environment where U.S. Combat Personnel—be they neoFights, seasoned BattlePersonnel, NCOs, officers or squads—can be trained and evaluated in a cost-effective and performance-effective manner in AWE situations of the most accurate, convincing and challenging kind, and where Tactics, Techniques and Procedures may be subjected to Extreme Action Testing. It is estimated the Demi-Monde® will save the U.S. military over $4.35 billion in training, hospitalization, welfare and mortuary costs in each fiscal year.

—THE DEMI-MONDE® PRODUCT DESCRIPTION MANUAL, *JUNE 14, 2013*

W*ha?D'oh?*
    "I'm sorry?"
    "I asked, Miss Thomas, if you would like to earn a million dollars."

Ella took a deep breath as her natural suspicion kicked in. She eyed the general skeptically, simultaneously shooing away all those very pleasant thoughts about how good it would be not to have to worry about raising the money she needed to get to college, not to worry about paying the rent, not to worry about Billy, not to worry about all the things an eighteen-year-old girl shouldn't have to worry about.

"Are you on the level? You're not just blowing me shit . . . winding me up?"

The general nodded enthusiastically, which Ella found a little confusing. "Why yes, Miss Thomas, I am *absolutely* on the level. I am deadly serious. Never more so! So I ask again, would you like to earn a million dollars?"

Ella mulled things over, trying to stay calm. The general *looked* like he was playing the straight shooter. But . . .

"That, in the words of my law teacher, Mr. General, sir, is a non sequitur. Of course I'd like to earn a million dollars. The question is, though, what would I have to do to earn it?" She smiled. "Who would I have to kill?"

The general frowned and gave his head a vehement shake. "No one, Miss Thomas, absolutely no one. No, you won't have to kill anyone. What the U.S. government wants you to do is *save* someone. We need you to go on a rescue mission."

This whole conversation, Ella decided, was getting a little bent out of shape. She had come to Fort Jackson, the U.S. Army's InDoctrination and Training Command Center, a week ago to audition—so they had told her—as a singer in a band being put together to tour U.S. military bases around the world. And now, here she was, being asked if she wouldn't mind playing Ella TrueHeart and being offered a million bucks for her trouble. It didn't make sense. But a million bucks was a million bucks.

"You don't want me to sing?"

"Oh, yes, that is vital. The woman we send on this mission has *got* to be able to sing. The only way she'll be able to infiltrate the enemy's position is by being able to pose as a jazz singer."

This was getting out of hand; Ella decided to give the general a reality check. "Look, General, sir, I'm just an eighteen-year-old high school student who sings in the evening to try to scratch up enough dough to put herself through college. I'm an ordinary girl. You've gotta realize that the name Ella Thomas ain't some kind of secret identity. I ain't sitting here in your office as my alter ego. I'm not Wonder Woman or Supergirl in disguise. People like me don't do 'rescue missions.' People like me wait tables and run checkouts."

The general gave Ella what she guessed was his take on a reassuring smile. She wished he hadn't; it made him look constipated. "I sympathize with your confusion, Miss Thomas, and I apologize for springing this on you so suddenly, but you really are ideally qualified for this mission. We need a girl like you to play a role in a computer simulation."

"What . . . a computer game?"

"A very, very sophisticated computer game."

"Okay, General, I'm listening." This didn't sound so bad: playing a character in a computer game might be a lot of fun.

And a million bucks was a million bucks.

The general didn't say anything. It was as though he didn't quite know how to proceed with the conversation; he just gazed out of the window and absentmindedly tapped his pencil on the desk.

Tap, tap, tap.

Finally he gave Ella a rueful smile and continued. "Before I begin, Miss Thomas, I am obliged to tell you that this mission has a certain element of danger attached to it."

Ah, shit . . . good-bye, college.

What was the old adage? Anything that seemed too good to be true *was* too good to be true.

Ella swallowed hard, trying to mask her disappointment. She didn't quite know what to make of what this general person was saying. This whole interview was teetering on the surreal. All she was was a singer trying to raise enough money to get to college and to keep her kid brother out of trouble. She wasn't a heroine. She didn't do danger. But then all they were asking her to do was play some stupid computer game. She asked the obvious question. "How dangerous?"

"Very."

What sort of computer game is this?

"Oh come on, don't be coy, General, sir: what are the chances I'll get to spend the million?"

The general sat back in his chair and massaged the bridge of his nose. He was a man under a lot of pressure. "Okay . . . the chances of you surviving the mission are fifty-fifty: one chance in two. But the million would be paid regardless of the outcome," he added quickly. "In the event of your failing . . ."

"Failing," or as it's better known in less polite circles, "getting slotted."

" . . . the money will still be paid to your next of kin."

Oh great, so I get a one-way ticket to Slab Central and Billy gets the chance to see how quickly he can shove a million bucks' worth of coke up his nose.

Ella pushed the idea of dying to one side; she'd worry about that later. Like in seventy years.

"Why me? You've got the whole American armed forces to choose from. There must be someone in the army with a decent set of pipes; there must be someone who can sing jazz. There must be *someone* out there better qualified than me."

The general shuffled uncomfortably in his seat. "Oh, the army is full of jazz singers, Miss Thomas, but unfortunately not one of them can match the requirements necessary to fulfill this mission. That is why we have undertaken this somewhat protracted audition process.

You, Miss Thomas, are a very special young woman, combining as you do vocal ability, intelligence, beauty, physical and mental resilience and a specific racial aspect."

Oh, come on, General, let's call a spade a spade. I ain't got a "racial aspect." I've got a black skin.

"This combination of talents means you are the only person who can undertake this mission. You are unique."

Tap, tap, tap.

The general finally realized he'd been playing with the pencil and put it firmly down on his desk. "So, Miss Thomas, before I go any further, I need to know if you are interested in my proposition."

Really she had no option. The life she could see stretching before her could be summarized in the declension "broke, broker, brokest." She was just a dirt-poor nobody with a junkie for a brother, and prospects that were zero and falling. People like her didn't turn down the chance to pocket a million bucks.

"Oh, I'm interested, General, sir. In fact I've got a million bucks' worth of interest. But before I sign on the dotted line I'm gonna need a *lot* more information."

"Very well, Miss Thomas; what I am about to apprise you of is highly classified. Divulging any of this information to nonauthorized personnel is a criminal offense ... a very serious criminal offense, one for which you could go to prison for a very long time. Do you understand?"

It was Ella's turn to nod and at that instant it seemed as though the walls of the general's office had closed in on her. She had the distinct impression that things were about to get a whole lot heavier.

"Do you know what Asymmetric Warfare is, Miss Thomas?"

Dumb Question #3.

"Yeah, I had one once but the wheels fell off."

The general obviously didn't do humor; he simply ignored Ella's quip. "Asymmetric Warfare is the U.S. military's name for all those messy little conflicts that our country keeps finding itself fighting in hellish places like Afghanistan, Iraq and Pakistan. They are wars without rules and without honor and, to be blunt, they are wars that the U.S. Army isn't particularly good at fighting. When the U.S. military began to study its performance in Asymmetric Warfare Environments it discovered that its soldiers, especially its officers, weren't effective because they had no appreciation or understanding of what sort of war they would be fighting. So in order to prepare them better the U.S. Army InDoctrination and Training Command came up with the idea of creating a computer simulation that would let our combat personnel experience what was waiting for them in Peshawar and desperate places like it."

"The Demi-Monde?" Ella ventured.

"Got it in one, Miss Thomas. The Demi-Monde is the most sophisticated, the most complex and the most terrifying computer simulation ever devised. It's a simulation that re-creates the visceral anxiety and fear of being in an AWE—"

"An AWE?"

"An Asymmetric Warfare Environment. To play the Demi-Monde you have to be hardwired into it and the hardwiring creates a full sensory bypass: you *believe* you are in the Demi-Monde. For those in the Demi-Monde it is the *only* perceivable reality: neo-Fights—military trainees—are utterly enveloped in the simulation."

"That sounds scary."

"It is and it's meant to be. It's also vitally important if the training paradigm is to be as realistic as possible. AWEs are scary so the simulation of them has to be scary. With conventional computer simulations the player always knows that what they are involved in is just a game, they know that if they get uncomfortable with what's happening in the simulation all they have to do is press 'pause.' This isn't an option for Demi-Monde players."

The general took a sip of his coffee as he gathered his thoughts.

"But this isn't the only remarkable thing about the Demi-Monde. The U.S. military has employed computer simulations for training purposes before, but the problem with modeling Asymmetric Warfare Environments is that they are so unpredictable, so chaotic, so *nonlinear* as to make modeling them almost impossible. Contrarily, the very act of programming AWEs means that we impose rules on the simulations and hence make cyber-representations of AWEs predictable. It's a catch-22 situation: we need a computer program to replicate the anarchy of an Asymmetric Warfare Environment but the very act of programming makes it unanarchic."

Unanarchic? Is that a word?

"The solution, Miss Thomas, was to make the Demi-Monde program heuristic."

"Heuristic?" asked Ella cautiously.

This is getting to be, like, Big Words 101.

"It means 'self-taught': we provided the initial programming to get the Demi-Monde up and running, we defined the basics of the cyber-milieu and the formatting modality of the simulation, but after that the computer did its own thing. The computer changed— optimized—the function and the actions of the Dupes who populate the simulation to make their performance more arbitrary and, hence, more realistic. What this means is that from a simulation point of view immediately the Demi-Monde was activated how it performed and developed was out of our hands. The Demi-Monde is an unpredictable environment, which is perfect when describing an AWE."

"Look, I'm no nerd," admitted Ella, "but this sounds kinda freaky. And aren't you gonna have to use a pretty big computer?"

"The Demi-Monde is the first program to be run by ParaDigm CyberResearch's ABBA class of quantum computers."

"ABBA?"

"ABBA is a computer developed by the British. It is the most powerful computer ever devised. It has an almost unlimited processing power . . . enough to simulate sentience in each of the thirty million Dupes that populate the Demi-Monde."

"Thirty million? That's one hell of a lot of Dupes." Ella might not have been a fan of computer games but she knew enough to realize that even the biggest and the best only ever had a handful of cyber-characters interacting at any one time.

The general put a piece of gum in his mouth. "That's ABBA for you: it can handle thirty million Dupes at a snap," he said with a self-satisfied chomp. "But that's only part of the magic that is the Demi-Monde. All Dupes active in the Demi-Monde are modeled on real people: they are what we call the NowLive. ABBA simply dipped into DNA and other databases around the world and modeled the Dupes from the composite data it gleaned from them."

"These Dupes, your NowLive, are *real* people?"

"*Modeled* on real people, Miss Thomas. But we've gone further than that. We wanted the enemy leaders our neoFights would face to be as accurate as possible. Our research has shown us that the warlords who lead enemy forces in Asymmetric Warfare Environments tend to be psychotics . . . madmen . . . fanatics, the type of charismatic lunatics we in the military call Singularities. To make the Demi-Monde's cyber-milieu ultra-realistic we needed to have enemy leaders who replicated the cunning and the callousness of these Singularities. So we had ABBA select appropriate individuals from history, model them and then seed them into the Demi-Monde. These PreLived Singularities look, think and act just like their Real World equivalents did, and as their Real World equivalents were horrible, horrible people, so are their Dupes."

"Lemme get this right," said Ella carefully, "the people you fight in this Demi-Monde game—"

"Simulation."

"Game, simulation, whatever. The people you fight in the Demi-

Monde are modeled on real people, but you've also introduced some characters from history."

"Correct."

"For instance . . ."

"The ones you are probably most familiar with are Henry the Eighth, Maximilien Robespierre and Ivan the Terrible."

"Oh, c'mon. That's impossible. No computer can re-create dead people."

"ABBA can," said the general flatly.

Ella laughed. "Nuts. I don't believe it."

"Your incredulity is understandable, Miss Thomas. So perhaps, before we go much further with our discussions, we should give you a taste of the Demi-Monde, we should show you just how lifelike it really is."

The Demi-Monde: 40th Day of Winter, 1004

RaTionalism is an avowedly and uncompromisingly atheistic creed developed by the renegade Rodina thinker and ardent Royalist Karl Marx, which strives by a process of Dialectic ImMaterialism to secure logical explanations regarding the Three Great Dilemmas: the Creation, the Confinement, and the Purpose of the Demi-Monde. RaTionalism denies all supernatural interpretations with respect to the Three Great Dilemmas. Though it remains a popular creed within the so-called Scientific Community (notably Future Historians and preScientists), RaTionalism is now outlawed throughout the ForthRight and dismissed as the nonsensical and perverse belief system it is by most Demi-Mondians.

—RELIGIONS OF THE DEMI-MONDE, *Otto Weininger,*

UNIVERSITY OF BERLIN PUBLICATIONS

tta gettin' much awful late, Miss Trixiebell. Message from your father wassa that you should be home by the soonest time . . ."

Trixie ignored Luigi's entreaties, ignored his ludicrous Roman accent that made him sound as though he would, at any moment, try to sell her an ice cream. Trixie hated to be hurried by slaves . . . she hated to be hurried by *anyone*. Once Trixie Dashwood started something, nothing, but *nothing*, would stop her finishing. Trixie Dashwood was famous for her resolute spirit. Or her pig-headedness, as her governess preferred to call it.

Trixie waved impatiently to Luigi to begin. The huge Slave-Guard removed his thick, fur-lined gauntlets, spat on his callused hands, took a firm grip on the handle of his pickaxe, shuffled his feet until they were shoulder-width apart and swung.

The crash as the steel of the pickaxe head met the Mantle-ite floor made Trixie flinch back. Instinctively she raised her arm over her eyes to protect them from flying stone chips.

But there weren't any.

"*Nor-thing*," said Luigi dolefully.

Trixie looked down at the spot where the pickaxe had struck the Mantle. Luigi was right, there was "*nor-thing*" to be seen there: not a scratch, not a chip, not a mark of any kind.

Ridiculous!

Stamping her foot in frustration, Trixie slapped the slave hard across his face. "You're useless, Luigi, absolutely useless. If you don't shape up I'll have to sell you!"

Despite the enormous difference in their relative size, the huge Italian shrank back from the girl's fury. No one wanted to be near Lady Trixiebell Dashwood when she was in one of her fits of pique.

Trixie threw down her gloves, grabbed the pickaxe out of Luigi's hand, gave him the lantern she had been holding and steadied herself to swing the axe. It was obvious to her that Luigi, big and powerful though he was, was so blood-starved that he couldn't wield the pickaxe with enough force to trouble the Mantle-ite.

Useless bloodless Quartier Chaudians.

Why can't I have a Chink Slave-Guard like all the other girls at the Academy? After all, an Eyetie is only one step up from a Shade. Shades . . . ugh!

With a resolute set to her mouth—usually a precursor to one of her famous tantrums—Trixie swung the pickaxe. Though physically best described as small and thin ("svelte," as her governess preferred to call her) Trixie was a very determined young woman ("girl," as her governess preferred to call her) and hence was able to bring the point of the pickaxe down on the Mantle with considerable force. Indeed, the axe struck with so much force that the jarring impact sent vibrations juddering up the handle, out along her arms, across her shoulders, to finally set her teeth dancing.

Hardly noticing the pain, Trixie tossed the pickaxe to one side and dropped to her knees, ignoring the damage done to her very expensive silk stockings—smuggled in from Paris—her gaze searching for the impact point. There wasn't one: the pickaxe hadn't even scratched the surface of the Mantle. Perfect and pristine it lay before her, glowing with its characteristic green sheen.

Damn and double-damn.

Disappointed though she was, the RaTionalist in Trixie told her that she shouldn't be surprised by the outcome of her little experiment. Her findings were at one with the results from all the other tests conducted on the Mantle by RaTionalist scientists in every corner of the Demi-Monde.

Trixie corrected herself: the Demi-Monde, being circular, didn't have any corners.

Corners or no, the point was that no matter where on the Demi-Monde they tried, Ratty scientists found it impossible to dent, chip or even scar the Mantle. Perplexed and bemused, Trixie slumped down on her pert bottom and pondered. Just what was the Mantle made out of if it could shrug off a blow as hard as the one she'd just administered? What was this mysterious substance, Mantle-ite?

Whatever it was, Mantle-ite was harder, tougher, more impervious than any rock that had been discovered anywhere in the Demi-Monde. It was harder, tougher and more impervious even than steel. And being harder, tougher and more impervious than anything known to man—or woman—meant that the Mantle, the crust that covered the Demi-Monde once the top coating of thirty feet of soil had been cleared away, wasn't natural.

But being unnatural didn't mean—as the UnFunDaMentalists would have it—that it was *super*natural. There was nothing magical about the Mantle; it was just unexplained. The Mantle might not be Demi-Mondian-made, but it had certainly been *made*, and that ruled out the involvement of gods, Spirits, Daemons and all the other silly entities that UnFunnies believed inhabited the Spirit World.

Find the explanation—the *RaTional* explanation—to this conundrum, Trixie knew, and she would go a long way toward solving the question that had bedeviled thinkers in the Demi-Monde since time immemorial: how had the Demi-Monde been created? And finding the answer to that would help solve the even more perplexing puzzle as to *why* the Demi-Monde had been created.

But if her delving had been unproductive regarding discovering the composition of the Mantle, it had been very fruitful in other ways. The runes she'd found embossed into the Mantle had been a real find, and that they were rendered in Younger Pre-Folk meant she had a chance of understanding them. Not even the great Michel de Nostredame had managed to decipher Pre-Folk A.

She took her notebook out of the breast pocket of her pinafore and after carefully measuring the runic inscriptions made a sketch of them. The irritating thing was that whilst uncovering the runes was quite a coup, with this being an illegal dig she would have to keep the discovery secret. Respectable women in the ForthRight were not expected to engage in intellectual activities, especially those prohibited by the Ministry of Psychic Affairs. And if they found anything interesting in the course of these prohibited intellectual activities then, of course, respectable women couldn't publish.

And what she had discovered *was* interesting. According to UnFunDaMentalism, the fact that runes were seen on the Mantle throughout the Demi-Monde indicated that the Demi-Monde had once been ruled by a Master Race of pure-blooded—*Aryan-blooded*—Anglo-Slavic godlings known as the Pre-Folk. So to have found runes so close to the Boundary was an amazing discovery. It suggested that once, long, long ago, there had been no Boundary Layer, that the Pre-Folk had lived in what was now the Great Beyond, the land *beyond* the Demi-Monde.

Sketches complete, Trixie scribbled down a brief summary of the tests she had conducted. Tomorrow she'd hire one of the steam-driven drop-hammers she'd seen being used to break rocks at the docks, get it hauled to the site, erected down here in her excavation pit, and then she'd see just how tough the Mantle *really* was.

But she'd have to be careful. To be caught using a steam hammer to smash a way through the Mantle would create a real scandal, one even her father wouldn't have enough influence to cover up.

And as for her governess . . .

No, she didn't even want to think of the hissy fit Governess Margaret would throw if she was Censured again. Then Trixie really would be unmarriageable. No respectable man in the ForthRight—now there was a contradiction in terms—would marry a Ratty. No respectable man would come near her.

Thrusting this unpleasant thought to the back of her mind, Trixie climbed to her feet and brushed the dirt off her knees. Her stockings were ruined but that wasn't a concern; she would blame her maid for that. Better a slave got a whipping than her governess discovered that her one and only charge was a closet RaTionalist who was conducting secret and very illegal experiments designed to overturn the supposedly inviolate beliefs of UnFunDaMentalism. RaTionalists weren't popular with the Party. Only *dead* RaTionalists were popular with the Party.

Lost in her cogitations, Trixie leaned back against the Boundary Layer, feeling it yield just a little as she did so. She had had Luigi dig the pit in an abandoned warehouse owned by her father that butted hard up against the Boundary. Digging her excavation pit here gave her the opportunity simultaneously to examine both the Mantle *and* the Boundary Layer.

The Boundary Layer.

If the Mantle was a Mystery, then the ninety-four miles of Boundary Layer that circled the Demi-Monde was the *Big* Mystery, the Mystery at the heart of the enigma that was the Containment. More learned men (men, hah!) had studied the Boundary Layer than any other of the Phenomena in the Demi-Monde. And what had their studies revealed?

Nothing.

Oh, after much deliberation and head-scratching the Party in the shape of His Holiness Aleister Crowley had officially classified the Boundary as a Selectively Permeable Magical Membrane, but that was just a fancy way of saying that neither the Party nor Aleister Crowley had a clue what it really was. All they—or anybody else, for that matter—knew was that the Boundary Layer was the transparent wall that surrounded the Demi-Monde and prevented Man from moving into the Great Beyond.

And as such the Boundary Layer was at the center of the schism that had divided the religions of the Demi-Monde and kept them at each other's throats. Was, as the UnFunnies had it, the Boundary Layer there to keep nasty things like Daemons out, or, as Ratties believed, was its purpose to keep Demi-Mondians in? That, in a nutshell, was the dilemma that was the Containment, the key philosophical question that had bedeviled thinkers since time immemorial: was the Demi-Monde a sanctuary or a prison?

Whatever the Boundary Layer's purpose, it was a wall that the harder you pushed against it, the harder it pushed back. The only things that seemed to be able to traverse the Boundary Layer were light, air and the waters of the five Spoke Rivers.

Nothing else.

It was an invisible and impenetrable wall that extended thirty feet below ground level, where it made a seamless join with the Mantle and extended up ... well, no one knew quite how far up into the sky the Boundary stretched. That daredevil Speke had ridden one of the new hydrogen balloons to an altitude of over six thousand feet and the Boundary had still been there, so it was anybody's guess how high it really went.

Trixie drew a hand lovingly over the surface of the Boundary, feeling it ripple slightly as she did so. The thirty feet of topsoil of the Great Beyond was clearly seen through the Layer . . . so close and yet so very far away.

The strange thing was that—as far as Trixie could tell—the nanoBites that inhabited the soil of the Great Beyond never got closer than twenty feet to the surface. That was why there were so many great trees in the forests of the Beyond: there weren't any nanoBites nibbling at their roots. Not like here in the Demi-Monde's Urban Band. There weren't many trees in the Urban Band as the nanoBites came within five feet of the surface and made short work of their roots. Luigi had only been able to dig the pit because it was Winter and the nanoBites were hibernating.

One day, Trixie was determined, she would penetrate the Boundary Layer and understand the mysteries of the Great Beyond. One day she would understand *all* the mysteries of the Demi-Monde. One day she would be the most famous of all RaTionalists.

"It really gettin' awful, awful late, Miss Trixie. We gotta be home real soon."

Luigi's whining voice cut through Trixie's reverie. With a sigh she dragged her fob watch out of her pocket.

Dancing Daemons!

"Why didn't you tell me that was the time, Luigi?" Trixie demanded as she scrabbled up the ladder leading to the top of the pit. "You stupid, stupid man! If I'm late it will be your fault. I'll have Governess Margaret tan the astral ether off your useless Eyetie arse!"

5

The Real World:
June 12, 2018

An α-Class Singularity (a.k.a. Dark Charismatic, Hi-Level Psychotic) may be defined as an individual demonstrating such distorted and aberrational force of personality and such singularity of purpose that they have the ability and the inclination to wrest power from existing governments, to overturn the politico-social status quo and to irreparably change existing cultural, moral and religious mores.

—The Demi-Monde® Product Description Manual, June 14, 2013

Captain Sanderson led Ella out of the general's office and back along Fort Jackson's labyrinthine corridors. Being out of the general's presence helped the captain relax: he chatted quite amiably to her as they walked. He even called her Ella. She didn't object; the captain was good-looking if a little on the small side, but then compared to her near-six-foot height, most men came up a little short. "You're going to be meeting two disturbing people, Ella," he said as they strode through the building, "but don't let either of them distract you too much. Everybody is a little upset by their first meeting with the Professor, and as for Heydrich . . ."

They walked for about five minutes and then descended—Ella had no idea how many floors—in a high-security elevator. When the elevator's steel doors finally opened they were met by a man who was excessively lanky and thin, his emaciated body clad in an exquisitely cut—if a tad old-fashioned—suit made from worsted wool of an uncompromising black. He looked like an undertaker, though his long, Roman nose, his dark button eyes that snarled out at Ella from behind shaded glasses and his oiled black hair made him an extremely aggressive-looking undertaker.

Weird.

Captain Sanderson effected the introductions. "This is Professor Septimus Bole, who developed the Demi-Monde. Professor, this is Miss Ella Thomas, our first-choice candidate for Operation Offbeat."

Operation Offbeat?

Ella held out her hand. The professor looked at it warily, then with what appeared to be extreme reluctance shook it. The man's fingers were cold and clammy and her feeling of revulsion was heightened when he squirmed them hurriedly out of her grasp. It was as though he was disgusted by her touch.

"I am delighted to meet you, Miss Thomas. I hope what you see today will persuade you to help us." This little announcement was made, unexpectedly, in an English accent, which had a strange mechanical cadence to it. The professor noted Ella's surprise. "Yes, Miss Thomas, I am a Brit, though I trust you won't hold that against me. I, for my sins, am head of ParaDigm CyberResearch's Demi-Monde Project Team, ParaDigm being the company behind the Demi-Monde. I am here on secondment from ParaDigm to help the U.S. Army sort out its problems."

Problems?

Introductions made, Captain Sanderson slotted his ID tag into a scanner set on the wall by the side of the elevator and placed his palm on the reader next to it. Immediately a door in the steel wall sighed open and Sanderson nodded Ella and the professor through to the conference room beyond. The door slid shut behind them.

The room they entered was small, cold and impersonal, and, rather disconcertingly, reminded Ella of a hospital waiting room. The only furnishings were a line of five very uncomfortable-looking plastic chairs set in front of a low stage which had a lectern standing at its center. At a sign from the captain, Ella took the middle chair. Professor Bole sat next to her, and after taking an age to coil his long body into the seat and ensure that the immaculate creases in his trousers weren't being compromised he turned to Ella.

"As I think the general will have explained to you already, Miss Thomas, the Demi-Monde was designed to replicate the chaos and anarchy associated with an Asymmetric Warfare Environment. The demonstration you are about to see will, I hope, inform you of two things. The first and most obvious will be to convince you of the realism of the Dupes populating the Demi-Monde, a realism so profound that they are as close to real life as makes no difference."

Yeah, yeah, yeah.

Ella kept her face bland; she would believe this when she saw it. There was no way she was *ever* going to believe that a computer-concocted Dupe was a real person.

"The second point," the professor continued, "which to my mind makes the Demi-Monde such a triumph, is that it accurately conjures up the type of people who rise to leadership positions in Asymmetric Warfare Environments. For the leaders in the Demi-Monde we have selected individuals from history famous for their brutality and their barbarism, and have mimicked their aberrational personalities using state-of-the-art DNA-mapping techniques. As a consequence these PreLived Dupes look, think and act just as their real-life equivalents did. I tell you this not to frighten you, but to prepare you."

The professor flicked a switch on the remote control he was holding. "I'll just dim the lights, Miss Thomas, and then I think our guest will be ready to present himself."

Even before the lights had fully faded a tall, slim man dressed in a perfectly fitting black uniform of an officer in the Nazi SS strode out of the right-hand wall. His jackboots shone, his leather belt and holster sparkled and the silver death's-head badge on the brow of his tall peaked hat twinkled under the room's fluorescent lighting. That the man was a Dupe, Ella had absolutely no doubt—no one she knew of could walk through a solid steel wall—but . . .

But in all other respects the man who came to stand on the stage behind the lectern was a perfect representation of a living, breathing human being. Ella stared at him, awed by the way in which the man's body—the *Dupe's* body—so precisely imitated the shadows and highlights that would have been seen if it had been rendered from solid flesh and blood. In sum, it was an amazing, disturbing display of computing power; a display of verisimilitude such as Ella had never imagined could be achieved. It was impossible to distinguish the Dupe from the real thing.

"Perhaps you would be so kind as to introduce yourself?" Captain Sanderson asked quietly.

The Dupe turned his bleached, narrow-set eyes toward the captain and smiled the most chillingly arrogant smile Ella had ever seen. And as he smiled he seemed to suck all the heat and goodness out of the room. She shivered in cold and fear; the man standing before her was the very personification of evil.

"As you wish." The man gave a sharp click of his heels and a slight bow of his head. This done, he took his cap from his head, placed it precisely to the left of the lectern, and slowly and deliberately ran a hand over his short, sleek blond hair. He wasn't a handsome man, decided Ella, but he *was* striking, what with his prominent nose and his long, narrow face. But what she particularly disliked was the way his cold, cold eyes didn't seem to look *at* her but *into* her.

"I am Reinhard Tristan Eugen Heydrich, SS-Obergruppenführer, Chief of the Reichssicherheitshauptamt, the Reich's Main Security Office, and Reichsprotektor of Bohemia and Moravia."

Jesus.

Ella sat openmouthed in amazement. The nuances of speech were so astonishingly correct that she was having trouble remembering that the man standing not six feet away from her was a piece of computer fabrication. Even the tone and resonance of his voice—a little too light and effeminate, she thought, for a man of his size—by its very wrongness added an authenticity to the masquerade.

She turned to the professor. "Just who is this Heydrich of yours? Is he a fiction?"

The professor tapped a button on his control pad and immediately a red sign illuminated over the Dupe: <PAUSE>.

The figure of Heydrich froze in mid-gesture.

Professor Bole smiled in a disdainful, condescending way. "I had thought the teaching of history in British schools was the worst in the Western world but . . ." He shook his head sadly. "No matter. Whilst Reinhard Heydrich has, as a consequence of his assassination by Czech resistance fighters in June 1942, not generated quite the public disdain and infamy of other leading Nazis such as Hitler, Himmler, Goebbels and Goering, Heydrich was, in my humble opinion, the most evil, the most callous and the most dangerous of the whole pack of them. The man so wonderfully represented here in this room is the individual whose organizational genius, superhuman capacity for hard work and total and utter disregard for human suffering made the triumph of the Third Reich possible. The man standing before you, Miss Thomas, masterminded the Holocaust. He was the man who enabled the Nazis to send six million Jews to their death." He smiled bleakly at Ella. "Shall we continue?"

<PLAY>

"I must congratulate you, Herr Obergruppenführer," said the professor in a ridiculously conversational tone, "on your recent promotion to Reichsprotektor."

The Dupe nodded his appreciation of the compliment.

"Perhaps," the professor continued, "you would be so kind as to describe your career for my young friend here? She is quite an admirer of yours."

The dead eyes of the German settled upon Ella and a contemptuous smile flickered over his full, fleshy lips. "I am wondering why I should be obliged to discuss my career with one such as her."

"One such as me?" asked Ella, unable to keep the tremor out of her voice.

"A black . . . a negro . . . a member of a more primitive race."

Ella was jolted back in her seat by the scorn in the Dupe's voice. Struggling to remember that Heydrich was just digital make-believe, she did her best to hide how upset she was by what the bastard had just said. Taking a deep, calming breath she continued the conversation in as equable a manner as she was able.

"I am student president at my high school. I have achieved an SAT score that places me in the top one percent of all students in the USA. I am intent on majoring in genetics at college. I am a skilled musician. Surely that gives the lie to your proposition that I am a member of an inferior race?"

Heydrich slid a silver cigarette case from his jacket pocket and with infuriating slowness went through the pantomime of selecting and lighting a cigarette. He drew heavily on the cigarette then breathed out, snaking a stream of perfectly imitated virtual smoke into the room. A miasma of malevolent vapor, ashen and feathered, settled around his head like a diabolical halo. "That you are capable of rote learning merely confirms the inferiority of your race. You are the exception that proves the rule. And anyway, I have seen chimpanzees performing in the circus. Even apes can, through diligent training, be made to perform tricks surprisingly well." He sneered. "Perhaps that is what you are: a trained ape."

If this guy had been for real Ella would have given him a real mouthful. But he wasn't for real: he was just a Dupe imitating the attitudes of a racist who had died almost eighty years ago.

Stay cool, Ella. Try to get yourself into this jerk's mind-set. Play the psychologist.

"I understand you are an officer, Herr Heydrich. Then surely your duty as an officer is to help those of lesser ability? If you scorn me as an African-American, perhaps you can assist me as a woman . . . as one of the weaker sex?"

The feminist in Ella almost gagged when she uttered this last phrase.

She felt those terrible eyes studying her, Heydrich slowly sliding his gaze over her body. She had the distinct impression that the Nazi liked what he saw . . . more than liked what he saw. In fact the way he was looking at Ella persuaded her to pull the hem of her short skirt further down her long legs. Heydrich's crystal-cold eyes watched her as she did so, a smile tugging at the corner of his mouth. She shivered again; there was something infinitely unsettling about the man . . . about the Dupe, she quickly reminded herself.

"Very well. As you are not a pure black, there being something of the *Mischling*—a person of mixed race—in your appearance, I am prepared to speak with you. May I be permitted to know the name of my interrogator?"

Ella looked to Professor Bole, who merely shrugged his assent. "My name is Ella Thomas."

"And you are intent on becoming a geneticist?"

"That's correct."

"Ah, most apt, the study of genetics is much favored by the *Untermenschen*, by the lesser races, by the Jews." He paused to enjoy his cigarette, all the time watching Ella as a cat might watch a mouse.

Eventually he deigned to continue. "Yes, the explanation must be that you wish to study genetics in order to appreciate why your race is so inferior to mine. I am told that self-knowledge can lead to improvement." He sniggered dismissively; he obviously found the idea of blacks being capable of improving themselves risible. "Regarding my career, I have recently been elevated to the position of Reichsprotektor of Bohemia and Moravia. This I take as a signal from the Führer that he holds me and my talents in high regard."

"So you are well thought of by Adolf Hitler?"

"Whilst I am loath to discuss the thought processes of the Führer with one such as you, Miss Thomas, I will say that this is an asinine question. I have served both the Führer and my immediate superior, Reichsführer Himmler, to the very limits of my abilities and would say with no little pride that these efforts have contributed mightily to the success the Vaterland has enjoyed in its struggle to bring order to the lesser nations of the world."

"And which of these successes has given you the most satisfaction, Herr Obergruppenführer?" asked Ella, slightly perplexed to be having such a freewheeling question-and-answer session with what was, after all, just a computer-driven Dupe.

Another sneer from Heydrich and another arrogant puff on his cigarette. "There have been so many. In the early days of my career I would cite the snuffing out of the protests planned by enemies of the Nazi Party at the time of the Berlin Olympics of 1936 as a signal achievement. Later I took a great deal of satisfaction in organizing the forging of the documentation which persuaded that animal Josef Stalin to liquidate so many of his most able officers on the eve of war."

"Heydrich speaks fluent Russian," Professor Bole added as an aside to Ella.

"You will not speak until you are spoken to!" snarled Heydrich, and smashed his fist hard against the wooden lectern. The sound of the blow caused Ella to flinch back in alarm.

Jesus! How the hell did they program that?

"*And* I am to be addressed by my titles and rank, not simply as 'Heydrich.' Do you understand?" His gaze flickered around the room, touching on each of the three members of his audience in turn. "Do you *all* understand?" The hatred and the contempt were redolent in every word the German uttered.

In the midst of the stunned silence an almost beatific calm drifted across Heydrich's face. "Now, what were we discussing, young lady? Ah, yes, my achievements. Another major success was my bringing of the Czech workers back to full production and the gaining of their support for the war against the Bolsheviks." A self-satisfied grin tugged at the corners of his mouth. "But I suppose my lasting memorial will be the freeing of Europe from the pernicious contamination of the Jews."

"It was you who organized the extermination of the Jews?" asked Ella incredulously, stunned by how casually Heydrich could talk about his involvement with the Holocaust.

"No, I am organizing their transportation to the east, where they will contribute to the success of the German Reich by building roads and laying railway tracks. The work will be . . . exacting and certainly many will die, but it is not my intention to 'exterminate' them as you so crudely put it. It would be too expensive of bullets to shoot, what, ten million people. In my opinion, bullets would serve a greater use if they were employed to kill Russians and other enemies of the Reich rather than being squandered in the dispatching of Jewish offal."

<PAUSE>

"You should realize, Miss Thomas," explained the professor, "that the Heydrich you are speaking with is the Heydrich of February 1942. He has no perception of what will be the future course of the war. At that moment everything in the Nazi garden was coming up roses: they had rolled back the Soviet armies and seemed to be on the brink of conquering Russia as easily as they had conquered mainland Europe. The 'Final Solution' to the Jewish problem as Heydrich perceives it is the shipping of every single Jew east and working them to death creating a German Garden of Eden in the lands of Belarus and the Ukraine. The mass execution of Jews in gas chambers hadn't yet been adopted as Nazi policy, though Heydrich had already set up gas chambers in Poland and Czechoslovakia. He had already initiated the Holocaust."

<PLAY>

"It will be an amazing logistical exercise to move ten million Yids east," Heydrich continued, seemingly unaware that he had been interrupted, "and to accommodate and to feed them . . . well, to feed them after a fashion anyway. But at least in this way they will be of some economic value to the Reich rather than just an expense. This is the proposal I made and had accepted at the Wannsee Conference of just a month ago. Within two years we will be living in a Jew-free world, ten million people moved out of the Reich and resettled somewhere where they can be of benefit rather than simply being a burden." Heydrich smiled a secret little smile. "A Jew-free world: that will be my greatest achievement."

Ella shook her head. "Don't you ever have sleepless nights about conniving to destroy the lives of millions of people? Do you never stop to consider whether what you are doing is right?"

Heydrich studied Ella carefully, as though he had difficulty understanding her question, as though perplexed by her obtuseness. Suddenly he began to laugh. It was an unnaturally high-pitched laugh, which reminded Ella of the braying of a goat. "Right? Morality is a mutable, a subjective thing. It is not whether a thing is right that matters, my dear Miss Thomas; all that matters is victory. Victory makes all that you do correct: success is the only criterion by which we judge what is right and what is wrong."

"But what you are doing is barbaric . . . uncivilized."

Heydrich shrugged nonchalantly. "As the Führer said, 'Why should man be less barbaric than nature?' You call me 'uncivilized' but the chief characteristic of civilized behavior is cruelty. So, let history judge me"—he laughed sardonically—"and as I am *making* history I have every confidence that I will receive excellent reviews."

<PAUSE>

"Have you seen and heard enough?" asked Professor Bole quietly.

"More than enough. It's terrifying." Ella felt empty inside . . . nauseous. Oh, she had met racists and rednecks before but their hatred had been playground stuff compared to what she had just heard. This man—this *monster*—didn't only hate those he considered his racial inferiors but was intent on destroying them.

<STOP>

The image of Reinhard Heydrich flickered and faded.

Ella took a handkerchief from her sleeve and wiped her sweat-sheened brow. "That was really freaky. The guy was totally and utterly off his head."

The professor nodded. "Heydrich was a classic psychopath: a man unable to form any friendships and utterly socio-apathetic except where it was necessary to further his personal ambitions and the desires of the two monsters who were his role models, Hitler and Himmler. He was a man who showed no remorse or regret, indeed this complete absence of any humanity was his defining characteristic. Reinhard Heydrich was, like all other psychopaths, damaged goods."

Just like Billy.

The professor rose from his chair. "But as Heydrich's psychosis was conjoined with a genius for administration and organization, his madness and his talent make him one of the most fearsome of his kind, an über-psychopath . . . what we call an α-Singularity."

"I thought Heydrich had been classified as a β-Singularity?" interrupted the captain.

"In the light of developments in the Demi-Monde since the OutSet of the simulation we have had to reclassify Reini. He has, after all, taken control of two of the five sectors of the Demi-Monde. A remarkable achievement. We have now flagged him as an α-Singularity, and when chaos and disorder are the order of the day, then α-Singularities like our friend Reini here come out to play their horrible little games."

"How many Singularities like Heydrich do you have loose in the Demi-Monde?"

"At the last count? Eighteen."

Jesus . . . eighteen of the bastards . . . eighteen like Heydrich.

Ella just hoped the cyber-walls they had built around the Demi-Monde were strong enough to contain that amount of evil.

6

The Demi-Monde: 40th Day of Winter, 1004

HerEticalism *is a Covenite religion based on female supremacy and the subjugation of men. Rabidly misandric in nature, the HerEtical belief is that Demi-Monde-wide peace and prosperity—an unfeasibly idyllic outcome given the tag "MostBien"—will only be realized when men ("nonFemmes" in Coven-speak) accept a subordinate position within society. HerEticalism has a more aggressive sister religion known as Suffer-O-Gettism (a contraction of Make-Men-Suffer-O-Gettism) which espouses violence as the only means of bringing change in the Demi-Monde. Suffer-O-Gettes are of the opinion that the removal of the male of the species from the breeding cycle is a vital concomitant to the securing of MostBien. Such are the unnatural and obscene sexual activities of HerEticals that they are lampooned throughout the Demi-Monde as "LessBiens."*

—Religions of the Demi-Monde, Otto Weininger,
University of Berlin Publications

Trixie barely had a chance to unpin her bonnet before Crockett, the Dashwoods' butler, attended her. "The master asked that you join him in his study immediately you returned home, Miss Trixiebell."

"Why the urgency, Crockett? Why does my father want to see me?"

"The comrade commissar has not seen fit to apprise me of the answers to those questions, Miss Trixiebell. I would simply observe that he seems a trifle agitated."

"Well, agitated or not, he'll just have to wait. I have to go and change . . ."

The butler sidled his considerable bulk between Trixie and the staircase. "The master emphasized the word 'immediately,' Miss Trixiebell. He was most insistent upon this point."

"But look at me. I can't be presented looking like this."

"The word *was* 'immediately,' Miss Trixiebell."

Her father, decided Trixie when she flounced into his study, looked decidedly unwell. His handsome face was pale and his curly hair, usually so strictly regimented by a thick dressing of Macassar oil, was disheveled. There was even—and here Trixie couldn't believe her eyes—a spot of blood on the lapel of his high-necked frock coat.

Something must be really amiss if the unbending Comrade Commissar Algernon Dashwood had felt the need to indulge in a little Solution so early in the day. He made it a rule never to imbibe until the sun was set.

Trixie took a seat on the couch to one side of the study, tucking her grimed shoes under her skirt as she did so; the less said regarding the expedition she'd been about that morning the better. Unfortunately her attempted subterfuge did her no good. "Where have you been?" her father asked suddenly.

Trixie had long ago come to the conclusion that when lying, it was better to stick as close to the truth as possible. "I went down to the docks to do some sketching."

"The docks? Are you mad, girl? The docks are one of the most dangerous districts in the Rookeries."

"I had Luigi . . . ," she began, but her father wasn't in the mood to listen to excuses.

"This madcap escapade is at one with the irresponsible, the downright unacceptable behavior of a young woman oblivious to and careless of the responsibilities of her rank. Spirits damn it, girl, you are the daughter of a commissar, not some mindless dolly-mop!"

Trixie flinched back from her father's fury. She was used to being told off by her governess but not by her father. He had always encouraged her to think for herself, he had always indulged her misdemeanors. Her father took a long sip from a glass filled, she fervently hoped, with port wine.

Pray to ABBA it isn't blood.

Whatever it was, it settled him. When he addressed her he seemed more composed. "I had a visit from Vice-Leader Beria this morning."

Trixie's eyes widened in amazement and her guts churned in horror.

"He has a file on you."

Trixie felt as though she was going to faint. Her senses swam. She slumped back into the couch, drained of strength and energy. Trickles of horror rippled over her skin. If the Checkya had found out she was conducting an unlicensed archaeological dig . . .

"I thought that piece of news might bring you to your senses."

"But . . . but . . . but . . ."

Oh, for Spirits' sake, Trixie, get ahold of yourself!

"A file?"

"Yes, a very thick file: a very thick file containing some very nasty jottings about the activities of a very silly girl."

"But why? Why did he show it to you?"

"Trixie, don't be so naïve. Beria wishes to coerce you into doing a job for him."

Trixie swallowed hard. Beria was famous—infamous—for liking young girls. She would kill herself before she let that debauched piece of shit touch her.

Her father obviously understood the foul thoughts Beria's name had conjured in her mind. "It's not like that, Trixie. Showing me the file was Beria's not-so-subtle way of making me appreciate the consequences of your *not* cooperating with him. Believe me, he will never touch a hair of your head . . . not whilst I'm alive, that is. No, they've captured a Daemon, a Grade One Daemon."

Trixie's mouth fell open. She almost laughed. Daemons were inventions used to frighten children into being good, monsters evoked by Crowley to keep the hoi polloi cowed and submissive. No one—well, no one educated or with a spark of intelligence—believed in Daemons.

"A Daemon? What, a *real* Daemon? But they're just figments of fantasy."

"Apparently not. And this one isn't just a common or garden-variety Daemon, this one's sentient. This one has a memory of the Spirit World."

"How did they catch it?" It was a stupid question; as far as Trixie was concerned Daemons didn't exist, so how could they be captured? It must all be twaddle.

"I don't know the details but it seems that Crowley used his magic to lure it from the Spirit World. We'll know more tonight. Crowley is delivering her—"

"Her?"

"Yes, it's a female Daemon, a she-devil, a succubus. Apparently the Daemon has taken the outward form of a girl of about your age. As I was saying, Crowley is delivering her here tonight."

"I'm sorry, Father, I'm having a little difficulty with this. I mean . . . Daemons don't *really* exist . . . it isn't RaTional."

Comrade Commissar Dashwood slammed his fist onto his desk so hard that he made both an ink pot and Trixie jump. "Are you so monumentally foolish, Trixie, that you can use the word 'RaTional' so openly? Have you listened to nothing I've said? The Checkya have a file on you: they think you're a proto-RaTionalist, a potential HerEtical. By the Spirits, Beria even insinuated that you might be a Suffer-O-Gette."

Shiver and shake time.

"You must be careful now, Trixie. One more slip and it's the Lubyanka for you . . . for us. And don't think I'll be able to save you: all of the Dashwood family will be traveling in the same tumbrel. Have you no idea just how evil these people are? Have you forgotten the fate of your friend Lillibeth?"

Trixie shuddered; she still had nightmares about what had happened during the Cleansing, the night when Heydrich and his henchmen had simultaneously assassinated King Henry and Tsar Ivan and seized power in the ForthRight, when they had rounded up all of the Royalists and their families and shot them as Counter-Revolutionaries. She still remembered the screams of the Marlboroughs—who had been dining with them that night—when the Checkya had come to arrest them, had dragged them outside and thrown them into the black, windowless steamers.

She remembered going to the Academy the next day and no one having the courage to ask where Lillibeth Marlborough was. Lillibeth Marlborough: Trixie's best friend. Overnight Lillibeth became a nonNix: someone never to be mentioned again, someone it was better never to think of again. Even the daguerreotypes showing the school teams that Lillibeth had captained had been removed. And when Trixie had protested they had Censured her.

"I haven't forgotten, Father, I'll never forget." A tear trickled down Trixie's cheek.

"Don't cry, Trixie. Crying isn't going to bring Lillibeth or any of them back. What we've got to concentrate on is surviving in this crazed world."

"So what does Beria want of me?"

"Apparently Crowley is unwilling to hand the Daemon over to

the Checkya for interrogation, which I think is quite sensible of the chap. Crowley might be as mad as a bag of bolts but even he knows that once inside the Lubyanka the chances of getting anything sensible out of the creature, Daemon or not, are negligible. Under torture, people . . . Daemons are liable to say anything. So Beria has suggested a more softly-softly approach: seduction rather than rape, so to speak."

"That must be a novelty for Beria," observed Trixie wryly.

"Indeed. Beria's suggestion is that the creature is held under house arrest, where it is given an opportunity to commune with a like spirit . . . that's 'spirit' with a small 's.'"

"Here?"

A nod from Trixie's father.

"Me?"

Another nod.

"But why me?"

"Beria has cast his eye over all the daughters of senior Party officials . . ."

I bet he has.

" . . . who are roughly the same age as the form taken by this Daemon. He was, so he says, looking for someone of high intelligence, strong character and who is loyal to the Party. Apparently you scored two out of three. He had you evaluated at Mrs. Albemarle's last social by an odious man named Captain Dabrowski."

That slimy Polish bastard.

"Was he the man you hit, Trixie?"

"Yes, Father. He was overly familiar with me."

"Bravo. Perhaps you should have hit him harder. Next time perhaps. Well, beaten or not, Dabrowski has recommended you to Beria. It seems the captain was quite taken by my little Trixie."

"So what do I have to do?"

"This Daemon, who calls itself Norma Williams, will be brought here to live with us. The house will be guarded, of course, but every effort will be made to make this guarding as unobtrusive as possible. The idea is that you and the Daemon will . . . bond, and gradually over a couple of weeks you will find out the truth about it and the Spirit World."

"I don't know if I like the idea of bonding with a Daemon," admitted Trixie. "What does this thing look like? Does it have horns and a tail? They always draw Daemons with horns and a tail on the covers of penny dreadfuls."

"No horns and no tail, or so I am told. Apparently it looks and acts just like a normal young woman."

"Very well; I don't suppose I have any option in the matter, do I?"

"None whatsoever," was her father's bleak answer.

The Real World:
June 12, 2018

The Memories of Dupes: each Dupe is provided with an appropriate and fully functional memory of his or her life as a Demi-Mondian prior to the OutSet of the Demi-Monde plus a realistically flawed ancestral memory.

—The Demi-Monde® Product Description Manual, June 14, 2013

Ella was back in the general's office in the company of the captain, the professor and, of course, the general. She was glad of the company; the meeting with Heydrich had shaken her, had frightened her. More . . . it had scared the shit out of her. Heydrich might have been just a virtually rendered Dupe but there had been something disturbingly real about him. No computer-programmed entity could walk into a room and dominate it like that; it wasn't natural. She shivered; the thought of being involved in anything that required her meeting or interacting with that madman again most certainly did not appeal at all. Not even for a million bucks . . .

"You met Heydrich?" asked the general.

Ella nodded distractedly. She didn't feel like talking. Meeting close-up and personal with such pure, undiluted evil had really taken the wind out of her sails. She felt empty . . . weak . . . vulnerable.

"Reini was at his despicably racist best," observed the professor. The professor was sitting in a chair stationed as far away from the general as the room's architecture would allow; it was obvious that they disliked one another. The frisson of their mutual loathing infected the atmosphere of the room.

"Is Heydrich typical of the Dupes you've used to populate the Demi-Monde?" asked Ella quietly. That there were more like Heydrich made her flesh creep.

The general shook his head vigorously. "Thankfully, no. Heydrich is what we classify as a Singularity. These, the ultimate class of high-performing psychopath, are very rare: we see only a dozen or so of them in a century. That's why we only seeded twenty into the Demi-Monde, four in each Sector. Unfortunately—or fortunately, depending on the way you look at it—two of them are already dead: Henry Tudor and Ivan Grozny were assassinated by Heydrich when he staged a coup to take over two Sectors of the Demi-Monde. A shame really; I thought Henry was one of the more interesting of the professor's PreLived creations. He was the only one with anything approximating to a sense of humor."

Hand shaking, Ella picked up her cup of coffee and took a drink, hoping the caffeine would bring her out of her funk. What sort of maniac, Ella wondered, thought these games up? She put the cup firmly back down on its saucer. "Okay, so I've met Heydrich. The question is: so what? What has all this to do with me? Let's cut to the chase, shall we, General?" Now all she wanted to do was put as many miles of interstate between her and the Demi-Monde as was humanly possible.

Screw the million bucks.

No amount of money would persuade her to come anywhere near Heydrich again.

The general glanced nervously at Ella; he was obviously discomfited by *her* discomfort. "As I've explained to you, the Demi-Monde is not a predictable simulation . . . it's a heuristic program that teaches itself. As soon as it was switched on four years ago it was independent, free of its creator's control, free to develop anarchically. Suffice it to say, Miss Thomas, that how the Demi-Monde operated post-initiation—or post-OutSet, as it is called technically—came as something of a surprise to *all* of us. We had designed the Demi-Monde to be a very hostile environment for our neoFights, to be a perfect replication of an Asymmetric Warfare Environment. What no one expected was that it would be a *life-threatening* environment."

Now, that was a phrase that made Ella's eyes widen. "Look . . . I really don't understand all this 'life-threatening' mumbo. I thought you told me that the Demi-Monde is only a computer game . . . that it's only a simulation. Surely if the shit hits the fan in a computer simulation you still have the ultimate power. You can always pull the plug."

"We *had* the ultimate power, Miss Thomas," said the general quietly. He turned to the captain. "I think, Captain, it might be useful if I give Miss Thomas a little more background to the Demi-Monde."

The captain illuminated a screen at the side of the general's office to show what appeared to be the picture of a crudely drawn dartboard. "This is a map of the Demi-Monde. It is, as you can see, a circular world stretching thirty miles across, which is home to thirty million NowLive Dupes. Each of these Dupes is, thanks to the colossal processing power of ABBA, a discrete, unique and independent individual who thinks, acts and interacts just like their Real World doppelgänger would think and act if placed in a similar environment."

"I'm having a problem with the word 'think.' Are you saying that these Dupes of yours have some form of intelligence?"

The captain smiled in a condescending way that Ella found hugely irritating. "It's only ersatz intelligence, but to neoFights operating in the Demi-Monde it does appear that the Dupes have the capacity to think and behave independently. And Demi-Mondians don't just interact with neoFights, they interact with each other." He took a deep breath, then continued his dissertation. "The Demi-Monde was planned from the OutSet to be a world that was intrinsically unstable and discordant, as only in this way could we be sure to provoke the type of war conditions we needed for our training. To do this we designed in a number of 'Areas of Tension,' the notable ones being race, religion and population density."

Ella found all this a little depressing. The USA had spent the last two hundred years trying to overcome the problems created by its citizens being drawn from different racial backgrounds and having different religious beliefs, and here was the U.S. military studying how to exacerbate these differences in order to provoke war.

The captain used a laser pen to indicate five segments of the map that radiated out from the center of the circular world like slices of cake. "There are five equally sized Sectors in the Demi-Monde: the Rookeries, the Coven, Rodina, the Quartier Chaud and NoirVille. Each of the Sectors is racially and religiously distinct. To the north we have the Rookeries. This Sector is populated by people of Anglo-Saxon descent—an equal mix of Americans, of English and of Germans—who speak English and have an ascetic religion—"

"Ascetic?" asked Ella.

"It's a religion built on the denial of pleasure called UnFunDaMentalism, a creed that your friend Heydrich has made his own. However Aleister Crowley, the black magician who was so famous in the first half of the twentieth century, is the religious leader we placed in the Rookeries so there's little wonder that UnFunDaMentalism has become suffused with aspects of the occult." He gave Ella a glance to check that she was following everything he was saying. "To the west of the Rookeries is Rodina. This Sector is largely Slavic in ethnicity: it's a mix of Russians, Poles and Ukrainians. They speak Russian in Rodina and they follow—*followed*—an avowedly atheistic creed called RaTionalism which looks, as the name suggests, for rational explanations of the creation, the purpose and the oddities of the Demi-Monde and rejects supernatural interpretations. Since Heydrich's coup RaTionalism has become an underground religion: UnFunDaMentalism is now the only official religion in the Forth-Right."

"The ForthRight?"

"The name Heydrich gave post-coup to the state that unifies Rodina and the Rookeries, the state he now controls."

"That's a pretty ballsy thing for Heydrich to have done."

A nod from the captain. "But then Heydrich's a pretty ballsy sort of guy and he was helped by a Russian β-Singularity called Lavrentii Beria."

"In real life he was head of Stalin's secret police, the NKVD," added the professor helpfully. "A really nasty piece of work."

"Thank you, Professor," said the captain testily. "Heydrich and Beria staged a revolution, assassinated the leaders of the two Sectors—Rodina and the Rookeries—"

"Henry Tudor and Ivan Grozny," murmured the professor.

"—purged their political rivals and took over. The whole revolution is called the Time of Trouble, or as it's more simply referred to in the ForthRight, the Troubles."

The captain moved his pointer around the rim of the Demi-Monde. "Clockwise from the Rookeries we come to the Quartier Chaud, where the inhabitants are of Mediterranean stock—mainly French, Italian, Venetian and Spanish—and where they all speak French. The Chaudians, as those who live in the Quartier are called, have a staunchly hedonistic outlook; they believe the pursuit of pleasure is the primary duty of mankind. Their religion is called ImPuritanism."

"Who's in charge there?" Ella asked.

"Maximilien Robespierre, the guy who ran the French Revolution, aided and abetted by a Singularity called Tomas de Torquemada who, when he was alive, was head of the Inquisition and tortured people on behalf of the Catholic Church. But the real power in the Quartier is in the hands of the doge of Venice, Catherine-Sophia, who seems to be giving our Singularities a run for their money. There's been something of a schism in the Quartier Chaud of late: for some reason Venice and the rest of the Quartier Chaud are at each other's throats."

"Not a holiday destination then," observed Ella drily.

"Well, funnily, for the sexually liberated, it is. The ImPuritans have a pretty free-and-easy attitude and as almost anything goes in the Quartier . . . well, it did until—"

There was a cough from the general, who obviously thought there wasn't any need for the captain to elaborate. "Moving on. The fourth Sector is NoirVille; the population here is mostly a mix of Arabs and Africans. The religion followed in this Sector is HimPerialism and the language Arabic."

"HimPerialism?"

"Yes, it's a religion based on male supremacy and the subjugation of women . . . terribly misogynistic, I'm afraid to say." He ignored the look of disgust on Ella's face. "We believe this developed because the gender mix in NoirVille is skewed toward men: NoirVillian men outnumber NoirVillian women by two to one. There are some very strong characters in this Sector. Shaka Zulu . . ." He paused. "Have you ever heard of him, Miss Thomas?"

Ella shook her head.

"He was the man who created the Zulu nation at the beginning of the nineteenth century. A remarkable man. It is his HimPis—his regiments—who have taken control of the black market in blood."

"Blood?"

"We'll come to that in a moment, Miss Thomas. NoirVille is also home for the WhoDoo religious cult, which the sociologists studying the Demi-Monde have been getting a real kick out of. They're into—"

Another cough from the general. *The guy must be consumptive.*

"The last Sector—" said the captain hurriedly.

"Lemme guess," said Ella, "we ain't gonna be meeting Benny the Bouncy Bunny in this next place, are we?"

"I'm afraid not. The fifth Sector is the Coven. The Coven is largely Sino-Japanese, with the gender mix skewed in favor of females. The religion of the Coven is called HerEticalism, which teaches that peace and prosperity will only come to the Demi-Monde when men accept a subordinate position to females within society."

"Sounds sensible to me."

The captain ignored Ella's aside. "Unfortunately this feminist bias has been taken to extremes: the Coven is a virulently anti-male Sector and avowedly pro-lesbian. As you might appreciate, HerEticalism is the antipode to HimPerialism: the two hate each other. HerEticalism has spawned a radically feminist terror wing called Suffer-O-Gettism—or to give it its full title, Make-Men-Suffer-O-Gettism—which is dedicated to the use of violence to achieve the triumph of women in the Demi-Monde. Funnily enough, despite this vehement gender bias, the Coven, under the tutelage of the empress Wu—a *very* strong-willed woman and the only woman ever to be emperor of China—has become a hotbed of radical thought. Most of the more unorthodox thinkers in the Demi-Monde have made the Coven their home, Karl Marx being one of them." The captain clicked off his laser pen. "And that, Miss Thomas, concludes my ten-cent tour of the Demi-Monde."

"You've forgotten the nuJus, Captain," the professor observed. "On top of the various peoples that the captain has described we also introduced some nuJu seasoning into the racial pot."

"Ah yes, how could I forget the nuJus? The professor is quite correct, there is a quasi-Jewish element in the Demi-Monde—the nuJus—representing a sixth of the total population and spread evenly over each of the five Sectors."

I wonder what else the captain has forgotten?

"But why did you set the Demi-Monde up like this?" asked Ella. "It seems like a recipe for chaos."

"That was exactly the point, Miss Thomas," answered the captain. "The Demi-Monde was designed to mirror the often divided demographics and religions of the populations and the enemies our forces meet in Asymmetric Warfare Environments. Oh, these disharmonics might have been taken to extremes when we were structuring the Demi-Monde, but remember we wanted the Demi-Monde to be an unstable and violence-prone world. And that's why we seeded four Singularities into each Sector: these are the type of individuals with the potential to provide the aberrational leadership necessary to ensure that the Sectors are continually fighting one another. The last thing we wanted was peace breaking out in the Demi-Monde. In short, Miss Thomas, the Demi-Monde is the most extreme and the most pernicious of dystopias."

"A hell on earth," observed Ella as the captain reclaimed his seat.

"Exactly," agreed the general, "and that's where we want you to go, Miss Thomas. We want you to go to hell."

8

The Demi-Monde: 40th Day of Winter, 1004

HimPerialism *is a religion, widely practiced in NoirVille—or NoirVile, as it is sometimes called—based on male supremacy and the subjugation of women (or, as they are known in NoirVille, woeMen). The fundamental HimPerialistic belief is that Men have been ordained by ABBA to Lead and to Control the Demi-Monde and that woeMen's role is to be Mute, Invisible, Supine and Subservient (the concept of subMISSiveness). Further, HimPerialism teaches that an individual's Machismo may be enhanced by the exchange of bodily essences—a practice known as going Man²naM—which has led to the vile and unnatural sexual practices for which NoirVillians are rightly condemned in the eyes of ABBA and of right-thinking people throughout the Demi-Monde. HimPerialism has a more aggressive brother religion known as HimPeril which espouses violence as the only means of securing the triumph of HimPerialism in the Demi-Monde.*

—RELIGIONS OF THE DEMI-MONDE, OTTO WEININGER,
UNIVERSITY OF BERLIN PUBLICATIONS

Beria's interpretation of what constituted an *unobtrusive* guarding of the Daemon whilst it was kept at Dashwood Manor was totally different from Trixie's father's understanding of the word. But then, mused Trixie, as she watched the fifty-strong Checkya detachment arrive that afternoon, Beria wasn't famous for being "unobtrusive." The Checkya troops, assisted by a gang of slave laborers, had rapidly and efficiently turned Dashwood Manor from a home into a prison. Every window in the rooms the Daemon would occupy was equipped with bars, and the locks on every external door were changed and substituted for ones that were considerably more formidable.

The Dashwood family was forced to endure five hours of frenzied hammering and bashing. Indeed, such was the chaos and the vast amount of mud that was tramped so uncaringly into her prized Coven-made carpets that Trixie's governess retreated to her room in a flood of hysterics. It was as well she did: what Trixie saw the Checkya doing to the manor's front gardens was enough to reduce anyone to tears. Obviously fearful that the house would be subject to a full-scale assault—by whom, Trixie had no idea—the silent mob of navvies dug and delved, burrowed and banged until a labyrinth of trenches, pillboxes and barbed-wire entanglements surrounded the house. The lawn where Trixie played croquet in the summer was no more; in its place was an implacable military emplacement.

The commander of the SS—Ordo Templi Aryanis, Colonel Archie Clement, came to inspect the works in the late afternoon, but whilst Dabrowski had been polite enough—and had the grace to look mildly embarrassed when introduced to Trixie—Archie Clement was not. Clement, Trixie decided, was a thoroughly disagreeable and disgusting piece of work. But then, what more could you expect from a Yank?

Clement strutted around the house and the grounds barking orders, kicking slaves and generally acting in a hugely obnoxious manner. And it was impossible to say him nay; the SS was, after all, the force dedicated to protecting the person of His Holiness Comrade Aleister Crowley and, by inference, the spiritual well-being of the ForthRight. They were UnFunDaMentalism's shock troops.

It was fortunate that her father was, by dint of breeding and education, so adroit at handling jumped-up popinjays like Clement. As a comrade commissar he was used to the rough and ready manners of some of the men who populated the upper ranks of the Party.

"Will you take coffee, Colonel Clement?" her father had offered. "I could have it served in my study, which has endured only modest restructuring at the hands of Captain Dabrowski's men."

Clement was oblivious to the sarcasm. "That'd be mighty choice of you, Comrade Commissar; ah'm partial to a cup of café au gore after a hard day."

"Perhaps it would be useful if my daughter, Lady Trixiebell, were to join us?" Dashwood nodded toward Trixie, who bobbed a curtsy. "She, after all, has a major part to play in the drama that is to unfold in this house."

Ignoring the scowl from Clement—UnFunDaMentalism taught that women should confine themselves to "Feeding, Breeding and MenFolk Heeding"—her father led the three of them (Dabrowski came too, much to Trixie's disgust) through to his study and had Crockett serve coffee with a blood chaser.

Immediately after he had drained his cup, Clement began. "You understand, Comrade Commissar, that while the Daemon is in your care, she . . . it . . . is to be your complete responsibility."

This was an example of a phenomenon associated with the rise of the Party that Trixie had often heard her father complain about. Heydrich was an uncompromising Leader, quick to reward success, but equally quick to punish failure. And as the consequences for failure in the ForthRight were so draconian officers and politicians had an aversion to taking responsibility for *any* action. Given a task to do, the first instinct of anyone in the ForthRight was to make sure that if anything went wrong there was someone else to take the blame, that it was someone else who disappeared—never to re-emerge—into the shadowed depths of Beria's Lubyanka Prison.

Dashwood was too experienced a politician to be fooled by such a crude attempt to avoid responsibility. "Not so, Comrade Colonel Clement; I understood that all security arrangements are the responsibility of Comrade Captain Dabrowski. No, whilst your Daemon is here, the responsibility for keeping it *here* is the captain's. And presumably, Comrade Colonel, as you are inspecting and approving the security arrangements then you are also shouldering, at least in part, some of this honorable duty."

Clement shook his head. "Nah, all the comrade captain is doing is *assisting* you . . . helping you make your house secure such that the Daemon can't escape. But the final responsibility for holding her . . . it . . . here is yours."

Trixie found the inability of her father and Clement to decide whether the Daemon was a "she" or an "it" somewhat troubling. To her mind Daemons—figments of supernatural fiction though she thought them to be—were, by definition, inhuman and therefore should be referred to using the pronoun "it."

Her father replied equitably. "The task I was given by Vice-Leader Beria was very clear: I am to provide an environment where the Daemon might feel less threatened and therefore more inclined to talk. To facilitate this loquaciousness, my daughter is to try and establish a friendship with the Daemon. Vice-Leader Beria made no reference to my being in charge of security." He shrugged to indicate his helplessness in the matter. "And how can I be? The good captain here . . ."

Good, huh!

" . . . is not under *my* command, Comrade Clement. If anything, he is under *yours*."

This verbal tennis proved to Trixie just how important this Daemon was considered to be by the upper echelons of the Party. For two such high-ranking officials as her father and Archie Clement to be squabbling about who should carry the can if the Daemon were to escape showed just how fearful they were. Which raised the question: if she couldn't get the Daemon to talk and to divulge its secrets what would be the consequences of failure to *her*?

His soft, boyish face red with anger, Archie Clement sprang to his feet, but before he could reply an imperious and cultured voice cut through proceedings.

"Comrade Commissar Dashwood is quite correct, Colonel Clement. His only obligation in this momentous endeavor is to persuade the Daemon to speak; all other matters are in your most competent hands."

How the speaker had entered the room without any of the four of them noticing was beyond Trixie's comprehension: he seemed to have materialized out of thin air. But then, she decided, if any man could perform such an amazing manifestation, such an extraordinary feat of magic, it would be His Holiness Aleister Crowley.

Trixie had never been close to Crowley before, but although he was standing swathed in shadows in the corner of the room, she recognized him. He was the man, after all, who stood at Comrade Leader Heydrich's left hand; he was the man who presided over all the Party's ceremonies and rites; he was the man who was head of the Church of the Doctrine of UnFunDaMentalism; and it was his UnFunnies who claimed to be leading the ForthRight toward the reclaiming of its Aryan birthright lost by the Pre-Folk to the wiles of Lilith.

But while it was one thing to watch the man awe-stricken from afar, it was quite another to be with him in the same room. At a distance of ten feet he looked disappointingly normal: just an ordinary man in early middle age running to fat.

Despite the arrogance that dressed Crowley's face, despite the intensity of his gaze and how dramatic he looked with his shaven head and his pointed ears, there was, Trixie decided, something weak about the man. Oh, he was tall and handsome enough in a fleshy, puffy sort of way, but he gave the impression of being less resolute than his proud, square jaw signaled. It was almost as though Crowley used his decidedly outré appearance—the shaved head and the flamboyant clothes and jewelry—as window-dressing to distract attention from the rather flimsy reality beneath.

But nonetheless Aleister Crowley was one of the most powerful and vindictive personages in the whole of the ForthRight. He was so vainglorious that he demanded his rank be acknowledged by lesser mortals—and acknowledged quickly. As one they dropped to the floor and genuflected. Crowley, a smile twitching at the side of his mouth, mimed a benediction over his audience.

"I must apologize, Comrade Commissar, for visiting you unannounced"—he waved away Dashwood's spluttered protests about the honor Crowley was showing his humble house—"but it behooves me to confirm for myself that everything is prepared for the arrival of the Daemon, and that the young lady"—a glance toward Trixie—"charged with uncovering its secrets is aware of the importance the ForthRight places on her success." He flicked a careless hand to signal everyone back into their seats and then seated himself behind Dashwood's desk.

After he had allowed Crockett to serve him with a glass of Solution, Crowley continued his address. "You will all know that since time immemorial, the Demi-Monde has been visited by Daemons from the Spirit World. Some are emissaries from ABBA but most are in league with Loki, the Lord of Darkness. These disciples of Loki have sought to disrupt and subvert the natural order of the Demi-Monde and it will not have escaped your notice that in recent months these visitations have been concentrated here in the Forth-Right. It is as though the Daemons sense the growing power—the growing certainty—of the ForthRight as it seeks to bring racial, political and religious order to the Demi-Monde. Such is the threat posed to the ForthRight by these troublesome Daemons that Comrade Leader Heydrich, in his ineffable wisdom, decreed that my priests bend their will to the breaching of the Mystical Integument that divides this, the physical world of the Demi-Monde, from the ephemeral Spirit World, and strike back at the Daemons." Crowley gave a self-satisfied little smile. "This we have done. But we have done more: we have lured a Grade One Daemon into the Demi-Monde."

"A Grade One Daemon?" asked Trixie.

Crowley's forehead furrowed; he obviously disliked being interrupted in mid-sermon. "The Daemons who entered the Demi-Monde before were little more than malevolent imps. They destroyed bridges, they incited unrest, they gave encouragement to the enemies of the ForthRight, but when captured and questioned . . ."

Poor swine.

" . . . they were found to be empty vessels. They knew little of the worlds that lie beyond the Mystical Integument; they knew nothing of the intentions of their dark masters. Most were unintelligent and bestial: lowly Grade Fives of no consequence. But now . . ." He paused dramatically. "The Daemon we have captured is different: it is fully cogent and aware. It is, we believe, privy to the deepest secrets of the Dark Daemons and to the ambitions of their Master, Loki, regarding the Demi-Monde."

Crowley gestured toward Crockett that his glass should be replenished. Trixie was disgusted that he should be indulging so heavily so early in the evening. Obviously the man had a huge and overwhelming appetite for blood; perhaps that was why, although he was still relatively young, his flesh had started to soften and his complexion to blotch.

"Unfortunately our experiences in interrogating lesser-ranked Daemons are that should they be subject to coercion, they become dysfunctional; it is as though their minds switch off. That is why we have determined on this new policy in which you, Lady Trixiebell, will have such a key role."

Trixie felt every eye in the room turn in her direction. She fidgeted uncomfortably under the scrutiny. "I am always ready to do whatever is necessary to help the ForthRight and to do the Leader's will," she said, mouthing the words her father had made her memorize.

"Excellent. But put your mind at rest on one thing, young lady: this Daemon, though duplicitous and conniving, is not physically threatening. It has manifested itself in the shape of a young woman and there is no record of a Daemon ever transmogrifying itself whilst in the Demi-Monde. There is no risk of you being confronted by a Daemon in its true and horrific guise."

Well, that's reassuring.

"But whilst there is no physical threat to your person, Lady Trixiebell, there is, I regret to say, a spiritual threat. The natural inclination of a Daemon confronted by a human is to try to corrupt their soul. Daemons are great deceivers. Make no mistake, Lady Trixiebell, this creature will attempt to fox you, to persuade you that it is not what it truly is. That is the one thing you must continually be on your guard against: feeling sorry for the Daemon. As you know, Lady Trixiebell, the aiding and abetting of a Daemon is one of the greatest of all sins against UnFunDaMentalism, so you must harden your heart against its trickery and its perfidy. You have been chosen, Lady Trixiebell, because you are a pragmatist, because you are, by inclination, a RaTionalist."

Crowley held up his hand to still the gasp of protest that came from Trixie's father. "Calm yourself, Comrade Commissar, it is not my intention to chastise Lady Trixiebell for her doubts. As I myself have noted, the Key of Joy is disobedience. It is the role of the young to be dubious of the teachings of their elders: the young are inclined to be impetuous." He smiled at Trixie and she was amazed to see that Crowley's canine teeth had been sharpened. The man, she decided, must be totally mad. "I am confident," he continued, "that the proto-RaTionalist that is Lady Trixiebell Dashwood will emerge from her communion with a denizen of the Spirit World a changed woman, perhaps even as a candidate for the SisterHood."

Over my dead body.

"But on a more practical note, it will be important for you, Lady Trixiebell, to record everything you discuss with the Daemon and to note down everything, no matter how trivial, the Daemon says. It is also vital that you adhere to all the security arrangements that Captain Dabrowski has put in place: it is imperative that the Daemon is not allowed to escape or to be rescued."

"Rescued?" asked Dashwood.

"You should be under no illusion as to what a prize you will have living with you, Comrade Commissar Dashwood. This Daemon possesses the secrets of the world beyond ours, and so it is almost inevitable that other Daemons will seek to rescue it. And then, of course, there are the more prosaic temptations the Daemon presents to our fellow Demi-Mondians. The Daemon is possessed of blood and it is not beyond the realm of possibility that Shaka's Blood Brothers will attempt to abduct the Daemon in order to drain it."

The thought of Dashwood Manor being assaulted by a Zulu HimPi made Trixie shudder. Maybe, she thought, the presence of Captain Dabrowski and his Checkya detachment wasn't such a bad idea after all.

"You have fifteen days. In fifteen days we will hold a reception, here in Dashwood Manor, to present the Daemon to Comrade Leader Heydrich and by then it is necessary that it is both docile and cooperative." Crowley turned to Captain Dabrowski. "Now, Captain, I would be grateful if you would release the Daemon from the steamer parked outside. It is time Lady Trixiebell met her companion."

The Real World:
June 12, 2018

Area of Tension #1, Population Density: *The OutSet density of population of the Demi-Monde®is almost 70,000 persons per mile², which comfortably exceeds the figure of 60,000 persons per mile² believed by sociologists to be the maximum density sustainable in an urban milieu without the disintegration of discipline and the breakdown of law and order. As a consequence it is confidently predicted that post-OutSet the AntiSocial Behavior Quotient (ABQ) registered in the Demi-Monde will accelerate, leading to social unrest, to violent disorder on a mass scale and, ultimately and inevitably, to the outbreak of inter- and intra-Sectorial war.*
—The Demi-Monde® Product Description Manual, June 14, 2013

Y ou want me to go to hell?"

"Perhaps that's a somewhat melodramatic way of putting it," admitted the general, "but in essence the answer is yes. We want you to enter hell. We want you to enter the Demi-Monde."

"Enter?"

"We want you to become a Dupe in the Demi-Monde."

Ella guffawed. "Look, General, I don't wanna rain on your parade but you and the captain have just finished telling me how the

Demi-Monde is mean as cat shit and twice as nasty, and now you're offering me the chance to mix and mingle. Pardon me if I give a big no to that offer."

"There is just one more . . . wrinkle I should explain before we discuss how we see you being able to help us, Miss Thomas."

The guy must be hard of hearing.

"As Captain Sanderson has explained, the design team led by Professor Bole was charged with raising the inter-Sectorial disharmonics evident in the Demi-Monde such that at least two Sectors would *always* be at war. Therefore it was felt necessary to promote intense competition between the Sectors, to have them vie for possession of a scarce commodity that they were *desperate* to possess. In the Real World this might be the control of oil deposits or water resources but the professor here was more mischievous in his choice of commodity: he chose blood."

"Blood?" Ella asked, nervously wondering where this question would lead.

"We programmed the Dupes that inhabit the Demi-Monde so that they had a craving for blood," the professor explained. "We made it so blood to the Demi-Mondian is like heroin to an addict, the only difference being that they can't go cold turkey. Without blood they die in a fortnight."

Ella stared at the professor wide-eyed in disbelief. "Are you saying that everybody in the Demi-Monde is a vampire?"

The professor gave a disdainful laugh. "Don't be ridiculous. Vampires indeed! There is nary an extended canine nor an aversion to daylight in the whole of the Demi-Monde. No, better to say that Demi-Mondians have a *requirement* for a dietary intake of at least ten milliliters of blood each week. Most of them take it mixed with alcohol, which they call Solution because it provides, literally, a 'solution' to all their cares and worries."

"But where do they get the blood from?"

"Oh, that was very simple to organize. There are a number of Blood Banks in the Demi-Monde and each week the Demi-Mondians are credited with twenty milliliters of blood. What they don't consume they can save, trade or convert into cash."

"I don't understand, Professor," protested Ella. "If they only need ten milliliters and they are being credited with twenty, how can blood be one of your disharmonics? There's an oversupply of the stuff."

"Ten milliliters is the absolute *minimum* a Demi-Mondian needs to survive; they crave much, much more. They can survive on ten milliliters a week but they don't find it much fun."

Ella eyed the professor carefully. "I hate to be obtuse, but so what?"

"Unfortunately there was a programming error." The professor ignored the glare this admission provoked from the general. "Whilst the Dupes inhabiting the Demi-Monde crave blood, they don't actually have any blood . . . not in their bodies, anyway. But whereas the Demi-Mondians are bloodless, ABBA programmed those visiting the Demi-Monde—the general's neoFights—to have their full quota of five liters of virtual blood . . . blood that on the Demi-Monde black market is worth a fortune."

"Ah . . ."

"Ah, indeed. The Demi-Mondians took to hunting down our soldiers—or Daemons as they call them—capturing them, strapping them to a drip and then milking them of enough blood to keep them docile but not enough to kill them. Their human POWs became not so much *milchcows* as *blutcows*."

"Jesus, that's horrible."

The professor nodded. "Unfortunately it was not as awful as the realization that if we unhooked the POWs from their connection to the Demi-Monde without them having 'returned,' so to speak, they would be left here in the Real World as vegetables. Remember that for our neoFights the Demi-Monde is the only reality: they are completely unaware of the existence of the Real World. The last thing we wanted was a grunt getting drunk in the Demi-Monde and spilling the beans to any locals in earshot that they were only a piece of digital mapping. That sort of snafu wouldn't be helpful to maintaining the integrity of the simulation."

"We have tried to amend this by giving neoFight officers some partial recall—"

"Protocol Fifty-seven," interjected the professor, but the general ignored him.

"—but as this is a facility available only to officers we won't burden you with it. Suffice it to say that for those unfortunate neoFights captive in the Demi-Monde, to bring them out prematurely would mean that though their bodies would be with us, their minds would be lost in cyberspace. They have become, in the parlance of the Demi-Monde, the Kept."

"Let me get this straight. You sent men into the Demi-Monde and they were captured by *Dupes?*"

The general didn't look happy. "I know it sounds a little farfetched, and believe me we have made efforts to remedy the situation, but the simple answer to your question, Miss Thomas, is . . . yes."

"But didn't you try to rescue them?"

The general sighed. "Yes, we did but the Dupe leaders were too quick for us. All the Sectors closed the access ports—the Portals—that lead to and from the Real World. As a result of this debacle we now have seventeen of our men trapped in the professor's little simulation."

Ella shook her head. "Look, I don't wish to seem brutal, but this Demi-Monde of yours sounds like a most trippy place. Why don't you just cut bait and close it down?"

"Well, apart from the fact that it would cost the lives of seventeen good men, there is another consideration. Somehow, Norma Williams, the daughter of the president, has become lost in the Demi-Monde."

Ella couldn't believe what she was hearing. "Norma Williams? Just what the fuck were you doing letting Norma Williams into this hellhole?"

The general nodded toward Professor Bole for an explanation. At least the professor had the good grace to look awkward. "As I have said, the Demi-Monde is a self-governing and self-supporting cyber-environment. It is also self-protecting. The leaders in the Demi-Monde—crazed and paranoid as they are—concluded, correctly as it happens, that we in the Real World were a threat to them and so they moved to abduct someone we would be unable to sacrifice: the president's daughter."

"But how did they do that?"

"We don't know," admitted the professor. "We believe the abduction was organized by Aleister Crowley but how he did it, we just don't know. What we *do* know is that Norma Williams is active inside the simulation."

"Well, send in another rescue squad."

"As I have told you," intoned the general gloomily, "the Demi-Mondians have closed all access Portals: we can't get anybody in. Fortunately there is still one *exit* Portal working but that's in the middle of NoirVille Sector and NoirVille is a *very* dangerous place."

"So, if there is no way into the Demi-Monde, why are we sitting here talking? You're screwed."

The general and the professor exchanged looks.

"Not entirely screwed, Miss Thomas," answered the general. "It would seem that Professor Bole here is of a whimsical turn of mind. In the early days of designing the Demi-Monde he persuaded one of his designers to create a Dupe jig that was never utilized. It was to serve, in the argot of the computer world, as a 'back door' into the Demi-

Monde." The screen on the side wall changed to show the picture of an alleyway. "This is an alley in the Rookeries, the Anglo-Saxon Sector of the Demi-Monde." The scene shifted, the view focusing on a doorway at the end of the alley illuminated by a red gas lamp.

"Gaslights?" queried Ella. "Why are they using gaslights?"

"We locked the Demi-Monde's technology at that which existed around the year eighteen seventy. The U.S. military insisted that the simulation display a fairly primitive technological modality, such as would be available to belligerents in Real World Asymmetric Wars. So it was agreed that the technology in the Demi-Monde be held at a Victorian-era level. That's why they're still using gaslights: they haven't yet figured out how to harness electricity."

Yeah, right.

As the camera zoomed in on the doorway, Ella saw the sign over the door, which read "The Prancing Pig."

"The Prancing Pig is a pub in the slum area of the London docklands," advised the professor. "A horrible pub in a horrible place."

The zooming didn't stop there; it kept going until it had tightly focused on a handwritten notice—rain-stained and tatty—nailed to the pub's door. The notice said:

THE PRANCING PIG PUB

WANTED

CHIRP

MUST BE YOUNG, SINGLE AND WILLING

TO MINGLE

ONLY SHADE FRAILS NEED APPLY

AUDITIONS EVERY SUNDAY

SPEAK TO BURLESQUE BANDSTAND

"A 'chirp' is—" began the professor.

"I know what a chirp is. A chirp is a female jazz singer." Ella shook her head. "Oh, you must be joking."

"I should explain," said the general evenly. "When the Demi-Monde was originally being populated, the good professor here thought it would be a great joke to advertise for a thing that could never be: to wit, a black jazz singer performing in a rabidly white Sector. And he created a Dupe to match."

Once again the general nodded to the captain and once again the screen shifted, this time showing the picture of a Dupe. The girl shown was tall, had tawny black skin, was slim, big-eyed and—ignoring the Victorian-style gown and bonnet the Dupe was wearing—looked a lot like Ella. It was almost as though ABBA had been expecting her.

"You must be out of your tree. I ain't going anywhere near your Demi-Monde or Reinhard I'm-a-Motherfucking-Racist Heydrich and that's final."

The general ignored Ella's protest. "We desperately need someone who is capable of posing as a jazz singer to go into the Demi-Monde, to rescue Norma Williams and to bring her out safely. As I think you might appreciate, we're under a lot of pressure from the president to save his daughter."

"You're assuming I'm willing to go, which believe me I ain't. You've got the wrong girl, General. Let me sum up the offer you're making me: I get to be jacked up to some über-computer and sent to a truly fucked-up war zone populated by vampires and run by a bunch of most undeluxe and undelightful psychopaths who hate— sorry, *HATE*—black cats like me. And once I'm in there all I've got to do is track down the president's daughter, rescue her and somehow find my way home. And if I foul up I get to spend the rest of my life plugged into a blood-sucking machine playing Brenda Blood Donor." Ella mimed being deep in thought. "Nah . . . I think I'll pass."

"You *must* go, Miss Thomas! You are the only person available who fits all the selection criteria: you are a perfect physical match for the dormant Dupe; you are intelligent; you are healthy enough to endure the rigors of the Demi-Monde; and you are, according to the captain, a talented jazz singer. You are ideal. You *must* go!"

"Well, ideal or not, I ain't going. You think I'm gonna let you drop me into the middle of Racism de Ville? Once those bastards spot my black ass I'm gonna have the life expectancy of a fruit fly. How do they dress in this ForthRight of yours, white robes and pointy hats? Do they have funny names like Mr. Ku and Mrs. Klux?"

"This is a most unhelpful attitude, Miss Thomas."

"Well, General, it might be unhelpful, but I've got a shrewd idea that it's a much more healthy one."

"I would remind you, Miss Thomas, that your life is currently a piece of shit."

"Well, that might be the case, General, but the prospect of spending the rest of my life pumping gas for Count Dracula and his pals makes it look like a mighty appealing piece of shit."

"Will five million dollars change your mind?"

It did.

10

The Demi-Monde: 40th Day of Winter, 1004

ImPuritanism *is a staunchly hedonistic philosophy—mainly practiced in the Quartier Chaud—based on the belief that the pursuit of pleasure is the primary duty of all Demi-Mondians. The ultimate aim of all those practicing ImPuritanism is the securing of JuiceSense: the experiencing of the extreme pleasure that comes from an unbridled sexual orgasm. To achieve JuiceSense requires that men and women are spiritually equal and that man's proclivity toward MALEvolence is controlled and muted. Such rampant and unrestrained sexual activity is, of course, vile and unnatural and violates the notion—enshrined in the UnFunDaMentalist creed of Living&More—that sexual union should only be undertaken for the purposes of procreation.*

—Religions of the Demi-Monde, Otto Weininger,
University of Berlin Publications

The *thing* that Captain Dabrowski pushed snarling and protesting into her father's study was to all outward appearances a normal and quite attractive girl of about eighteen years of age, but even without being told, Trixie would have known it for the Daemon it was. The girl—the Daemon—was different.

It was difficult for Trixie to quite put her finger on what made the Daemon look quite so wrong. It was modest in stature. Its hair was a raven black, which was unusual in the ForthRight but quite common in the Demi-Monde: it was the sort of hair color sported by some of the lesser races like the Chinks and the Shades. The hairstyle the Daemon had adopted was odd too, pushing back its hair to leave its ears exposed, ears that were circled with studs. This affectation was really too disgusting for words: the studs were almost—she shuddered at the thought—ImPure.

The Daemon walked in quite a masculine way too. The fashion amongst ForthRight girls was to make small rapid steps, not the great hulking strides the Daemon took. Certainly the thing moved with a decided limp, but that only seemed to emphasize its strange and wholly unfeminine athleticism.

But for Trixie the thing that indicated that the Daemon wasn't a *real* girl was the way it stared at everybody. There was no modest dropping of the eyes when a man looked at it; the Daemon glared angrily back. It might have hidden its Daemonic ugliness beneath the form of a quite pretty girl—though Trixie thought its nose a trifle too long and its chin just a little too square for it to be *really* pretty—but there was no mistaking that it was most certainly not the coy and respectable ForthRight gentle-girl it was dressed as.

Yes, the Daemon was a determined-looking individual. It might have had an ugly bruise on the side of its face, and its arms might have been decorated with a huge number of cuts and scratches, but it carried itself in a decidedly haughty manner. The cuts and scratches were curious too. They appeared to be crusted with dried blood and this, more than anything, confirmed that the girl was, in fact, a Daemon. Cuts on Demi-Mondians—on *real* people—healed as thin white lines, not as ugly red welts.

And its decorum was as appalling as its appearance. Indifferent to the protocol that demanded a woman remain silent until addressed by a man, the Daemon spoke first.

"Ah . . . Aleister Crowley, so we meet again. I wondered when you would come crawling out from under your rock. So how is the

Wickedest Man in All the World? Still promoting your poisonous nonsense no doubt, still meddling in the forbidden arts."

Trixie was aghast. No one spoke to Comrade Crowley like that; the man's temper and his peevishness were legendary. But, astonishingly, Crowley seemed, if anything, to be cowed by the girl: he actually reddened a little.

"I am unsure as to what I have done to deserve such an unflattering sobriquet," he said almost apologetically.

The Daemon laughed, revealing a set of the most abnormally— supernaturally?—white and even teeth. No one human had such perfect teeth . . . no one in the Rookeries anyway. "Perhaps I am just anticipating an honor yet to be bestowed upon you, Crowley. Perhaps you have yet to develop the full menu of brute appetites you were famous for. But I'm sure that together with that psychopath Heydrich you will be able to arrange things so that history will view you as the evil bastard I know you to be."

By the Spirits, this Daemon really is intent on occupying an early grave.

But then presumably, as the Daemon occupied the Spirit World, it was *already* dead.

Dead or not, no one—no one sane, that is—openly criticized Comrade Leader Heydrich. Criticism of the Leader implied doubt and doubt signaled that the citizen was not convinced of the rightness of the Leader's will. And a citizen who doubted the Leader relinquished all claims to be a citizen; they became non-citizens. And in the ForthRight a non-citizen was a nonNix, just like the nuJus and the Poles and the Shades . . . and Lillibeth Marlborough.

Amazingly Crowley simply shrugged off this slur on the Leader's infallibility. He waved a heavily beringed hand in the direction of Trixie. "May I introduce Lady Trixiebell Dashwood, who will be your hostess for the next two weeks? Lady Trixiebell, this is Miss Norma Williams."

Both the girls—well, the girl and the imitation girl—stood examining each other from across the room. Truth be told, Trixie was unsure as to quite what was acceptable behavior when being introduced to a Daemon. But the remembrance of her father's request that she form a "friendship" with this creature persuaded her to dispense with the niceties of etiquette. Trixie took a deep calming breath and walked across the room in order to allow the Daemon to curtsy to her. "Good afternoon, Miss Norma"—*Norma? What a stupid name, even for a Daemon*—"I'm Lady Trixiebell Dashwood. My friends call me Trixie."

To Trixie's astonishment the Daemon didn't curtsy; instead it merely took Trixie's hand in its own and shook it in an alarmingly familiar fashion.

To be touching a Daemon!

"Hi."

High? What in the Demi-Monde is this salutation "high"?

"I'm Norma Williams and my friends call me Norma." The Daemon paused. "But you, my little fifth columnist, may call me Miss Williams."

Though Trixie was somewhat nonplussed by both the Daemon's grossly impolite behavior and her confusion as to just what exactly a "fifth columnist" was, she did, however, take the opportunity to smell the Daemon. The journals had it that Daemons could be recognized by their stench; the tang of their blood was, apparently, unmistakable. Disappointingly Trixie couldn't smell anything untoward in the room except the pong coming from Archie Clement's boots.

"And this is Comrade Commissar Algernon Dashwood," said Crowley, nodding toward Trixie's father.

Distracted by her failure to detect a blood odor on the Daemon, Trixie wasn't prepared for the Daemon's next insult, this one directed at her father.

"Dashwood, eh?" observed the Daemon in a contemptuous voice.

"Then I guess your great-great-grandfather must have been Sir Francis Dashwood." The Daemon didn't wait for an answer. "Now he was a *real* reprobate. As I recall he was founder of the Hellfire Club, which had the motto *Fais ce que tu voudras* enshrined over its doorway. This was, of course, plagiarized from the writings of François Rabelais." The Daemon turned to Crowley. "So you see, Crowley, your own slogan 'Do what thou wilt shall be the whole of the law' is twice stolen: once by you and once by the Dashwoods."

Crowley laughed. "You are too clever by half, Miss Williams; the maxim of the UnFunDaMentalist Church is 'Let the *Leader's* will be the whole of the Law.' If you are to censure me then you could at least do me the honor of being accurate."

This observation seemed to surprise the Daemon. "The little tweaks ABBA has made to the Demi-Monde never cease to amaze."

ABBA? Why would a Daemon in thrall to Loki speak of the Lord God, ABBA?

"So, what's to be my fate, Crowley? You say that this girl ..."

"This girl"! You impudent cow!

" ... is to be my hostess? What for? Are we just going to sit around discussing bustles and bonnets? That's all the women in this patriarchal ForthRight of yours seem to be good for. From what I've seen and heard they've had any independence of thought brainwashed out of them."

Brainwashed? What is a brain?

Crowley gave an indulgent smile. "I thought it would be more pleasant for you, Miss Williams, to spend your time as my guest in the company of someone of your own age. Of course, if you prefer, I can return you to the Lubyanka, but you were very outspoken in your criticisms of its amenities."

Now it was the Daemon's turn to laugh. "I get it: Princess Trixiebell here is going to be my stable pony, brought in to keep the troublesome Norma Williams docile and cooperative." It shrugged.

"Okay, I'm relaxed; anyplace has got to be better than a ten-by-five in that shithouse you call the Lubyanka."

A gasp from Trixie at the use of a profanity by the Daemon . . . and that she'd used it in front of men!

The Daemon obviously noted her consternation. "Yeah, little Miss Milksop over there looks as though she could use a little loosening up."

"I should warn you, Miss Williams," said Crowley carefully, "that you will be under constant supervision whilst you are living in Dashwood Manor and that the grounds are constantly patrolled. Your confinement is the responsibility of Colonel Archie Clement. If you try to escape he has been empowered to punish you most severely."

The Daemon's eyes hardened and its mouth tightened. "Then as we're in 'giving warnings' mode, Mr. Aleister Crowley, you better understand that if that piece of human excrement you call Archie Clement comes within ten feet of me I'm gonna rip his arm off and beat him to death with it."

Stunned though Trixie was that a *woman* could issue such a threat, the most remarkable thing was that she was utterly convinced that the Daemon meant every word it said. This wasn't just empty saber-rattling.

Archie Clement's face darkened and he made to rise out of his chair, but he was waved back by Crowley. "There will be no need for you to speak to or to socialize with Colonel Clement, Miss Williams, provided you do not try to escape."

All he received by way of reply from the Daemon was the merest of smiles.

11

The Real World:
June 12, 2018

The Demi-Monde[®] is the first simulation product to employ ParaDigm CyberResearch's Totally Realistic User Envelopment (TRUE[®]) technology to ensure full and all-pervasive Player–Simulation meshing. TRUE is the only product foundationed on ParaDigm's BioNeural-Kinetic Security Sensor (PBN-KiSS[®]), optimized for the probing, gathering, predicting and processing of neural, cerebral and autonomic bodily responses. TRUE also employs ParaDigm's own FAST/TRAK[®] Neurobahn-Network and its 2ndSkin[®] Total Immersion Shroud.
—THE DEMI-MONDE[®] PRODUCT DESCRIPTION MANUAL, JUNE 14, 2013

Somehow Ella had assumed when she agreed to undertake the mission to rescue Norma Williams from the Demi-Monde that she would be subjected to weeks, months even, of training, familiarization, role-playing exercises and total immersion in her new persona before she was sent on her way.

She was wrong.

A mere hour after her final meeting with the general, forty minutes after the session with the army lawyer signing numerous waivers and disclaimers—a little unnerved that for "benefits accruing upon death" she had been allocated the notional rank of captain in the U.S. Marines—and twenty minutes after a very upsetting meeting with an attorney to draw up her will, Ella was led to the professor's laboratory, where she would be prepared to enter the Demi-Monde.

The laboratory was situated at an even lower level than the room where she'd met Heydrich, which meant, so far as Ella could judge, that she was now standing just a few yards up from the earth's core. It was a modest enough room: white-painted walls, plastic-tiled floor, and furnished with just an examination couch, a control panel with a few monitors set in it and a chair for the use of the professor.

The professor smiled, displaying a set of brilliantly white teeth standing like tombstones behind his thin lips; ushered Ella onto a couch; clipped an electrode to the lobe of her ear and began. "If you will just lean back and relax, Miss Thomas. I am going to place a drop of liquid in your right eye. Don't worry, it's a totally painless procedure." It was such an innocuous request and Ella was still so distracted by matters legal . . .

Putting the money in trust for Billy was definitely the right thing to do. That way he can't try to spend it all in a single week.

. . . that before she quite realized what she was doing, she had complied.

"What was that for?" she asked a little belatedly as she dabbed a tear from her cheek.

"Contained in that drop was a miracle of cyber-science developed by my team of cyber-engineers at ParaDigm: a miracle known as PINC . . ."

One more acronym and murder will be done.

" . . . or Personal Implanted nanoComputer. Four years ago we were tasked by the U.S. military with finding a means of radically reducing training times and of more efficiently inculcating troops with the specific knowledge sets needed to make them more effective when operating in AWEs—a quick and easy way of teaching them things like foreign languages and giving them an understanding of idiosyncratic patterns of religious and social behavior. What we developed were Memory Supplements: nano-sized memory chips that are biologically compatible with the human brain. Once in contact with the brain these PINC chips fuse with the organic tissue of the brain and are able to graft information—painlessly and seamlessly—onto a person's memory bank."

Using one of his bony fingers he tapped one of the monitors on the control panel. "Excellent! You, Miss Thomas, are now the proud possessor of a PINC, a microbe-size computer which contains all the information you could ever require regarding the Demi-Monde, including fluency in all the major languages. But as you are the first player we have sent into the Demi-Monde who is fully au fait with the Real World, PINC will also give you an ability to know everything about everybody in the Demi-Monde. This will optimize your Dupe-to-Dupe effectiveness." The professor nodded toward a female nurse who was hovering at the side of the room. "If you would follow Nurse Green, she will equip you with your Total Immersion Shroud."

"Do I really wanna know what a Total Immersion Shroud is?"

He ignored her. "The TIS ensures full and all-pervasive player–simulation meshing. The TIS has three main purposes. First, it blocks out all external, Real World, stimuli. Second, it allows ABBA to receive feedback along a neurobahn from the player's body as it reacts to events in the Demi-Monde, which in turn enables ABBA to mimic these reactions in the player's Dupe. This raises the player's perception of the reality of the Demi-Monde. Third, the TIS protects the player. The safety of our players is of prime importance . . ."

Ella had the distinct feeling she was now in Bullshit Central, but then five million bucks bought a whole heap of bullshit tolerance.

". . . so not only does a player's TIS help sustain the player's bodily functions—body temperature, blood pressure and so on—and give our medical staff real-time feedback on the player's vital signs, but it also *maintains* the player's body. Whilst in the Demi-Monde the player will be, here in the Real World, comatose. The TIS manipulates the player's body to obviate the development of pressure sores, the contraction of ligaments, the attenuation of muscles and all the other ailments a bedridden body is prey to."

To Ella this sounded less than appetizing: bedsores and attenuated muscles had not been mentioned in the promotional brochure.

"At the end of his or her sojourn in the Demi-Monde, the player is as healthy and fit as he or she has ever been."

"Unless they can't get out of the place," observed Ella wryly.

"Well . . . let us hope for the best in that regard."

Yeah, right.

"Now, Miss Thomas, Nurse Green will prepare you for entry to the Demi-Monde."

The nurse led Ella through to a large room swathed in stainless steel and equipped with a couch, yet another control panel, a shower unit tucked in one corner and, oddly, a large black circle inscribed on the floor.

"If you would strip yourself naked, Miss Thomas, and remove all body ornamentation," the nurse asked in what Ella thought was an excessively casual manner.

"Naked?"

"Why, yes; in order for the TIS to do its job correctly it must be directly in contact with your skin—*all* of your skin. And anyway, we need access to your orifices. We have to place evacuation ducts into certain . . . places to eliminate waste products. We won't be able to interrupt you in the Demi-Monde to allow you to take a comfort break, now, will we?"

Silly me.

"We will, of course, feed and nourish you through a drip. But don't worry; all these connections—both for nutrients and for waste products—will be made once you are in the Demi-Monde. This will minimize discomfort and embarrassment."

Terrific.

"So if you would undress, then I will shave you."

"Shave me?"

"Of course. Hair prevents TIS making a true connection in two very important parts of your body: your head and your—"

"I get the picture."

The nurse shaved her. When a shorn Ella looked at herself in the mirror she decided that it was a look that suited her. Even the sight of all her beautiful long black hair lying discarded on the floor didn't upset her as much as she thought it might.

"If you will shower thoroughly, Miss Thomas"—the nurse nodded toward a shower cubicle in the corner—"then we can start. You can remove your glasses. You won't need them in the Demi-Monde: ABBA will ensure that your Dupe has twenty-twenty vision."

Ella did as she was asked and then, showered and dried, came to stand in the middle of the room. "Now, Miss Thomas, please step onto the black disc." She pointed to the shiny black circle on the floor. It seemed to be just a disc of thin black plastic, perhaps eighteen inches in diameter, that had been absentmindedly tossed onto the floor.

"This disc is the compressed TIS. When you are standing on the disc and I put an electrical current through it, the TIS will rise up over your body to form a wafer-thin body-encasing film. I am told that the sensation is strange but not unpleasant. The word most commonly used to describe it is 'ticklish.'" Ella stepped onto the black disc. "Now, if you will stand perfectly still, I will begin on the count of three. One, two, three . . ."

The nurse threw a switch. Ella felt a trembling under the soles of her feet as the shiny blackness of the disc began to crawl slowly up over her. It was akin to being gradually dipped in a vat of luke-warm black treacle. The TIS crept over her feet, up along her calves, around her thighs, past her midsection—*Now, that did tickle!*—over her torso and her chest, to halt its progress just below her chin. Now when Ella gazed down at herself it seemed that she had been re-created in shiny black Perspex.

The nurse circled Ella, searching, she presumed, for flaws in the TIS covering. "Excellent. Now, Miss Thomas, please pop yourself up on the couch and place your bottom over the hole in the middle and the back of your head over the one at the top."

As Ella climbed onto the couch she was surprised to find that her TIS had dried; to all intents and purposes now she had a second skin. When she was comfortable the nurse tethered a steel band across her forehead. "The band is simply to hold your head steady when we make the hook-up to ABBA. Now I'll activate your TIS."

Ella felt the TIS begin to vibrate over her body.

Oh, my. If the porno industry ever gets their hands on this they'll make a fortune.

It was at this moment that the professor entered the room. After running an appreciative eye over Ella's TIS-covered body—*Pervert*—he made a thorough check of the readings shown on the control panel monitors. "Excellent. You may proceed, Nurse Green."

The nurse came to stand next to where Ella's head was resting. "Now to plug you into ABBA." Out of the corner of her eye Ella saw the professor press a button on a control panel. She felt a nudge at the back of her head. "You see, Miss Thomas, completely painless," said the nurse with a little swagger in her voice. "All that remains before we send you on your way is for the professor to say a few words."

The professor remained motionless at the control panel. Ella had met furniture with more empathy. "You're now ready to become a player in the Demi-Monde, Miss Thomas. When I press this"—he wagged a finger toward a large red button—"you will be *in* the Demi-Monde. Although it is superfluous—PINC contains all your instructions and parameters relating to Operation Offbeat—I will summarize what you will see immediately when you arrive there. You will materialize in the London District of the Rookeries Sector at seventeen hundred hours on the fortieth day of winter, in the Demi-Mondian year one thousand and four, in an alleyway next to the building where your client Dupe has rooms. I would suggest you go immediately to your lodgings and take forty minutes or so to acclimatize yourself. Players have complained of a feeling of dis-orientation—of *ill-ucination*—when first entering the Demi-Monde. The auditions being held for the 'chirp' will take place at eighteen hundred hours at the Prancing Pig pub five blocks from your home. It is an easy fifteen-minute walk. After that you're on your own. All you have to do is locate and rescue Norma Williams and transport her to the one remaining Portal that we have functioning, which is situated in NoirVille. Again PINC has all the parameters necessary to find the Portal."

The professor made it sound like a walk in the park.

"Where do I find Norma?"

"Unfortunately with Norma Williams being a renegade Dupe we are unable to track her accurately, but our last intelligence was that she was active in the Rookeries."

Marvelous.

"One final piece of advice, Miss Thomas: the only thing distin-guishing you from the other Dupes that populate the Demi-Monde is that you can bleed. We will be introducing a hormone into your body to suspend your menstrual cycle, which would otherwise be mimicked in the Demi-Monde, but we can do nothing to stop bleed-ing from accidental cuts. I would suggest that you make every effort *not* to be cut whilst in the Demi-Monde, otherwise your fellow Dupes will know instantly that you are a Daemon." He gave Ella what he must have thought was a reassuring smile. "All that remains is for me to wish you the very best of luck." He turned to the nurse. "You may complete the TIS envelopment."

The nurse placed a mouthpiece between Ella's lips. Ella felt the black skin of the TIS begin to flow over her chin, over her mouth, her nose, her eyes and then . . .

Part II

ENTRANCE

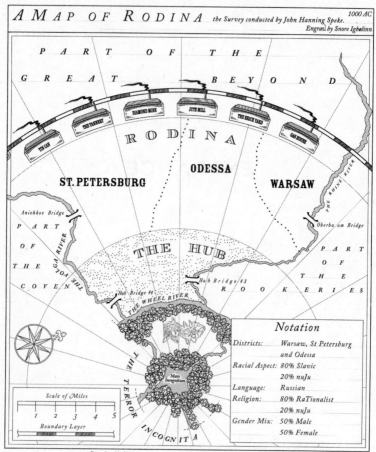

MAP OF RODINA.

PLATE 2

12

The Demi-Monde: 40th Day of Winter, 1004

It is hereby announced that as from the thirty-first day of summer 1003 all use of conjurations, witchcrafts, sorceries and enchantments (including but not limited to the enacting of séances, the making of 4Tellings, the devising of calculations relating to preScientific prognostications, the use of crystals and wands, and the employment of scrying and other forms of divination) is declared illegal (on pain of being declared nonNix) within the frontiers of the ForthRight EXCEPT when said conjurations, witchcrafts, sorceries and enchantments are performed by psychics examined and licensed by the Ministry of Psychic Affairs.

—Decree 8989, relating to the Control and Licensing of Psychic and Occult Practices within the ForthRight, ForthRight Law Gazette, Summer 1003

Of all the seasons in the Demi-Monde, Vanka Maykov liked Winter the best. Oh, he hated the bitter, biting cold, he detested the ankle-deep snow, he abhorred the frosty winds and simply loathed the ice-treacherous pavements. But there were compensations, the principal ones being that during Winter it was permissible for him to wander through the streets of the Rookeries with the collar of his coat turned high, his fox-fur *chapka* pulled hard down on his head and a thick woolen *sharf* wrapped around his face. And dressed like that it was impossible for anyone to recognize him.

Which, when you had Comrade General Mikhail Dmitrievich Skobelev and his bully-boys combing the ForthRight in search of you, was very handy.

Not that Vanka was *too* concerned that General Skobelev was on the lookout for him; in his opinion the general could *look* for him for as long as he liked. What Vanka was worried about was the general *finding* him. That and the small part of Vanka's anatomy the general had promised to lop off if he did find the psychic.

Vanka had never really understood the emotion of vengefulness, and anyway, how was he to have known that the lady (lady, ha!) in question—Madam Alisha Petrovna Andreyeva—had been General Skobelev's *sister?*

The general's lust for revenge seemed totally ridiculous to Vanka. Why would anyone go to so much trouble just because of a *woman?* It wasn't civilized. There were *lots* of women in the ForthRight and since the Troubles there were a damned sight more women than men. And despite the Party's urging that they all follow the teachings of UnFunDaMentalism and disport themselves in a modest and ladylike manner, girls would be girls.

Or, as in Madam Andreyeva's case, very *naughty* little girls.

At the end of the shadowed street, Vanka made an absentminded left turn into the shit-strewn alleyway that led to the Prancing Pig. He shuddered at the thought of being reduced to asking Burlesque Bandstand for help.

But when Vanka had escaped the general by sliding through the concealed door, out of the back window of his apartment in St. Petersburg and down the fire escape, the quandary he faced was where to run to. And he had to run for it; he had to get out of Rodina while he still had the use of his legs.

He'd immediately corrected himself: while he still *had* his legs. The general's boys were meant to be really handy with their hatchets.

It hadn't been much of a stretch to decide to head for the Rookeries. Running to NoirVille was a no-no: Shaka and his gang of cutthroats hated Blanks with a vengeance, and anyway he didn't fancy being buggered bandy by all the zadniks living there. And an equally unpleasant, if somewhat different, problem confronted him if he was to exit in the direction of the Coven: the Suffer-O-Gettes were so anti-men—well, anti-*ordinary*-men; Empress Wu had a soft spot for geniuses like Karl Marx and Pierre-Simon Laplace—that trying to hide there would necessitate his having to sing falsetto for the rest of his life. Letting those mad-cow LessBiens chop his bollocks off and turn him into a NoN did not appeal.

The Quartier Chaud had been a possibility. All he would have had to do was pinch a boat and scull across the Thames. His French was pretty good too. And it *was* over a year since he'd sold Godfrey de Bouillon that consignment of adulterated blood. That's what had finally ruled the Quartier out: Godfrey de Bouillon never forgot and even wearing a mask like all the other CitiZens in the Quartier wouldn't stop Vanka being recognized. De Bouillon was a mad, vicious bugger and without Madam Alisha Petrovna Andreyeva's fortune to pay him off . . .

So the Rookeries were really the only place that Vanka could hide. His English was perfect and with the Rookeries being part of the ForthRight he didn't need any new documents. He'd done business there too, so he had contacts. The problem Vanka had was blood.

He was sure that the Checkya monitored the Blood Banks, that they had cryptos hanging around noting who was doing what in the Transfusion Booths, trying to spot when transfers and withdrawals were made. And if the Checkya knew, then sure as eggs were eggs General Skobelev would know: someone as important as the general was bound to be able to access Checkya files. If Vanka couldn't make withdrawals legitimately then he'd have to buy blood on the black market and that was expensive and dangerous, because the black market was run by Shaka's Blood Brothers.

The other problem he had was that having skedaddled at such short notice all he had to his name was what he stood up in and what he'd squirreled away in his safe-deposit box at the St. Petersburg Blood Bank. Enough to keep him going for a month, tops. A month, that is, if Burlesque didn't get greedy, didn't get wind of just how desperate Vanka was for a place to lie low. If he did, then the price of the two shitty garret rooms Vanka now called home would rocket. Burlesque was a master at squeezing people dry. The bastard had really stiffed him on the blood trade they'd done at the end of autumn.

The odd thing was that yesterday, when Vanka had shown up at the Prancing Pig pub—the dive that Burlesque used as the headquarters for his pub empire—the fat Anglo had been almost friendly, almost as though he was pleased to see Vanka.

Remarkable.

Vanka arrived outside the Pig, stepped over the frozen body of the drunk that was decorating the doorway, took a deep breath and pushed his way inside.

BURLESQUE BANDSTAND WAS SITTING IN HIS BOOTH AT THE SIDE OF the pub, dolly-mop at his side, toying with a glass of 20 percent Solution. He was wearing his usual hangdog expression, the dog in question being peculiarly mangy and flea infested.

"Afternoon, Burlesque, how's things?" Vanka said by way of a greeting.

Burlesque looked up from his examination of the hugely fat

comic who was fiddling around with the megaphone on the stage and blinked in Vanka's direction.

"Hello, Wanker, glad to see the swelling's going down. Yous look almost human."

Thanks.

"My name is pronounced 'Van-ka,'" protested Vanka for the umpteenth time, moderately relieved that in the two days since he'd been beaten up by Skobelev's boys he had, at last, regained the ability to talk without dribbling down his shirt front. "I was born and raised in Rodina."

"Vanka, Wanker, Spanker . . . it's all the same between friends."

Vanka grimaced at the thought of being classified as a "friend" of Burlesque's. Burlesque didn't do friends, he did debtors.

Waving him into a seat, Burlesque turned his attention back toward the comic and Vanka was—unfortunately—obliged to do the same. It took only a few moments for him to decide that of all the truly diabolical variety acts that Burlesque put on at the Pig—which he laughingly called "entertainment"—Maurice Merriment, the Monarch of Mirth, was perhaps the most dire.

The comedian wasn't just bad; he'd left "bad" behind several jokes ago and was now exploring that seldom-visited and deathly unamusing hinterland that existed somewhere between "terrible" and "fucking awful." So bad that even the fifty-strong audience in the back room of the pub was becoming restless, which was quite remarkable given that Vanka was convinced two of them were dead, and the remainder so blasted by the adulterated Solution Burlesque sold that their relationship with the reality that was the Demi-Monde was tenuous at best. Only those with a truly outrageous death wish drank "Bandstand's Best Blasting Solution" and even then they did it with reluctance: no one wanted to go to the Spirit World with nary a tooth in their head.

Fortunately for Vanka's sanity and Maurice Merriment's continued good health (the audience was getting *very* restless), the manager of the Pig, the huge and uncompromising Blowback Trundler, strode onto the stage and grabbed the megaphone away from the comic. "Thank you, thank you and . . . thank you. Now, ladies and gentlemen, a big round of applause for Horace Humor, the King of Comedy."

"It's Maurice Merriment, the Monarch of Mirth." The comic's protests were truncated as Blowback's kick up the arse encouraged him to vacate the stage.

BURLESQUE BANDSTAND LEANED BACK IN HIS CHAIR AND SPREAD HIS hands contentedly over his ample stomach. The chair gave a protesting groan: Burlesque wasn't so much round as blobby. "So whaddya fink, Wanker?"

"Think about what?"

"Abart Maurice bleedin' Merriment, ov course," said Burlesque, twitching his head toward the now-empty stage.

Vanka looked at Burlesque for as long as he was able to stomach it. "What do you mean, what did I think? He was terrible, useless, arse-clenchingly bad. It was a uniquely awful performance."

Burlesque beamed and nudged him in the ribs. Vanka winced; he was still very tender from the kicking Skobelev's goons had administered. "Unique, eh? That's good, ain't it? To be unique's good, ain't it?"

"The answer to that question, Burlesque, is both yes and no, or more accurately in the case of Maurice Merriment: no."

"So what do you fink 'e'd 'ave to do to improve 'is act?"

"I'm tempted to suggest suicide."

Burlesque descended into a sulk: he hated to have his acts criticized. Finally though, after a slurp of Solution, he roused himself to continue the conversation. "I'm sorry you fink like that, Wanker. I arsked you 'ere to get an appreciation ov the standard of artiste I 'ave performing at the Pig."

"Yeah, Burlesque, I appreciate them all right. I appreciate that they're shit. But I knew that already."

"I fort 'e wos funny," observed the girl sitting to Burlesque's right. Reluctantly Vanka turned his attention to Burlesque's *trollop du jour* and studied the girl for the first time. Burlesque changed his tarts as often as he changed his socks—more often, decided Vanka, judging by the smell drifting up from under the table—and as the brasses he used and misused were always the most vacuous and stupid of doxies there was little point in engaging them in conversation. But as this one had deigned to express an opinion, Vanka felt obliged to reciprocate with a show of interest. She was just the type of girl that Burlesque preferred: blond, with a body that looked as though it had been inflated to bursting and then viciously constrained around the neck, waist and ankles. It was like sitting across the table from a sexy blimp, a sexy blimp blessed with the most stupendously enormous tits Vanka had ever seen.

Knowing that his finances were as precarious as the grip the girl's dress had on her tits, Vanka determined to be as pleasant as possible. He thrust out a hand in greeting. "I'm delighted to meet you. I'm Colonel Ivan Ivanovich Maykov, licensed psychic, but my friends call me Vanka."

The girl's eyes widened. "A psychical? Wot, like them seers and such everywun's bin talkin' abart? Well, chuffed to meet cha, Wanker; me name's Sporting."

An awful feeling of inevitability descended on Vanka. "I don't suppose your surname is Chance by any . . . er, chance, is it?"

The girl's dull eyes widened in amazement. "Gor blimey, 'ow d'ya know that? Yeah, that's me: Sportin' Chance. You really are one 'ell ov a psychical, ain't cha, Wanker?"

Vanka just smiled a fatalistic smile.

Burlesque smiled too, which was a mistake. Burlesque's face wasn't built for smiling. The exertion of smiling caused his face to strain in a very odd way, making his potato of a nose twist in a most peculiar fashion and his piggy eyes become engulfed by his chubby cheeks. The best word Vanka had ever found to describe Burlesque's appearance was "ugly" but now, on closer inspection, he was veering toward amending this to "fucking ugly."

But what he found most alarming was the way Burlesque's thin, harsh lips pulled back to reveal his three remaining teeth, a consequence of his success in the entertainment business. There was a lot of competition in the entertainment business, competition that expressed itself in a very physical manner.

"You wan' anovver drink, Wanker?" asked Burlesque, smacking his lips in anticipation of downing another glass of Solution.

Vanka eyed Burlesque suspiciously. For Burlesque to be buying drinks meant he wanted something. Burlesque *never* bought people drinks. By reputation he had the shortest arms and the deepest pockets of anyone in the Rookeries.

"Yeah, I'll have a double b-and-t."

Burlesque scowled and then gave a reluctant wave to a scabrous waiter. When the blood and tonic had been served he leaned toward Vanka in a conspiratorial sort of way. Vanka rather wished he hadn't; the smell coming from his armpits was repellent.

"So yous still in this psychical lark, Wanker?" Burlesque asked casually.

"Might be," answered Vanka cautiously. Whilst he *was* a Licensed Psychic, the way he had obtained said license had been rather unconventional. Not wanting to trouble the busybody officials of the Ministry of Psychic Affairs with having to squander their time examining and interviewing him, Vanka had negotiated his license directly with the chief psychic. That he had possession of a set of daguerreotypes showing the chief psychic examiner in congress with someone who most certainly wasn't his wife had certainly helped the negotiations, as had the fact that that someone hadn't even been of the same species as the examiner's wife.

"Well, iffn you is, then I might 'ave a job for you."

Vanka suppressed a shudder. The prospect of having Burlesque Bandstand as an employer made Vanka's teeth itch . . . the ones he had left anyway. Burlesque was, as far as Vanka was concerned, the foulest individual to walk the Demi-Monde. He might be the biggest impresario operating on the Rookeries' "Blood, Grub, Shrub and Pub" circuit but he was still a horrible, disgusting man . . . near-man.

But as Vanka was on the run and in four weeks would be destitute, he decided to put his aversions and olfactory prejudices against noisome and hydrophobic people like Burlesque to one side. Preferably the upwind side.

"What's the job?"

"I'm trying to take the Prancing Pig upmarket, Wanker," said Burlesque, without a trace of irony in his voice.

For a moment Vanka was speechless: the association of the words "Pig," "up" and "market" was at best risible and at worst worrying, possibly implying that Burlesque had relinquished his grip on any vestigial trace of sanity he might once have had. He looked around the pub. Even in the gloom it was easy to see that the back room of the Pig—the "Best Room" as Burlesque insisted on calling it—was dirty, careworn and, if the brown tracks covering the top of the scarred and chipped table Vanka was sitting at were any indication, vermin infested. It was difficult for him to imagine how much shit someone's life would have to be in for them to consider the Pig "upmarket."

"Burlesque, believe me, the only way you'd be able to take this place upmarket is by the use of a steam-powered hoist. The Pig isn't so much downmarket as subMantle." Vanka shook his head and took a sip of his freshly delivered drink. As he had anticipated, it was so watered down fish could live in it. "Anyway, why would you want to do that? I thought you had found your niche"—he nodded toward the motley collection of individuals making up the customers of the Pig—"fleecing those of diminished intellect."

"Because some bugger is trying to kill me, Wanker," answered Burlesque with a rather overtheatrical look around the pub.

"I'm not surprised, Burlesque; I've seen the acts you've been putting out."

"Nah, I'm serious, Wanker, I've had two potshots taken at me in the past week and I got this today." He delved into the inner recesses of his voluminous black coat—well, it was black now; originally, as best Vanka could tell, it had been light gray—and pulled out a grubby piece of paper. "Scared the shit outta me it did."

Wishing he was still wearing his gloves, Vanka carefully unfolded the letter and read:

> For Burlesque Bandstand
>   We know it was you who betrayed the Daemon.
>   You are a malevolent individual who is using his Houses of Infamy to promote the subjugation of women and to propagate hedonism and dissolute living amongst the working classes. If you don't abandon your pernicious and misogynistic ways within the next two weeks we will execute you.
>   I am prepared to make you Suffer.
>   A Friend

Burlesque took a swig of his Solution. "It's a poor world when a respectable businessman like wot I am 'as to put up wiv bin threatened. Comes to somefink when an honest bloke like wot I am 'as got to go around heeled." He pulled back the side of his frock coat to display the Webley revolver holstered on his belt.

Vanka gulped, ignoring the pain in his damaged jaw. He didn't

like violence. He didn't even like the thought of violence. So he decided not to think about it and just shrugged his broad shoulders
dismissively. Anyway, he saw threatening letters like this virtually
every day, usually sent to him by aggrieved husbands. "What's all
this about a Daemon?"

"Nuffink important," murmured Burlesque in an offhand
manner as he gnawed at a fingernail that had already been bitten
down to the quick.

Bloody liar.

"Nothing important? Oh come on, Burlesque, how can a Daemon
be classified as nothing important?"

"Look, Wanker, I can't say nuffink abart it, okay? It's confidential." Burlesque tapped the side of his nose.

"But was it a *real* Daemon?" Vanka persisted.

Burlesque took a quick gander around the pub. "Yus."

Vanka looked at the fat man with something approaching admiration. Daemons—not that he believed in Daemons—were things
only important people in the ForthRight got involved with.

"Awful, ain't it?" whined Burlesque. "An' it don't make sense neither. Wot's 'misogynistic' mean, Wanker?"

"It means you hate women."

"Well, that's bollocks, ain't it, Burlesque?" scoffed Sporting.
"Wot you an' me wos doin' this lunchtime—"

"Never mind wot we wos doing," interrupted Burlesque, as ever
worried that one of his wife's cronies might overhear. "The important fing is that I've got to take it seriously, ain't I, Wanker? It's awful,
ain't it?"

Vanka nodded sympathetically. The word "Suffer" was the clue.
Presumably this indicated that the author was a Suffer-O-Gette and
Suffer-O-Gettes had to be taken very seriously indeed. From what
he'd heard there was a whole army of LessBien terrorists ready to die
for the cause of women's rights and take people like Burlesque with
them as they did so.

Sensible of them.

"More accurate than awful, Burlesque. I mean a man in your line of work is bound to accumulate a few enemies."

Burlesque wouldn't be consoled. "The Suffer-O-Gettes 'ave got it in for me."

"So what are you planning to do?"

"Like I said: I wanna move the Pig upmarket—knock the filthy comics and the pawno-contortionists and the donkeys on the head and introduce a bit ov tone to the Pig." Burlesque ignored Vanka's derisive snort. "I was finking of 'aving a sorry," he said quietly.

13

The Demi-Monde: 40th Day of Winter, 1004

Biological Essentialism is a cornerstone of the UnFunDaMentalist doctrine. It is predicated on the principle that the sexes occupy Separate Spheres of intellectual, economic and social functionality within the Demi-Monde, and that these Separate Spheres are ordained by ABBA and are thus natural, fixed and immutable. ABBA, by making the sexes biologically, psychologically and intellectually different, has equipped them for different tasks in life. UnFunDaMentalism teaches that the preservation of these distinctive Spheres of Activity is vital if social harmony is to be maintained and for women this means adherence to the mantra of "Feeding, Breeding and MenFolk Heeding" given to them by ABBA.

—Cogitations on the Superior Male Essence, Thomas Aquinas, Party Rules Publications

B link.
  Daylight . . .
   Blink.
Cold . . .
Blink.
Noisy . . .
Blink.

Smelly . . .

Blink.

Confused . . .

Ella staggered, her head spinning. Her mind seemed to be a whirling muddle of facts and information.

Ill-ucinating . . .

Her brain was struggling to come to grips with PINC and the mass of data it was trying to upload regarding the Demi-Monde. Only gradually did the torrent of information subside, allowing Ella a chance to reassert control over her thought processes. And as she did so, so PINC's enthusiasm was subdued: now it simply lurked at the back of her mind, waiting like some overeager puppy dog to tell her things she might need even if she didn't want to know them.

Happier now, Ella took a look around. She was standing in a filthy alleyway pressed between two filthy tenement buildings. It was cold, the pavement was covered with thick snow, and the wind, sharp and biting, cut at her cheeks—so cold that the light from the gas streetlamps seemed to have taken on an almost crystalline clarity. She huddled deeper into the thick fur collar of her coat and tied her bonnet a little more securely about her ears, noting as she did so that ABBA had kindly replaced the hair that had been shaved off in the Real World. She wrinkled her chilled nose: the alley stank. It seemed to be the place where the back entrances of a couple of restaurants whose owners were careless about hygiene regulations let out. Waste and refuse overflowed the bins and, even as she stood there, Ella saw a couple of fat rats scurry around. She shivered from cold and disgust.

But although it was an unappetizing place, there was no denying that it was very, very real. If Ella hadn't known that she was now occupying a computer-generated simulation there would have been nothing to suggest that this world wasn't as real and as substantial as the one she had been inhabiting just a moment before. It even *smelled* right.

But there *were* differences.

The colors of the Demi-Monde were out of kilter with those of the Real World. It was as though she were looking through a filter that leached out some color intensity but at the same time made the light just a little brighter. ABBA had obviously tinkered around with the spectrum: maybe the computer just wanted to add a sepia tone to the Victorianesque atmosphere of the simulation. It was meant to be 1870, after all.

The fact that the gaslights were lit worried her. It seemed too dark to be five o'clock in the afternoon. But even as she pondered she felt herself being given a mental nudge from PINC (she knew it was PINC; it was as though a brand-new piece of information had elbowed itself eagerly into her consciousness) to check the fob watch pinned to the lapel of her coat. The watch showed six o'clock, an hour later than the time the professor had told her she would be manifesting.

That ABBA had gotten things a little wrong Ella found simultaneously worrying and reassuring. Worrying in that maybe the data held on PINC was similarly flawed and reassuring in that when all was said and done, ABBA was just a machine.

Unfortunately ABBA's screwup over the time meant she'd have to go immediately to the audition. There was no time for "acclimatization," no time for her to chill out in her room; she'd have to jump straight in at the deep end. Taking a long, calming breath—noticing as she did so that the air, laden with soot from the belching chimneys, tasted foul—she marched toward the main street that ran at right angles across the mouth of the alleyway.

She stood there for a moment gathering her courage. Truth be told, she felt just a little panicky; she really had no idea how to go about *finding* Norma Williams, never mind rescuing her. She was just a girl from the wrong side of the tracks being asked to do something that was way out of her league.

Stop it . . . think positively.

She adjusted the veil that covered her face. Now *that* idea of ABBA's—equipping her bonnet with a veil—was a good one. There was no point in announcing her ethnicity: this *was* Heydrich-ville after all.

She swallowed hard, trying to displace the lump that had formed in her throat.

God, she was scared.

Ella, baby, just what have you gotten yourself into?

Getting a grip on herself, she stepped out of the alleyway.

Not even PINC could prepare her for what she experienced when she emerged. It was one thing to talk about how congested the Demi-Monde was, about it being a Deep-Density Urban Environment, but it was quite another to experience it. The street—Mile End, according to the grimy sign set high above her head—was full to overflowing with humanity. Never could she have imagined that so many people could be compressed into so confined a place. Oh, she knew from PINC that the Mile End was an important road leading to and from the wharves and docks that lined the Thames on the east side of the Rookeries, but even so . . .

The pavements were jam-packed with pushing, rushing, shouting, screaming people: bewhiskered men in somber suits and towering top hats, workmen wearing cloth caps and sullen expressions, women in bonnets and skirts that scraped along the pavement and children dressed in rags and oversized boots chasing through the press of the crowd. There was also a disproportionate number of soldiers—easily identifiable by their red coats—strutting around looking brave and arrogant.

But the most disturbing thing was that the Dupes populating the Demi-Monde looked so amazingly lifelike: they were indistinguishable from the real thing. This was all the more remarkable because, according to PINC, Demi-Mondians weren't flesh and blood: although they had a skeleton, over this was layered stuff they called

Solidified Astral Ether—SAE in Demi-Monde-speak—a pale white organic matter that provided the musculature that allowed the Dupes to move and to think, equipped them with the five senses they needed to interact with the world about them and gave them the means to take in nutrients and excrete waste products.

For Ella though, the saddest fact was that, just like in the Real World, the color of a Demi-Mondian's SAE divided people. UnFunDaMentalism taught that the finest, the superior form of the human species was the Anglo-Slavic race—the Aryan race—because theirs was the only race whose external SAE color matched the internal one. Because this white color was adulterated in the other races of the Demi-Monde—the UnderMentionables—by UnFunDaMentalist thinking this signaled that all other races were unclean and inferior.

Racial prejudice was alive and well in the Demi-Monde.

Hardly daring to surrender the lee of the alleyway for fear of being swept away by a tide of faux-humanity, Ella took a moment to orientate herself. The Prancing Pig pub was off Sidney Street, which lay on the opposite side of the Mile End, and to get to the pub she'd have to cross the road. And that was a daunting prospect.

If the pavements were crowded, they were as nothing to the maelstrom of carts, omnibuses, cabs and steamers that were trying—ineffectually—in a storm of honking and shouting and swearing to force their way along the traffic-choked thoroughfare. God, it was noisy: the Demi-Monde was a cacophony of ersatz humanity and all its works.

She shook her head; the thought of trying to lizard through the almost solid jam of vehicles most certainly did not appeal, especially as the road's surface seemed to be covered by a thick compote of soot, mud, slush and horse shit. One slip and she knew her mission would be ended before it had begun, with her crushed under the wheels of a careless cart or the hoofs of a neglectful dray horse.

Then . . .

Suddenly the traffic paused as though taking a breath, and grabbing her chance she ran, slipping and sliding as she went, on the snow-slick cobbles, dodging between the carts of two costermongers parked at the side of the road, sidestepping the steel wheels of a steam tractor, ducking under the flicking whip of a carter as he urged his horses into a nonexistent gap in the traffic, ignoring the obscene shouts of a cabbie as she obliged him to rein up, swearing as she stepped into a puddle of ice-cold and very scummy water, and finally, with a sigh of relief, skipping—soiled, sweaty and shivering—to the sanctuary of the other side of the road.

For a moment she sheltered in the entrance of a haberdasher's shop to get her breath back and still her jangling nerves. The Demi-Monde, she decided, was a nightmare. She had never felt so threatened or so endangered by a place in all her life; even Flatbush at its worst had nothing on the Rookeries. Everything about the Demi-Monde seemed designed, if not to kill her, then to make her wish she was somewhere else. She slumped back against the wall, then, cursing herself, stood straight up again; she'd forgotten that every vertical surface in the Rookeries was coated with slimy soot. Now her beautiful fur coat had a beautiful black line down the back.

Terrific.

With a resigned sigh Ella pushed herself back into the current of people, elbowing and shoving in what PINC told her was the direction of Sidney Street. She made it, though her bonnet was knocked askew in the mêlée and she thought her bustle would never be the same again. Here the street was jammed with swarms of people coming back from the ForthRight Union Day celebrations in Hyde Park. It seemed that any appearance by the Great Leader Reinhard Heydrich was an event that all loyal ForthRightists were expected to attend, and anyway, people seemed very taken with all the marching and community singing.

A crowd of laughing kids—their faces pinched tight with cold—swarmed past Ella, each of them holding a balloon decorated with the ForthRight's motto "Two Sectors Forged as One" in one hand and waving a paper flag emblazoned with the Valknut's three interlocking triangles in the other. The ForthRight Party was big on balloons and flags.

One thing it wasn't big on was Daemons.

It was that thought that persuaded Ella to pick up her pace. The sooner she got to the Prancing Pig the better.

14

The Demi-Monde: 40th Day of Winter, 1004

Efforts by Occultists (also known by the archaic term Ocularists) are directed toward the resuscitating of the Third Eye and restoring the Aryans' lost metaPhysical powers. All the metaPhysical powers of the Pre-Folk emanated from the Third Eye, the organ situated in the middle of the head and embedded in the Solidified Astral Ether. The Third Eye gave connection to ABBA and to the metaPhysical forces flowing through and around the Demi-Monde. After the Fall of the Pre-Folk, the Third Eye diminished in size to such an extent that it was presumed to have vanished; however, surgeon John Austen Hamlin has found vestigial traces of this wondrous organ in Aryan cadavers ("Examination of the Cranial SAE of Aryan Soldiers Killed in the Troubles," The Lance It Magazine of Surgery, Spring 1003).

—Rediscovering the Third Eye, Grigori Rasputin, Occult Books and Scrolls

A sorry?" queried Vanka as he tried to stop the contents of his stomach from making a return visit. The stench from Burlesque's fouled mouth as he whispered in Vanka's ear was overpowering.

"Yeah, that's right. Like wot the Frogs in the Quartier Chaud 'ave."

"Ah . . . a soirée," exclaimed Vanka as the penny dropped. The linguistic ability of all Anglos was appalling; they were famous for it . . . or actually for their lack of it. They were the only Demi-Mondians who couldn't speak all five of the world's languages. The rumor was they had never really mastered English.

"Yeah, dat's wot I said: a sorry," said Burlesque, proving the rumor correct. "A better class of people come to sorries, nice people who are dead keen on speaking wiv their loved ones wot inhabit the ovver side."

Vanka concluded that Burlesque didn't see the irony involved with anyone being "dead keen" to attend a séance.

"You're a Licensed Physicalist, Wanker, you're an occultist, so I wos wondering..."

So *that* was why Burlesque had been so pleasant. But when Vanka thought about it, it wasn't that bad an idea.

Since the ending of the Troubles, and thanks to Crowley's enthusiastic promotion of UnFunDaMentalism, attending séances had become very fashionable in the ForthRight. Business for Vanka—pre-Skobelev, that is—had been booming. Everyone, it seemed, wished to commune with the dead, and as the fighting during the Troubles had been so ferocious—or so Vanka had heard; he'd made a point of staying as far from the front line as possible—there were a great many dead to commune with. Not that Vanka believed in a life after death. Rather he believed in life *before* death ... a luxurious and comfortable life before death.

Spiritualism—*Faux-Spiritualism*; Vanka was nothing if not a realist—provided him with a handsome income. To put it at its most blunt, Vanka ran séances the true purpose of which was not so much to contact the dead, but rather to fleece widows out of their fortunes and, whenever possible, out of their knickers.

True, relieving the rich, the stupid and the credulous—and Madam Andreyeva, Skobelev's sister, had managed, miraculously, to be all three—of their wealth didn't make for a pleasant way of earning a living, and true, Vanka had very few friends, but when it came to a choice between friendship and a full stomach he always came down on the side of dinner.

But still Vanka hesitated before replying. In truth he was beset by something of a dilemma. On the one hand he was so desperate for money that the prospect of holding a few séances for Burlesque to help refill his coffers was mightily appealing. On the other, the one place General Skobelev and his thugs were sure to be looking for him was at séances.

But without blood he was a dead man.

"You're correct, Burlesque," he said in a low, conspiratorial voice, "I *am* a Licensed Psychic and Occultist." He leaned as close to Burlesque as the man's novel ideas about hygiene would allow. "I have studied at the feet of a master who taught me the mysteries of Russian cosmology and now, as an adept, I am able to connect with the esoteric forces that tie the past with the present and the present with the future. But more: I am able to link the living with the dead."

"Blimey," gasped Burlesque.

"Gor," said Sporting, and with a shaking hand she drained her glass of 5 percent Solution or, more accurately as this was the Pig they were sitting in, her glass of 2.5 percent Solution.

"So, wot you is saying, Wanker," began Burlesque as he wiped a terminally filthy handkerchief across his flaccid mouth, "is that yous can speak wiv the dead?"

"Certainly," said Vanka emphatically, "but you must realize that séances are difficult and expensive to run."

As was his wont, Burlesque skipped over the word "difficult" and homed in on "expensive." "'Ow expensive?"

"Let's say ten guineas a session."

"Let's say something a damn sight less bleedin' expensive."

"No . . . it's ten guineas or nothing. I am sorry, Burlesque, but that is my price. You have no idea the amount of mental anguish conducting a séance entails."

"Yessen I does," protested Burlesque. "It's abart the same as the mental anguish I experience when I 'ave to part wiv ten guineas ov my 'ard-earned loot. 'Ow about we say *five* guineas a show for the first week, then let's see how it goes."

"Okay . . . eight guineas for the first week and then ten thereafter."

Burlesque thought for a minute, but Vanka knew he would agree. No Licensed Psychic worth his salt would perform for less than ten guineas, so Burlesque knew he'd gotten a good deal.

"Done," he said at last, spitting on his hand and offering it to shake. Vanka looked at it with contempt; even from across the table he could smell whatever it was that Burlesque had been chewing and the last thing he wanted was to come into physical contact with it. In his opinion anything that came out of Burlesque's mouth was a biological hazard. The only way he'd shake the man's hand was if he was wearing a reinforced leather gauntlet.

"Never mind the handshake, Burlesque, there's one small problem."

Burlesque scowled; he wasn't a great fan of "problems."

"As I'm performing in the Rookeries, I want to use an Anglo name." Perform as "Vanka Maykov: Psychic" and he would become, in very short order, "Vanka Maykov: Dickless Psychic."

"That's fine wiv me, Wanker."

"And I need an assistant to help me commune with the Spirit World. I need a PsyChick. The girl I normally use, Svetlana, is nursing a sick relative in St. Pete's." Or more probably, if General Skobelev had found her, she was nursing part of the foundations propping up the new railway bridge the ForthRight had just built over the Rhine. "I need to hire a new girl."

"There's always Sportin' 'ere," suggested Burlesque. "I bet she's a natural PsyChick, wot wiv the amount ov spirits that 'ave manifested themselves in 'er. An' she's always very willin'."

Vanka gave Sporting a quick look; if ever there was a girl who could confidently be described as "willing" it was Sporting.

"I need a girl that can read."

"I can read," said Sporting hopefully.

"I mean something other than your name."

"Oh."

Burlesque took a huge drag on his cigar and then pushed the bowler hat that was permanently planted on top of his grease-drenched hair back on his head. His nasty little eyes settled on Vanka and for a moment he was reminded of just what a vicious bastard Burlesque really was.

Be careful, Vanka, be very careful.

"I've gotta idea, Wanker. I'm 'aving an audition this evening. I'm looking for a chirp, see, a new singer—someone classy. I'm looking for a jad singer . . . a *Shade* jad singer. Why don't cha stick around, Wanker, an' see 'oo turns up. Maybe you'll find a PsyChick amongst that lot."

Vanka sighed. He knew the sort of girls who came to auditions at the Pig: most of them had been around the block so many times they could only walk in right angles.

But Vanka needed a PsyChick. To pull off a séance he would need an assistant of such mesmerizing loveliness that the men in the audience wouldn't be able to keep their eyes off her. All good psychics knew that a pretty girl wearing not much more than a big smile was the ideal way to distract an audience's attention, and distraction was the psychic's most powerful weapon. But there was more to it than that. The girl—mentally Vanka emphasized the word "girl"; she had to be young—also had to be intelligent enough to help Vanka work his tricks and, most importantly, be so terminally naïve that she didn't realize that if they were caught running a bent séance they would both be for the high jump.

Not a chance . . . but then hope springs eternal.

ELLA TOOK A LEFT DOWN BOTTOMLEY ROAD, THANKFUL THAT IT WAS quieter here and that there were fewer people jostling her. With the noise of Sidney Street reduced to a background grumble, she took a moment to gather herself. The Prancing Pig was easy to spot at the end of the road; it was an oasis of light in the thickening gloom. But though it was well lit, judging from the expression on the face of the urchin swathed in an old army coat several sizes too big for him who was guarding the entrance, it wasn't very welcoming. Crouched in the pub's doorway out of the winter wind, the boy looked about ten years old and was, rather incongruously, puffing on a pipe.

He glared out at Ella from under his tatty *chapka* as she tried the door and then spat into the gutter. "Yous one ov them singing tarts?"

"I've come to audition," said Ella, tapping a finger against the soiled notice pinned to the door, "if that's what you mean."

"Don't get shirty wiv me, luv," admonished the boy with an angry puff on his pipe. "Sos yous sing jad, right?"

Ella referenced PINC. Jad was the swing music popular in the JAD—the nuJu Autonomous District of NoirVille—and it was widely thought in the Demi-Monde that only Shades could sing jad in anything approaching an authentic manner.

"Yeah, I'm a jad singer."

"Burlesque 'as left me 'ere to tell yous chirps that yous is to go round to the back room." He nodded down an alleyway that flanked the Pig.

She flipped the boy a penny for his advice and trudged down the dark alley. Twenty yards along she came to a pair of red doors. Ella had never been in a real—well, as real as anything could be in the Demi-Monde—English pub before and she was taken aback by the concoction of smells she was subject to: the sweet stench of rancid sweat, the tart aroma of spilled Solution and the undercurrent of damp and decay. And if her nose took a moment to adjust to the Pig so too did her eyes. She had to squint against the glare of the dozens of gaslights that illuminated the place, the light reflected, in turn, by the huge mirrors that decorated the walls.

As it was early in the evening there were only about thirty or forty people in the pub. Most of the clientele seemed to be workmen enjoying an after-work pint and taking the opportunity to chat up the somewhat flyblown girl idly polishing glasses behind the bar. There was also a circle of five or six heavily made-up women in rather risqué costumes drinking Solution—pinkies held out from the glass in an imitation of refined behavior—around a table on the far side of the room. A trio of musicians were setting up on the low stage to the front of the bar.

When she walked in every eye in the room turned in her direction.

A quick reference to PINC told Ella that Burlesque Bandstand was the fat and scruffily dressed man seated at the table near the stage. He had a rather too well-endowed blond girl—a floozy called Sporting Chance—by his side and a long-haired man sitting across from him. Long-haired or not, unfortunately—and worryingly—PINC couldn't tell her anything about him. He was a mystery: a tall, lean mystery with a big bruise on the side of his face. Despite the bruise she thought Mr. Mystery to be rather good-looking and she liked the careless way he had draped himself over his chair; the word that came to Ella's mind to describe him was "louche," closely followed by "rascal."

She strode across the sawdust-strewn floor of the pub and presented herself at the booth.

"Excuse me, sir, but would I be correct in thinking that I am addressing Mr. Burlesque Bandstand?"

15

The Demi-Monde: 40th Day of Winter, 1004

nuJuism *is the religion practiced by the Demi-Monde's Sectorless nuJu community. nuJuism is an unrelentingly pessimistic religion which teaches that suffering and hardship is life-affirming and necessary to prepare nuJus for the rigors to be experienced during the Time of Tribulation (a.k.a. the End of Days). It is a central tenet of nuJuism that there will arise a Messiah who will lead the nuJu people safely through Tribulation and to the Promised Land. As with everything to do with the nuJus this is, of course, pernicious nonsense.*

—Religions of the Demi-Monde, *Otto Weininger*,
University of Berlin Publications

Vanka looked up. It was difficult to see the girl who was addressing Burlesque as she had a light directly behind her and she was wearing a veil. All he could make out was a silhouette. It was a very *nice* silhouette though, without any of the usual humps and bumps that were de rigueur for women who frequented the Pig. From what he could see, the woman—girl!—was everything he had ever dreamed of in an assistant. Okay, she was a bit scrawny, but still . . .

He shuffled his chair around to get a better look, hoping, as he did so, that she didn't have a beard. He held his breath as she pulled back the veil that so completely covered her face. She didn't have a beard. She was quite lovely. Young, slim *and* lovely: perfect.

Except that she was black. Well, not black exactly; she was a wonderful light caramel color. But there was no denying she *was* a Shade and this *was* the Rookeries.

And if any of Archie Clement's SS thugs ever saw her, there would be Hel to pay: Shades weren't popular with the SS, who were liable to deal with them pretty viciously. As far as they saw it the ForthRight was a Shade-free zone and they would fight to keep it that way. But as a PsyChick the girl would be perfect. Even her color would be useful: it'd bring a touch of the exotic to the proceedings. He could bill her as a WhoDoo mambo. It'd hide the bruising too, if the SS ever caught up with her.

Burlesque didn't seem to notice the girl's skin color; in fact as Vanka remembered it he had specifically wanted a Shade singer. The punters liked Shade birds; they were sexier than the fat Anglo items Burlesque usually employed. In fact this girl was so sexy that even Burlesque was persuaded to be pleasant. "Good evening, m'dear," he crooned as his eyes made a professional inventory of the girl's body. "I am indeed Burlesque Bandstand: purveyor of alcoholic beverages an' fine victuals, an' impresario extraordinaire. An' to 'oo do I 'ave the pleasure of introducing myself?" Burlesque used a boot to shove a chair out from under the table and gestured the girl into it. She sat down and now, illuminated by the candle that sputtered in the middle of the table, Vanka could see her better.

She wasn't lovely.

She was more than lovely. She was beautiful and very, very *clean*. He couldn't remember when he had seen anybody that clean before or who smelled so . . . nice. The bouquet of violets and strawberries that shrouded the girl reminded him of days in the park and walks in the woods, which was remarkable because, as far as he could remember, he had never been in a park nor had he ever walked in a wood. She was so clean that he had to resist the urge to stretch out a hand

and touch her shimmering black hair. The girl smiled—revealing the whitest teeth he had ever seen—and thrust out a slim, elegant hand in the direction of Burlesque, each finger adorned by a beautifully manicured and varnished nail.

Burlesque looked at the hand in bemusement and then, reluctantly, took the girl's fingertips in his own mitt and gave the hand a cautious shake. Vanka could understand Burlesque's trepidation: when people shoved a hand in your direction in the Rookeries it was usually wrapped around the handle of a knife.

"My name's Ella Thomas," the girl said softly.

"An' I'm Sportin' Chance," said Burlesque's girlfriend, sticking out a hand whilst simultaneously giving her beau a filthy look. Sporting obviously wasn't keen on competition, especially good-looking competition.

"Delighted to meet you, Miss Chance."

"An' I'm delighted to meet yous, Miss Thomas," interrupted Burlesque. "An' this is my mate, Wanker."

"Colonel *Vanka* Ivanovich Maykov: Licensed Occultist," Vanka corrected as he took the girl's hand and shook it. He cursed himself as he did so; he had been so smitten by her beauty that he had forgotten to use an alias, and for all he knew she could be an agent of Skobelev. But gazing into those wonderful limpid eyes, he didn't think so; no one so lovely could be so venal. As he shook the girl's hand his cold-reading techniques came into play. Her skin was so soft that he knew she'd never done a decent day's work in her life; she was either a gentlewoman fallen on hard times or an expensive hooker. Unfortunately his instincts told him to put his money on her being the former.

Shame.

"'Ow may I 'elp you, Miss Thomas?" smarmed Burlesque.

"I've come to audition as a jad singer." The girl's voice tinkled like a bell through the room.

"A jad singer?" Burlesque almost choked.

A frown creased the girl's perfect forehead. "Yes, you have a notice on the door of your pub. It says you're looking for a chirp . . . a jad singer. I understand the auditions are being held here."

"Well, forgive my surprise but yous don't look much like a jad singer. They tend to be bigger than wot yous is."

The girl smiled her wonderful smile. "Well, I guess I'm one of the new generation of less-big jad singers." She thought for a moment. "People tell me, Mr. Bandstand, that I've got a good voice and I can sing just about anything, so why don't you try me out?"

Burlesque eyed the girl sidelong. He was probably, Vanka thought, trying to establish if the girl's suggestion that he "try her out" was a double entendre. Disappointment flared on the impresario's face; he'd obviously decided it wasn't.

"D'you dance?" Burlesque asked suspiciously.

"Sure, I can dance."

Sure?

From the moment she had opened her mouth Vanka had known she was just *too* good to be true. There was definitely something of the Yank about her, and Yanks, as everybody knew, were too independently minded to be reliable. Most of the bastards were Royalists too.

Her being a Yank would definitely be a problem: Burlesque didn't like Yanks. But Vanka had never heard of a *Shade* Yank before. Maybe Burlesque didn't like Shade Yanks. But then Burlesque didn't like *anybody*, be they Anglos, Slavs, nuJus, Shades, Polacks, Krauts, Russkis, Frogs, Eyeties, Wogs, Chinks or Nips. Burlesque was an equal-opportunity racist. He was probably wondering if the girl might be an undercover agent working for Shaka . . . or, worse, a Suffer-O-Gette assassin.

Burlesque continued his interrogation. "You tell jokes?"

A moment's consideration. "I guess I could."

"Right, let's see you outta that shooba," said Burlesque, nodding toward the girl's thick fur coat.

The girl paused, then with a shrug stood up from the chair and wriggled out of her coat. She shuffled self-consciously on her feet as Burlesque gave her body his usual forensic examination.

Looking at her without her coat, Vanka was sure his guess that she was a down-on-her-luck gentlewoman was correct. She was wearing a very sober outfit, just the sort of thing a young lady from a more refined background might wear. The dress was the epitome of decorum, being restrained in both its coloring (dark gray) and its skirt length (only an inch above the floor). Unfortunately the decorum didn't end there: her bosom was ensnared in an all-encompassing bodice—which was unusual for women in the Pig. Even the bustle was small. All in all it was an outfit that only those of the most proper and conservative of outlooks would be seen dead in; it was the sort of outfit women got buried in.

But proper and conservative though her dress was, it couldn't disguise the fact that the girl's figure went in and out in an appealing manner ... very appealing indeed.

Burlesque was less than impressed. "Gor, your frock's a bit drab innit and you're a bit skinny for this singing lark. People coming to see a singer wanna see a bird wiv a bit ov flesh on 'er. 'Course you 'ave got a nice set of charms."

"Charms?" the girl asked in a puzzled way.

"Tits," explained Burlesque with commendable brevity. "Yeah, it's good that you've got a decent upper 'amper. My punters like their singers to bounce around a bit, iffn you knows what I mean." He winked at her and miraculously she didn't run for it. "You've got to wiggle 'em abart when yous singing." Suddenly he stopped and looked at the girl suspiciously. "Yous ain't a Suffer-O-Gette is you? I've been getting sum funny letters from Suffer-O-Gettes lately."

"I most certainly am not a Suffer-O-Gette, Mr. Bandstand. And with regard to my ... charms, I came here this evening to audition as a singer, not a stripper."

Spirited. Vanka liked that. He decided to come to the girl's aid. "You were saying you wanted to take the Pig upmarket, Burlesque, that you wanted to get out of the bump-and-grind business. Miss Thomas, here, certainly looks refined."

"All right," said Burlesque with a resigned sigh, "let's see wot you're abart. 'Ave a word wiv Arthur." He nodded toward the stage. "He's the bloke on the piano. You got your book wiv you?"

The girl had, and with a confidence that belied her youth she gave Burlesque a determined nod and walked to the stage.

Vanka had never heard the song before. It was a jaunty little number called "Falling in Love Again." It seemed that the band hadn't heard it either, and to begin with they were foxed by the song's peculiar waltz time. Eventually though they got into what the girl called "the groove" and her performance, to Vanka's untrained ear, was remarkable. Remarkable and highly unusual.

She didn't have one of the big blowsy voices usually possessed by women singing in Burlesque's pubs; hers was more subtle and nuanced. She managed to quiet the room, even the gabbling hookers sitting gossiping at the back of the pub. She was a stunningly different singer. The problem was that Burlesque wasn't comfortable with "different."

When the final notes of the song faded away he sat immobilized by indecision. "I dunno," he said eventually. "People coming to the Pig like their singers big an' loud. Waddya fink, Wanker? Should I give 'er a gig?"

Vanka gave an incredulous shake of his head. "Burlesque, she's the most amazing singer I've ever heard. Of course you've got to give her a gig. Give it a couple of weeks and the Pig will be packed."

Burlesque remained unconvinced. "I dunno . . ." He trailed off and then, obviously struck by inspiration, his face lit up in a smile. "I tell you wot, luv," he shouted toward the girl, who was still standing rather awkwardly on the stage, "as this is a burlesque show yer auditioning for, 'ow would you feel about singing charms out? I could bill you as the 'Naked Nightingale' or some such."

Vanka buried his face in his hands. His interpretation of "up-market" and Burlesque's were obviously very different.

"Absolutely not." There was a decided frost in the girl's voice.

Burlesque's face darkened. "Why not? It'd get a lot ov punters in."

"I don't care. It isn't dignified. It's not jad singing. It's pornography."

Burlesque wasn't used to being told no by a woman. Like most men in the Rookeries he was used to women doing as they were bloody well told, especially women who wanted a job from him.

"Don't be a soppy cow. It ain't pawnography; it's show business. And the fings I want yous to show are your tits."

"No," said the girl even more firmly.

Burlesque was totally perplexed by her intransigence. "You sure you ain't a Suffer-O-Gette?" Vanka knew why he was confused: most girls offered a gig at one of Burlesque's pubs would be more than delighted to take their clothes off . . . and more.

"No. I can assure you, Mr. Bandstand . . ."

The girl's refusal seemed to convince Burlesque that his suspicions were correct. "I bet you're a Suffer-O-Gette come 'ere to do me in."

"Mr. Bandstand, please."

"I bet it wos you sending me all them poison-pen letters."

Vanka sensed Burlesque's mood becoming decidedly more malevolent. He'd probably been drinking all day, trying to dampen his worries about being assassinated, and now all that drunken anguish was welling out. It was a dangerous moment: Burlesque's podgy and slightly comical appearance often tricked people into forgetting just how tough and vicious he actually was. No one became as big a duke as Burlesque was in the East End pub trade without being able to fight their corner.

"Well, let me tell yous this, Miss 'Oity-Toity Thomas, 'oo ain't inclined to take 'er clobber off, that iffn yous is a Suffer-O-Gette then I ain't just some no-account 'erbert. Yous an' your cronies come after Burlesque Bandstand an' yous gonna get a real 'ot reception." And for emphasis Burlesque drew the oversized Webley pistol he had hidden under his coat and placed it firmly on the table in front of him.

There was a scrabbling of chairs around the pub as punters sought to place themselves out of the line of fire, which they knew from experience generally meant sitting in another pub at least half a mile distant. A drunk Burlesque was that lousy a shot.

"I'm sorry," spluttered the girl on the stage, her eyes goggling at the sight of the gun. "I don't know what you're talking about."

The remarkable thing for Vanka was that the girl's confusion was perfectly genuine. She was without doubt the most incredibly naïve creature he had ever met.

She was, in a word, perfect.

16

The Demi-Monde: 40th Day of Winter, 1004

The Seventh nuCommandment: *You shall shun all those who are base in the sight of ABBA. You shall revile and disdain all those who are cursed to be UnderMentionables in the knowledge that all UnderMentionables—be they nuJu, Shade, Pole or Chink—are as animals in the sight of ABBA. You shall not know any UnderMentionable carnally. There is no greater sin than the Sin of Miscegenation driven by the Daemon Lilith.*

—The UnFunDaMentalist Prayer Book *(1004 edition)*

What a screwup.

But then no one had warned her what a flake this Burlesque Bandstand item would be. Not even PINC, which was odd because PINC seemed to know everything about everyone in the Demi-Monde.

Ella looked up and down the narrow street outside the Prancing Pig. It was dark now and everything looked infinitely more dangerous than it had just an hour before. Who knew what horrors were waiting to pounce out on her from the shadows?

The nerve of that guy . . . asking me to sing topless!

Squinting her eyes to see beyond the penumbra of the gas lamps, Ella looked around her. It wasn't the sort of place she liked to be at night. She was lost in some sort of Dickensian madhouse: wherever she looked all she could see was squalor, dirt and corruption, the whole sorry mess suffused with the stench of horse shit and rotting garbage. And she had the sneaking feeling that it wasn't just rats of the four-legged variety that came out to play at night.

She shivered as a swirl of snow carouseled around her.

It was then she realized that, in her hurry to get out of the pub, she'd left her coat inside. Her coat that had all her money, her room keys, her identity papers and her derringer in its pockets. She couldn't believe how stupid she'd been and because of that stupidity she was now back on the streets of the Rookeries with no gig, no home and not a fucking clue as to what to do next.

Terrific.

Now she really was up to her ass in alligators.

She'd have to get her coat back but the thought of going any-where near that madman Burlesque Bandstand did not appeal. He'd probably put a bullet through her head as soon as he saw her. For a second she had half a mind to forget about Norma Williams and simply to hit the bricks. It was hopeless. Better to slink off to the docks, jump on a barge going to NoirVille, find the Portal and get back to the Real World. Five million bucks was a lot of money but not if she was going to be trapped in this cyber-rathole for the rest of her life.

"Excuse me, Miss Thomas, might'n I have a word?"

She recognized the man who was addressing her. He was the long-haired item who had been sitting next to Burlesque Bandstand in the pub, the good-looking one with the bruise on his cheek and a glint in his eye that suggested that he knew things other people didn't. The one PINC knew nothing about.

Trying desperately to disguise her shivering, Ella glowered at the man. "What can I do for you, Mr. . . . ?"

The man doffed his top hat and performed a somewhat over-elaborate bow. "I am Colonel Vanka Ivanovich Maykov, latterly commander of the ForthRight Army's Fifth Regiment of Foot, at your service."

Yeah, right.

This Vanka Maykov was never a soldier. He had the look of someone who wasn't comfortable with taking orders.

"And with regard to what I might do for you, Miss Thomas . . ." The man held out Ella's fur coat. "I believe you forgot this in your quite understandable haste to leave the pig. That's pig with a small 'p.'"

Despite herself Ella laughed, took the coat and slid herself gratefully into its warmth. "You are very kind, Colonel Maykov."

"I would prefer it if you would call me Vanka. And as for thanks, I would be grateful for a few minutes of your time, Miss Thomas. I have a business proposition I would like to discuss with you."

"I've had a bellyful of being propositioned tonight, Vanka. As I think you heard when I was in discussion with your friend Burlesque Bandstand, I ain't that sort of girl."

"Oh, I appreciate your sensibilities, Miss Thomas, and what I wish to propose would require you doing nothing untoward."

He took a step closer to Ella. Too close. She snaked her hand around the butt of the derringer concealed in the inside pocket of her coat.

"Stop there," she said. "One step closer and I'll burn you down." To emphasize the threat, she hauled the derringer out and brandished it threateningly.

The man stopped as he was ordered and made the halfhearted gesture of raising his hands to demonstrate that he was unarmed. "I apologize if I have alarmed you, Miss Thomas, but believe me, my intentions are strictly honorable."

A steamer trundled past clanging its bell, its headlights washing over the man, giving Ella a better look at him. He was tall—over six foot—lean and impeccably dressed. He looked rather dashing. And though a little old—she guessed he was mid-twenties—he was handsome in a bashed-about sort of way. He wasn't an Anglo; his English was too good for him to be that and from his slight accent Ella guessed him to be a Russki. A good-looking Russki. Ella liked the mischievous twinkle in his eye; the man, unless she was very much mistaken, was a rogue. And Ella had a soft spot for rogues, even computer-generated ones.

Shame about the mustache. Well, nobody was perfect.

"So what can I do for you, Vanka?"

That impudent smile again. The man was a real charmer. "As I intimated to you in the Pig, I am a Licensed Psychic and Occultist and as such I am permitted to conduct séances to enable members of the general public to communicate with the Spirit World. I have been engaged to conduct a series of séances here in the Rookeries but unfortunately, due to illness, my regular assistant is incapacitated. I therefore find myself in need of a PsyChick to help me with my performances. Having seen you perform in the Pig, I am convinced that you are ideally suited to the position I have to fill."

Ella found herself believing him. He certainly looked genuine enough and he had brought her coat back without—as best she could establish—removing any of her valuables. And she was alone, at night, in one of the most dangerous parts of the Rookeries.

"I'm listening," she said, adding a flavor of indifference to her tone. It wouldn't do to seem too enthusiastic.

"Might I make so bold as to invite you for a cup of coffee? It seems a little déclassé for us to be standing negotiating in the middle of the street."

Déclassé . . . oh là là.

"Okay, there's a coffeehouse across the road from my rooms. We can take our coffee there, Colonel Vanka Maykov, and we can talk as we walk."

—‑⁀⁀‑—

FORTUNATELY THE STREETS OF THE ROOKERIES WERE CONSIDERABLY less crowded at night and the pair of them were able to amble along side by side quite comfortably. It also seemed that the big, bluff Vanka Maykov with his broad shoulders and his cane deterred even the most determined of those who prowled the night in the Demi-Monde.

"So, Vanka, perhaps you might begin by explaining to me just what a 'Licensed Psychic and Occultist' is."

Vanka chuckled and gave his cane a playful twirl. "I am blessed, Miss Thomas, with certain strange abilities," he intoned gravely. "These abilities give me the power to communicate with the Spirit World, with the souls of those who have gone before us."

"Gone where?" asked Ella sweetly.

"If you are familiar with the works of His Holiness Comrade Crowley, you will appreciate that beyond the reality of the Demi-Monde is a realm inhabited by the Spirits of the Dead. My gift allows me to open channels through to that Spirit World and speak with those who once lived in this Vale of Tears but who have now passed on."

Ella had to look away. As part of her psychology studies she had done a paper on how faux-spiritualists fooled the gullible and the vulnerable into believing their mumbo jumbo, but she had never for the life of her thought she would ever be asked to work as an assistant to a real huckster . . . well, as real as any *Dupe* huckster could be.

"And how would I be able to assist you in your channeling? As far as I know I have no great facility with regards to Spiritualism."

Vanka halted at the edge of the pavement and made a great show of looking about for oncoming traffic before stepping carefully into the road. "Unfortunately the practice of Spiritualism has been tarnished—adulterated, if you will—by the activities of a number of sharps who mask their lack of talent with theatrical tricks."

"Tricks? What sort of theatrical tricks?" prompted Ella, dressing her face with the most disingenuous of smiles.

Vanka nudged Ella lightly around a pile of horse manure that adorned the middle of the road. "These shysters are prone to stoop to such low contrivances as table rattling, levitation and the manifestation of ghosts and ectoplasm to convince their audiences that they are indeed gifted with the same powers as those possessed by adepts such as myself." He shook his head dolefully. "It is a sad reflection of the world in which we live, Miss Thomas, that without such artifice and theatricality, the audiences at a séance are now somewhat disappointed."

As she stepped up onto the pavement, Ella eyed the man carefully. "So, let me see if I've got this straight, Vanka. All these tricksters, in order to hide the fact that they have no psychic ability, fool their clients with a flimflam display of tricks and gimmicks . . ."

"Exactly."

" . . . but they have been so successful that now, in the public's mind, these tricks and gimmicks are such an indispensable part of the ritual of Spiritualism that without them a true adept such as you . . ."

An appreciative nod of the head.

" . . . finds it difficult to be taken seriously."

"A most pithy and insightful summary."

"So where do I come into all this?" Ella asked.

"I need an assistant, Miss Thomas—a beautiful, vivacious and intelligent assistant—who can assist me in the execution of certain elements of theatricality I, through necessity, have been obliged to incorporate into my performances."

Ella smiled. "So you want me to be your assistant flimflammer?"

"That is a somewhat palsied way of describing your duties, but I suppose, in essence, the answer is yes."

"I see. And would this beautiful, vivacious and intelligent assistant flimflammer be remunerated for her efforts?"

"One guinea a performance . . ."

Ella laughed derisively.

" . . . payable in advance and a further guinea payable after the successful conclusion of each séance."

"Two guineas at the end of the performance," Ella riposted, "three guineas in total."

"Very well, but your costume comes out of your advance. I'm not having you scalp me for a new dress and then play the forgetful truant."

"I'll think about it. I'm not really in the mood for making career decisions at the moment. I live just around this corner and over there"—she pointed across the street—"is where you'll find the coffeehouse I was telling you about. Let's get together at noon tomorrow to discuss—"

The words died in her mouth. As she turned the corner she could see the building where she had her rooms but she could also see the three Black Marias stationed outside and the swarm of black-uniformed Checkya officers milling around the building's entrance. A large crowd had gathered to see what the excitement was all about. Instinctively Ella looked up to the fifth floor where, so PINC advised her, she had her rooms, and what she saw there set her nerves jangling. Her apartment was ablaze with light and through the windows—no one had bothered to draw the drapes—she could see Checkya officers searching her bookshelves.

Her blood ran cold.

"Those are my rooms they're searching. I've got to see what's happening . . ."

Vanka took a firm grip on her arm. "I think that might not be a sensible thing to do, Miss Thomas. With the Checkya it is better to know what is going on in advance rather than trusting to those two mythical beasts, luck and the law. Why don't you stay here, tucked away in the shadows of this doorway, and I'll just go over and ask a few questions."

Ella was so upset by this development—through PINC she knew just how unprincipled and evil an outfit Beria's Checkya was—that all she found the energy to do was nod. What troubled her most was the thought that the Checkya had come so soon after her arrival in the Demi-Monde. From what she understood from the professor, as long as she wasn't cut, as long as no one discovered that she could bleed, she was safe. He had assured her that her identity and her background were foolproof. But if this was the case, why were the Checkya looking for her?

She shrank back into the darkness of the doorway and watched as Vanka sauntered across the road to stand with the crowd of rubberneckers. For about ten minutes he chatted with the people around him, he laughed, he pointed out events happening in Ella's room, he cracked jokes, he politely made way for ladies as they meandered into and out of the crowd and finally, unbelievably, he shared a cigarette with one of the Checkya officers. The man might be a rascal but he had the balls of an elephant.

It was when Vanka began chatting with an enormously tall and very thin man, dressed in a long frock coat and high top hat, both colored a severe black, that Ella took especial notice. She had to do a double take: the man might have had his back to her but for a moment she could have sworn Vanka was talking with the doppelgänger of Professor Septimus Bole. Then the crowd shifted and the man was gone, swallowed up in the mob. Most peculiar . . .

She shook her head. It couldn't be him. Surely he would have told her he had a Dupe loose in the Demi-Monde.

Finally, after doffing his hat to one of his new female acquaintances, Vanka meandered back across the road to Ella. "I would be grateful, Miss Thomas, if you would secure your veil snugly about your face." He slid his hand through her arm and steered the shaking Ella toward the coffee shop.

"You look cold, my dear," he purred as he pushed his way through the revolving doors. "Let's see if we can get a table near the fire." They could: money was exchanged and she found herself being seated at a table at the back of the restaurant next to the fireplace.

Distracted though she was, Ella couldn't help but be impressed by the elegance of the room in which she was sitting. It reminded her of the pictures she'd seen of Viennese coffeehouses: all gilt, mirrors, stiff white tablecloths and uniformed waiters. Vanka ordered coffee and gateau and once they had been served he insisted that she sample both before they spoke.

It was good advice: as she ate and drank, Ella found herself becoming calmer and much of this she attributed to her new friend. Vanka Maykov *was* a charmer. It was impossible to feel distracted or depressed in his company; he had a certainty about him that was immensely reassuring. Moreover, he was a very *attentive* charmer, who bustled around her making sure that she wasn't sitting in a draft and that her coffee was prepared in just the way she liked it.

Finally he turned to business. "It would seem, Miss Thomas, that you have attracted the attention of the Checkya. They have a warrant for your arrest and are currently searching your apartment."

"But why?"

"The commander of the Checkya squad charged with your arrest informed me that you are wanted on suspicion of being a Suffer-O-Gette crypto, an agent provocateur working for the Coven to disrupt the peace and tranquility of the Rookeries. These are serious charges."

"I am not a Suffer-O-Gette!" Ella protested for the second time that evening.

"Shh!" Vanka raised a finger to his lips. He used his chin to indicate the packed tables surrounding theirs. "I would be obliged if you would keep your voice down." He leaned back in his chair and stretched his long legs. "In my career as a psychic, Miss Thomas, I have met a great many people and have developed an almost infallible nose for the liar and the scoundrel. You are neither of these; I believe you are telling the truth."

For some perverse reason Ella found these words oddly comforting.

"Unfortunately the opinion of Vanka Maykov has no weight in Checkya circles. Clearly you are being sought in connection with a political crime; the Checkya do not lower themselves to become involved with day-to-day villainy. So we must assume that you have been traduced . . . dangerously traduced. Someone, for whatever reason, has convinced the Checkya that you are an Enemy of the People." He took another nibble at his gateau. "Mmm, excellent, but one must be alive to the need to keep the girth of one's waistline under reasonable control." Reluctantly, he laid his fork down. "I have to ask, Miss Thomas, for my own safety as much as yours, have you in some way insulted or discomfited one of the ForthRight's movers and shakers?"

"No. I've never even met any of them."

"Heydrich? Beria? Crowley?"

"No, no, no."

"You are a beautiful woman, Miss Thomas; have you rejected the advances of one of these people?"

Annoyingly, Ella found herself blushing. "No."

"Could it be that you are the victim of the revenge of a jilted lover or a jealous wife?"

"Don't be ridiculous."

"Then you must be in possession of information that is of a compromising nature."

"Absolutely not."

"Are you an agent of Shaka's? You are, after all, a Shade."

"No!"

Vanka took a thoughtful sip of his coffee. "As it would seem that you have committed no crime nor upset any in authority, I am left with two alternatives. The first is that the Checkya's interest in you is the result of mistaken identity." He shook his head. "No, they are too efficient for that and, to be blunt, your complexion is not common in the Rookeries. I am therefore left with only one other possibility."

"What's that?"

"That you, Miss Ella Thomas, are not all you seem. That under that carapace of innocence and femininity there is someone who threatens the ForthRight. I say this because the Checkya committed over thirty men to the raid on your rooms, when to the best of my knowledge, generally they would only have sent a pair of agents on such an errand. This indicates that Beria—and only he could have authorized such a large operation—wants you in custody very badly. He must regard you as an extremely dangerous person."

Ella's gaze locked with his. "And if I am a dangerous person . . . what are you going to do about it?"

Vanka held up his hands. "Please, Miss Thomas, I would be grateful if you wouldn't flourish your pistol again. I abhor violence: I find it disrupts my digestion. To my mind, the need to resort to violence indicates a lack of wit. Understand that you are in no danger from me, quite the contrary, in fact. For good or ill we find ourselves united. The Checkya have a simpleminded approach to law enforcement and hence will interpret my association with you as complicity in whatever crimes you have been accused of. As a consequence, my fate is now enmeshed with yours, which gives me a vested interest in your remaining free."

He called for fresh coffee, waiting until it had been served before continuing. "I have a philosophy which convinces me that anything that undermines the ForthRight and the reprobates who administer it is to be encouraged. So I will do what I can to protect you, Miss Thomas." He took a sip of his coffee and frowned. "That protection extends to a plea that you do not drink this coffee; it is stale." He pushed the cup disdainfully aside. "And, of course, in the interim I am still interested in securing the services of a PsyChick. Have you had an opportunity of considering the offer I made in this regard?"

"Do I have any choice in the matter?"

"None whatsoever; I see it as a quid pro quo for any trouble you might cause me . . ." He stiffened and his face took on a serious expression. "For the trouble you are *about* to cause me. Miss Thomas, I beg you to trust me implicitly. Do exactly as I say and we will survive the night, and I emphasize the 'we' here."

"What's wrong?"

"A Checkya officer has just entered the coffeehouse and is examining the papers of all the customers."

17

The Demi-Monde: 40th Day of Winter, 1004

UnderMentionables in the ForthRight are only permitted to live within the walls of the Warsaw Ghetto. UnderMentionables are classified as Category B citizens and may only be educated up to the age of fourteen years, and must not receive medical treatment beyond the age of fifty years. No places of worship other than those consecrated by the Church of the Doctrine of UnFunDaMentalism are permitted within the Warsaw Ghetto. All UnderMentionables working or traveling outside the Warsaw Ghetto must be in possession of a valid visa, issued by the Checkya. All nuJus working or traveling outside the Warsaw Ghetto must be in possession of a valid visa, issued by the Checkya, and must wear an armband (not less than five inches in width) displaying a black five-pointed star on a white background.

—Decree 7823, relating to the Control and Confinement of
UnderMentionables within the ForthRight,
ForthRight Law Gazette, Spring 1003

There was no escape.

One look at her skin color and she would be arrested, and the last thing she wanted to do was spend the rest of her life in a Demi-Mondian prison. Unfortunately there was no way to hide her color: her veil might mask her face but she wasn't wearing any gloves. Desperate to keep her hands out of sight and stop them shaking with fear, Ella placed them on her lap and knotted her fingers. She could feel the color drain from her face—an unfortunately inaccurate description—and the sweat pooling under her armpits.

"The man is two tables away," said Vanka idly. "When I say laugh I want you to laugh out loud, I want you to guffaw. And then I want you to raise your napkin to your mouth as though embarrassed. Doing this will help mask the nervousness that has started to manifest itself in your body language." He looked up. "One table away. Oh, yes, and if you are asked, you live at Twenty-three-A Morgan Street, and your name is Delores Delight. Now laugh!"

It was hysteria that drove the laugh and once Ella had started she found she couldn't stop. She found that she *had* to raise the napkin to her mouth to try to muffle her squawking. It took the appearance of the huge, black-uniformed Checkya sergeant alongside their table to terrify her into silence. She pushed the napkin and her hands back under the table.

"Papers, Comrade," he snapped.

Vanka handed his over and the man, beetle browed and sporting a huge handlebar mustache, studied them carefully. "Says 'ere you're from Rodina."

"That's right, Sergeant, I'm in the Rookeries on business."

"And where are you residing whilst in the Rookeries?"

Vanka flipped a card out of his top pocket. "At the Hotel Metropolitan, it's—"

"I knows the Metropolitan," the sergeant interrupted brusquely. "Wot business is you about 'ere in the Rookeries?"

"I'm a Licensed Psychic, Sergeant." Vanka flashed his license and a smile. "I'll be giving séances at the Prancing Pig all next week." He gave the sergeant another smile. Vanka was a great smiler. "If you let me have your name I'll arrange for complimentary tickets to be left at the door."

"I ain't a great one for the occult, Comrade, it gives me the heebie-jeebies, it does. Best left to experts like His Holiness Comrade Crowley." The sergeant turned to Ella, letting his eyes wander leeringly over her body. "Papers, miss."

Ella almost passed out, but realizing that this might be her last act as a free woman she dug her hand into the right-hand pocket of her coat to retrieve her papers.

They were gone!

A wave of ice-cold panic washed over her.

"I've lost them!" she spluttered.

All Vanka did was chuckle. "Calm yourself, Delores, my dear, the sergeant won't bite. Don't you remember, you gave your papers to me for safe keeping?" And with that he pushed his hand into his inside pocket and produced Ella's papers. Well, not her papers exactly but certainly *a* set of papers. He handed them to the Checkya sergeant, who studied them carefully. "Address?"

"Er . . ." For a heart-stopping instant Ella thought she had forgotten the address Vanka had given her. "Twenty-three-A Morgan Street."

A disappointed sniff from the sergeant. "And wot is your relationship wiv this man, Miss Delight?" he asked brusquely.

Before Ella could utter a word, Vanka had answered for her. "Delores is my assistant onstage and my fiancée off it," he said, beaming a puppy-dog look at Ella.

"Seems to me, miss, that you ain't much cop as a psychic's assistant iffn you don't even know which pocket your papers was in." He handed them back, and Ella was obliged to reveal her hands in order to take them.

Ella tried her best to make her reply as normal as possible. "Oh, even a PsyChick can be forgetful, Sergeant."

"You ain't wearing no engagement ring neither," observed the sergeant. It was then that he noticed the color of Ella's skin. "Would I be right in finking that you are ov the Shade persuasion?"

Vanka didn't miss a beat. "Ours is a somewhat unofficial engagement, Sergeant."

"Yous, being a citizen ov the ForthRight, sir, must be aware ov the Seventh nuCommandment that condemns the practice ov miscegenation. I would be grateful iffn you would raise your veil, Miss Delight, so that I might confirm your racial bone fids."

Ella's heart sank. Now there was no escape. She slipped her left hand into her pocket and closed her fingers around her derringer. If necessary she would shoot her way out.

She could hardly believe this was happening. Two hours ago she had been a student, a part-time singer, and now here she was contemplating murder. She caught herself: it was an indication of how real these Dupes were that she could think of killing one as murder. The Demi-Monde was so persuasive a place that it was almost impossible for her to suspend belief.

"Sergeant," interrupted Vanka very sotto voce, "I would prefer it if my fiancée did not do that. Our tryst here tonight has not met with the approval of my family nor of the authorities." He smiled and pushed a five-guinea note across the table in the direction of the Checkya sergeant. "You're a man of the world, Sergeant."

"Is yous trying to bribe me?" asked the sergeant disdainfully.

"Yes," confirmed Vanka as he added a second five-guinea note to the first.

"Then look here, I am a member of the Checkya and we's—"

In desperation Ella reached out and grabbed the sergeant's hand. "Please . . . Sergeant Stone . . . I implore you—"

"'Ere, 'ow do you know my name?"

Fuck!

Thank you, PINC!

That's the problem with knowing everything about everybody: I have to remember what I shouldn't know about somebody.

Or something like that.

Swallowing hard, Ella tried desperately to think of a way out. There was only one thing for it. "I know your name because I'm a clairvoyant, Sergeant. My abilities allow me to commune with any man or woman I meet and to know their innermost secrets."

The sergeant eyed her suspiciously. "That right?"

"Yes, Sergeant, perfectly right. If you really want to know what fate holds in store for you, why don't you take up the colonel's kind offer of those tickets and come along to see us at the Prancing Pig?"

"Very kind ov you, I am sure, miss. But that does not alter the fact that yous a Shade and your identity papers state yours racial type to be Grade One: Anglo-Slavic, and this being the case I 'ave no alternative but to—"

"I'll make sure there are *two* tickets waiting for you; you will, after all, be accompanied by Arthur."

The sergeant eyed Ella carefully. "'Ere . . . wot do you know about Arthur?"

"Everything," said Ella, the single word replete with ominous meaning.

The sergeant's face blanched. "But . . . you won't be saying nuffink to nobody about Arthur, now, will you?"

"My lips are sealed, Sergeant. If you forget all about having met me, then your wife and your superiors will never hear about Arthur." Ella touched the sleeve of Sergeant Stone's black uniform. "And we both know how severe Vice-Leader Beria is regarding members of the Checkya engaging in zadnik-like activities, don't we, Sergeant?"

"How . . . ?" began Vanka as he watched the bemused Checkya sergeant shuffle, with a couple of worried backward glances and ten guineas of Vanka's money in his pocket, out of the coffeehouse.

"You first, Vanka. How did you pull that stunt with the papers?"

Vanka shrugged dismissively. "Nothing to it. I knew there was a chance that the Checkya would start checking papers so I found the girl in the crowd that was the closest match to you in terms of age and hair color and lifted her papers. Of course she was a Blank, but in the circumstances it was the best I could do. There aren't that many Shades in the ForthRight."

Ella bridled at the use of the word "Shade" but decided to let it roll. After all, the man had just saved her life.

"Amazing; you must be a very accomplished pickpocket, Vanka."

He chuckled. "All stage magicians—close-up magicians, that is—are good with their hands. If you can't palm things then you've no right calling yourself a magician." His gaze settled on Ella and his face took on a more serious cast. "Now it's your turn, and make it good."

"I have special powers, Vanka. I *know* about people."

"What? You're telling me that you're a *real* clairvoyant?"

"Exactly. Please don't ask me how, but I have an instinctive knowledge about everybody I meet in the Demi-Monde. It seems that the closer I am to them the more powerful my reading becomes and if I touch them—"

"Oh, fiddlesticks. Don't try and gull me, young lady. Come on, admit it, you already knew this Sergeant Stone, didn't you? Maybe he's interviewed you before, maybe you saw his name somewhere on his uniform."

"Then how did I know about Arthur?"

"A lucky guess. Arthur is a pretty common name. Maybe he had it engraved on his watch chain or something."

"I'm sorry to disappoint you, Vanka, but there was no lucky guessing and no engraved watch chain, just insight."

"Twaddle. Look, Miss Thomas, I've been around the Demi-Monde too long to believe in this sort of nonsense. Maybe Crowley and his sorcerers are the *real* magicians they claim to be, but for my part I've never seen anything magical about the Demi-Monde."

"But aren't you a Licensed Psychic and Occultist? So you must have powers."

Vanka looked around the coffee shop to make sure no one was eavesdropping on their conversation, then leaned closer to Ella. "As you so rightly observed, Miss Thomas, Spiritualism is just flimflam. It's Party-inspired sleight of hand to have people believe that there is some point in enduring the sorry excuse of a life they have here in the ForthRight. All Spiritualism does is give the poor and gullible the belief that their horrible, mundane, painful lives are not meaningless and random, that there is some purpose to human existence, that there is a better life after death. So don't tell me you're a medium or a clairvoyant or a bloody sensitive, Miss Thomas, because I can't—I won't—believe you."

"What you will or won't believe, Vanka, is immaterial. The fact remains that I have such powers."

"Very well, tell me about me. Give me some insight about myself that only I could know."

Ella shook her head. "I can't. I don't know why but I can't read you. You're a mystery to me."

"Hah! Typical."

"Ask me something else. Ask me something about Burlesque Bandstand. When I shook his hand I learned an awful lot about him, and some of it, I freely admit, was *bloody* awful. The man is a walking bag of corruption."

"All right, Burlesque had a fling with someone, just before Winter set in. He kept it very hush-hush. So who was it?"

"Oh, that's easy. Burlesque Bandstand and Julie the Jug Juggler were an item for nearly two weeks. Burlesque got quite spoony over her. He really liked her jugs."

Vanka's face took on an expression a little like the one on the face of a cat who has been presented with a very large bowl of cream. "Now *that* is amazing. I thought I was the only one who knew about

Julie." He fell silent, lighting one of the pungent French cigarettes he favored. She was about to object when she noticed that virtually all the other men in the café were smoking. Puffing contentedly on his cigarette, Vanka studied Ella carefully. "Maybe, Miss Thomas, I might be able to do a bit better than three guineas a séance."

The Demi-Monde: 47th Day of Winter, 1004

The two-year Civil War which beset Rodina and the Rookeries between 1000 and 1002 ("the Troubles") saw the revolutionary forces of UnFunDaMentalism—led by that visionary genius Reinhard Heydrich—triumph over the Royalist faction fighting in support of Henry Tudor and Ivan Grozny. With the establishment of the ForthRight on the 40th day of Winter, 1002, all religions other than UnFunDaMentalism were banned and those religious dissidents and counterrevolutionaries who failed to secure refuge in neighboring Sectors were executed. All UnderMentionables were declared nonNix and relocated to Warsaw, where they are held pending a "Final Solution" being found to the problems they pose. The victory of the Party over the reactionary, atheistic forces of RaTionalism during the Troubles is a vindication of the belief that ABBA is on the side of UnFunDaMentalism.

—WITH ABBA ON OUR SIDE: THE FINAL VICTORY
OF THE REVOLUTION IN THE FORTHRIGHT,
LAVRENTII BERIA, PARTY RULES PUBLICATIONS

Trixie gazed in a disinterested way over the manor's ruined garden that stretched so forlornly beyond her bedroom window. Fortunately for her—and the sensibilities of the Dashwoods' head gardener—the garden wasn't at its worst: it had snowed heavily during the night and the white covering conspired to make the earthworks and the gun positions look almost attractive. But she knew it was a transient beauty that would be destroyed just as soon as the Checkya detachment roused themselves, shook off the indolence caused by a cold night spent under canvas and began patrolling and marching in earnest. Then the pure white snow would be churned to a disgusting khaki color.

She glanced at the grandfather clock ticking away in the corner of the room; it was still not yet seven o'clock.

For Trixie this was the perfect time of the day. It was the only time when she could be alone and untroubled, the only time when she was free of the obligation to "do something" about or with the Daemon, when she could stop worrying.

A movement at the side of the house caught her attention. She scrubbed the window free of the ice that had formed on the inside of the glass overnight. What she saw irritated her: Captain Dabrowski and the Daemon were taking their early morning constitutional. Every morning since it had been a guest in the Dashwoods' house the Daemon had insisted on being allowed to walk around the gardens for half an hour, and as it was unthinkable that the creature would be allowed to do this unguarded, the Polish captain had been given the task of accompanying it. To Trixie's mind there should also have been an older gentlewoman accompanying the pair to act as chaperone, but, as they walked in full view of the house and as this Norma Williams creature wasn't a real girl, etiquette had been abandoned.

As she watched, the Daemon stumbled—it was using a walking stick; apparently it had injured its leg when attempting to escape the SS—and held out a hand to grab the captain's arm. It was an obvious piece of coquettish dalliance and Trixie was aghast that the captain would be so naïve as to fall for it. The Daemon, it seemed, was not above using its faux-feminine wiles to have the captain forget she—it—was an Enemy of the ForthRight. Trixie gave a disdainful sniff, picked up the journal she had been keeping regarding the Daemon and made a note in her large, precise handwriting.

DAEMON ENJOYS EARLY MORNING CONSTITUTIONAL WITH CAPTAIN DABROWSKI, COMMENCING 06.27 AND ENDING . . .

She checked back through the journal; the pair's walks were becoming lon.ger and they were certainly talking more during them. During the first few days of the Daemon's stay the couple had hardly exchanged two sentences when they made their promenades, but now they seemed to converse nonstop.

It had been a real puzzle for Trixie to understand what they could find to talk about. Her own attempts to chat with the Daemon had been rebuffed in a most impolite manner. It had said that it would under no circumstances answer questions regarding where it had come from and what it was like there. It would not, the Daemon had said sternly, act as a quisling. Trixie had no idea what a quisling was but it sounded quite revolting.

As a consequence their time together—and they were obliged to endure ten hours a day in each other's company—was spent with Trixie sewing and the Daemon reading. Daemons, it appeared, were avaricious readers. That was another thing to note in her journal.

In the end, taking her pride in both hands, Trixie had sought Captain Dabrowski's advice regarding possible subjects of conversation. He had smiled that aggravatingly condescending smile of his and said that he simply let the Daemon ask him questions. The Daemon, it seemed, had an unquenchable thirst for information about the Demi-Monde.

"But how does that help *our* understanding of *it*?" Trixie had asked.

"Quite a lot, in an indirect sort of way," the captain had replied.

"The questions it asks me give an indication of what the Daemon is interested in and the extent of its knowledge of the Demi-Monde. When it interrogates me its main topics of inquiry relate to the functioning of the Demi-Monde . . ."

Maybe all Daemons are RaTionalists? Trixie had wondered, but as RaTionalists denied the existence of a Spirit World from which the Daemons like this one supposedly came, this was a contradiction in terms.

" . . . and the role of women in the running of the ForthRight."

That, Trixie decided, *must make for a short conversation.* The role of women in the running of the ForthRight was precisely nil.

"And what have you gleaned from these question-and-answer sessions, Captain?"

"That the Daemon is perplexed that we in the ForthRight are content to live in what it calls a 'totalitarian regime' and that it is disgusted that women here are so 'disenfranchised.'"

Although it would never do to admit it openly, Trixie knew what the word "disenfranchised" meant; overcoming women's disenfranchisement was the watchword—the rather-too-long watchword in Trixie's view—of the Suffer-O-Gettes. Nevertheless she thanked the captain when he defined the word for her; in the company of "outsiders" she had, after all, to play the dutiful and politically correct young woman of breeding. RaTionalism was a dangerous belief for a ForthRight woman.

According to the captain the Daemon thought that everybody, both men and women, should have a say in the running of the Forth-Right, that the Leader should be elected by the adult population of the two Sectors. The Daemon called this "democracy."

To Trixie's mind this was a ridiculous idea. Nowhere in the Demi-Monde (except, perhaps, in the nuJu Districts, and everybody knew nuJus were naturally perverse creatures) had there been a challenge to the concept that the Sectors should be ruled by a Leader, who by dint of his—and more often than not it was a "his"—genius and energy rose through political osmosis above the rest of the population. Certainly in the ForthRight and NoirVille they embraced a more primitive notion that their leaders were, somehow, ABBA-ordained, but the concept was the same, as was their belief that the success and the well-being of a Sector's citizens rested on the shoulders of the man who led them.

Trixie had shaken her head. "But surely under this democracy of the Daemon's anyone could be Leader . . . even men who are unsuited to lead. All that democracy would result in is a Sector being led by someone who is not up to the job. As Comrade Leader Heydrich says, great men are the rarest thing that can be found in the Demi-Monde, and they certainly are not a thing to be discovered by the haphazard voting of the hoi polloi."

"Oh, I agree with you, Lady Trixiebell, the idea is outrageous," the captain replied, "but the very fact that the Daemon asks about it gives us an indication of how the Spirit World functions."

That conversation with the captain had taken place yesterday and, ever diligent, Trixie had noted it in her journal.

Another ten minutes dragged past before she saw the captain and the Daemon turn back toward the house. It was a signal that she should be stirring herself; breakfast would be being served and her father was a stickler for punctuality. And since the Daemon had been in residence, breakfasts had become amusing events—amusing but quite testing. It was one thing to debate current affairs over the breakfast table with her father, it was quite another to do it in front of a Checkya agent like Dabrowski.

When Trixie bustled into the dining room, she found her father already seated at the breakfast table. He grunted a "good morning" in response to Trixie's greeting, then retreated back behind his paper. Captain Dabrowski and the Daemon joined them shortly afterward, having removed their *valenkis* and changed into their indoor shoes.

"I have persuaded Cook to provide you with a better selection of fruits this morning, Miss Williams," Trixie announced as the Daemon seated itself. "I am assured that the dates and the apricots are quite edible and that the apples are of passable quality." Here she could barely conceal her revulsion; the thought of anyone eating the rather desiccated apples that Cook had retrieved from the cold store was disgusting.

And then there was the *way* the Daemon ate the fruit.

"You are very kind, Lady Trixiebell, to go to all this trouble on my account," murmured the Daemon as it took one of the apples onto its plate.

"Not at all, Miss Williams, but you must be aware that consuming so much fruit is liable to give you colic."

The Daemon laughed. "I don't think we'll ever agree about what constitutes a healthy diet. I don't have your penchant for dairy products and fried foods."

"Vital if one is to survive the Winter," sniffed Trixie's father from behind his paper. "Everyone needs a covering of fat. It helps keep out the cold."

"Well, where I come from, Comrade Commissar—"

"And where might that be?" inquired Captain Dabrowski as he ladled bacon and kidneys onto his plate.

"Never you mind, Captain Dabrowski," replied the Daemon lightly and rather too teasingly in Trixie's opinion. The creature was actually *flirting* with Captain Dabrowski! "As I was saying, where I come from there is a belief that a surfeit of fat can raise cholesterol, which in turn can lead to a blockage of the circulatory system."

Circulatory system? What in the Demi-Monde is a circulatory system? Another note for the journal.

"Stuff and nonsense," muttered Dashwood as he brusquely turned the page of *The Stormer.*

Unperturbed, the Daemon proceeded to slice the apple neatly

into quarters and to eat each piece in turn. This was the part of breakfast that Trixie found most upsetting. That the Daemon didn't peel and core the apple first was disgusting and potentially very dangerous to the maintenance of a healthy astral ether: everyone knew that the eating of pips and skin led to the most profound constipation.

"Coffee, miss?" inquired the maid, and the Daemon nodded. "Black, please."

A shudder of revulsion from Trixie. Black coffee, as she had been taught in her Living&More lessons, had a most deleterious effect on a young woman's complexion. There had been studies done that suggested that it could even *darken* the complexion. Trixie never drank coffee; the prospect of having a skin color that could be mistaken for that of a Shade filled her with horror.

"I see the headlines in *The Stormer* continue their criticism of Empress Wu and the Coven. It's pretty belligerent stuff. Is there going to be war?" It was another idiosyncrasy of the Daemon that though it had manifested in the form of a young woman it conducted itself in a peculiarly masculine manner. Trixie felt a moment's envy; the Daemon was lucky to come from a world where it was possible for a young woman—even an ersatz young woman—to express an interest in matters outside the home.

Ever the gentleman, Trixie's father didn't allow himself to be distracted by the Daemon's rudeness. He lowered his paper and smiled at it. "Unfortunately, Miss Williams, my position in the Party precludes me from commenting publicly on articles carried in newspapers. Suffice it to say that, although there are immense religious and political differences between the Coven and the ForthRight, I have every confidence in the abilities of Comrade Beria to bring the negotiations currently being held with Empress Wu to a successful conclusion."

Immense religious and political differences: now that, to Trixie's mind, was an understatement. Crowley was always banging on in his speeches about the "unnatural" and the "perverse" practice of LessBi-enism promoted by the HerEtical Church. He *hated* the Covenites.

The Daemon was, as ever, impertinently persistent in its questioning. "And what, from the point of view of the ForthRight, would constitute a 'successful conclusion'?"

"Well, as that discussion is in the public domain," answered Dashwood with a sigh, "I suppose there is no harm in answering your question. The ForthRight requires that the Coven cease its harboring and support of those LessBien terrorists the Suffer-O-Gettes, and that it hand over Royalist fugitives who sought sanctuary in the Coven after the Troubles." He took a sip of his tea. "The ForthRight also requires that its ration of coal be doubled."

Coal.

After blood, coal was the most precious commodity in the Demi-Monde. Without coal the steamers stopped, without coal people went cold in Winter. And the Coven controlled the world's supply of coal.

"And what is the ForthRight offering in return for these concessions?"

"The precise details are, of course, confidential, but it is common knowledge that the restoration of diplomatic relations is one of the many things being discussed."

"That doesn't sound terribly generous," observed the Daemon.

"The Coven has also been lobbying hard for the supply of M4s."

"M4s?"

Dashwood laughed. "Your compatriot Daemons, when they came to the Demi-Monde, were armed with rifles far superior to those then available to our own soldiers. When the Daemons were captured these weapons were taken, studied, and ForthRight engineers managed to replicate them. *Only* the ForthRight engineers have been able to do this and hence only the ForthRight is able to manufacture these M4s."

"And will the ForthRight supply them to the Coven?"

With another, louder, sigh, Dashwood closed his newspaper, folded it carefully and placed it beside his plate. "Who knows, Miss Williams? Diplomacy is designed to achieve a resolution of differences between two Sectors such that both are, to a greater or lesser extent, content with the outcome. That, I am sure, is the objective of Comrade Beria in his discussions with the Coven."

"There is a saying where I come from"—the Daemon made an impish glance at the captain—"that war is diplomacy pursued in a more physical manner. The Stormer is being very antagonistic toward the Coven and as it's the mouthpiece of Heydrich I can only assume that it's preparing the people of the ForthRight for war."

"The ForthRight is a peace-loving state. Comrade Leader Heydrich signed a nonaggression pact with Empress Wu only last Autumn."

"Pacts are made to be broken. Are the two railway lines you are building part of this pact, Comrade Commissar?"

"No, that is a wholly ForthRight initiative. Comrade Leader Heydrich is of the opinion that railway lines connecting Hub Bridge Number Two and Hub Bridge Number Four will enable the ForthRight to open up the economic potential of the Hub."

"I thought the nanoBites precluded anything being built in the Hub."

Trixie decided to join in the conversation. "My father has developed a novel means of laying railway tracks on 'floating' sleepers so that no part of their construction ever goes below six inches and hence they are immune to nanoBite attack. It's very clever."

"But won't the lines also enable the ForthRight to make war on the Coven? Won't they make it easier for the ForthRight to maneuver its soldiers?"

The comrade commissar stood up from the table. "You seem determined to malign the motives of the Great Leader, Miss Williams. I think that is enough political chitchat for one day. Young ladies should not, in my opinion, concern themselves regarding the machinations of the ForthRight's leadership. I am confident that, as ever, Comrade Leader Heydrich is intent on leading the ForthRight in a manner consistent with the needs and aspirations of his people."

Trixie smiled. Her father was a great man. No one else she knew would be able to announce such twaddle and still be able to keep a straight face.

19

The Demi-Monde: 47th Day of Winter, 1004

As Aryans are largely of superior Pre-Folk stock they have evolved more rapidly and further than the UnderMentionable races. This, in turn, has caused their more primitive instincts (of which sexual desire is one) to wither. Eugenical science (see Francis Galton: Eugenics: The Final Solution) informs us that as a race evolves, these primitive powers— so readily seen in the instinctive behavior of animals—atrophy because they are no longer necessary to enhance the survival of the species. That is why UnderMentionables (especially Shades, who are considered the most primitive of all the races of the Demi-Monde) excel in such fields as athletics, dancing, WhoDoo and in all matters of the flesh, these Lilithian abilities being known as Atavistic Animal Talents.

—Why Shades Run So Fast: A Study in Atavistic Anatomy, Nathan Bedford Forrest, ForthRight Publications

Despite what he'd told Sergeant Stone, Vanka wasn't staying at the Metropolitan Hotel. Actually he was camped out in a couple of rooms provided, at an eye-watering rent, by Burlesque. Anonymity didn't come cheap.

It was in truth a pretty miserable pair of rooms, positioned in the attic of a pretty miserable house located down a pretty miserable backstreet just around the corner from the depressingly miserable Prancing Pig. The rooms were also dark and cold. Dark because a number of the glass panes in the windows were broken and had been replaced by plywood, and cold because the putty had fallen out from around the remaining panes, allowing the frigid winter wind to whistle in.

Ella was sure it was colder in the rooms than outside in the street.

Vanka was totally unapologetic. "You've got the couch in the living room," he said, pointing to the lumpy sofa resting in front of the fireplace. "If you get cold at night . . ."

Here it comes, thought Ella, *this is when he hits on me*.

But he didn't.

" . . . you can light the fire but you'll have to lump your own coal up from the coal cellar."

As Vanka went on with his description of their domestic arrangements, Ella didn't know whether to be relieved or disappointed.

"You empty your own pan." He used the toe of his boot to nudge a rust-stained bedpan in Ella's direction. At least she hoped it was rust. "If the Checkya come calling then it's out of the window and over the rooftops. Under this veneer of wood the front door's got a solid steel core." He gave the door a hefty kick and it hardly quivered. "It's strong enough to give us a ten-minute head start. Other than that my only advice is for you to stay in the rooms as much as possible. We don't want the neighbors complaining about Zulus moving in and giving the district a bad name, now, do we?"

Fortunately for Vanka, Ella sensed he was being sarcastic.

It seemed straightforward enough, but after a couple of days' confinement she began to feel herself going a little stir-crazy. Her worries about the Checkya gave way to nagging doubts about her ability to find Norma Williams. She had a sneaking feeling that hiding out in a couple of slum rooms wasn't the ideal solution to that particular problem.

It was all very discouraging but this, the seventh day of her self-imprisonment, seemed to promise a break in the boring routine she had settled into: Vanka had taken an interest in cooking and had been laboring over the stove all morning. Unfortunately whatever it was he was cooking up was horribly noisome.

"What's that smell, Vanka?" she asked warily, not quite certain if she wanted an answer.

"Which smell?"

Ella was just about to give a pointed riposte when she realized that it was, in fact, a pertinent question. There were any number of repulsive smells competing for her attention and it was an indication of how adapted she was becoming to life in the Demi-Monde that now the odors of damp, of urine, of boiling cabbage, of overflowing drains and of horse shit that were wafting up from the streets below warranted hardly a mention. No, what unsettled her was the new and distinctly chemical fragrance drifting from a cooking pot resting on a table at the back of the room.

"That chemical smell. You're not cooking up crack, are you?"

"What's crack?" Vanka asked. Then, following the direction in which her nose was pointing, he realized what she was talking about. "Oh, *that*. I'm making the luminous paint I use in manufacturing my ectoplasm."

Now it was Ella's turn to play the naïf. "What's ectoplasm?"

"The magical stuff that forms around mediums when they go into a trance. No good psychic can perform without being able to materialize oodles of ectoplasm." The look on her face persuaded Vanka to expand his explanation. "When mediums are in communion with the Spirit World they produce a luminous aura which the audience at a séance can see glowing in the dark. Ectoplasm signals that the medium is at one with the Spirit World, that they have been possessed by their Spirit Guide."

"Can *you* do that, Vanka?"

"I'm surprised at you, Miss Thomas. Of course I can't, but then no one can. Ectoplasm, like everything else to do with Spiritualism, is total and utter bollocks. Unfortunately ectoplasm has become so famous that if customers at a séance don't see it drifting around they start asking for their money back."

"So how do you make it?"

He looked at her suspiciously; the recipe for ectoplasm was obviously one of his trade secrets. "It's simple really. You cut the heads off a boxful of matches and drop them into a pan of water, which you bring up to a gentle simmer. The phosphorus dissolves off the match heads, and if you give the solution a good stir, the phosphorus mixes in with the water. All you do then is strain off the match stems and, hey presto, there you have it: phosphorescent paint. If you soak a couple of lengths of calico in that and let them dry you'll find that they glow yellow in the dark. Wave the calico around in a séance and everybody goes away happy."

"But surely people aren't fooled by a bit of luminous cloth? Don't you have customers grabbing at it?"

Vanka gave a derisive laugh. "What you've got to understand, Miss Thomas, is that people go to séances in a frame of mind that makes them *want* to believe in the supernatural. The last thing they want is to come away disappointed; they *want* to experience something special, to feel something marvelous has happened, and if that involves them mentally turning a blind eye to the grubby reality of everyday magic, then so be it. As a psychic all I've got to do is to give them the chance to convince themselves, to let their own desperation to believe persuade them to ignore the crudity of it all."

"That seems a little cynical."

"Possibly because I *am* a little cynical." Vanka paused to light one of his foul French cigarettes. "No, that's wrong: I'm *very* cynical. And regarding your other well-made point about people making a grab for the ectoplasm, that's why, at the beginning of the séance, I always tell my audience that to make contact with the Spirit World we need to have all joined hands and hence to be physically and spiritually united with one another. Then I go on to say that anyone deliberately breaking the circle will bring the wrath of the Spirits down on their head. That's usually enough to stop even the bravest punter from letting go of their partner's hand."

"So you rely on the customers convincing themselves that what they are seeing at one of your séances really is magic."

Vanka warmed his hands by the fire. "Exactly. But it *is* magic in a way, in that I cast a spell over the audience. And it's the same when I do cold readings, when I make predictions about people without having met them before. At any individual reading I might make twenty educated guesses about a subject and eighteen of them will be wrong, but what the customer goes home remembering are the two I guessed right. It's called 'selective memory.'"

"And it really works?"

"Let me show you; I've got to begin your training as a PsyChick sometime and now's as good a time as any." He sat down next to Ella on the couch. "I want you to pretend you've come to me for a psychic reading."

Ella nodded but kept as much space between her and Vanka as the couch allowed. The man was a rascal and she was determined to keep their relationship strictly professional. After all was said and done he was just a Dupe, even if he was a particularly *handsome* Dupe.

Stop it, Ella; the man's a Dupe, if that isn't a contradiction in terms.

Vanka's soft voice brought her out of her daydream. "As I'm a psychic who specializes in contacting the dead, in all probability you'll have come to consult with me because someone close to you has recently died. Now, even before I ask you a question I know a lot about you: you're young, attractive, well dressed, well spoken and you're not wearing a wedding ring or an engagement ring."

"So what?"

"Think about it. At your time of life, Miss Thomas, probably the only people whose death would warrant a consultation with a psychic would be your father, your mother or a sweetheart. In the case of a girl as young as you I'd put my money on your coming to see me to contact the Spirit of a boy who died in the Troubles."

"Okay, that seems reasonable but how would you find out for sure?"

"I'd ask."

"But you're meant to be the psychic."

"Just bear with me a moment. When I do a reading I always ask the client to place their hands in mine." Vanka took Ella's hands gently in his. She tried as best she could to still the tremor of excitement she felt as his fingers closed on hers. It was difficult to keep reminding herself that he was just a computer-generated Dupe. "I can tell immediately that you're well-to-do."

"How?"

"No calluses."

"You haven't got any either."

"I'm allergic to hard work, Miss Thomas, just as I'm allergic to girls who keep interrupting me."

Ella took the hint and kept quiet.

"But there's more to holding your hands than that. When a person is being asked questions or is listening to statements being made about themselves or their loved ones their body reacts. These aren't deliberate reactions but automatic—autonomic—reactions the client is often unaware that they are making. Often these reactions, these telltales, are almost undetectable but with practice a good cold reader can spot them. Do you want to try?"

"Sure."

"May I call you Ella while I ask my questions? It's a little less formal."

"You may." She was pleased by this development, though she

immediately worried that her reaction had been communicated to Vanka.

"Good. So if you were here to have me contact a 'dear departed,' I'd probably start with a general statement, something like 'I see a man in a red jacket.'"

"Why a red jacket?"

He gave her an odd, quizzical look. "Because all soldiers in the ForthRight army wear red coats. I'm surprised you didn't know that, Ella."

She tried to mask her annoyance at making such a silly mistake. PINC had already told her that.

"I'd immediately follow this up with the question 'Does this signify anything to you?' You see, if my guess is correct you're amazed at my perspicacity and if it isn't, well . . . I'll just frown and move on. Shall we see if it works with you?"

"Why not?"

"So . . . I can see an older person in your life, Ella, someone who is directing you: a mother, a father, a teacher, a professor . . ." He smiled. "Eureka: I got the most subtle of flinches from your fingers when I mentioned the word 'professor,' so that encourages me to pursue that line of questioning. I sense, Ella, that sometimes your relationship with your professor isn't all that it should be."

"Whose relationship with their professor is ever perfect?"

"True, true. But the message I am receiving is that you are *very* unhappy with what he has asked you to do. You feel as though he's put you in danger."

Try as she might, she couldn't quell the start she gave in reaction to the word "danger."

"Now that *is* a positive reaction. So you feel endangered because of what your professor has asked you to do?"

Alarm bells started to sound. He was finding out too much about her. "Look, I'm really not comfortable with this."

"I'm just trying to show you how cold reading works, Ella," he said in an oh-so-reasonable voice. "There's nothing to be frightened of. Maybe if I just ask a few, more specific questions. After all, I know very little about you and we are going to be partners. Where shall I start? Tell me, which part of the Yank Sector are you from?"

"Why do you think I'm a Yank?"

"Your accent for one, the way you use your fork when you eat for another. The trouble is, you're a Shade."

"I don't like the word 'Shade,' it's demeaning."

He laughed. "I can tell. So what should I call you: darkie, black, sambo, coon, nigger—"

"Stop! I'm a woman of color."

"Very well: the trouble is I've never met a Yank *woman of color* before. You're a real enigma, Ella, you look like you're a NoirVillian but you sound like you come from Washington."

For an instant she didn't quite know what to answer. Fortunately PINC cut in and her faux life history flashed before her. "I was born in NoirVille but adopted by a Yank couple. I was brought up in Fairmont Heights."

"Interesting," murmured Vanka as he caressed her fingers between his. It was really quite distracting. "So your family must have been caught up in the Troubles. There was some vicious fighting in and around Washington."

"I'm an orphan. My adoptive family died when I was a baby."

"Of course."

Ella ignored the sarcasm. "I went to school in London during the Troubles."

"But you never lost your Yank accent?"

"No."

"It must be difficult to be a Yank *and* a Shade amongst the Anglos. The Yanks were the most fervent of all the Royalists; they were the last to surrender to the Party during the Troubles. As I understood it the Anglos hate the Yanks and animosities in the Forth-Right die hard. And as for how Anglos view Shades . . . sorry, people of color . . ."

"London had its moments, but I've never had any real problems."

"Until a few days ago when you had your little contretemps with the Checkya."

She shrugged.

"Why are you so interested in Daemons, Ella?"

"I'm not!"

"Then why did you tear out that article about them from yesterday's *Stormer*?"

Cursing herself for leaving the newspaper lying around, Ella pulled her hands away from Vanka's and glowered at him.

He selected another cigarette, lit it and blew smoke toward the ceiling. "That's something else you'll need to understand about doing cold readings: lies are almost invariably signaled by a pause before they are made. Even the most accomplished of liars needs a moment to get their lies in order before they answer. You have been lying to me, Ella." He flicked some ash into the fire. "As I say, you're an enigma. You're a woman of color, born in NoirVille but adopted by Yanks who had the distinct lack of consideration to die when you were a baby. You're a fashionable girl brought up in fashionable London but who didn't adopt a fashionable Anglo accent. You went to a school in London when I know for a fact that none of them would ever accept a Sha—a *girl of color* as a pupil. And yet, having been brought up in London, you are still unaware that ForthRight soldiers wear red coats. You have a professor who you are more than a little frightened of and who you believe has placed you in danger. You have a peculiar interest in Daemons but you want to keep that interest a secret. You don't believe in Spiritualism but you are the only true clairvoyant I've ever met. And, last but not least, you are being pursued by the Checkya. What an enigma you are, Ella, what an enigma you are."

"You've just got a very suspicious mind, Vanka."

"Suspicious, perhaps, but being a suspicious bastard has kept me alive when some truly horrible people have been determined to kill me." He held up a hand to still her protests. "Look, young lady, I don't know who you are but one thing I am certain of is that what you have just told me is a pack of lies. I've a real suspicion that you're bad news, so let's cut to the chase. I've been thinking about you a lot these last few days and my feeling is that you're a crypto working for NoirVille. Am I right?"

Ella hesitated. It was impossible to admit who and what she really was, but she sensed that unless he got something approximating to a believable explanation Vanka might, just might, throw her out onto the streets. But with a man as sharp as he was . . .

"Okay," she said finally. "I admit it: I'm a crypto, here in the ForthRight on a mission to rescue a Daemon who has been abducted by Aleister Crowley and take her to NoirVille."

Vanka stared at Ella, dumbfounded, then slowly stood up, poured himself a tumbler full of Solution and downed it in one. "No wonder the Checkya are after you."

"Look, Vanka, I've been straight with you. The question is, will you help me?"

"Quite frankly, Miss Thomas . . ."

Miss Thomas? What had happened to "Ella"?

" . . . I don't give a hoot about your politics, but what I most certainly do give a hoot about is my neck and ensuring Beria isn't given an excuse to lengthen it. Therefore I think our partnership is destined to be a short one; I want nothing to do with rescuing Daemons in distress from Aleister Crowley. Crossing that bastard is as good as signing your own death warrant. You can stay here until the Checkya heat has died down and in return you'll help me do a few séances. Let's say a month." He gave Ella a lopsided grin. "Then, Miss Thomas, we go off in opposite directions and I never, ever want to meet up with you again. As you Yanks—and here I am assuming that you *are* a Yank—would say, do we have a deal?"

The look in his eyes convinced Ella that further demurral would be a waste of time. "It's a deal. And thanks, Vanka."

20

The Demi-Monde:
47th to 50th Days
of Winter, 1004

Operation Barbarossa: Case Red

Case Red is to be undertaken by the ForthRight Army under the command of Comrade General Mikhail Skobelev. Commencing on the first day of Spring 1005, the campaign will last thirty-nine days. Case Red involves the invasion of the Coven, the defeat of the Covenite army and the imposition of total and uncompromised political, economic and military control on that Sector. Once said control is achieved the intelligentsia of the Coven is to be eliminated. Those eliminated are to include, inter alia: all members of Empress Wu's Court, Imperial NoNs, army officers, politicians, government officials, HerEtical Priestesses, Suffer-O-Gettes, RaTionalists, scholars, teachers, businessFemmes, journalists, artists, playwrights, writers and others demonstrating leadership or creative potential.

—Minutes of the PolitBuro meeting held under the guidance
of the Great Leader on the 39th day of Winter, 1004

Vanka might have been a cynic when it came to the more supernatural aspects of Spiritualism but he was a *professional* cynic. And if Ella was to be his assistant then he demanded that she aspire to the same professional standards he evinced in his act.

Over the next few days he made Ella practice hard until she knew her cues, her lines and her tricks from back to front. As she discovered, her role as a PsyChick was something akin to being a stooge who helped Vanka do some of the things that added a little pizzazz to his performance as a psychic. Specifically she was to attend his séances posing as a customer, gasp in amazement at crucial points in the performance, use the toe of her boot to set the table rattling at the instant Vanka was possessed by his "Spirit Guide," and, most importantly of all, produce the calico ectoplasm from where it was hidden in her bustle and wave it around in the darkness of the séance room.

Learning how to conjure and then handle the ectoplasm was tricky but it had educated her as to why all séances were conducted in the dark. To pull out the luminous calico from the back of her dress, extend the thin metal rod hidden under her skirts, attach one to the other and then wave the calico around high in the air *without anybody noticing* was a nightmare to master. It also required her to have the use of both her hands, so Vanka had to teach her how to trick the couple she was sitting between and hand in hand with at the séance table into believing that they had an unrelenting grip on *her* hands when, in fact, Ella had arranged things so that they were gripping *each other's* hands.

But she managed it.

And as they worked, Ella began to appreciate why Vanka was such a successful Spiritualist. Besides being handsome and very charming, he was a natural flatterer and a very good listener. She could easily understand why the customers at his séances—especially the women—would be convinced that they were in the presence of someone who could truly commune with the Spirit World.

Finally Vanka pronounced her ready. Two days later she found herself standing in the back room of the Prancing Pig as the customers began to arrive for their first séance. They were, so far as she could judge, a well-heeled group, but then to afford the one-guinea entrance fee that Burlesque demanded they had to be. As it was still early, only about fifteen people had gathered, and they milled around the room eyeing the séance table rather sheepishly, waiting for the show to begin.

The role Vanka had given Ella for her first performance was that of a recently bereaved widow. So it was a heavily veiled Ella, dressed in an all-enveloping black gown—her veil, her gloves and her widow's weeds doing an excellent job of camouflaging her skin color—who sat amongst the audience waiting for Vanka to make his appearance. But despite her rather unflattering costume, there was no disguising that she was slim and young, and inevitably one of the male attendees wandered over to Ella and, doffing his hat, introduced himself. "Good evening, madam, I see we are to be co-travelers on this journey to the Spirit World." He held out a hand. "Allow me to introduce myself. I am Nathaniel Warrington."

They shook hands and immediately Ella knew everything there was to know about Nathaniel Warrington.

Knew that he was a liar.

Knew that his real name was Samuel Morris.

Knew that Morris had adopted an alias because he was a senior psychic assessor at the Ministry of Psychic Affairs who was attending the séance not to journey to the Spirit World but rather to unmask Mephisto—Vanka's new stage persona—as a fraud.

Knew that Morris was attending the séance with his boss, an equally odious-looking man called Tomlinson, who was lurking on the other side of the room pretending not to know his colleague.

But Ella didn't need PINC's help to know that she had to warn Vanka. Reading Morris's mind told her the fate of fraudulent psychics and it wasn't pretty.

It took all her self-control to sit calmly through a few minutes of inconsequential chitchat, before she made her excuses. "You must forgive me, Mr. Warrington, but I'm quite overcome by the excitement of the séance . . . by the prospect of communing with my recently departed husband. Oh dear, I feel a little queasy." With that she scuttled off to find Vanka.

Even the normally unflappable Vanka Maykov was stunned by the news.

"You're certain?"

"Yes. I touched his hand. I get my strongest insights when I do that."

"Then I can't go on. I've heard of Morris; he's a devil for detail. He'll spot my tricks for certain and then I'll be for the high jump." He paced up and down the room. "But if I pull, Burlesque will blow his top. Anyway, sure as eggs are eggs, my nonappearance will only make Morris more determined to find out who I really am. And once he finds out that Mephisto is none other than Vanka Maykov there'll be Hel to pay; stage names are meant to be registered with the Ministry."

"There is one solution," Ella said quietly.

"Under no circumstances!"

"Put me on, Vanka. No tricks, just me. You've seen what I can do."

"I can't . . . he's already seen you."

"I was wearing my veil; he'll never recognize me. And you can introduce me as the mambo Marie Laveau, a WhoDoo mambo."

Marie Laveau? WhoDoo? Now where had PINC conjured that from?

Ella could almost hear Vanka's mind whirring. "You're sure you're up for this?"

"Don't worry, Vanka. Leave everything to me."

"Ladies and gentlemen," announced Vanka as he strode out before the audience seated around the séance table, "I am Mephisto."

There was a polite round of applause to which Morris, on whom Ella was spying from the wings of the stage, did not contribute.

"In my quest as a psychic to achieve ever more profound union with the Spirit World I have sought others whose abilities complement my own. It is a given that two psychics who are able to achieve spiritual union with one another are able to delve more deeply into the strangeness that lies beyond the reality that is the Demi-Monde. Unfortunately such spiritual union is rare, but, ladies and gentlemen, during my travels around the Demi-Monde I have found a woman of such power and ability that together we are able to do what no other Spiritualists have ever been able to. The magical abilities of WhoDoo mambos of NoirVille are much derided, but tonight you will be witness to the most remarkable feats of psychic divination ever performed. I say this to warn you: if you do not wish to see the shadowed secrets of the future that awaits you, withdraw now before it is too late."

No one moved but the atmosphere in the room became distinctly more serious. Ella, as she watched Vanka work his audience, was lost in admiration: when it came to dishing out bullshit, Colonel Vanka Maykov was without equal.

"Very well," he continued in an increasingly somber tone. "Could I have all the lights in the room turned off with the exception of the one situated over this stage?" One of Burlesque's minions performed the duty. "Now, ladies and gentlemen, I have the very great honor of presenting the amazing, the unprecedented, the awe-inspiring, the high priestess of all WhoDoo magic, the great mambo herself . . . Miss Marie Laveau!"

Hearing her cue, Ella swept out into the room to stand beside Vanka under the pool of light afforded by the single gas lamp that sizzled overhead. It was really quite a blast to be onstage, playing the clairvoyant and having an audience of twenty people hanging on her every gesture.

And Ella knew she looked the part.

Considering she had had only ten minutes to concoct a costume, she thought she had done pretty well. She had torn down one of Burlesque's new blue and gold brocade curtains, folded it in half and, using a knife, cut a slit in the fold. When she pushed her head through the slit the curtain enveloped her like a huge tabard that draped down to her feet. It gave her, she thought, a vaguely Oriental air, especially when worn in conjunction with her all-encompassing black veil.

If the gasps emanating from the audience when she stood, arms outstretched, in the middle of the stage were anything to go by, the people seated around the table set in the middle of the room were impressed.

Vanka moved to stand behind her with his hands on her shoulders.

"If you would all join hands, we will begin," he commanded the audience.

Once this was done, he chanted a long, rambling incantation to the Spirits to leave the sanctuary of the World Beyond to journey to the Demi-Monde. There was something almost hypnotic in the rhythm of his voice and even Ella, who had heard Vanka rehearsing this piece of hocus-pocus a dozen times, found herself drifting off into a fugue. Indeed she was so lost in her daydreams that it came as a shock when the gaslight above her head began to flicker.

"The Spirits are come," announced Vanka.

Or, more accurately, one of Burlesque's boys was buggering around with the gas tap.

His grip on her shoulders tightened, the signal for her to go into her act. "Ooooooh!" Ella wailed and she was pleased to see several mouths drop open in nervous astonishment. "Who calls?" She used a voice that she hoped was a good imitation of the spooks she had seen in late-night horror movies. "Who calls me from the Sphere of Shadows?" Immediately the room seemed to become colder, as though the manifesting of the Spirit had drained the room of its warmth.

That, Ella presumed, would be Burlesque opening one of the pub's windows behind the stage.

"It is I, Mephisto," intoned Vanka, in a voice about an octave lower than his usual speaking voice. "I am an Adept of the Fifth Circle, Magus of the Esoteric Arts, and as an Ipsissimus of the Temple of Odin, I call you and I command you. What is your name, Spirit?"

"Hear me. I am Lilith, Goddess of Nature and of the True Magic." The words tumbled out of Ella unbidden. It was as though she were tapping into some primeval memory of a life lived long, long ago.

Weird.

She paused to do a little shaking of her head and body, then with a shriek she stretched out her arms as though trying to embrace some invisible Spirit. Being possessed, Ella decided, was quite good fun. "Why, oh magus, do you call me from the sanctuary of the Spirit World?"

"There are those gathered here who wish to see the future."

"Ooooooh! There are many futures: the future that could be, the future that will be . . ."

"Will you answer our questions?"

"I will."

Vanka addressed the audience. "Who amongst you has the courage to ask the first question?"

As was to be expected, the questioner was Samuel Morris. "I have a question."

"Your name?" asked Vanka.

"I am Nathaniel Warrington."

"Ooooooh. You lie," Ella keened. "Your name is Samuel Morris."

Morris's eyes popped open in wide amazement. "How the Hel . . ." he spluttered, and then recovered himself. "This woman don't know what she's talking about. My name is Nathaniel Warrington."

"Again you lie," cried Ella. "Know you that nothing can be hidden from the Spirits! Your days are spent in deceit." She raised her hand and pointed a finger tipped by a black-varnished nail at the senior psychic assessor. "Oh woe unto those who practice deceit, for they are in thrall to the Dark One." Even in the gloom she could see that Morris had gone as white as a sheet. "This deceit has infected your soul, Samuel. Now you are unable to be true to yourself. I see your future and it is infused with the consequences of your duplicity. I see ruin and despair."

"This is all tripe. You've been spying on me!"

"You have given false witness to those who trusted you. You have cheated those who placed their faith in you. You have placed avarice before honor and you have deceived those who love you. If you do not repent then you will be damned to suffer torment and humiliation when your soul passes beyond this Vale of Tears."

That shut Morris's protests up for a moment as he wrestled with the words "false witness" and "cheated."

"What do you mean? I haven't done anything." The fact that Morris was now giving his boss nervous looks across the room gave the lie to that proposition. "I don't understand." There was real panic in his voice. He looked desperately around the audience for support but all he saw was people edging away from him.

"Those above you know of the crimes you have committed. They know you have issued licenses to those without true power."

"That's a bloody lie."

"They know that your lusts have turned your soul black. Beware, Samuel Morris, beware. They know of the ledger you keep in the locked drawer of your desk. They know of the gold you have hidden at your brother's house."

"I don't know what you're talking about."

"They know of the blood bribes that are held in the Bank in Odessa."

Samuel Morris sprang to his feet. "I'm not sitting here listening to all this claptrap."

"Beware . . . retribution stalks your footsteps. Death walks behind you."

"Shut your gob, you fucking WhoDoo witch. You're just making this up."

"I know of the son that does not bear your name. You have been unfaithful to your wife and to the teachings of UnFunDaMentalism you are oath-bound to protect and uphold." That was a revelation that hit home. Morris flinched back as though he'd been physically struck. "I see deep, deep, deep into your tarnished soul. And there I see your doom."

"Bollocks."

"You have so little time, Samuel. You must make your peace with ABBA."

"Shut up!" Samuel Morris shouted as he shook off the grasp of the two women seated next to him, who in fear of offending the Spirits had doggedly kept hold of Morris's hands all through Ella's wailing. Immediately when the circle was broken, Ella pitched forward, tumbling to the stage as though in a swoon.

As Morris tried to make his escape, a voice boomed out, and, from the look on his face, for him it really was the Voice of Doom. "Stay where you are, Morris," came the shouted command from the man's boss, Tomlinson.

Samuel Morris obviously wasn't of a mind to do much staying. Quick as a flash he drew a pistol from the back of his belt and pulled back the hammer. "Stand your ground or by the Spirits, I'll—"

That was as far as he got before the cudgel wielded by Burlesque Bandstand smashed down on his head.

"THAT WOS ONE 'ELL OF A SORRY, WANKER," crooned BURLESQUE as
he plied Vanka with drinks thirty minutes after the last customer
had left the Pig. "Most of the punters 'ave already bought tickets
for tomorrow's performance." He glanced nervously at Ella. "Yous
wos good too," he admitted. "I liked all that wooing and wailing and
shit." He took a slurp of his Solution. "So c'mon, Wanker, tell Burlesque 'ow you did it. That Morris item wos a plant, wosn't 'e?"

Vanka gave a half smile. "Trade secret, Burlesque, but for your
information neither Miss Thomas nor myself had ever met Samuel
Morris before tonight's performance."

"Then you must've bin 'aving 'im followed. Yous bin using the
Pinkertons to dig the dirt on 'im? Wos that 'ow it wos done?"

"Nope."

"Then 'ow the 'ell?" Burlesque's brow furrowed. "You'll be tellin'
me next that Miss Thomas 'ere really 'as got physicalist powers."
He started to chortle but when neither of his guests joined in he
stopped. "Aw, c'mon, Wanker, yous can tell yer old mucker Burlesque: 'ow d'you do it?"

Slowly and very seductively, Ella leaned across the table and took
Burlesque's hand in hers. "I really am a clairvoyant," she crooned
in her best femme fatale voice. "I can see into your soul, Mr. Bandstand. I can see all your darkest secrets."

Burlesque pulled his hand away. He'd gone a little paler than
usual. "Nah . . . no one can do that. Yer just pullin' my plonker." He
looked at Ella suspiciously. "Yous on the level?"

A nod from Ella.

"Go on then, Miss Thomas, tell me sumfink that only a physicalist person would know."

"I can tell you where Kurt Vangler's body is buried."

That little statement turned out to be a real show-stopper. All the remaining color drained from Burlesque's face. He was so distressed that he spilled his drink. "Shit, 'ow the fuck did yous do that? Fuck me gently, you really is a physicalist ain't yous?" He shook his head in bewilderment and emptied the remaining, unspilled Solution down his throat in one loud gulp. This done, Burlesque looked nervously around, checking that there was no one eavesdropping on their conversation, then gave Ella a very hard and very dangerous look. "Keep yer voice down, will you? An' let me tell you sumfink, Miss Thomas, yous wanna be careful, cos knowin' fings like that can get yous scragged."

Vanka edged protectively closer to Ella. "And you should remember, Burlesque, that us knowing things like that can also get *you* hanged. Just think, if either Miss Thomas or I were ever to get a surprise visit from the Checkya, what interesting information we could give them in exchange for a reduced sentence."

From the look on his face that was the last thing Burlesque wanted to think about.

"That also goes for your talking to your buddy the Witchfinder about things you shouldn't," warned Ella.

This provoked an even deeper scowl.

"And that's why it's so lucky that we're all such good friends," Vanka added with a smile. "Now where's the money you owe us?"

"Wot money?"

"Money for the gig and for our expenses."

"Wot bleedin' expenses?"

"Never you mind, but they're less than the expenses you'll incur if I tell Kurt Vangler's father where his son is buried."

"Fuck. Okay, 'ow much?"

"For tonight's performance? Ten guineas plus another ten for expenses."

If there was one thing that Burlesque hated doing it was parting with money, but the determined glint in Vanka's eye decided him to pay up. Slowly and reluctantly he counted out nineteen guineas.

"The deal was for twenty," observed Vanka.

"I 'ad to deduct a guinea for the curtain the young lady 'ere used as part ov 'er costume."

"I also know where you disappear to on a Sunday afternoon when your wife thinks you're counting stock," said Ella quietly.

Burlesque quickly decided to add another golden guinea to the pile in front of Vanka. "You know, Wanker," he mused idly, "once word of 'ow talented this young lady is gets out, you're—we're— gonna be able to charge a fortune to attend wun ov your sorries. You knows wot yous wants?"

"More money to perform in this shithole?" suggested Vanka.

"Nah, yous wanna manager, that's wot yous want."

And Ella had a horrible feeling she knew just who Burlesque was going to suggest as the ideal candidate for that role.

21

The Demi-Monde: 52nd Day of Winter, 1004

Into the pre-Containment Demi-Monde came a woman—sometimes cited as being a Shade—called Lilith who was skilled in the dark arts of Vanir magic, Seidr. Lilith used her powers to journey to the furthest reaches of Yggdrasil (also called the Tree of Knowledge) to secure occult powers denied to the Pre-Folk by ABBA. There—at the very edge of Space and Time—Lilith met Loki (also called Satan, and the Trickster), who was so intoxicated by her sexual charms that he revealed to her the Secrets of the Living. Upon her return to the Demi-Monde, Lilith used her newfound powers to stir the base passions of the Pre-Folk to a frenzy, whereupon they lost all sense of racial propriety and wantonly engaged in the sin of miscegenation. Intermingling the seeds of the Pre-Folk and of the UnderMentionables, Lilith employed her occult powers to remodel and remake the people of the Demi-Monde, thus precipitating the Fall.

—TALK GIVEN BY PROFESSEUR MICHEL DE NOSTREDAME, MINUTES OF THE TENTH ANNUAL CONGRESS REGARDING THE MYTHS AND ORAL TRADITIONS OF THE PRE-CONFINEMENT DEMI-MONDE, *1003*

Despite all her best efforts Ella could find neither hide nor hair of Norma Williams. She was fast coming to the conclusion that her mission was a wild goose chase. But in the end, in a roundabout way, Norma Williams found Ella.

That particular lunchtime, two days after her first séance, Ella was sitting in the Prancing Pig, enjoying—if that was the correct word—the dubious food on offer. The Pig wasn't a particularly salubrious pub but as it was popular with the lascars and the Shades—she hated herself for lapsing into Rookeries-speak—who crewed the barges that plied up and down the Thames, Ella's skin color didn't seem quite so out of the ordinary. Nevertheless she still wore her leather gloves and a broad-brimmed bonnet with a—fortunately—very fashionable veil draped over her face. The veil made eating her sausages a nightmare but anything was better than being noticed by the Checkya.

She had just pushed her disgusting plate of sausage and mash to one side when Vanka bustled in and tossed a thick envelope onto the table. "That's a little thank-you present." He sat down and signaled the barmaid for a glass of Solution.

"A thank-you for what?" Ella opened the envelope to reveal a NoirVillian passport in the name of Marie Laveau complete with a ForthRight visitor's visa stamped on the first page.

"For getting me out of that jam with Morris the other night. If it wasn't for you he'd have spotted me for sure, and then . . ." He trailed off in uncomfortable consideration of how the ForthRight dealt with fraudulent psychics.

"That's very kind of you, Vanka."

"It's nothing really, Burlesque's ten guineas of expense money paid for it and what with Beria promoting his Festival of Friendship with NoirVille, there are so many Shades coming into the Forth-Right that slipping one more visa through the system wasn't that big a deal. Anyway it'll help explain why you're wearing a veil: all Noir-Villian women wear veils when they're out in public."

"Still, it's very thoughtful of you." Before she quite realized what she was doing Ella had leaned forward and kissed him on the cheek.

The reaction wasn't at all what she expected from a man of the world like Vanka Maykov: he blushed!

For a moment she wondered if he was embarrassed by being

kissed by a black girl in public, but from the way he was looking at her she didn't think so. He raised his fingers to his cheek and touched the spot where Ella had kissed him, then stretched out a hand and gently eased back her veil. "Miss Thomas," he began in a very serious tone, "I should warn you that beautiful young ladies being so free with their affections might find themselves in danger of having those affections reciprocated."

Their eyes met and Ella felt an oddly pleasant sensation welling up inside her. Oblivious to the crowds pressing around them, she leaned forward.

She froze and her eyes widened in terror. "Oh, Vanka . . ."

VANKA SPUN AROUND IN HIS CHAIR AND FELT FEAR TRICKLE DOWN his spine. Even as he watched, four large, black-uniformed and heavily armed SS StormTroopers led by a hard-faced captain barged into the Prancing Pig, two of the StormTroopers peeling off to stand guard at the back entrance to the pub. Then, with legs akimbo and automatic rifles held across their chests, they stood glowering at the thirty or so men and women who made up the pub's lunchtime clientele.

Vanka took a quick look around; there was no way out. They were trapped.

Maybe, he thought, it was just a routine raid, but as those were usually conducted by the Militia—the ForthRight's police force— this, he decided, was infinitely more serious than an ordinary shakedown. Some poor bastard was for the high jump.

His suspicions were confirmed when, at a signal from the captain, a small SS colonel, flanked by ten members of the SS–Ordo Templi Aryanis, strutted in through the door. The SS–Ordo

Templi Aryanis didn't do ordinary or routine; they were the crack regiment that made up His Holiness Comrade Crowley's own personal bodyguard. When Vanka saw that the SS colonel was no less than Archie Clement himself he knew something big was going down, although the adjective "big" was difficult to use in connection with Archie Clement.

He was tiny.

The man the newspapers called "Crowley's Hammer" was an unprepossessing individual; he looked little more than a boy, not at all the Hero of the Revolution he was billed as. But if the legends about him were to be believed he was an extremely dangerous boy. For the commander of the SS to be personally supervising a raid on the Prancing Pig meant they were hunting an Enemy of the State.

Vanka darted a look at Ella and his heart sank. He had an awful suspicion just who that Enemy of the State was.

Clement clapped his hands to signal that he wanted silence. "Ah am SS Colonel Archie Clement," he announced in a drawl of a voice. "This here establishment is now under the control of the SS–Ordo Templi Aryanis. You are asked to have your documents ready for inspection."

"I don't care 'oo the fuck are you, I ain't finished me grub," came the drunken complaint from one of the pub's patrons, a huge lascar bargee up from NoirVille.

There was a nod from Clement and one of his SS gangsters stepped forward, unclipped a long baton from his belt and proceeded to smash the man to the ground. He kept raining blows down on the bargee's head until he had stopped twitching and lay silent and broken on the pub's floor.

"Does anyone else wanna make a comment?" asked Clement.

No one said a word.

"Good. Ah wish to have known to me the psychic who disports himself by the name of Mephisto."

Vanka felt his spirits sag. To have justified such a high-ranking SS delegation coming in search of him meant that they wanted him very, very badly. Images of being tortured in some SS Hel-hole flashed before Vanka's eyes but he shooed them away; he had to stay focused.

He gave Ella's hand a surreptitious squeeze signaling that she should be silent. There was a chance they could bluff their way out; the only other person who knew that Vanka Maykov and Mephisto were one and the same person was Burlesque Bandstand.

At that moment Burlesque barged his way into the Pig looking even more florid faced than usual. "Good afternoon, yer 'ighnesses, Comrades . . . sirs. I am delighted to 'ave yous honor my establishment wiv your esteemed presence. As yous knows, Comrade Clement, I am always ready to do my duty for the ForthRight so iffn there's anyfink you might require . . ."

Clement looked at Burlesque as he might look at something that had just been scraped from the sole of his shoe. "Ah'm searching for the psychic known as Mephisto."

Now there was *no* chance of Vanka working a bluff. When it came to loyalty to friends, well, Burlesque didn't have any friends.

"Oh, in that case then you'll want to speak to Wanker Maykov." Burlesque nodded Clement in their direction.

Bastard.

Clement strode across the room to stand by Vanka's table. "Are you the psychic who performs under the name Mephisto?" he snarled.

It was useless to deny it. "I am," said Vanka quietly. He slid his hand under the table and around the butt of the Cloverleaf he had in his belt. He detested violence, but if things got really bent out of shape . . .

Clement nodded toward Ella, his nostrils twitching as though he was offended by some unpleasant smell. "And this Shade; who is she?" he sneered.

"This is my PsyChick, Miss Marie Laveau."

"Ah didn't think NoirVillian women were allowed to travel outside their Sector."

"She's from the JAD."

That was explanation enough: the nuJu Autonomous District was the only place in NoirVille where women were free of HimPerialism's rabid misogyny.

A sniff from Clement. "Black scum ain't welcome in the ForthRight."

"Miss Laveau has a visa to visit the ForthRight," interrupted Vanka, thanking the Spirits that Ella now had papers to support her *nom de magie*. "She is here as part of the cross-cultural exchange organized by Vice-Leader Beria to foster a better relationship between the ForthRight and NoirVille."

Clement spat on the floor. "Ah don't give a damn about Comrade Beria's good works." He turned to the SS captain. "Clear the room; only the psychic Mephisto and the Shade girl are to remain."

"Wot abart me, yer 'ighness?" inquired a groveling Burlesque.

"Get out!" A disgruntled Burlesque and his thirty customers were pushed and shoved out of the pub, leaving Vanka and Ella to the tender mercies of the SS. The pair of them sat waiting for almost ten minutes, sitting in splendid isolation in the center of the deserted pub with only the silent and sullen SS StormTroopers for company. It all, to Vanka's mind, seemed a little odd. As he understood it, usually those arrested by the SS were simply manacled, dragged out to a steamer and then . . .

Well, there was never any "then"; people taken by the SS were never heard of again. Once they were inside the SS stronghold of Wewelsburg Castle their existence was over. They became nonNixes.

A thought struck him: the real oddity was that neither he nor Ella had actually been arrested. In fact Clement had been—by SS standards—remarkably restrained: he hadn't hit Vanka once. And as he understood it the SS's usual treatment of Shades—especially young, attractive female Shades like Ella—was a lot more physical than the scowls and the black looks Clement and his men were shooting at the girl.

They hadn't even searched him.

No, their treatment of him and Ella had been almost respectful. *Strange.*

The explanation for this softly-softly treatment came striding through the door of the pub a moment later, when His Holiness the Very Reverend Comrade Crowley swept into the Prancing Pig.

Oh, fuck, thought Vanka, *anybody but him.*

Crowley: the Demi-Monde's preeminent expert on the occult and all things relating to the Spirit World. Crowley: the most exalted prophet of UnFunDaMentalism. If there was one person who would be able to spot a scam or a phony Psychic Practices License, it was Aleister Crowley.

Vanka used the opportunity afforded by the distraction Crowley's entrance caused amongst the SS—he had never seen so much bowing and scraping in his life—to lean toward and whisper in Ella's ear: "That's Crowley. Call him 'Your Holiness.' And be careful, he hates Shades."

Crowley looked around the Prancing Pig in disgust. It wasn't often, Vanka guessed, that someone of so elevated a rank came so close to the ForthRight's blood poor; normally he would have his steamer's armored glass between him and the hoi polloi, but today he was seeing how the have-nots really lived. And despite Burlesque's best efforts to tart the Pig up, the pub's back room was still the epitome of poverty chic.

Raising a scented handkerchief to his nose, Crowley held a quiet conversation with Clement, then looked in their direction, threw off his golden cloak and walked across the pub. Immediately Vanka sprang to his feet, made the Party salute and recited, "Two Nations Forged as One."

Crowley didn't even do Vanka the honor of returning the salute. "You are the psychic who presided over the séance where that scoundrel Morris was unmasked as a seller of fraudulent Psychic Indulgences?" he asked, and indicated to one of the StormTroopers that he should be brought a chair.

Vanka's courage nearly failed him, then with a great effort of will he answered in as casual a voice as his strangled guts would allow: "I am, Your Holiness."

"And this is the PsyChick, Marie Laveau?"

"Yes, Your Holiness. She was instrumental in the unmasking of Morris."

To Vanka's astonishment he saw that—ABBA only knew how—Ella had managed to unbutton the top buttons of her bodice, revealing her long, slender and very tempting neck. As she was introduced she began to squirm around on her chair like a lovesick schoolgirl, wriggling her remarkable body in a really quite coquettish way. She giggled and simpered and if he hadn't known her better, Vanka would have been positive that she was making a pass at His Holiness. His Holiness seemed to be of the same opinion.

What the Hel is she playing at?

"You will instruct her to remove her veil," Crowley ordered with a decided catch in his voice.

Artfully, Ella did as she was told, throwing His Holiness several lascivious little glances when her beauty was revealed. She sat there looking simultaneously coy and vampish, batting her huge eyes and looking impossibly sexy. Vanka watched as conflicting emotions danced across Crowley's face: there was revulsion at being in such close proximity to one of the races UnFunDaMentalism proclaimed to be little better than animals, and then there was lust. Shade or no, Ella was a beautiful woman, and even someone as racially myopic as Crowley appreciated beauty when he saw it.

Lust must have triumphed over revulsion because, amazingly, he demeaned himself to address Ella directly. "I am informed by Comrade Colonel Clement that you are in the ForthRight at the behest of Comrade Beria. Am I to presume that you are one of those Shade witches skilled in the WhoDoo arts?"

Ella bobbed in acknowledgment, managing to give her interrogator a disconcerting peek down the front of her bodice as she did so. When she answered, to Vanka's surprise she adopted the accent of a WhoDooist. "Ah am, Your Holiness, ah am de WhoDoo Queen Marie Laveau, de most powerful mambo in de whole of NoirVille. Ah am able to speak wit Papa Legba, de Lord of de CrossRoads, who guards de doorway dat divides de people of de Demi-Monde and de *loa*, de Spirits of my people. It is Papa Legba who has bestowed upon me mah powers of clairvoyance."

To Vanka what Ella was spouting sounded like arrant nonsense but it certainly had an impact on Crowley. He sat down in his chair and the quite obscene expression on his face segued into one of respectful caution; something had certainly struck a chord with His Holiness. But he still seemed unconvinced. He turned back to Vanka. "I give you a chance to admit that the unmasking of Morris was accomplished through artifice. Admit that you exposed Morris's villainy by means of trickery and legerdemain rather than by use of occult talents and I will be moved to be lenient."

Bollocks.

"Your Holiness, there was no artifice. Miss Laveau has the ability to read the thoughts of all those she touches. For corroboration of this you must speak with your man Tomlinson; he witnessed the séance."

"I have spoken to Tomlinson. He has been interviewed rigorously."

Poor bugger.

Crowley ran a finger idly along the edge of his mildewed teeth as he struggled with a decision. "I would like a demonstration of your

PsyChick's ability. I wish to be convinced of her talent as a clairvoyant."

Now this should be interesting.

"Then I must counsel you, Your Holiness, that to commune with
the Spirit of another, the mambo Laveau must connect with them,
flesh against flesh."

Vanka saw the man's eyes sparkle as his imagination kicked in.
But excited or not at the thought of being flesh against flesh with the
beautiful Ella, he still hesitated. It was Ella who—literally—took
matters into her own hands. She used a finger to push a wisp of
hair back from her face and then began, very theatrically, to strip
her leather gloves—slowly, oh so slowly—finger by finger from her
hands. It was one of the most erotic acts Vanka had ever seen performed and its effect on the men in the room was electric: every eye
was fixed on her. The girl was a born show-woman.

This done, she stretched out her naked hands to Crowley, invit-
ing him to take them in his. Like a man in a trance, he did as he was
bade. Immediately Vanka stood up and positioned himself behind
Ella, lifting his hands and placing one on each side of her head, his
fingertips touching her brows. She let out a low moan. "Mah, mah,
ah am in communion wit a most powerful soul. Hum, hum, Your
Holiness, sah, yous a strong, strong *houngan*, full of mucho de vitality and de manly essences. Wooo-whee . . . yous make mah little
heart go pit-a-pat."

Brilliant.

"Mambo Laveau," crooned Vanka, "I command you to journey to
the Other Side, to commune with the Spirit World. Are you ready
to do this?"

"Yeeesss, ah is."

Ella began slowly to roll her head. Gradually the tempo of the
rolling increased and as her head rolled so too did the volume of the
low moan she was emitting. Suddenly she slumped back in her chair

and began to shake, her body quivering in a most extraordinarily exciting fashion. Vanka tore his attention away from the girl's trembling bosom and back to the job at hand.

"I am here."

Even Vanka was startled by the voice that Ella managed to find within her. There was nothing mock NoirVillian about this accent; it was perfectly enunciated Anglo spoken in an amazingly deep voice. It was certainly not the sort of voice that one would believe could emanate from a girl, even one as tall as Ella. It drew astonished gasps from the SS guards, and out of the corner of his eye Vanka saw Clement raise a grubby hand to make the protective sign of the Valknut across his chest.

"Who calls me from across the Abyss?" groaned Ella. "Who is the one who disturbs the peace and tranquility of Aiwass?"

From his long experience in running séances Vanka knew that no matter what happened, no matter how confused events became, no matter what surprises presented themselves, it was vital for the psychic to remain aloof and confident throughout. But even Vanka couldn't prevent his eyes widening when he heard what Ella said; where the girl was conjuring all this nonsense from he had no idea.

But his reaction was as nothing compared to the effect her words had on Crowley. Even as the name Aiwass was uttered it seemed that the mask of arrogance that decked his face crumbled.

"Aiwass?" he muttered.

Again Ella rolled her head but now when she spoke it was as though the words were being unwillingly wrung out of her, as though the uttering of each reluctant syllable was a trial. "Yeeeess. I am Aiwass: Minister to Hoor-par-kraat, Keeper of the Great Seal of Horus the Child, and Guardian Angel to those who seek to take up the burden of Truth. I am the One Who Sees."

"What do you see?" asked Crowley in a hoarse voice.

"That Which Is Yet to Come." There was a silence as Ella seemed to struggle with the Spirit possessing her. "Who calls Aiwass from the Realm of Shadows?"

"I-I call you," came the stuttered reply. "Aleister Crowley c-c-calls you."

"I know you, Crowley!" Ella uttered the name as a strangled scream. There was an immediate shuffling of feet as her SS audience backed away. "Behold," she gasped as her voice sank so low that it was no more than a whisper. "I am your Guardian Angel, sent to guide you on the path of Unification." Once again her voice mutated; now the vowels were clipped and ill pronounced but powerful nevertheless, projecting the animal force of the woman to the corners of the room. "Oooooooh . . . I have been sent from the World Beyond to guide you and to teach you. Heed me. Follow me and I will show you the Way, show you the Way to enlightenment and to resurrection. I hold the keys to the doors which seal the Demi-Monde from the Spirit World." More head-rolling, which Vanka thought was a little excessive. "You, Aleister Crowley, are destined to lead the Chosen to the Ark of the Reborn, to guide the Children of the Second Coming."

From somewhere to the side of the room there was a solemn "amen": the SS audience was really getting into the spirit—the Spirits—of what was happening in the room. Ella's voice rose higher and spittle glistened on her lips.

"Reject asceticism, let what you will be the whole of the law. Do nothing that restricts you or confines you. Through your guidance, the Demi-Monde will merge with the Spirit World, with the World of Shadows. You have that power in your hand. You have the Spirit Maiden. You have the Daemon."

"The Daemon?" uttered an incredulous Crowley.

"Yeeeeessssss . . . the Daemon. You have her in your power but yet you do not know all her secrets. She remains mute and unyielding. She is the great enigma. But I, Aiwass, will help you. It is the will of the Spirits that you understand all. Ask your questions."

"What is the Daemon's name?"

"She calls herself . . . she calls herself . . . Norma."

An astonished gasp from Crowley.

"Beware: she is of the highest level. She sits at the left hand of Loki himself. Beware of this Daemon for she is a succubus, sent to trick and deceive. In the Spirit World she is known as Naamah and is one of the most powerful of all the Daemons. Guard her well, Crowley, but do not harm her lest her consort, the fearsome Daemon Asmodai, journeys from the Darkness to take revenge." Ella's voice was now so low as to be almost inaudible. Vanka found himself having to lean forward to better hear what she said.

By the Spirits, she's good.

"I, Aiwass, have been sent to guide and protect you. I must commune with Naamah and I must make her cower before your wisdom and your strength. Then and only then will all her secrets be yours."

"What secrets?"

"I know she is the daughter of a Daemon possessed of much power. He is a Daemon who calls himself 'the president.' He is powerful, but know you this, Crowley, there are ways in which he can be made your servant, there are ways he can be made to do your bidding. We must tease these secrets from the Daemon . . . secrets that will allow you to control the Spirit World."

"What are these secrets?" Crowley urged.

"Ooooooh . . . the veil between the Spirit World and the Demi-Monde closes . . . my strength . . . fails . . . summon me . . . again . . ." And with that Ella slumped forward across the table as though unconscious.

Brilliant, brilliant, brilliant; always leave the mark gagging for more.

"The Spirit Aiwass has gone, Your Holiness," said Vanka as he gently pulled Ella back into her seat. "It must have been a most potent Spirit the mambo Laveau was communing with to have drained her so quickly."

"Oh, it was, it was." Crowley slowly withdrew his hands from

Ella's grip. Then he too sat back in his chair, a look of stunned incredulity on his face. "That was remarkable, Mephisto. Your PsyChick is a woman of profound ability. I used all my powers to block her but still she penetrated my psychic defenses."

He twisted around on his chair and signaled that he wanted—needed—a drink. It took the downing of three large glasses of Solution before the color returned to his cheeks and the confidence into his voice. "I wish your PsyChick to have a sitting with a Daemon."

"A Daemon?" Even Vanka couldn't keep a tremble of apprehension out of his voice. Daemons were meant to be terrible, hideous things that came to the Demi-Monde from out of the darkest depths of Hel.

"We have captured a particularly powerful Daemon and I wish to use the mambo Laveau's powers to discover all the Daemon's secrets and concealments."

"Then I must ask the mambo Laveau if she believes her powers to be sufficient to deal with such a mighty Spirit."

Hearing her cue, Ella mumbled, "Water."

Remarkably it was Archie Clement who played waiter. The sight of an SS colonel waiting on a Shade was one, Vanka decided, that would live with him for a very long time. Ella drained the glass and, refreshed, she raised her head and stared in an unfocused sort of way at Crowley. "Oh my, yo set me de most mighty of challenges, Your Highness, sah. De Daemons have de great powers and to conquer dem ah must call on *all* de Spirits to aid me. Man, ah'll have to call on de Great Lord Bondye to help me and to do dat, Your Holiness, ah must commune wit de Daemon in a *hounfo*, in a WhoDoo temple."

"Is there such a temple in the ForthRight?"

Stupid question. It was Crowley himself who had banned all churches in the ForthRight except those dedicated to the worship of UnFunDaMentalism.

"No, sah, dere ain't."

"Can this temple be built?"

"Yes, Your Holiness, if ah am given a room big enough."

"Very well. In three days you will come to Dashwood Manor to perform a sitting with the Daemon."

WHEN CROWLEY AND HIS SS ENTOURAGE HAD SWEPT OUT OF THE pub, Burlesque bustled back in and after cursing and swearing about the bottle of Solution that Crowley had drunk but not paid for, he had been at pains to tell Ella that the appearance of the SS had been nothing to do with him. He had obviously taken her warning to heart.

"I know, Burlesque," Ella had reassured him, "I know."

"So wot did Crowley want?"

"Crowley wants me to perform a séance at Dashwood Manor."

"Dashwood Manor? That's wun ov them big 'ouses in Kensington where all the nobs live. Gor, that's great. I'll be able to charge fifty guineas."

"The séance Crowley is talking about is to be performed before the Leader, Reinhard Heydrich." As statements went, Ella knew it was a real revelation. Vanka's mouth flopped open in astonishment.

"Heydrich?" he gasped. "Are you sure? How do you know?"

"I'm a clairvoyant, remember?"

Vanka shook his head. "No . . . not Heydrich . . . I'm not going anywhere near that fuck . . . no . . . bollocks to that."

Burlesque, by contrast, was enthused. "Gor, that's even greater, that is. The Leader, you say? That trick yous pulled on that Morris bloke musta really got the feathers flying in the Ministry an' no mistake." Burlesque called over to a passing barmaid for a glass of Solution. "We'll be able to arsk a fortune in fees."

"Are you fucking insane?" snarled Vanka, abandoning his usually cool demeanor. "Perform a séance for Heydrich? If there's even a hint of trickery then we'll be arrested on the spot."

Burlesque wasn't listening. "Maybe I should ask a century, wot wiv it bin the Leader an' all."

"I don't care if they're offering a thousand fucking guineas. I can't spend it if I'm banged up in Wewelsburg Castle hanging from the ceiling by my scrotum, now, can I?" Vanka shook his head even more firmly. "No, I'm not doing it. I've one rule in my life and that's to keep as much distance between myself and those fucking"—his instinct for self-preservation kicked in; he gave a quick look around to make sure there was no one in the pub listening to what he was saying— "lunatics who run the ForthRight as is humanly or, in their case, as is inhumanly possible." He shoved his half-finished glass of Solution across the table. It seemed his thirst had suddenly deserted him. "Now, if you'll excuse me I've got to get home urgently."

"Wot? But we've got fings to discuss, Wanker, like wot share ov the takings I'm getting. As your manager—"

"Fuck your discussions, Burlesque, I'm going home to pack."

"Pack? Where yous goin'?"

"A place called Somewhere-Else-in-the-Demi-Monde."

"Ah, don't be like that, Wanker. I'd 'ave thought you'd 'ave bin pleased." Burlesque took a stone-cold sausage off Ella's plate and gave it a ruminative gnaw. "Iffn Miss Ella here can do the business wiv a *Daemon*, well, the sky's the limit. We'll be able to charge—"

"Are you totally fucking crackers, Burlesque? Can you imagine the amount of shit we're going to be in if our séance goes wrong in front of Comrade Leader Heydrich?"

"Yeah, but fink abart it, Wanker: wot iffn it goes *right*! I can see the handbill now. 'Burlesque Bandstand Entertainments proudly presents, by royal—'" He stopped. "Nah, I can't use the word 'royal,' the Party's still twitchy." He paused to scratch his groin, presumably, Ella decided, searching for inspiration. "That's it: 'by *Imperial Warrant*: Wanker Maykov an' the Amazing Miss Marie Laveau, the Demi-Monde's Foremost Physicalists.' You'll be a star, Wanker. Make a fortune we will: twenty guineas an 'ead we could charge to attend wun ov your sorries, no problem."

"I'm not doing it."

"I think we should, Vanka."

The two men turned to look at Ella. Men in the ForthRight weren't accustomed to being interrupted by women, especially when they were discussing business.

"Now yous talkin' sense, Miss Thomas."

"Under no circumstances," Vanka continued to protest.

"I *need* to, Vanka," insisted Ella. "It might be the only way I have of finding the friend of mine I was telling you about, the one who is missing."

Vanka shot Ella a venomous look and when he answered his voice had a distinct edge to it. "No way. We've created far too big a stink as it is. The last thing you want to do is attract *more* attention. You start being paraded around in front of Heydrich and the Checkya will nab you for sure, and if they nab you, they'll nab me."

"Is that your final word, Vanka?" said Ella in an equally determined voice.

"Damned right it is."

"Then I'll do it without you," she said quietly.

The mouths of the two men flopped open. "You can't do it without me," protested Vanka.

"Oh, yessen she can," interjected Burlesque quickly. "I've seen 'er. She don't need yous, Wanker. I'll get you a new assistant, Miss Thomas . . ."

Vanka glared at Burlesque, obviously angered by the abrupt way he'd been demoted from "star" to "assistant."

" . . . maybe even a new frock. That old bit ov curtain ain't suitable for a *star* like wot yous will be."

"Wait a minute, Burlesque. Ella here is *my* assistant. This is *my* act."

Burlesque shrugged his protests aside. "Times change, Wanker. Opportunities like wot this is don't come around very often and when they does, they've gotta be grabbed wiv both 'ands. Gor, I can see it now, Miss Thomas 'ere playing the Palladium."

Burlesque lapsed into a lucrative daydream, leaving Ella to deal with a scowling Vanka. "Vanka, it's a great opportunity. We've got to do it. I need your showmanship, Vanka; I need you to work the audience."

Vanka shook his head. "I can't, Ella, there might be people there, people I don't want to meet."

The penny dropped; *now* Ella understood Vanka's reluctance. "For the love of God—for the love of ABBA," she quickly corrected herself, "there are people *I* don't want to meet either." Wasn't that the truth; the prospect of being in the same room as Reinhard Heydrich certainly wasn't flipping her bananas. "But that's not a problem, Vanka. I've been thinking about how we could spice up our act and I've come to the conclusion that we need to be a bit more theatrical. You've already been billed as Mephisto so no one will know your real name and if we come onstage wearing masks—"

"Masks?" asked Vanka incredulously. "Like they wear in the Quartier Chaud?"

"Yes, that way no one will be able to recognize either of us."

"I like the idea of making your act a bit more theatrical," mused Burlesque. "We could 'ave a coupla birds wiv really big charms wandering around in the—"

"Shut up, Burlesque," snapped Ella, and to her amazement, that's just what he did. "I need you, Vanka, I need you to help me design a trick so big that no one will ever imagine that it *is* a trick." Ella suddenly became aware that Burlesque was hanging on her every word. "I need you to help me design the temple, the *hounfo.*"

"Wot's a *hounfo?*" asked a suddenly nervous Burlesque. "Is it expensive?"

AN HOUR LATER ELLA AND VANKA—HAVING LEFT A HALF-PISSED AND very happy Burlesque asleep in the Pig—were sitting back in Vanka's rooms.

Vanka had lapsed into a fretful silence as though he knew what he should do but couldn't bring himself to actually do it. It took half a bottle of Solution and nearly an hour's worth of dark brooding before he pulled himself out of his mood. "Is this Daemon—the one Crowley was talking about—the one you want to take back to NoirVille?" he asked.

There was no point in lying. "Yes, I got that much out of Crowley. He was a tough one to read and he blocked most of his mind off to me, but I found out about the Daemon and one or two other bits and pieces of useful information. The main thing though is that Crowley has given me a golden opportunity to rescue the Daemon."

"So come on, tell me: why is it so all-fired important that you abduct this Daemon? Are you mixed up with the Blood Brothers? Are they making you do this? Do they want the Daemon back in NoirVille so they can milk it of its blood?"

Ella sighed. "It's too difficult to explain, Vanka. All I can tell you is it's something I *have* to do; I have to help the Daemon escape Crowley and take her to NoirVille."

"I don't like this, Ella. I think all this milking of Daemons is wrong."

"Vanka . . . please . . . you'll just have to trust me: this has got nothing to do with stealing the Daemon's blood. I don't mean the

Daemon any harm, quite the contrary in fact. But I do need your help to rescue her."

Vanka shook his head. "It's madness, you know. To kidnap a Daemon from under the nose of Heydrich is . . . madness. And even if you succeed, the SS will hunt you down."

"The Demi-Monde is a big place. And once I get to NoirVille I intend to disappear."

Isn't that the truth?

"Yeah, but anyone helping you will have to disappear too. They'll need a new name, a new identity, a new home, a new life. To evade the SS will cost a lot of money. It'll take a fortune in bribes and hush money."

"How much?"

He shrugged. "I dunno. Probably half a million guineas."

"Vanka, how would you like to earn a million guineas?" inquired Ella quietly.

Vanka looked up from the doleful consideration of his near-empty glass of Solution. "A million guineas?" He laughed. "No one's got a million guineas. That's more money than in all of the Forth-Right."

"No it isn't. The Ministry of Psychic Affairs has over fifteen million guineas to its credit in the Blood Bank in Berlin."

"You learned that while you were holding Crowley's hands, didn't you?" There was a distinct flavoring of admiration in Vanka's voice.

"Correct. I now know all the Ministry's bank account details, all the passwords they use to access it . . . everything. I could clean out their account like that." She snapped her fingers.

"Then why are you telling me this?" asked Vanka suspiciously. "Why aren't you down at the bank now, making yourself a very rich woman?"

"Because I need your help. I need your help to make that Daemon vanish from Dashwood Manor."

"A million guineas?"

"Yeah."

"Just tell me why you put on that act with Crowley. Why did you vamp him?"

"Crowley is suspicious of me so I acted out what he expected me to be: a pantomime WhoDoo mambo. It worked too; he just dismissed me as a brainless, oversexed Shade. And a man who's thinking what it would be like to jump my bones ain't thinking about the things he should be thinking about." She gave Vanka a grin. "I thought I vamped him pretty good; what do you think?"

"I think you could . . . well, never mind what I think."

For five minutes Vanka strode up and down the shabby room lost in thought. Finally he turned to Ella. "Okay, Miss Thomas, you've got a deal."

Ella leaped up out of her chair, threw her arms around Vanka's neck and pressed her lips firmly against his.

It was Vanka who broke away. He gave Ella a sideways look. "Remember, Ella, I'm only human."

And *that*, Ella decided, was the big problem.

22

The Demi-Monde: 55th Day of Winter, 1004

The greatest and most compelling aim of UnFunDaMentalism is to reclaim the racial purity of the Aryans (as the direct descendants of the Pre-Folk) lost during the Fall and to eliminate all contaminating UnderMentionable aspects from the population. Whilst modern Eugenical studies contend that, over ten generations, it will be possible to breed out the UnderMentionable impurities from the Aryan people, it will also be necessary to supplement these more considered aspects of Eugenical policy with Exterminationist strategies designed to eliminate—finally and totally—UnderMentionables from the breeding pool. This policy of Extermination I call the Final Solution.

—My Struggle, Reinhard Heydrich, ForthRight Free Press

I t was bad enough when word came that Comrade Leader Heydrich would be personally interviewing the Daemon and that the interview would be taking place at Dashwood Manor. That, by itself, was enough to throw the household into panic.

It was the codicil to the message that had threatened to reduce Trixie's governess to gibbering insensibility. The instruction that His Holiness Comrade Crowley was intent upon holding a séance in the manor's ballroom, a séance that the Leader and other notables would be attending, had been almost too much for the woman's fragile constitution to bear, especially as it was to be, according to the note, "*a séance designed to unlock the Daemon's darkest secrets and to use whatever conjurations and adjurations are necessary to make said Daemon pliant and obedient.*"

Trixie's governess almost crumbled under this weight of responsibility and the thought that the manor would soon be the venue for something as outré as a WhoDoo séance. To have her home playing host to a psychic and—so they had been warned—a *Shade* witch was intolerable. And when the gang of rather uncouth workmen had arrived to construct this mysterious thing called a *hounfo* in the manor's ballroom she became nigh on hysterical. But after a quiet word from the master and a glass of 20 percent Solution, she rallied and turned all her nervous energy toward preparing Dashwood Manor for the Leader's arrival.

Under Governess Margaret's impassioned—and often tearful—instruction the servants polished and scrubbed, swept and tidied until the manor was immaculate and smelled of beeswax and bustle. Never had the manor been so clean and polished nor the wooden floors buffed to such a dangerously lustrous sheen. But for Trixie the most singular aspect of this premature spring cleaning was the servants being instructed to take down all of the mirrors that hung in the hallway and in the drawing room.

Her father noted Trixie's confusion. "The Leader has an aversion to mirrors. He will not look into them," he said by way of explanation. This only fueled her curiosity.

"But why?"

A shrug from her father. "Who knows, Trixie? The Leader is different from the rest of us mere mortals. Perhaps," he added in a whispered aside, "he does not wish to see what he has become." This thought made the comrade commissar pause for a moment and then he edged closer to his daughter. "And *we* must be careful of what Reinhard Heydrich has become. As my daughter, Trixie, you will be introduced to the Leader, but it is doubtful whether he will deign to talk with you. But if he does, you must answer his questions correctly as a good Daughter of the ForthRight. No demurral and none of your famous sarcasm. You may be young, Trixie, but your youth will not protect you; just remember it is treason to express doubts about the rightness of what the Leader says or does. For a female to question the ForthRight's ultimate victory over the other peoples of the Demi-Monde is HerEsy." He paused for a moment as though running through a mental checklist. "You know your Un-FunDaMentalist catechisms? You may be asked to recite them by Heydrich; the man is a stickler for Party dogma."

A nod from Trixie.

"Excellent." He placed a hand on her shoulder. "And keep that Eyetie slave of yours out of sight. Heydrich hates the Medi races almost as much as he hates Shades and nuJus."

Despite their having been advised that the Leader would not be arriving at the manor until the evening, Heydrich's cavalcade swept into the grounds a little after one o'clock that afternoon, the Leader's Mercedes steam-limo set in the middle of a phalanx of armored pan-technicons full of SS militia.

Captain Dabrowski had drawn up his company in front of the house to provide an honor guard, but he and his men were ignored by the four black-uniformed men who clambered out of the steam-limo and across the driveway's swept gravel to the steps that led to the main doors of Dashwood Manor. Trixie knew them all; their engravings were forever on the front page of *The Stormer*. All were Heroes of the Revolution: Vice-Leader Comrade Beria; His Holiness Comrade Crowley; Colonel Clement, the head of the SS; and, of course, the Comrade Leader himself.

Trixie was beside herself with excitement; to be actually meeting the Leader in the flesh! It was the dream of every good member of the RightNixes—the ForthRight's youth movement—to meet with the Great Leader face-to-face.

She tried to calm herself. The Leader's arrival had been so unexpected that she and her father had had to rush to greet their distinguished guest, but now she stood with her presentation bouquet and dressed, a little uncomfortably it had to be admitted, in a stylized peasant's dress—the Party was encouraging women to shun the "decadent" styles coming out of Paris—embroidered with blue Valknuts. Trixie hated the dress, but her governess had insisted.

Her father gave the Party salute, intoned the Party oath and then bowed a greeting. "Good afternoon, my Leader, you do my home tremendous honor."

"You are not wearing a uniform, Dashwood," said Heydrich, who then proceeded to make a critical study of the garden, obviously assessing the defenses. "I require all members of my government, when on official business, to wear their uniform. By wearing a uniform we signal that we are all of one accord. It demonstrates, Comrade Commissar Dashwood, that you have sublimated your individuality to the will of the Leader and of the Party." He tapped at the side of his highly polished boot with the riding crop he was carrying. "One day all men in the ForthRight will be obliged to wear uniforms, and when they do it will signal that their identity is in the Party's gift, that individuality and independence of thought are decadent and obsolete, that their only function in life is to obey."

The Comrade Leader spoke very quickly, as though his mouth had to hurry to keep pace with his mind. Trixie was still musing on what he said—trying to memorize it for repetition at the Academy—when he moved to another subject. "I have come to interview the Daemon," said Heydrich abruptly. "You have a study I might use for this purpose?"

"Why yes, Comrade Leader."

"Then have the creature brought there." Heydrich's gaze drifted toward Trixie. "Is this your daughter, Dashwood? Is this the girl who has been assisting with the Daemon's interrogation?"

"Indeed, Comrade Leader, may I present my daughter, Lady Trixiebell Dashwood."

Trixie curtsied and automatically recited the mantra of the RightNixes, "One Race Defines Us, One Party Unites Us and One Leader Commands Us." She held out the bouquet and one of the Leader's flunkies took it.

"Charming," murmured the Leader as he held out his hand to Trixie. "You are to be congratulated, Comrade Commissar, on siring such a perfect flower of Aryan womanhood. With girls as beautiful and as racially pure as this I am confident that the bloodstock of the ForthRight will soon be free of the contaminants of the UnderMentionable races." He smiled at Trixie. "You must always remember, Lady Trixiebell, that ABBA has given the women of the ForthRight the divine task of breeding out the racial impurities that defile our Aryan birthright. My advice is that you marry young and be fruitful."

During the moment when the Leader had shaken her hand she had a chance to study him more carefully. He was tall, narrow hipped and lithe—his svelte body wonderfully presented by his ink-black uniform—and his long face was dressed with an imperious nose and narrow-set, very pale eyes. He was a perfect specimen of the "ForthRight man," the Aryan male.

An impish, unpatriotic and decidedly dangerous thought popped into Trixie's head: perhaps, though, he could even be considered *too* perfect. It might have been how soft his hand was when he had shaken hers. It might have been that his uniform was *too* immaculate or that his eyes contained no humor or humanity. There was something almost doll-like about him, as though she were meeting with an emotionless, soulless automaton.

The slap of the Leader's riding crop against the black leather of his jackboot snapped Trixie out of her reverie. "So to work, Comrade Commissar; we cannot, through indolence or the squandering of time, allow the reins of government to slip from our grasp."

As Heydrich and his party were shown into the house, Trixie and her father trotted after the Leader's delegation. Trixie was just in time to see the Leader being shown into her father's study and Crowley, with Clement at his heels, wandering off in the direction of the ballroom, presumably to check on the construction works being done in advance of the evening's séance. As soon as the study door was shut, Beria began barking out orders, demanding that the Daemon be summoned.

Five minutes later the creature was escorted down from its room by two of Clement's SS troopers. As Trixie watched it descend the staircase, she was amazed by how sanguine the Daemon seemed. It even bade her a jaunty "good afternoon."

Doesn't the silly thing know it's going to meet the Leader?

Once the Daemon was shown into the study, Beria shut the door and stationed two large and imposing SS soldiers to guard it. As Beria forcefully reminded Dashwood, no one was, in any circumstances, to disturb the Leader whilst he was in conference with the Daemon.

The Dashwood household settled into a sort of hyperactive indolence, everyone ready at an instant to do the Leader's bidding but not daring to do anything whilst they waited. Trixie decided to return to her embroidery, but as she was climbing her way up the staircase that led to the upper floors of the manor and her bedroom, she saw Captain Dabrowski dodge back into one of the guest bedrooms on the second floor.

Odd . . .

But not as odd as what she saw when she peeked through the door's keyhole. The captain was kneeling next to the empty fireplace, apparently listening to the wind whistling up the chimney. She turned the doorknob and to her amazement found that the captain had bolted the door from within. Perplexed and not a little aggrieved by his antics, she rapped on the door. A second later the bolts were pulled and the door was edged open. "Yes?" said the captain in a decidedly disrespectful and impatient tone.

"What are you doing in there, Captain?" Trixie demanded in a loud and imperious voice. "I know you have jurisdiction over this house regarding security but what I saw you doing—"

She wasn't allowed to finish. The Polish captain reached out, grabbed her by the wrist and hauled her into the room. Trixie gave a squeak of complaint but when she saw the revolver in his hand and noted that it was pointed in her direction she decided that any more squeaking might not be a good idea.

"Be *very* quiet, Miss Dashwood, or I will be obliged to silence you." He shot the bolts to the door, then pulled a handkerchief out of his pocket and stuffed it into the keyhole to deter any more would-be voyeurs.

"Are you mad? My father—"

"Miss Dashwood: shut up! I have been presented with an ABBA-sent opportunity to find out what that bastard Heydrich . . ."

Bastard? Trixie flinched away from the dangerous insult.

" . . . is up to. If you are quiet and do what you are told, then I will leave here without harming you. But if you attempt to call out or to raise the alarm then I will silence you . . . permanently. Make no mistake, these are desperate times and I will not hesitate to sacrifice one life to save millions. Do you understand?"

The look in Dabrowski's eyes convinced Trixie that he was in earnest. She nodded her agreement.

"Very well," said the captain, "if you will come and sit with me by the fireplace, I think we will hear history being made."

"What?"

"The chimney at this side of the house runs up from your father's study. By sitting quietly we can hear everything that is said in that room."

"You can't eavesdrop on the Leader," Trixie protested.

But they could.

"Good afternoon, Miss Williams, would you take a seat?"

For an uncertain moment Norma Williams stood by the door of the shadow-draped room. No one had told her who she was to meet, but from the panic that had enveloped the house she guessed it was someone important. She moved toward the desk and took the leather tub chair indicated. Closer now, she could see who her host was.

Oh, sweet Lord.

"Perhaps I should begin by introducing myself—"

"I know who you are. You're Reinhard Heydrich. I've read about you."

"I am gratified that the exploits of my doppelgänger in the Real World should still have resonance so long after my death. One does not wish one's efforts in life to have no impact on history."

"Oh, you're remembered all right: you're remembered as one of the most evil, hateful men who has ever lived, as the perpetrator of the greatest crime ever committed against humanity, as the man who industrialized genocide. Yeah, history remembers you, Heydrich, remembers you as a mad, bad, psychotic mass murderer." A disturbing thought struck Norma. "But how do you know about having a doppelgänger?"

Heydrich gave an arrogant smirk. "All in good time, Miss Williams, all in good time." He took a cigarette from the silver box set on Dashwood's desk, tapped it absentmindedly on a thumbnail and lit it using a gold lighter he tricked out of the top pocket of his uniform. For several seconds he smoked silently, as though cogitating on what to say next. Finally his attention returned to his guest. "I came here today because I wanted to see you for myself. You are a very remarkable young woman, Miss Williams, unique in fact. You are the first Daemon we have ever been able to draw from the so-called Real World into this, the Demi-Monde. All the other Daemons came here to play their sordid little war games but you are different. You were brought here to play a leading part in one of *our* games." He blew smoke idly toward the ceiling. "You, Miss Williams, are our hope for the future."

There was something about the way he spoke the last sentence that frightened Norma. Why, she wasn't quite sure, but Heydrich gave the impression that he was laughing at her behind his hand, that he knew something that she didn't. The feeling she had as he sat there smoking his cigarette and sipping his coffee was that he was toying with her.

"And what future is that?"

"A future where the past is rerun, where mistakes of history are rectified and errors of judgment eliminated and where what *should* have been . . . is. A future that will be reshaped and remodeled to match the template of that Aryan paradise envisaged by Adolf Hitler."

"Adolf Hitler?" Norma tried to make her question sound as off-hand as she could, but in truth she was really disturbed by a Dupe talking about a person who, as far as Norma knew, had never been re-created in the Demi-Monde.

"Oh, come now, Miss Williams, let us not be coy or naïve; we both know who Adolf Hitler is. The time for dissembling is over." He took a long, enjoyable drag of his cigarette. "You are wondering, perhaps, if I am feigning a knowledge of the Führer, if I am on what Yanks like you so picturesquely call a fishing expedition. Perhaps you think that it is a name given to me inadvertently by one of the other Daemons we have captured and interrogated? But in this you would be mistaken. I knew the Führer intimately and had the honor of serving him in many capacities, the final one being as Reichspro-tektor of Bohemia and Moravia. It was in the Czech lands that my life in the Real World was so prematurely brought to an end. Yes, I knew Adolf Hitler. He was a great man, if emotionally flawed."

"Hitler wasn't a great man; he was a monster. He was mad as they come. He was a homicidal maniac."

Heydrich gimleted Norma with a savage look. "I really am not accustomed to being contradicted, Miss Williams, especially by those who do not have the intellectual capacity to appreciate the profundity of the Führer's teachings."

Now it was Norma's turn to be silent, to take a few moments to cogitate, to wonder if, perhaps, this Dupe sitting in front of her really did have knowledge of what his "real self" had been when he was alive. But surely, she thought, that was impossible. As she understood it, one of the immutable programming instructions ABBA had been given was that none of the Dupes populating the Demi-Monde would have any remembrance of what they were—or in the case of the PreLived Singularities, what they had been—in the Real World.

An awkward thought struck her: *she* was a Dupe and she had a remembrance of what *she* was in the Real World. It was all rather confusing and very, very disturbing.

Norma decided to play it cool. "Okay, so you've heard of Adolf Hitler. Big deal. Okay, so you think that lunatic was the best thing since the wheel. The question is: so what?"

"An apposite question, Miss Williams, a very apposite question. And I understand from the disdainful manner in which it is posed that you have little appreciation of my talents. Indeed, if I were a normal man possessed of normal abilities and normal ambitions the answer to your question would be 'not much.' It would matter not a fig that I have knowledge of the Real World denied my fellow Demi-Mondians. But I am *not* a normal man, Miss Williams, I am one of the *Übermenschen,* one of the Supermen whose destiny it is to rule the world. I am the Messiah sent to reestablish the hegemony of the

Master Race—the Aryans—and to purify the world of the contamination of the lesser races. I am charged by Fate to enact the Final Solution. And being an *Übermensch*, I am a quirk of Nature, Miss Williams. Oh, I do not allude here simply to my genius and my skills as a leader but to the fact that uniquely in all of the Demi-Monde, I am the only one with memories of what the man on whom I am modeled achieved. I remember who and what I was."

That shook Norma up. It was easy to dismiss the inhabitants of the Demi-Monde as just figments of ABBA's fevered quantum imagination but not so easy when the bastards started to talk about having memories of their previous existence in the Real World. That the Dupe of Reinhard Heydrich should somehow be all-aware seemed to be a dangerous occurrence. The son of a bitch was bad enough when his malignant, Luciferian personality was confined to the Demi-Monde, but when it seemed suddenly to have become Real World–perceptive . . .

"How do you know all this?"

Heydrich gave a nonchalant wave of his hand. "Who knows? It might be that my personality—my will—is simply too powerful for ABBA to contain."

ABBA? The bastard knows about ABBA.

"ABBA?" she asked, hoping against hope that Heydrich was talking about the Demi-Mondian deity rather than the supercomputer running the simulation she was trapped in.

Heydrich carelessly flicked the ash from his cigarette onto the carpet. "Please, do not play the naïf with me, Miss Williams. ABBA is the immensely powerful difference engine that designed and created the Demi-Monde as a playground for the American military to train their soldiers and to test their pathetic little theories about urban warfare."

Jesus.

"Okay, so if you know about ABBA then you must know that

you're just a computer glitch, a ghost in the machine. How does it feel, Heydrich, to be nothing more than a computer programmer's wet dream? How does it feel to know you can be edited out with one click of a mouse?"

Heydrich shrugged. "There is no difference between how I felt when I was active in the Real World and how I feel here, in the Demi-Monde. *Cogito ergo sum*: I think, therefore I am. In both realities my existence hangs on the whim of Fate. What difference does it make if I am killed by the bullet of a Czech terrorist or the whim of a computer programmer? In both existences I would still be very much dead. But"—he gave a chuckle—"here in the Demi-Monde, I am very much alive."

"That still brings me back to my original question: so what?" Norma gave Heydrich a careless smile, as though what he was saying had little import. The last thing she wanted was this lunatic to appreciate how unsettled he was making her feel.

"Your problem, Miss Williams, is that you are unable to understand or appreciate what it is like to taste power and have it snatched from you. I sit here agonized by the thought of 'what if?' What if those Czech terrorists hadn't succeeded in assassinating me? What if I had been on hand to wrest the levers of power from Hitler when he faltered and his will crumbled? What if *I* had become Führer?"

"You would have been hanged with all the other Nazi war criminals at Nuremberg, that's what."

"Perhaps. But then, perhaps not."

"Unfortunately for you, Heydrich—"

"You will address me by my title."

"And you can kiss my ass."

There was a sour silence for a moment as the pair of them glared at one another. Finally Heydrich broke the silence. "No matter. Call me what you will. We are alone."

"Then I'll tell you what you are: you're a computer-drawn chimera. You're a nothing, just a piece of digital doodling. And that being the case all of your psychotic what-if scenarios will have to be played out here in the Demi-Monde. And you better enjoy it while you can because one day someone in the Real World is going to pull the plug on this shitty little world of yours."

Heydrich laughed scornfully. "How pathetic you are. Do you really believe a person of my will, my genius, of my ambition, would be content to be imprisoned in this . . . nothing of a place? Do you really imagine I will be content to be condemned to live my life—my second life—in a world that is little better than a digital sandbox built for the education of military incompetents and the amusement of armchair generals?" He shook his head. "Impossible; when man has feasted on steak he is no longer satisfied with mince."

"You don't get it, do you, Heydrich? So let me spell it out: you ain't real."

"If I had more time and more patience, Miss Williams, it might be interesting to debate how a sentient entity, as I undoubtedly am, can ever be considered *not* to be real. But unfortunately time is pressing and the interesting must yield to the important. We were talking about Adolf Hitler. Hitler believed that the principal aim of Germany's foreign policy was to ensure that Germany's living space was that necessitated by the size and needs of its population. This is the notion of *Lebensraum* that persuaded him to invade Czechoslovakia and Poland. During my exile here in the Demi-Monde, I have had a chance to ponder upon this and I now believe that in this matter the Führer was wrong. In my view the foreign policy adopted by a nation has nothing to do with the needs of the people; rather it must be designed to enable a nation to achieve a size that is consistent with the will, the genius and the energy of its leader. Nations wax and wane, grow and contract, not because of the needs of their people, nor because of that nation's political, economic or military success but because of the scale of the ambitions of the one who leads it."

"Look, Heydrich, fascinating as all this is and much as I would just love to sit around here all day shooting the breeze . . ."

Heydrich ignored her. "I will be frank with you, Miss Williams, I wish to conquer the Real World."

Norma laughed uproariously. "Your ambition runs ahead of itself, Heydrich, you haven't yet gained mastery of the Demi-Monde."

"That is just a question of time. My crushing of the Demi-Monde is an historic inevitability. I have already initiated Operation Barbarossa—"

"Unfortunate pick: Operation Barbarossa was the invasion of Russia that led to the downfall of Hitler in the Real World."

Heydrich scowled. "There will be no such 'downfall' in this world. Soon I will have conquered the Demi-Monde and then I will change it."

"Change it?"

"I will remake it in my own image. By the imposition of my Final Solution I will eliminate all the sub-races from this world. In the microcosm that is the Demi-Monde I will construct my world of the *Übermensch*—of the Superman—who will, in turn, claim the Real World. That is my task here in the Demi-Monde: the purification of the human race."

"You Nazis tried that once. Tried and failed."

"No, we did not fail, rather the Führer failed us. Ultimately he was proven to be weak. He was a false Messiah. But I, Miss Williams, am not weak. And I have learned from the failure of the Führer. I will mold the Demi-Monde into a perfect Aryan world. All sub-races—the nuJus, the Poles, the Shades, the Orientals and the Arabs—will be scoured—"

"Scoured?"

"Eliminated. Shortly, in a matter of days, Operation Barbarossa will begin here in the ForthRight. The nuJus and the Poles—the scum of the ForthRight—have been packed together in the Warsaw Ghetto and soon I will unleash that madman Archie Clement and his SS–Ordo Templi Aryanis, their mission to destroy all of the *Untermenschen* gathered there. Clement will be my Eichmann."

"You will kill your own people?"

"No, I will kill those of my own people who are inadequate or racially degenerate. Only the strong will be permitted to live in order that those who come after are stronger still."

"Why do you hate the Poles so much?"

"It is an instinctive thing, a manifestation of the hereditary hatred of the Teuton for the Pole. Of all the people of the world—of this and the Real World—the Pole is one of the basest. After the Jew and the black, the Pole is the lowest form of the species *Homo sapiens*. To eliminate such a vile creature is merely an expression of the Darwinian doctrine of the survival of the fittest. The Poles, the nuJus and the Shades are not fit to cohabit this—or any other—world with the Aryan people, and hence it is only logical and fitting that they be expunged."

"You are totally mad, you know, Heydrich."

"Not mad, Miss Williams, I am merely gifted with the ability to perceive the reality of Nature and with the force of will to act on that perception. Great men like Genghis Khan, Tamerlane and Alexander are not remembered for the millions they slaughtered but for the grandeur of their ambition. The eradication of the three million stupid and worthless Poles and nuJus cowering in the Ghetto will, in fifty years, barely warrant a footnote in the books recording the history of the Demi-Monde. And once the Poles have been dealt with it will be the turn of those degenerate and perverted LessBiens who inhabit the Coven."

"But to what end? All this suffering, but you and your *Übermenschen* will still be marooned here in the Demi-Monde. You're still just a Dupe like everyone else living in the Demi-Monde!"

Heydrich gave a scornful laugh. "It is now time for you to meet, or should I better say, to *remeet*, a friend of yours, Miss Williams."

Heydrich rang a handbell on Dashwood's desk and immediately

Beria entered the room accompanied by a girl whose identity was shrouded beneath a heavy veil that cascaded from the top of her bonnet, over her face, to pool at her shoulders.

After Beria had bowed out of the room, Heydrich made the introductions. "Miss Williams, I have the great pleasure in presenting my daughter, Aaliz." The girl drew back the veil and Norma found herself gazing at . . . herself.

She had to do a double take. To her amazement this Aaliz Heydrich was her perfect twin, her exact duplicate. But there was more to the girl's mimicry than simple physical resemblance: with the exception of the color of her hair, of the absence of body piercings and the lack of tattoos, this girl *was* Norma. Every mannerism, every reaction, every nuance of expression was a precise match for those Norma saw every morning in her bathroom mirror.

But the most troubling thing was that she had met Aaliz Heydrich before in the Real World. Aaliz Heydrich had been the girl in the store, the girl who had coaxed and cajoled Norma into playing the *Demi-Monde* computer game.

And the tragedy was that Norma hadn't recognized her . . . hadn't recognized herself. Oh, she had known, instinctively, that there was something wrong about the girl but she had been so skillfully disguised that Norma hadn't realized that she was looking at and talking with *herself*. What a fool she had been.

"You're the girl in the shop."

When Aaliz Heydrich replied, she spoke in a voice that was identical to Norma's; the thick New York accent she'd used in the Real World had vanished. "Yes. It's amazing what a haircut, hair dye, glasses and rather outré makeup can do for one's appearance, Norma."

Heydrich chuckled at Norma's confusion. "It would seem, Miss Williams, that the creators of the Demi-Monde had a peculiarly puckish sense of humor. They used as the digital jig for the creation of my daughter the image of the eldest daughter of the president of the United States. It was a piece of serendipity that has opened great possibilities for one as ambitious as I am."

He gestured his daughter into a seat and lit yet another cigarette. Maybe, Norma hoped, there was a chance that the bastard would smoke himself to death before much longer. But then, of course, as Demi-Mondians didn't have lungs the chance of the maniac developing lung cancer was minimal.

"Aleister Crowley has long been of the belief that the Demi-Monde is surrounded and manipulated by a Spirit World, or, as you call it, the Real World. Although Crowley propounded his beliefs in magical terms, in essence he has been proven correct. You, the denizens of the Real World, Miss Williams, are Crowley's Spirits and we know how mischievously you delight in testing and tormenting us poor Demi-Mondians. But there was one thing that seems to have been beyond the wit of the creators of the Demi-Monde and that was an appreciation of the psychic bond that would exist between the Dupes of the Demi-Monde and their Real World twins. Crowley, though, sensed this, and using his occult powers, he has striven to achieve a melding of the Demi-Mondian self and the Real World self."

"Look, Crowley's out to lunch."

"The unfortunate thing from your point of view, Miss Williams, is that Crowley has succeeded in bridging the divide between the Demi-Monde and the Real World. Your presence here is proof of that. Admittedly, my daughter's excursion into your world was Crowley's first and, thus far, only successful attempt to manifest a Demi-Mondian in the Real World. And although the experiment highlighted certain limitations, it did enable us to lure you here to the Demi-Monde."

"But why?"

"Initially to prevent your masters from destroying the Demi-

Monde. When I took power in the ForthRight my first task was to preserve the Demi-Monde from the threat you so eloquently describe as 'pulling the plug,' and to do this I had to have a hostage, one of such importance that the Real Worlders would be deterred from closing the Demi-Monde. You are that hostage, Miss Williams. But having accomplished this, I then identified other opportunities arising from your presence amongst us."

"Other opportunities?"

"Indeed. It came to me in a moment of inspiration," said Heydrich with a triumphant little smile. "*All* Demi-Mondians are exact replicas of persons in the Real World and that means that not only do people in the Real World have doppelgängers here in the Demi-Monde but Demi-Mondians have doppelgängers in the Real World. It's a sort of digital quid pro quo. And as you Real Worlders, in your arrogance, imposed your personalities on the people of the Demi-Monde, I wondered whether it would be possible to reverse this process and have Demi-Mondians impose their personalities on their Real World doppelgängers."

Norma gawped and then an awful, chilling realization dawned. "You want to swap your daughter for me!"

"That is the intention," said Heydrich blithely. "Aaliz here is to be my Trojan horse. Of course, this Rite of Transference, as Crowley rather melodramatically calls it, is as yet unproven, but he is very confident that it can be made to work. We Demi-Mondians might not have the faculty of the Real Worlders in the manipulating of the digital universe but we are very adept at manipulating the psychic one. And once Aaliz is in the Real World—posing as the daughter of the most powerful man in the world—she will be able to lobby very effectively for the preservation of the Demi-Monde ... amongst other things."

"I think you overestimate the influence I have."

Now it was Aaliz's turn to laugh. "And I think you underestimate how capable I am. I am my father's daughter, Norma. Whilst you squander your intelligence and your time cultivating your image of antiestablishment emo, losing yourself to self-pity and self-loathing, I have applied my will to shaping this world. Here, in the Demi-Monde, I am leader of the Party's youth wing: the RightNix."

"Oh, good for you; I stopped being a Girl Scout years ago."

"More fool you. The work of the RightNix is vital in forming the attitudes and the beliefs of the young people of the ForthRight. I am alive to the fact that the youngster of today is the Party member of tomorrow. As leader of the RightNix I am responsible for inculcating a belief in the ForthRight's children that to be true Aryans they must display an unquestioning obedience to the Leader. They are taught that denying the doctrine of UnFunDaMentalism as set out in the nuCommandments is a Betrayal of their FatherLand. They are taught that the Strong have command over the Weak, and that the Aryan race is the Master Race. When my RightNixes come of age they will show no mercy to the ForthRight's enemies: whoever blocks the ForthRight's path to Purity and Oneness with ABBA will be destroyed." Aaliz stretched over and took Heydrich's hand in hers. "My father has taught me well. And I think *your* father, Norma, will be delighted to have a daughter suddenly willing to take a more active, a more committed role in the running of America. He must be sick of your selfishness and your glowering introspection. Having an emo for a daughter is hardly an electoral asset, especially with your father struggling for support in the more conservative Midwest."

It was a nightmare. It was bad enough for Norma to be stuck in the Demi-Monde, but to have a Dupe talking about taking over her body—taking over her life—was mind-blowingly awful.

"You'll never be able to pull off a stunt like that. You might look like me, you might talk like me, but you know squat about me and my life. It's impossible. You don't know anything about the Real World apart from what you learned serving behind the counter of a clothes shop. They'll spot you as a fraud straightaway."

Heydrich gave Norma a crooked smile. "Unfortunately, Miss

Williams, there is much in what you say: even someone as intelligent and as diligent as Aaliz will have difficulty in performing in a manner that does not arouse at least *some* suspicion. That is why, Miss Williams, we have had you kept here at Dashwood Manor in the hope that Comrade Commissar Dashwood's daughter would be able to persuade you to speak about your life in the Real World."

He paused to take another draw on his cigarette. "Unfortunately your intransigence defeated Trixiebell Dashwood. I am not surprised; Comrade Commissar Dashwood is a Royalist recidivist and hence an Enemy of the People, and as for his daughter . . ." Heydrich laughed. "She is nothing more than a stupid, idle, vacuous nonentity. It will be better when the pair of them have been arrested and shot. I will have Beria purge the Dashwoods immediately after this evening's séance is complete. He will enjoy that: Trixie Dashwood is a trim little piece."

Heydrich stubbed out his cigarette. "Happily for us, Miss Williams, Fate has presented us with another, more certain means of unpicking your memories. Crowley has located a clairvoyant of immense power who will be able to delve into the deepest and most private recesses of your mind. Tonight, Miss Williams, we will drain you dry." He glanced at the grandfather clock ticking in the corner of the room. "Look at the time. I have other matters to attend to. You, Miss Williams, will spend the afternoon with Aaliz getting to know one another. After all, soon the pair of you will be inseparable."

The Demi-Monde: 55th Day of Winter, 1004

Operation Barbarossa: Case White

Case White will be undertaken by the SS–Ordo Templi Aryanis under the command of SS Colonel Archie Clement. Commencing on the 59th day of Winter 1004, two divisions of SS–Ordo Templi Aryanis StormTroops will surround and seal the Warsaw Ghetto. Once this is achieved, the SS will enter the Ghetto and systematically exterminate all UnderMentionables (approximately three million subhumans) living within the walls of the city. The legal basis for this extermination is given by the Racial Classification and Control Law, which removed the protection of ForthRight Law from UnderMentionables, nonNixes and those demonstrating hereditary physical and mental disabilities. Case White is to be completed by the 90th day of Winter, 1004.

—MINUTES OF THE POLITBURO MEETING HELD UNDER THE GUIDANCE
OF THE GREAT LEADER ON THE 39TH DAY OF WINTER, 1004

Immediately Captain Dabrowski heard the door of the study shut behind Heydrich, he very carefully replaced the steel fire screen across the fireplace and swept up the small fall of soot that had collected on the hearth. When he was finished there was nothing to show that anything had ever been disturbed.

Not that Trixie took much notice of the captain's housekeeping;

all she had the energy to do was sit slumped on one of the armchairs scattered around the room desperately trying to make sense of what she had heard. Her head was spinning.

Of course, much of it had been gibberish, especially the discussion between Heydrich and the Daemon about this man Hitler. And the part about Demi-Mondians being replicas of Real Worlders and Aaliz Heydrich being sent to the Real World as a replacement for the Daemon sounded like the stuff of trashy scientific romance.

But some of what she had heard couldn't be dismissed so easily, especially the part when Heydrich had stated his intent to destroy the poor people living in Warsaw.

Or that tonight she and her father were to be arrested and executed. *That* was a cold-blooded observation she couldn't ignore. Tonight she and her father were to be purged, just like her friend Lillibeth Marlborough and her family. It seemed hardly believable that she was going to be touched by the terror that had taken so many of her friends.

"He's going to kill us," she breathed, hardly able to understand the horror of what was happening.

It seemed unreal.

Dabrowski nodded and then added, "Yes. He means to exterminate my people."

My people?

Of course; the Poles. The captain was one of the UnderMentionables; it was his people that Heydrich was talking about murdering in Warsaw. As she looked at the pale, trembling Dabrowski, for the first time in her young life Trixie understood the full horrific implications of the philosophy of racial purity that was UnFunDaMentalism. It was not a rather farcical and non-RaTional exercise in religious whimsy but something much more serious. Now she understood that UnFunDaMentalism was simply an excuse for genocide.

Before she had simply accepted the undeniable need for the ForthRight to achieve the racial purity propounded by UnFunDa-Mentalism—it had, after all, been drummed into her throughout her life. She had unthinkingly accepted that it was a violation of nature for an Anglo-Slav to interbreed with one of the UnderMentionables, just as it would be against nature for a dog to breed with a cat. The Seventh nuCommandment was, after all, explicit in its condemnation of miscegenation. Every day she thanked ABBA—not that she believed ABBA existed—that she had been born an Anglo-Slav, that she was one of the Master Race. By being born an Aryan she had won first prize in the lottery of life. But never had she thought that to preserve and promote the racial purity of the Anglo-Slavic people the Party would destroy the UnderMentionables wholesale.

Segregation: of course. Condemnation of miscegenation: naturally. The abortion of mixlings: certainly. Control of race through the State Register of Racial Purity: without a doubt. But genocide . . .

The Party condoning the killing of three million or more men, women and children living in the Warsaw Ghetto was unbelievable. But now the unbelievable had been made believable: she had heard Heydrich himself talk with casual indifference about slaughtering these poor innocent people.

"What will you do?" she asked.

"I'm not sure," admitted the ashen-faced Dabrowski. Usually so decisive and energetic, he sat becalmed in his chair, numbed by the words that had come drifting up from the study. "Oh, we knew that the situation wasn't good. We knew that we Poles were classified with the nuJus as Second Class citizens of the ForthRight, but none of us ever thought that Heydrich was so deformed of character as to contemplate mass murder. The man is obviously mad." He shook his head, trying to clear it. "I have to get to Warsaw. I have to warn my people."

"Will they listen?"

"I don't know. How can anybody believe such a monstrous thing? But I have to try. The first thing we have to do is get out of here. And that won't be easy."

"We'll speak to my father. He'll know what to do."

THEY FOUND TRIXIE'S FATHER SITTING ALONE IN THE MORNING ROOM going through his red boxes of Ministry papers and doing the best he could to forget the baleful presence of Heydrich stalking the house. That he was surprised to be interrupted by his daughter and the Polish captain was an understatement: it was an unbreakable rule in the Dashwood household that the comrade commissar was not to be disturbed when he was working.

Dashwood's surprise mutated into real concern when he saw Trixie lock the door and approach with a finger pressed to her lips. "The captain and I have overheard something, Father," she whispered, "something so terrible that we felt obliged to come to warn you. It is imperative, father, that no one eavesdrop on our conversation."

Comrade Commissar Dashwood, a survivor of the Troubles and of the Royalist purges that followed, had lived for too long in the ForthRight to disregard such warnings. He gave a nod and waved his guests over to an alcove set in the corner of the room. As soon as they were settled, he pulled a heavy curtain across the alcove, effectively sealing the three of them from the rest of the house. "We are safe here from prying ears," he said quietly, "but speak softly. They say Beria hears every word uttered in the ForthRight, even the whispers of lovers. Very well, Trixie, what are these secrets that you are so determined to share with me?"

Trixie gave a breathless synopsis of what they had heard when Heydrich was meeting with the Daemon. Through the five minutes of Trixie's monologue her father sat silent and impassive, occasionally glancing to Captain Dabrowski for his nodded confirmation of what Trixie was saying. At the end of Trixie's speech her father lit a cigarette and spent a minute or so in ruminative reflection. Eventually he turned to the captain. "So, Captain Dabrowski, it would appear I have been nurturing a viper in my bosom. Am I right in assuming that you are a crypto . . . one of the Cichociemni perhaps?"

"The Cichociemni?" asked Trixie.

"It is the name we Poles give to the dark, silent ones," explained Dabrowski. "We are a group of Polish patriots who are dedicated to securing the freedom of the Polish people from the bondage of the ForthRight. As your father correctly surmises, I am one of the Cichociemni. I am a Polish crypto, my mission being to infiltrate the ForthRight hierarchy and learn their plans."

Trixie looked at the captain with surprise. The man was a counterrevolutionary. A *Polish* counterrevolutionary!

Dashwood gave a mirthless chuckle. "An accurate if somewhat disingenuous summary, if I might say so, Captain. I have an inkling that your intentions are somewhat more robust than simply the gleaning of information. Checkya intelligence reports indicate that in the event of the ForthRight moving against the Warsaw Ghetto the Cichociemni are sworn to eliminate specific targets within the Party's senior personnel." He took a long draw of his cigarette. "Presumably, Captain, you intended to assassinate me."

The captain had the good grace to blush. "I make no apology for being a Polish patriot, sir, nor for my ambition to defend my people from tyranny. You are, sir, a legitimate military target: our information is that you are the foremost expert in the ForthRight regarding matters of logistics. You are, after all, the man who refashioned the ForthRight's road network; your ministry supervises the traffic moving along the Thames, the Rhine and the Volga. You are the genius behind the ForthRight's new railway network, you are the man responsible for the suffering of the ten thousand men of the Polish Slave Labor Division forced to work through the Winter building the new railway spurs connecting the ForthRight to the Hub."

"You were going to murder my father?" interjected an incredulous Trixie.

"There are nearly three million people confined to the Warsaw Ghetto, Miss Dashwood, their lives made a living Hel by the Forth-Right. Is it any wonder that we have been provoked into the contemplation of such an ignoble action? But in my defense, Miss Trixie, understand that your father and *only* your father was targeted. We are not like the Party: we would not eradicate a man's family in senseless retaliation. This was to be a military operation, not a purging."

Dashwood gave a wry laugh. "It is a fine distinction, Captain Dabrowski."

"But an important one, Comrade Commissar!" retorted Dabrowski. "I am a Polish officer and a gentleman and as such I would not deliberately endanger your daughter. Unfortunately, as your daughter and I have heard, Heydrich is not of the same mind. Once this evening's séance has taken place he intends to have Beria place both you and your family under arrest. Your daughter, sir, is to suffer for your supposed misdemeanors. That is the Party's way, is it not: collective responsibility for all crimes? And we both know what will be the fate of your daughter once she is in the hands of that monster Beria."

Dashwood glanced nervously at Trixie. "I would prefer it, sir, if you would refrain from discussing such matters in front of my daughter." He drummed his fingers on the arm of his chair. "I suppose I have been lucky to survive as long as I have. No matter how careful I was, I knew that someday they would come for me. In Beria's book, once a Royalist, always a Royalist. It's just a shame they have come sooner than I had planned."

"Surely this is nonsense, father; they can't arrest you!" Trixie protested. "You have been a loyal member of the Party. They would be insane to eliminate you simply on suspicion of your being a Royalist reactionary, just on a whim. You must appeal to the Leader. You must convince him there has been some dreadful misunderstanding."

"Unfortunately, Trixie, there has been no misunderstanding. You must realize that Heydrich and his cronies *are* mad." It was a simple statement but so replete with treason that Trixie was shocked into silence. Her father had always been so careful not to criticize the Party or its leadership in front of others. "But their madness," he continued grimly, "should not blind us to the fact that they are accomplished people, that their intelligence apparatus is the most efficient in the Demi-Monde."

There was something in the way her father said the words that made Trixie look at him afresh. It was as though he had sloughed off a mask to reveal something different and far more deadly beneath. Whereas before she had only seen the dutiful Party apparatchik—a little dull and stuffy, it had to be admitted—now there was a man of action, determined and strong. It might have been the spark in his eyes or the resolute set of his mouth but suddenly he was different. Very different . . .

"You're a Royalist!" Even as the words tumbled out of her mouth, Trixie knew they were true. He was one of the people that Miss Appleton at the Academy had lectured them so fiercely to be on their guard against. He was one of *them*.

Dashwood nodded. "Yes, Trixie, I am a Royalist, I am one of the Silent Opposition. King Henry might have been unbalanced, but he was never as evil as Heydrich. Heydrich can't be allowed to succeed. I and others like me have been planning—" He stopped, looked up at Dabrowski and gave him a half smile. "Perhaps it isn't too late. The opening phase of Operation Barbarossa—the destruction of Warsaw and all the people in the Ghetto—by Clement's SS–Ordo Templi Aryanis begins in three days. In three days the Party will take its first step toward seizing control of the Demi-Monde and imposing its lunatic ideas regarding racial hygiene on the whole world."

"Clement won't find the Ghetto easy. We Poles will fight—"

"And you will lose! What will you and your fellow Poles use to oppose the SS–Ordo Templi Aryanis, rocks and coarse language? The SS are the finest shock troops in the ForthRight, they are the mindless bastards selected for their brutality and susceptibility to thought reform. They believe that by killing anyone who isn't an Anglo-Slav they are doing ABBA's work."

"Get us the guns and we will fight."

"Get you the guns . . ." repeated her father. "Yes, there might be a way." He pierced the captain with a hard stare. "Answer me truthfully, Captain: if your Poles have weapons, will they fight?"

"We will fight, Comrade Commissar, make no mistake of that. We will fight to the last man and to the last breath. We will die with our hands around the throats of those who seek to destroy us."

"You are organized?"

"The Warsaw Free Army is ready. I have the honor of being a major in the WFA."

"Then know this, Captain: though I cannot offer you salvation, I can help you and your people die as a proud people." Her father turned to Trixie and smiled ruefully. "Trixie, you are my greatest love and my greatest treasure. I am proud to be the father of such a strong and independently minded girl, but now I implore you to display all this strength and independence and ignore what your heart might tell you. The Demi-Monde is faced with a great evil and it is the responsibility of everyone to oppose that evil, even at the cost of their life. My life is over . . ."

Trixie gasped with astonishment. "What are you saying, Father? We can run, we can hide."

Dashwood shook his head. "No, for me the die is cast. I cannot escape, Trixie. If I were to try I would be caught and then there would be no hope for you. And anyway, I have a higher mission." He turned back to Dabrowski. "Amongst your detachment here in the manor, are there men you can trust implicitly, men you would trust with your life?"

The captain thought. "My sergeant and four others."

"Not enough."

"Enough for what?"

"There are two barges laden with rifles and ammunition moored just below the Oberbaum Bridge on the Rhine. These are obsolete weapons intended for export to the Quartier but though they are obsolete they are serviceable. A resolute and daring captain, with a company of soldiers equally uncaring as to whether they live or die, could board the barges and, under cover of darkness, sail them upriver to the Ghetto."

The captain could barely contain his excitement. "Give me an hour in Warsaw and I will have such a company of men. We will take the barges or we will die trying. All that I ask is that you tell me where they are moored."

"In a moment. First I need an undertaking from you, Captain. I need to hear you swear an oath as an officer and a gentleman that when you escape from the manor you will take my daughter with you."

"No," exclaimed Trixie. "I'm not going anywhere without you."

She couldn't believe what she was hearing. The man who had been the rock in her life, the man who had carried her through the loss of her mother, the man who had stood unflinchingly beside her when she had been Censured, the man who had taught her—convinced her—that she was the equal of any man, was talking of leaving her. That was impossible: she would live and, if necessary, die by his side.

But her father was equally determined.

"You must. It is imperative that I attend the séance this evening. If I were to disappear before then there would be a hue and cry, but your absence, Trixie, can be explained more easily. I can say you've been overcome by the excitement of meeting the Leader; you are only a girl after all." Dashwood reached across and took Trixie's hand in his. "There is no alternative, Trixie. If you stay we are both lost, but with the captain's help, you at least might survive. Do I have your word, Captain, that you will do everything in your power to save and protect my daughter?"

"You have my word."

Dashwood opened a drawer, extracted a file and passed it across the desk to the captain. "This contains the details of the mooring location of the barges."

The captain took the file and flicked through the pages. "Thank you, sir, thank you on behalf of the Polish people imprisoned in the Ghetto. This will give them hope." Dabrowski shut the file and looked sternly at Dashwood. "You should be aware, sir, that it is my intention to try to make my escape during the séance. When Heydrich and his entourage are in the ballroom the garrison will relax and its guard will be lowered. I will try to organize some form of distraction, some sort of ruse to draw all the guards away from their posts."

"I think I might be able to help you there, Captain. I had been hoping—planning—to disturb Heydrich's Operation Barbarossa, but now it seems I must bring these plans forward. I have already sent word to Royalist exiles in the Coven warning them that the ForthRight will attack in early Spring but now it seems I must take more concrete action." Dashwood drew a small revolver from the drawer where the file had been lying. "Although, like my daughter,

I am something of a RaTionalist and take Crowley's talk of Spirits and Daemons with several grains of salt it is apparent that the Daemon, Norma Williams, is of great importance to the Party. Of course, all this talk of doppelgängers and infiltrating the Spirit World is moonshine but . . ." The comrade commissar split open the revolver and checked that it was fully loaded. "At Heydrich's insistence I am to attend the séance this evening in full-dress uniform and that necessitates my wearing a sidearm. I will use this to assassinate the Daemon and, if I am able, Heydrich as well. That, I think, Captain, will provide a sufficient disturbance for you to make good your escape."

"And what about you, Father?" asked Trixie, a tear gently coursing down her cheek.

"I, my darling Trixie, am a dead man. It is your responsibility to ensure that I don't die in vain."

24

The Demi-Monde: 55th Day of Winter, 1004

The afterglow of Seidr ritual and of Lilithian worship is found in the WhoDoo magic practiced by the mambos of NoirVille. Being so heavily suffused by Lilithian folklore, WhoDoo magic is a strongly sexual magic. Mambos (and all of the most powerful practitioners of WhoDoo are female) believe that the interregnum dividing the Spirit World from the Demi-Monde is most readily traversed when the body and the soul conjoin at orgasm. To the WhoDoo mambo at the point of orgasm all things magical are possible because that is the moment when they commune, albeit briefly, with ABBA, or as the WhoDooists know him, the Great Lord Bondye.

—Religions of the Demi-Monde, Otto Weininger, University of Berlin Publications

S o waddya fink, Wanker? Fucking big, innit?"

For once in his life Burlesque Bandstand was guilty of understatement. The *hounfo* wasn't big, it was huge. When Vanka had designed it never for the life of him had he thought it would turn out to be so *monumental*. It was one thing, he had discovered, to put measurements down on a piece of paper but it was quite another to see those measurements conjured up in wood and steel. Black and menacing, the *hounfo* took up over half of Dashwood

Manor's massive ballroom, the floor area of which must have measured a hundred feet by fifty. It was the biggest piece of flimflam the Demi-Monde had ever seen.

"Yeah, it's big all right."

"Sumwun wos saying they thought it wos the biggest illusion thingy ever built in the Demi-Monde."

"How many times have I got to tell you, Burlesque, not to say it's an illusion? It's a *hounfo*, a temple dedicated to the practicing of WhoDoo magic. I don't want it called an illusion."

"Yeah, all right, Wanker. No need to get yer knickers in a twist. Only me an' yous and, ov course, Miss Ella know it's an illusion"—a withering look from Vanka—"a *hounfo*. The lads who built it didn't 'ave a clue wot it is, 'cept, that is, for Alf an' Sid an' they've got to know cos they're working the levers. But go on, tell us wot yous fink, Wanker. Me and the lads ain't done bad, 'ave we?"

In Vanka's judgment Burlesque and his gang of workmen had done very well indeed. In the space of a day they'd built something quite remarkable. But then, he supposed, the half-million guineas Ella had promised Burlesque for his help in freeing the Daemon bought a lot of enthusiasm.

The *hounfo* was made up of two forty-foot-long, ten-foot-high wooden walls arranged in a V shape, with the widest, open part of the delta formed by the walls extending from one side of the ballroom to the other and the delta's point almost touching the furthest end of the ballroom, where the room's windows looked out onto the manor's grounds. It was within the open space enclosed by the arrowed walls of the *hounfo* that that evening's séance would be performed.

"No, you've done a good job, Burlesque; I'm impressed."

Burlesque beamed. "But do you fink it'll fool the nobs?"

"It might," was all Vanka could bring himself to say.

He knew he was right to be cautious. Despite the strange emblems and decorations that Ella had had daubed over the *hounfo* and the black netting covering the walls it was still just a piece of stage magic writ large. He had the feeling that any illusionist worth his salt would see through the flimflam in an instant. And Aleister Crowley *was* a master magician. All Vanka could hope was that its sheer immensity would persuade Crowley that it was simply too big to be just a prop in a vanishing act.

He began a slow walk around the structure, pushing and shoving at the walls as he went, testing them for strength. "I never thought it would look this big," he admitted, "or this strange."

He gave the *hounfo* a kick. The walls were so heavy—it had taken five steamers to deliver all the timber used in its construction—that it didn't even vibrate when he booted it. But was it enough to fool Crowley?

If Crowley should suspect for an instant . . .

There had already been one heart-stopping moment when Crowley and Archie Clement had come snooping around earlier that afternoon, but fortunately that had been before the *hounfo* had been fully erected. After that Vanka had made bloody damned sure that the ballroom door was locked and he had spread the rumor that anyone who came near it before the séance would be cursed by the mambo Laveau. There had been no more snoopers.

Vanka rubbed his chin thoughtfully. "Yeah, it might just do. And all this WhoDoo mumbo jumbo Ella's tricked the place out in is a distraction." He nodded toward the kabbalistic designs painted over the black walls of the *hounfo*. "And, of course, it'll be evening and we'll have the lights turned low."

"Miss Ella tells me she's planning to 'ave a couple ov braziers at the sides ov the ballroom burning stuff that gives off a lot ov smoke."

"That's good thinking. Lots of smoke and mirrors, that's what we need." Vanka stopped alongside the gate that was hinged midway along the right-hand wall of the *hounfo*. "If you would close the left-hand gate, Burlesque, I want to check that the gates meet in the middle."

The two of them pulled the gates closed, Vanka surprised by how easily the ten-foot-tall gates swung on their hinges. They met perfectly, enclosing the pointed part of the WhoDoo temple from midway along the *hounfo*'s walls. Now Burlesque stood in the triangular space formed on the inside of the gates and Vanka stood on the outside, but even with the gates closed they could see each other clearly through the gaps between the thick wooden bars. What had Ella said? The gates reminded her of a gigantic version of the picket fence that had surrounded her grandmother's front yard. Vanka had trouble imagining a district where there was so much space that ordinary people could have gardens.

They reopened the gates and set them back ready for the evening's performance. Vanka gave the *hounfo* a final pat and stepped back to admire the construction. "Yeah, I think it'll do, Burlesque. It's big enough to awe even the most dubious of cynics and clever enough to fox even the most hardened of disbelievers, including, I hope, Aleister Crowley. We'll put the altar as far in as we can, right back hard against the pointed end of the temple." He glanced around the room yet again making sure that, except for him, Burlesque and Ella, the ballroom was empty. "That'll make the vanishing easier."

"I can't wait to see the punters' faces when yous an' the Daemon disappear inna puff ov smoke."

"I wouldn't hang around too long after we disappear, Burlesque. Chances are Heydrich will be a little bent out of shape when he finds his prize Daemon has done a runner."

"Don't worry abart me, Vanka. Me an' the Witchfinder are like that." He showed Vanka a pair of crossed fingers. "They ain't never gonna believe that their mate Burlesque Bandstand 'ad anyfink to do wiv it."

Vanka kept his face as bland as he was able; he found Burlesque's optimism almost unbelievably naïve. "I hope you're right, Burlesque, I hope you're right." He gave the *hounfo* another pat. "You know, this will make an amazing swan song to the career of Vanka Maykov: Licensed Psychic."

"Wossa 'swan song,' Wanker?"

"BURLESQUE STILL HASN'T TWIGGED JUST HOW PISSED OFF HEYDRICH'S going to be," said Vanka as he came up alongside Ella. She was staring out of one of the windows at the rear of the ballroom, watching the SS troopers marching up and down in the garden.

"Oh, don't worry about Burlesque, Vanka, he'll be all right. He's done so much work for the Witchfinder he's practically a member of the SS so the way he sees it he'll be able to talk his way out of any aggravation that might come his way. All he's interested in is getting to a Blood Bank and laying claim to the half a million guineas I'm paying him."

"I just hope we survive to get to a Bank. To my mind making the Daemon disappear is the easy part; escaping through that gate is the *real* problem."

Through the ballroom's windows Ella could see what he meant. Neither she nor Vanka, even in their wildest imaginings, had anticipated that the Daemon would be quite so well protected. The gardens were crawling with black-uniformed SS troopers, these goons supplemented by a detachment of red-coated regular soldiers. And as the only exit to the outside world seemed to be via the very heavy and very heavily guarded gate they'd passed through when they'd arrived that morning, the inevitable conclusion Ella was coming to was that escaping with Norma Williams would not be easy.

Scratch "would not be easy" and substitute "would be nigh on impossible."

So it was little wonder that Vanka was so concerned. As he had so succinctly put it when he had first seen Dashwood Manor, Ella was giving him "a terrific chance to be the richest fucking dead man in the whole of the fucking Demi-Monde."

Ella felt Vanka shuffle awkwardly.

"We haven't got a prayer, you know," he said in a conversational sort of way. "I thought the Daemon would be guarded, but this is ridiculous. It must be the presence of Heydrich that's got them spooked. There's a small army garrisoned here."

"We're going to have surprise on our side, Vanka," she suggested encouragingly.

Vanka's expression turned to one of disbelief. "Surprise, Ella? We could have total fucking *bewilderment* on our side for all the fucking difference it's going to make. *If* this *hounfo* of mine works correctly and *if* we are able to wriggle through a window without being spotted we've *still* got to run fifty yards across a wide-open lawn that's guarded by a hundred or so of the best troops in the ForthRight and *if*, by some miracle, we manage to do that"—a nod toward the gate leading to the world beyond the manor—"we've *still* got to find a way to vault over a fifteen-foot gate."

Ella was determined to remain upbeat. "It'll be dark by then."

"I don't want to be a party pooper, Ella, and correct me if I'm wrong but my understanding is that it's fucking difficult to see in the dark. So difficult that I would give good odds on us all finding ourselves pitching arse over tit into one of the trenches these SS bastards have dug or getting entangled in the barbed wire these sods have been so enthusiastic about spreading around the garden."

Ella had never heard Vanka so pessimistic and she found his mood affecting hers. "Do you think we should call it off?"

Vanka laughed ironically. "Nah. Life's too short to pass up the opportunity to piss Crowley off as much as you intend to. Anyway, a million guineas *is* a million guineas. Don't worry; something will turn up, it always does."

—⁓—

TRIXIE LEFT THE MORNING ROOM IN A STATE OF SHOCK. SHE HAD started the day as a schoolgirl, the daughter of a high-ranking and highly respectable member of the Party, a girl who expected her life to proceed in a well-ordered and predictable manner. She looked to be ending it as a fugitive, with her father arrested for being a counterrevolutionary and a Royalist, and with her safety—even her continued existence—depending on a Polack who was an admitted spy and would-be assassin.

It was almost too much to bear.

It was as though she had wandered into a nightmare. Drained and bemused, all she felt like doing was sleeping and crying. When she reached the sanctuary of her bedroom the temptation to throw herself onto her bed and abandon herself to despair was almost overwhelming, but something stopped her. In that moment Lady Trixiebell Dashwood: schoolgirl and closet RaTionalist, mutated into Trixie Dashwood: resolute young woman.

With an act of will she took all her misery and all her heartbreak and sealed them up inside a ball of hate. It was Heydrich and the ForthRight who were intent on killing her and her father and she swore that she would have her revenge on them. And those seeking revenge had no use for regret or remorse, no use in squandering time and energy on if-onlys. Her old life was dead—gone—and if she was to have a new life then her first task was to survive. And to survive she had to be strong. She would never cry again.

She stood up straight and threw back her shoulders, then, with a determined nod to herself in the mirror, went to her wardrobe and pulled a box from the bottom shelf. Inside was the costume she had worn in the Academy's 1003 Spring Eve drama production performed in celebration of the Party's defeat of the Royalists during the Troubles. Entitled "Forward to Victory," Trixie had played the villain of the piece—a Royalist soldier—and as such she'd had to wear a uniform. It had been the first time she had ever worn trousers, and despite the rather spiteful teasing she'd endured from the other girls, she had thought them eminently practical. And if ever she was in need of a costume that was both practical and a good disguise it was tonight.

She hauled herself into the black serge pants and strapped on the boots she wore when the RightNixes went on their "Winter Walks" into the Hub. She completed her outfitting by donning a thick woolen sweater and an old, but very serviceable, shooting jacket. Then, having packed a small haversack with one or two precious pieces—under no circumstances was she leaving the wedding daguerreotype of her parents for the SS crows to pick over—a change of clothes and a purse of golden guineas, she settled down to wait for Captain Dabrowski.

And as she sat she wondered what her new life in the Warsaw Ghetto would be like. The comfortable, pampered life she had enjoyed in this house was over and a new one, a much harder one, was beginning. She didn't know a lot about the Ghetto except that it was the sinkhole of the ForthRight: it was where all the unclean races—the Poles, the nuJus and, *ugh*, the Shades—were confined; where all the mongrels, the reviled mixlings, hid themselves; where the HerEticals, Royalists, RaTionalists, Suffer-O-Gettes, ImPuritans, HimPerialists and all the rest of the disaffected and the just plain lunatic had scuttled off to in an attempt to avoid the attention of the Checkya. It was a cesspit where all of the ForthRight's shit was dumped.

It was most certainly not a place where a respectable young woman ventured. Trixie laughed; she wasn't a respectable young woman anymore. If she was captured she would be charged with Complicity in the Execution of Crimes Against the State and that would mean she forfeited all rights as a citizen of the ForthRight. She would be nonNix, just like Lillibeth Marlborough. But the difference between her and Lillibeth was that the Checkya had caught Lillibeth. And if there was one thing of which Trixie was certain, it was that the Checkya would never take her . . . not alive anyway.

THE SÉANCE WAS SCHEDULED FOR EIGHT THAT EVENING.

Vanka checked his watch; there was less than an hour to showtime. As he strapped his mask over his face and wrapped his silk scarf about his neck, he took a deep breath, trying to settle his jangling nerves.

He felt Ella snake her hand through his arm and when he turned toward her he found himself being given the broadest of reassuring smiles. He wasn't reassured. He was beyond being reassured. But, by the Spirits, she was beautiful. He stopped himself. Surely, he wasn't doing this because . . .

He shook his head: Vanka Maykov didn't do love.

"I like your mask, Vanka, very dashing. Do you like my makeup?"

"You look lovely, Ella," he admitted. Even swathed in a neck-to-ankle, all-enveloping black cloak she looked lovely. Even with her face daubed with really quite outrageous stage makeup she looked lovely. Even wearing that strange half mask she looked lovely.

"There's time for one final check," Ella said, and kissed him on the cheek. The kiss and the sensation of that deliciously soft body pressed against his sent shivers of excitement coursing through him. He wished she'd stop doing that; whenever she kissed him he stopped thinking straight. In desperation Vanka turned his attention to the *hounfo* and, looking at it in the shadowed half-light of the ballroom, he began to believe that maybe, just maybe they could pull this stunt off.

Dressed in shadows and black netting, the *hounfo* looked ominous, just like Vanka imagined a temple dedicated to the celebrating of WhoDoo magic should. It was an effect enhanced by the lighting Ella had insisted on using: the ballroom's gas candelabras were turned down to their lowest setting and limelights had been used to flood the bottom of the walls. It looked decidedly sinister and decidedly spooky.

Which, Vanka supposed, was the whole point.

The sound of loud and insistent hammering from the back of the *hounfo* brought Vanka out of his reverie. "Is everything all right back there, Burlesque?" he shouted.

"Yus," said Burlesque Bandstand as he appeared from behind the *hounfo*, where he'd been making what he called "last-minute adjustments," which appeared to necessitate his hitting things very hard with a big hammer. "Everyfing's right as ninepence, Wanker. Straight as a die." He wiped his oil-blackened hands on the arse of his trousers and leered at Ella. "Nice mask, Miss Ella. Iffn you're innerested I knows a coupla punters who'd pay good money for a bird who'll dress up like that an'—"

"Do you remember your instructions?" interrupted Vanka.

"Yus. Cors I does. First Miss Ella shouts out, 'Lord Bondye 'as come,' then I let off the bangers and Sid and Alf throw the levers. An' then I just stand around lookin' all innocent when the dust 'as settled and they twig that you two 'ave 'ad it away on your toes wiv the Daemon." A frown crossed Burlesque's brow, and his voice dropped to a conspiratorial whisper. "Yous got the details ov my bank account in Venice all snug, ain't cha, Miss Ella?"

"I have, Burlesque, and as soon as I'm able I'll transfer your money."

Burlesque beamed.

"Excellent," muttered Vanka.

The three of them stood for a couple of minutes in silent consideration of the *hounfo* and what they were about to do . . . to try to do. Their musings were interrupted by an unexpected visitor.

"Most impressive," sneered a voice from the back of the ballroom.

All three of them jumped in surprise. The doors of the ballroom were locked; Vanka had seen Ella lock them behind her. No one was meant to be able to get into the ballroom.

But Aleister Crowley had.

Crowley, dressed in his ceremonial robes, appeared out of the darkness and gestured toward the *hounfo*. "I had no idea that WhoDoo *hounfos* were quite so profound."

Disturbed though Vanka was by Crowley's sudden materialization, he didn't miss a beat. "Good evening, Your Holiness. A *hounfo* of this size is needed because, as the subject for tonight's séance is a Daemon, it is important that all the astral energy the mambo Laveau conjures is concentrated. That is the purpose of this *hounfo*: it better enables her to commune with the *loa*—the good Spirits—and so encourage them to possess her body. The *loa* are needed to aid her to dominate the Daemon's will." As Crowley edged closer to the *hounfo*, Vanka could feel his heart starting to flutter. If he made too close an examination of their box of tricks, he would be sure to spot its none-too-subtle secrets. Vanka gave Ella a quick, anxious glance and then, remembering the rigmarole she had taught him about WhoDoo magic, he did his best to distract the man. "The *hounfo* also keeps out the *djabs* and the *baka*, the devils and the evil Spirits that are associated with Daemons," he said at a rush.

Unfortunately Crowley didn't seem to be of a mind to be distracted.

"Is that important? Surely a mambo of Miss Laveau's power won't be troubled by evil Spirits?" Crowley mused as he tested one of the gates.

Please . . .

It was Ella—or rather Ella in her role of Marie Laveau—who

saved the day. "If any ov dem mischievous *baka* mount me, Yous Holiness," she said in a very dusky voice, "den dere ain't no telling what will happen."

Crowley paused in his examination of the *hounfo* and turned to look at Ella. "*Mount* you?"

Ella nodded. "Sure ting, Yous Holiness. Dat's what it's called when de bad *baka* take possession of a *serviteur* like me. But as ah'm up against a Daemon tonight ah need to conjure de Great Lord Bondye himself to help me and to do dat ah've gotta look mah best. De trouble with looking mah best is dat if a *baka* was to see me he might be liking a taste ov some ov what ah've got on offer. That's why I need a *hounfo* to protect me."

Crowley's interest in the *hounfo* faltered; he eyed Ella carefully. "And what would happen if you were possessed by one of these *baka?*"

She dropped her eyes as though embarrassed. "Well, wit you being such a mighty mystic, Yous Holiness, yous know dat de most powerful incantations are made when dere is a lot of sexual energy in de air. Dat's what ah've got to do tonight . . . rouse de desires of de Spirits."

"Why?" asked Crowley, his voice having risen an octave or two.

Again the coy lowering of Ella's gaze; the girl was such a tease. "WhoDoo magic is de magic ov sex. De union between de Spirit World and de Demi-Monde is best made when de body and de soul are conjoin at orgasm. To be a mambo you gotta search fo' de constant, de unfailing, de eternal orgasm."

Vanka pulled at his collar. *By ABBA, it's getting hot in here.*

"So yous see, Yous Holiness, iffn an evil *baka* was to take me . . . well, there's no knowing what ah might do."

"And how do you intend to rouse the desires of the Spirits?" There was more than a hint of excitement in Crowley's voice.

Ella reached up and unhooked the tie that held her cloak. The cloak sighed to the floor, revealing Ella—or, more accurately, the mambo Marie Laveau—in all her glory.

The three men stood stock-still examining the vision of loveliness that stood before them. Vanka had seen such costumes when he'd been to some of the more risqué revues in the Quartier Chaud but he'd never thought any woman in the ForthRight would be brave enough to wear one.

Ella's costume was remarkable more for what it showed than for what it hid. The black chiffon material flowed over her long, stunning body like a dark mist. From what he could see in the half-light, the costume consisted of a loose dress gathered around Ella's waist by a five-inch-thick black leather belt. That the chiffon was virtually transparent and that she seemed to be naked beneath it was unsettling enough, but the slits cut artfully into the dress meant that most of her legs and a considerable part of the rest of her body were uncovered. There was a lot of firm young flesh on display, flesh which Ella had decorated with strange symbols and images of snakes drawn in thick black ink.

The ephemeral fabric of the costume left no doubt as to the wonders concealed—partially concealed—beneath. For a moment Vanka wondered whether he should play the gentleman and avert his eyes.

Fuck that.

Crowley had no such reservations: he stepped closer in order to get a better look at Ella. "You are a remarkably beautiful woman, Miss Laveau," he oozed, his voice thick with lust, "and I can see why these *baka* of yours would try to possess you. You look positively . . . Lilithian."

Lilith.

Crowley was right. When Vanka thought about it the way Ella was dressed did remind him of the pictures he'd seen of Lilith. Lilith was meant to have been the most powerful, the most evil woman who had ever walked the Demi-Monde and she'd been a Shade too.

He wondered if Ella had adopted the guise of Lilith deliberately. That was when he remembered that she'd pretended to channel Lilith during their first séance.

Funny he'd never thought of it before.

Crowley edged nearer to Ella. "You confirm to me that your race, being more brutal and bestial than the Anglo-Slav people, is more closely in tune with the earthier appetites that Demi-Mondians are sometimes—unfortunately—prey to. And this pandering to these inclinations, as you so rightly say, is vital in the performance of magic. My own investigations have led me to the conclusion that magic is fueled by sexual energy and I sense an enormous erotic potential in you, Miss Laveau." He stretched out a hand and drifted a finger across Ella's right breast. "You have the Mann rune drawn here. Why?"

"De Mann rune," breathed Ella as Crowley's fingers orbited her nipple, "is de sign ov sensual, erotic love and ov de wearer being one who indulges in de most dissolute sex. Tonight, to conjure de Great Lord Bondye, ah must show him ah am ready to pay for his services. And Great Lord Bondye always demands de use of mah body as payment."

This Bondye's no fool, decided Vanka.

Crowley swallowed hard. "Perhaps, after the performance, we might meet to discuss WhoDoo magic further?"

Ella curtsied. "Dat would be mah honor *and* mah pleasure, Your Holiness. A mambo like me is always ready to commune wit a powerful magician like yous."

With that a very red-faced Crowley swept out of the ballroom.

When the door had shut behind him, Ella began to giggle. "By the Spirits, he had me worried there. He got a little too close to the *hounfo* for comfort." She giggled again. "But then it's always so easy to distract men!" She smiled at Vanka and Burlesque and gave them a twirl. "So, guys, what do you think of my outfit?"

"Nice tits," was Burlesque's verdict.

THE KNOCK ON THE DOOR OF TRIXIE'S BEDROOM CAME JUST BEFORE eight o'clock. When she unlocked it and peeped outside she saw Captain Dabrowski standing there. He examined her.

"Excellent. Maybe you're not as stupid as I thought. The trousers are good and the boots look very practical." He handed her a cap. "If you would push your hair up under this, I think we will have a better chance of passing you off as a soldier."

"A soldier?" asked Trixie as she quickly pinned her long hair up and covered it with the cap.

"You're very popular with my men, Miss Dashwood; they think you're very good-looking. So to avoid you being recognized it's best that we try to smuggle you out disguised as my batman. You'll need this as well." The captain handed Trixie a leather holster, which, when she unbuckled its flap, she found to be holding a small Colt revolver.

"I have no use for this," she announced.

"This is no time for feminine niceties, Miss Trixie. You must learn to protect yourself."

"Oh, believe me, Captain, I understand that. It's just that I have no use for such a small-caliber revolver." She pulled back her jacket to show the huge Mauser she had holstered on her belt. "When I shoot at the SS, Captain Dabrowski, I intend to kill them, not frighten them."

"Have you ever used a pistol before?"

With a deftness that belied her soft, delicate fingers Trixie pulled her revolver from its holster, snapped it open and checked that it was loaded. "Yes, I can fire a pistol, Captain. My father considers me quite the sharpshooter."

"Good. Just remember, if things go badly don't hesitate to shoot. But if I were you, I'd be inclined to save the last bullet for myself. Now, if you're ready . . ."

———

Vanka stood in front of the *HOUNFO*, waiting for the audience to arrive, desperately trying to calm himself, to still the trembling in his hands and stop himself conjuring up images of Checkya torture chambers. It was too late now for something to turn up. He was a dead man.

How could Vanka Maykov, the cat who always walked by himself, have gotten himself into such a dangerous muddle? It was all Ella's fault. Everything had started to go wrong the moment she'd entered his life. He tried to stop thinking about her, to concentrate on the job at hand; the thought of her in that costume didn't do anything for his peace of mind.

Ella.

Ella who was now crouched on the floor in the middle of the *hounfo* completely covered by her cloak. Boy, was the audience in for a surprise.

A wisp of acrid smoke tugged at his nostrils; it was a horrible smell that tickled at the back of his throat. Burlesque had lit the two braziers set up in the ballroom and heaped on dried leaves from a plant Ella called epimedium. Vanka had never heard of the stuff but it was making his head swim, as was the rhythm the drummers were beating out from up in the minstrels' gallery. ABBA only knew where Burlesque had conjured these maniacs from but they were playing their drums VERY LOUDLY. Ella called the music—music?—she had written for them *rada* music and said it was a vital ingredient in WhoDoo rituals. Vanka had his own name for it.

He didn't know how much longer he could handle this unrelenting assault on his senses. He gave his head a shake but couldn't seem to drive away the fug that was clouding his mind and if ever there was a time to remain sharp-witted, this was it.

Suddenly the doors of the ballroom crashed open: their audience had arrived and it was an august audience at that. Even as he bowed his greeting, Vanka spotted Heydrich, Crowley, Clement, Beria . . .

Beria.

Foul up tonight and Beria would ensure that his days on the Demi-Monde were very short.

Very short but unbelievably fucking painful.

Striding arrogantly into the hall, Heydrich took the tall chair directly in front of the *hounfo* with Beria seated to his left and a slim and heavily veiled woman to his right. Next to Beria was Crowley, who was looking decidedly out of sorts, with Comrade Commissar Dashwood perched uncomfortably alongside. There were a couple of other dignitaries making up the rump of the audience but with one exception Vanka didn't recognize any of these supernumeraries.

The exception was General Mikhail Dmitrievich Skobelev, unmistakable in his trademark white uniform and ridiculous whiskers.

Skobelev, commander of the ForthRight army and the man who had fought the Royalist Poles to a standstill at the Battle of Warsaw. The general was a living, breathing hero and, more importantly, the man who had come within an ace of killing Vanka, the man who had sworn to revenge his family for the insult Vanka had inflicted by bedding the general's sister.

Of all the rotten fucking luck. Of all the people I didn't want attending the séance.

Vanka almost panicked and for a moment wondered whether he shouldn't just grab Ella and run for it. Then he remembered that he was wearing a mask and managed to get control of himself. It was impossible for Skobelev to recognize him; the mask completely covered what was left of the bruise on the side of his face.

He stood up straight and made a signal to the percussionists pounding away in the minstrels' gallery. The music stopped but unfortunately the hammering in Vanka's head kept right on going.

Taking a deep, calming breath, he strode forward to the front of the *hounfo*, acutely aware that every stride he took brought him nearer to Skobelev. He was sure the bastard was studying him.

"Comrade Leader . . . Comrade Vice-Leader . . . Your Holiness . . . comrades and ladies." He pitched his voice as low as he dared, hoping that Skobelev wouldn't recognize it.

The bastard *was* studying him.

"Tonight, the mambo Marie Laveau, the foremost practitioner of WhoDoo magic in all of NoirVille, will commune with a Daemon. She will use her occult power and her psychic wiles to dominate the Daemon's will and bend it to her bidding."

Skobelev leaned forward in his chair trying to get a better look at Vanka. Automatically he edged back as far into the shadows as he dared.

"Behind me you see a *hounfo*, a WhoDoo temple built especially for tonight's performance. Using the *hounfo*, the mambo Laveau will entice the *loa*, the Spirits, into this, the physical world. Then by her spells and her incantations and her feminine allures"—*That got a reaction . . .* —"she will persuade the mightiest of these *loa*, Great Lord Bondye, to possess her. Only the Great Lord Bondye has the power to overcome the will of a Daemon. Once possessed by the Great Lord Bondye, no secret can be withheld from Mambo Laveau."

Such was the intensity of Skobelev's interest that Vanka decided to cut things short. He made a hurried bow and glanced toward Aleister Crowley. "Your Holiness, if you will bring forward the Daemon."

Crowley grunted up out of his seat and clapped his hands. From the side of the room two SS guards used their batons to prod a young girl—slim, medium height with raven-black hair—forward, persuading her to limp across the polished wooden floor of the ballroom until she was standing in the middle of the *hounfo* facing the audience.

Vanka was a little disappointed. He had always imagined Daemons to be great hulking creatures with tails and horns, creatures who breathed fire and smelled of brimstone, but instead he was being presented with a rather nondescript and skinny girl.

Daemons obviously weren't all they were cracked up to be.

Nondescript and skinny though the Daemon was, from the way it struggled with its guards it showed it was a feisty little piece. But its struggling didn't last long; one of the guards gave it a backhand slap across the face that sent it spinning to the floor. For an instant the mask of defiance the Daemon wore slipped and Vanka saw a frightened girl beneath. Instinctively he stepped across the *hounfo* to take the creature by its arm and help it back up onto its feet. Unfortunately that necessitated stepping out of the shadows.

Seeing him in the limelight, Skobelev started forward in his seat like a dog scenting a rabbit. He beckoned to one of Crowley's aides and began an animated discussion with the man. Vanka tried to keep calm.

After a moment's hesitation the Daemon accepted his help but it obviously wasn't happy about it: from the glare it gave Vanka he was certain that if its hands hadn't been bound it would have tried to scratch his eyes out. He was also pleased it was gagged; his head was pounding and he wasn't in the market for a lot of screaming and shouting. He gave a second signal to the musicians and immediately the drumming began again, but now it was slower, more ponderous and more ominous.

Vanka led the Daemon to the altar at the furthest end of the *hounfo* and indicated that it should lie on it. The Daemon tried to refuse but as Vanka pushed it forward he managed to get close enough to whisper in its ear. "We're here to rescue you, so don't struggle. Understand?"

The Daemon's eyes widened and it gave an almost imperceptible nod.

Vanka moved back to the front of the *hounfo*. Skobelev was now whispering instructions to two Checkya guards.

He was saved by Ella. As the drumming gained in volume, Ella, hidden under the cloak, began to twitch.

The séance had begun.

WHEN ELLA'S MOTHER HAD BEEN ALIVE, SHE HAD INSISTED ON HER daughter taking dancing lessons. But that was a long, long time ago. Now all Ella had to guide her in her WhoDoo dance was her own imagination, the remembrance of any number of music videos she had watched, the clips she had seen of Josephine Baker performing her *danse sauvage* and the beat of the drums. All this informed her that she should emerge from beneath her cloak slowly, sinuously, undulating her long supple body to the rhythm pounding through the ballroom. So, like some strange serpent sloughing off its skin, Ella wriggled off the cloak covering her, to emerge, spiraling and squirming, into the half-light. And as she emerged, she drew astonished gasps from the audience.

The astonishment might have been because she was black. She knew from her discussions with Vanka that for a black woman to perform before that architect of racial purity Reinhard Heydrich was simply unprecedented. When she had met the man—the *Dupe*—in Fort Jackson she had seen firsthand how Heydrich felt about blacks and she had come to understand that he had poisoned the ForthRight with this hate. She could *feel* the audience's revulsion. The vibes she was experiencing told her that Heydrich and his crew didn't just hate blacks, they abhorred them.

As she lissomed to her feet, stretching her arms up . . . up . . . up toward the ceiling high above her head, she wondered how intelligent, educated people, as those in her audience presumably were, could come to think like this. Maybe, as her mother had often told her, it was true that when people believe others are their inferiors all they do is demonstrate their concerns about their own inferiority. True or not, Ella couldn't have made a bigger impression if she'd just stepped out of a flying saucer.

But Ella knew that it wasn't simply that she was black that had disturbed the audience. What they found equally disturbing was her costume, or rather the near-naked body they could see under it. When she had been designing her outfit for tonight's performance she had wanted it to be so shocking that her audience would forget everything else. The last thing she wanted was for them to wonder whether what they were witnessing was just a piece of magical the-ater. And to do that she knew she would have to tantalize, to tease and show a lot of flesh.

Not that Ella had any concern about being near-naked; what she had an objection to was her nakedness being exploited by people like Burlesque Bandstand. But she was perfectly relaxed about exploit-ing it to her own ends. She knew she was a good-looking woman and had no compunction at all about using her sexuality to control men, to bend them to her will. And from what she could see of the expres-sions on the faces of the men watching her, she had them all in the palm of her hand. Especially Heydrich . . .

His eyes never left her. It might have been that he was entranced by her ephemeral costume—all the other men seemed to be—or by the salacious moves she was making, but it was more than that. It was as though Heydrich was trying to remember something. It was as if he recognized her, almost as though he remembered her from their meeting at Fort Jackson. But that was impossible. Well, she *hoped* that was impossible.

She let out a wail to signal that her soul was in torment and spun on her heels, turning her back on him, taking a moment to settle herself. She gave her ass a wiggle, hoping that would distract him. The bastard certainly hadn't seen *that* before.

The dance she had choreographed was difficult as it necessitated the pretense that she had an invisible partner, that she was dancing with the Great Lord Bondye. For five long minutes she danced, imbuing her body with ever more suggestive, ever more lascivious moves, drawing her audience's eyes to her, demanding that they watch her and her alone.

And as she danced something remarkable seemed to happen. It was as though the Spirit of Lilith began to take hold of her. Now she wasn't just dressed as Lilith; she actually *was* Lilith. She reveled in the power that her beauty and her eroticism gave her over her audience. She delighted in making her moves and her twists ever more wanton. She tantalized by snaking nearer to the limelights to let the light wash over her, revealing, for just a provocative instant, all the secrets of her body. She swayed and undulated across the floor, allowing her figure to flicker and shimmer in and out of sight under her flimsy costume. She screamed and she moaned, she sang and she wailed.

And as she danced and ululated, so she edged closer and closer to Norma Williams, who lay on the *hounfo*'s altar.

It was the first time Ella had seen Norma Williams in the flesh, though of course her picture had adorned the front covers of lots of gossip magazines. She didn't disappoint. She was the epitome of the teenage rebel, all dyed hair, tattoos, piercings and an expression that seemed to suggest that she went through life with a bad smell under her nose. Even the bruise that covered half her face was a perfect complement to her whole demeanor.

Without for one moment pausing in her undulating, Ella began to circle the altar, wailing and screaming as though locked in a struggle with the Spirit who had come to possess her. Suddenly she collapsed to the floor, shaking and moaning.

That was Vanka's cue. He made the sign to Burlesque, who was standing in the wings. Immediately the limelights were dimmed; now only the flickering candelabras illuminated the room, giving it a fragile, uncertain ambience.

Once again Vanka addressed the audience. "Comrade Leader . . . Comrade Vice-Leader . . . Your Holiness . . . comrades and ladies . . . this edifice"—he waved his hands to indicate the tall walls of the *hounfo*—"is designed and constructed to confine and to concentrate the psychic waves which emanate when that most powerful of mediums the mambo Laveau communes with her subject. So powerful is the energy to be contained in this *hounfo* that, if the Spirits are willing, the mambo Laveau will merge with the Daemon and together they will journey to the Spirit World. This moment of merging will be signaled by a thunderclap and it will appear that the Daemon and the mambo Laveau have vanished. But, please, do not be alarmed; it is only that their physical presence in this realm of the flesh is cloaked by waves of psychic energy." Vanka turned toward Burlesque. "If you will close the gates to the *hounfo*."

Ella watched as Alf and Sid shuffled across and pushed the gates of the *hounfo* shut, sealing Norma Williams, Vanka and herself inside. But though the gates were closed she knew that the three of them could still be seen through the bars. She waited until Vanka had come to stand behind her and the drumming from the trio in the minstrels' gallery was as loud as it ever would be, then, confident that she wouldn't be overheard, she leaned forward and whispered to Norma. "Norma"—the girl's eyes started at the sound of her name—"my name is Ella Thomas, I've been sent here from the Real World to help you escape."

She pulled the gag away from the girl's mouth.

"Escape? How?" spluttered Norma.

"In a few moments there will be a terrifically loud bang. As soon as you hear the explosion, I want you to get up and walk through the wall behind you."

"Walk through the wall?"

"There's a secret panel," advised Ella. "Once through the wall, you'll see the window at the back of the ballroom. It's been unlocked. We must climb through that and then make our way across the manor's grounds."

"That's impossible. This place is crawling with soldiers."

"I'm sorry, Norma, but that's the best we can do."

Norma was quiet for a moment and then smiled a triumphant little smile. "I think I can do a little better than that."

ELLA STRETCHED OUT HER ARMS, BEGAN TO MAKE A LOUD KEENING noise and screamed out, "Lord Bondye has come!" It was the signal to Burlesque to start the countdown.

Five.

Burlesque lit the fuse to the fireworks hidden in the walls of the *hounfo.*

Four.

Vanka released the catch securing the hidden door.

Three.

Sid and Alf took a firmer grip on the levers controlling the mirrors set in the bars of the gates.

Two.

Ella nodded to Norma to ready herself to move.

One.

BANG!

The fireworks exploded, sheathing the front of the *hounfo* in thick, cloying smoke. Immediately Burlesque's men threw the levers and the mirrors hidden in each of the wooden bars of the gates snapped across. With the mirrors angled so that they reflected the sides of the hounfo rather than the audience seated directly in front of it, what the audience would see when the smoke cleared was a reflection of the outside walls, which were, of course, a duplicate of the walls inside the gates. To the audience it would appear that those inside had vanished. Confident now that they couldn't be seen, Ella leapt to her feet, grabbed Norma by the arm, cut the girl's bindings and waited while Vanka scrabbled the concealed door open. As soon as he was through the door, Ella shoved Norma after him. Almost blinded by the acrid smoke from the fireworks, she was only just able to spot Vanka as he rushed to the back windows and threw one of them open.

"Quickly, quickly, get out," he whispered, seizing Norma by the waist and almost tossing her out through the open window. A second later Ella found herself sprawling on top of the president's daughter. She had a moment to appreciate that a chiffon costume wasn't an ideal outfit to wear during a Demi-Mondian Winter before there was a grunt to her right and Vanka landed in a heap by her side. He ripped off his mask and gestured to the drive that snaked out into the night, disappearing in the direction of the main gate. "Come on, you two . . . this way . . . keep to the shadows by the wall . . ."

"No!" said Norma emphatically. And then she did something quite unexpected: she pulled Vanka's silk scarf from around his neck and wrapped it about her head, hiding her black hair. "Follow me," she ordered, and to Ella's amazement, she started to walk toward the *front* of the house

"What the fuck . . ." whispered Vanka, but before he could do anything to stop her, the girl had turned the corner and, making no effort to hide herself from the guards patrolling the manor's grounds, sauntered up—hiding her limp as best she could—to the steam-limo parked puffing and panting at the bottom of the steps of the manor.

"You," she called out in an imperious voice to the steam-limo driver who was lounging against one of the columns enjoying a sly cigarette. "You. Come here."

The man nearly passed out. He threw his cigarette away and scuttled over to the girl. "Why, yes, m'lady."

Norma gave a contemptuous wave of her hand in the direction of the Leader's steam-limo. "My father wishes me to return home early. I am to use his steam-limo."

"Well, I don't know about that, my Lady Aaliz. My orders . . ."

TRIXIE STOOD TO THE SIDE OF THE MANOR, SHROUDED BY SHADOWS and thickly falling snow, and guarded by the bulky presence of Captain Dabrowski's sergeant. It was so cold that Trixie was shivering under her thick woolen traveling cloak.

She stiffened her shoulders and in an act of will ordered herself to stop trembling; people would think she was frightened. She was a Dashwood and no one would accuse a Dashwood of ever being frightened, especially not this idiot of a sergeant. If an ordinary soldier could show no fear then neither would the daughter of a commissar.

But it was difficult not to be scared. Up until a few moments ago the whole evening had had a surreal quality. It had been as though she had been caught up in a dream—a nightmare, really—that what was happening to her wasn't *actually* happening to her. But the sergeant had brought her crashing down to earth: there was nothing dreamlike or whimsical about Sergeant Wysochi. He was a huge man, broad shouldered and with hands like paddles. He also stank, possessing that wholly masculine odor conjured from the mixed smells of tobacco, Solution, sweat and leather.

Trixie hated him.

"What's happening?" she whispered. "Where's Captain Dabrowski?"

"Shut up." As Trixie was fast discovering, Sergeant Wysochi was a man of few words and most of them curt and unpleasant.

There was a crunch of snow under a boot to Trixie's left and Dabrowski, wearing a camouflaged *dublonka* and toting a repeating rifle, stepped out of the shadows. "The occultists are in the ballroom, Sergeant, so it's any moment now. Are the men ready?"

"Yes, sir." It seemed that the Sergeant wasn't any more garrulous with his captain.

"And the bombs?"

Bombs?

"Zajac is manning the detonator. As soon as he hears the shot he'll blow the gates."

By the pale moonlight Trixie saw the captain work the bolt of his rifle, sliding a round into the breech. He flicked off the safety catch and gave Trixie a meaningful look. "You will do exactly as the sergeant here tells you, Miss Trixie, nothing more and nothing less. That way you'll survive. Understand?"

Trixie's throat was suddenly so dry that all she could do was nod.

"May ABBA be with us," muttered Dabrowski.

And then things *really* became surreal.

A window next to where they were standing was thrown open and a small figure fell through it onto the soft snow. Trixie jumped back in shock.

The sergeant thrust out a strong arm and pushed Trixie protectively behind him. From behind Wysochi's comforting bulk, she was amazed to see this first fugitive being followed in short order by two others, one of them a girl wearing not very much at all and the other a tall, long-haired man. The three of them began to sneak around the side of the building, and as they did so light from a lantern caught the face of the smallest of the three. It was the Daemon!

A wide-eyed Trixie watched the Daemon march around to the front of the house and begin shouting orders.

With a silent signal to Captain Dabrowski, Sergeant Wysochi, with Trixie following him, began to creep after the three escapees. As they reached the corner of the manor, Trixie could hear the Daemon speaking with the driver of Heydrich's steamer, but before she quite realized what was happening, Sergeant Wysochi strode forward to take control of the situation.

For Ella, everything seemed to be coming unraveled.

As Norma began arguing the toss with the steamer driver, a red-jacketed sergeant came marching up.

"Do as the Lady Aaliz . . ."

Lady Aaliz?

" . . . orders, you fool, and jump to it," the sergeant snarled as he turned to address Norma. "I have been asked to accompany you, m'lady. Your father ordered that I bring two men with me to act as escort." He nodded to the two soldiers standing in the darkness behind him.

Ella had to admire Norma Williams's aplomb: she handled a situation that was fast descending into farce with a degree of imperturbability Ella had never seen equaled. "Very well, Sergeant, I suppose you can serve drinks," Norma sneered, "whilst I and my friends play bridge." This girl, Ella decided, was a Vanka-class bullshitter.

For a second the steam-limo's driver was paralyzed by confusion. It might have been that all of a sudden the Blood Hounders patrolling the grounds of the manor began to howl or that he wasn't used to being given orders by Poles, but whatever it was, this confusion cost him his life. Ella had never seen anybody killed before, but she had never imagined that murder was an act that could be performed with such cold-blooded efficiency. The enormous sergeant conjured a long, vicious-looking knife out of nowhere and drove it straight through the driver's throat, forestalling any noise or protest he might have been inclined to make.

"I'll drive, Captain." Without waiting for a reply the sergeant stepped over the still-twitching body of the driver, hauled himself up into the steam-limo's cabin and began to shift levers. Immediately the puffing of the steamer's pistons increased in tempo.

"Get in," the captain ordered. They needed no second telling: Vanka bustled first Ella and then Norma into the passenger compartment and then dived in after them. They were joined an instant later by the captain and a second soldier.

"Are you ready, Sergeant?" called out the captain as he scrabbled inside.

An answering grunt came from the sergeant, who immediately pushed open one of the steamer's windows and fired a single shot into the air. In reply there were two explosions. The first ripped open the large wooden shed that was serving as a temporary barracks for the SS garrison and the second—the larger one—smashed open the gates that guarded the manor's grounds.

The steamer gave a lurch and began to shudder forward, steam from its mighty cylinders enveloping the vehicle. It seemed to take an age for it to pick up speed. As the huge wheels crunched over the gravel, all Ella could hear through the armored glass windows was the ringing of alarm bells and the yelling of running men. It was the sergeant who seemed to know what to do: he leaned out of the window and calmly shouted at the SS guards who were streaming out of the manor, "Don't shoot, you fools. I have the Leader's daughter with me."

As the steam-limo sailed unopposed around the manor's drive and out through the shattered gates, Ella sat back, stunned by the realization that she had done it, she had rescued Norma Williams.

She had really, really done it!

She looked up to congratulate Vanka and was surprised to see him leaning out of one of the steamer's windows giving the finger to a white-uniformed officer who had just emerged on the steps of the manor.

Part III

WARSAW

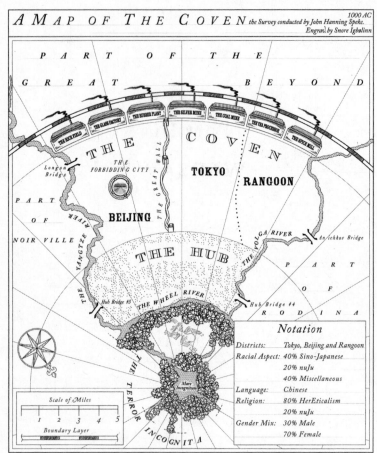

MAP OF THE COVEN.

PLATE 3

25

The Demi-Monde: 55th Day of Winter, 1004

"UnderMentionable" is the ForthRight term for an individual who has—because of supposed racial deficiency or religious, political or sexual deviancy—been illegally stripped of all rights and protection he or she formerly enjoyed as a citizen of the ForthRight. However, the deprivations suffered by the ForthRight during the Troubles—it is estimated that over two hundred thousand fighters died during this vicious and senseless civil war—has resulted in the relaxing of certain of the criteria normally used in determining whether an individual is or isn't an UnderMentionable. The major concession made was with regard to the GoldenFolk—a highborn sector of the Polish race—who have been retrospectively reclassified as Aryan.

—An Exercise in Futility: A PeaceNix's Assessment of the Human, Economic and Social Costs of the Troubles, William Penn, Warsaw Underground Press

I t took a few moments for Trixie to pull herself together.

The realization that with every passing second the steam-limo was trundling her ever further from the life she had enjoyed in Dashwood Manor and toward an uncertain and dangerous future was an unsettling one. And that, coupled with the chilling thought that she might never see her beloved father again, meant that she sat silent and pensive in a corner of the steam-limo's cabin.

She took a surreptitious look at her companions. They were a strange bunch. In the driver's seat was the huge and intimidating Sergeant Wysochi and sitting next to him, cradling a rifle on his lap, was a very nervous Captain Dabrowski. The Daemon was huddled in the opposite corner of the steamer's cabin, looking very unhappy and very piqued by everything that had happened. Beside the Daemon sat the two people Trixie hadn't yet been introduced to: the rather dashing young man with the long brown hair, and the Shade dressed in a most inappropriate and very revealing costume. These two, she guessed, were the psychic and his assistant, the PsyChick, who had been performing for the Leader. What they were doing involved in this little escapade, Trixie had no idea. It was an ill-met group and, as she was to discover, a particularly fractious one.

The problem, she decided later, was that there had been just too many would-be leaders in the steam-limo, just too many people who were determined to get their own way. The arguing began even before they had put a mile between themselves and Dashwood Manor.

"We have perhaps ten minutes before the Checkya realize what's happened and semaphore an alert to all the CheckyaPoints in the ForthRight," advised Dabrowski as the steamer puffed and panted its way onto one of the Sector's new autobahns. "We'll abandon this steamer maybe a mile from the Rhine, walk from there to the river and then bribe our way across the Oberbaum Bridge. That's the quickest way to the Ghetto."

Although she was too lost in her worries about her father to take much of an interest in what was being said, even a distracted Trixie bridled a little at Captain Dabrowski's rather arrogant assumption that he was in command of their group. It appeared that she wasn't the only one.

"That's the quickest way to the Lubyanka if you choose the wrong Militia officer to try to dash," grumbled the long-haired man. "I'll handle the bribing. It needs to be done with finesse: the Militia are sensitive about people leaving the ForthRight and entering Warsaw."

"We're going to the Warsaw Sector?" asked the Daemon.

"Of course," replied Dabrowski curtly. "Every Checkya officer in the ForthRight will be out looking for us. Warsaw is the only safe haven within striking distance."

Safe? wondered Trixie. In her book the Ghetto didn't qualify as a place where you went to be safe.

"Is the nearest Portal in Warsaw?" the Daemon asked the Shade.

How does the Daemon know the Shade?

It was the first time Trixie had been in close proximity to a Shade and she didn't like it. Everything she had been taught informed her that they were not to be trusted. Shades were the spawn of Lilith.

The black girl, who was struggling to get into the coat she had been offered by the tall psychic, shrugged a reply. "There isn't a Portal in Warsaw, Norma . . ."

Norma? How did the Shade know the Daemon's human alias? And what is this thing they called a "Portal"?

"Then why are we going there?" the Daemon snapped. "Are you stupid or something?"

The Shade glowered at the Daemon. "Okay, Norma, we're all a little uptight, so I'm gonna cut you a little slack and ignore that 'stupid' jibe. And for your information the only working Portal in the whole of the Demi-Monde is in NoirVille, but right now—"

"NoirVille? Well, that's where we've got to go," the Daemon announced, and then leaned forward and tapped Dabrowski on the shoulder. "I'd be obliged, Captain, if you would order your driver to head for NoirVille."

"No," he replied firmly. "We've got to get to the Ghetto. I've got to warn my people about the impending attack by the SS."

"Oh, don't be ridiculous," snapped the Daemon. "The only thing of any importance is getting me to NoirVille."

"We're going to the Ghetto," answered Dabrowski, introducing a distinct note of finality into his reply. "The lives of three million people are at stake."

The Daemon studied Dabrowski for a moment as though trying to establish whether he was being serious. "This is ludicrous. I'm not going to argue the toss with a Dupe. Stop this steamer right now, Captain. My . . . colleague"—the Daemon shot a sneering look at the Shade—"and I will get out and make our own way to NoirVille from here."

Colleague? How could the Daemon be a "colleague" of the Shade?

White people didn't have Shades as colleagues, they had them as slaves, and even then only if they couldn't afford Chink slaves.

The tall man was persuaded to rejoin the conversation. "We haven't had a chance to be formally introduced, young lady. My name is Colonel Vanka Maykov, Licensed Psychic, and I'm the man who just helped rescue you from Crowley." He offered his hand, but the Daemon petulantly shrugged it aside. "Well, young lady, if you won't take my hand, maybe you'll take some advice. The captain's right: with the Checkya on our heels the only place to hide is the Ghetto. And as for NoirVille . . . well, I've a feeling that as you've got no papers and no money that makes getting there by yourself virtually impossible. And while I don't give a damn about you or your welfare, I do care a great deal about my friend Miss Thomas, here."

Has everyone gone mad? How could an Aryan announce that he has a Shade as his "friend"? It isn't natural.

"Right now," Vanka went on as he pulled out his cigarette case, "there'll be semaphore messages batting back and forth across the ForthRight warning every CheckyaPoint to be on the lookout for a girl who looks a lot like Aaliz Heydrich . . ."

Trixie gawped; the Daemon *did* look like Aaliz Heydrich. She was amazed she hadn't noticed the resemblance before. If the Daemon had blond hair instead of black and fewer of those terrible facial mutilations it would be the girl's twin! It must have been the bruise on the side of her face that had foxed her.

" . . . a girl who may or may not be traveling in the company of a Shade." The man stopped abruptly. "I'm sorry, Ella . . . a girl of color."

The man actually apologized to the Shade!

"Don't worry about it, Vanka," said the Shade, twitching her head in the direction of the Daemon, "I've got bigger problems than a little low-rent racism."

"The upshot is, young lady—"

"For your information, my name is Norma Williams," the Daemon said with a haughty shake of her head.

"Very well. The upshot is, *Miss Williams*, if you get out of this steamer, you get out alone. I'm not letting Ella here sacrifice herself because of your pigheadedness. We've saved you once but I wouldn't bank on us being around to save you again."

"But I've *got* to get to NoirVille," the Daemon persisted. She glared at Vanka as he lit a cigarette. "And I'd appreciate it, Colonel, if you didn't smoke."

Vanka ignored the Daemon and blew smoke up toward the roof of the steamer. "And I'd prefer it if you did a little more thinking and a little less demanding."

"I think we should take Vanka's advice, Norma," the Shade said in a conciliatory tone.

"I don't need *you* to do my thinking for me, thanks very much," snapped Norma.

The Shade bridled. "Don't play the high-handed, high-and-mighty president's daughter with me, honey. And I'll do whatever thinking is necessary to get us out of here. It wasn't me who got my ass caught in a sling."

"Don't call me 'honey,'" Norma snarled.

"I'll call you anything I damn well want."

Trixie couldn't stand it any longer. "Please, please, can we stop this squabbling? Whether we like it or not, we're all in this together. Perhaps we should start by introducing ourselves?" There were no protests, so Trixie decided to start the ball rolling. She pulled the cap off her head and shook out her mane of blond hair. "I am Lady Trixiebell Dashwood—"

"I think you can forget the 'Lady' bit," sneered Norma. "After tonight's little set-to I don't think your father's going to be doing much lording about in the future. In fact, I don't think he's gonna have much of a future."

A stunned silence descended on the group, everyone shocked by the Daemon's crass indifference to Trixie's feelings. Trixie felt her cheeks going red with anger. "That, *Daemon,* was unnecessary. My father treated you with respect and I would be obliged if you would do the same." One day, Trixie resolved, she'd make the Daemon pay for that insult.

"That was an incredibly cruel thing to say," the Shade said quietly.

Norma was totally unabashed. "Oh, come on, baby, get with the program . . . the computer program. These are Dupes, they don't have real emotions."

"For your information, Miss Williams," Dabrowski snapped, obviously as outraged as all of them by the Daemon's vulgar behavior, "Comrade Commissar Dashwood helped to organize your escape this evening, help which has probably cost that brave man his life. So I would be obliged if, despite your obvious antipathy toward us 'Dupes,' you show some respect for Miss Dashwood's feelings."

There was another unpleasant silence.

"What's a Dupe?" asked Vanka.

"It's what Daemons call people who live in the Demi-Monde," answered Dabrowski. "That's what Miss Williams called us this afternoon when Miss Dashwood and I overheard a conversation between her and Reinhard Heydrich."

"What else did you hear, Captain?" asked Vanka.

"That the SS are planning to attack Warsaw in the next few days."

"And *that's* where we're escaping to?" sneered Norma. "Oh, well done, Captain, but don't you find the words 'frying pan' and 'fire' springing to mind?" With a disparaging laugh the girl turned to look out of the window at the scenery streaming past the steamer.

"Is that why you were hanging around outside the manor?" asked Vanka.

Dabrowski nodded. "Miss Dashwood and I were waiting for a signal to make our own escape. Your somewhat unconventional arrival was simply a coincidence—a happy coincidence. Without the presence of mind of the Daemon—"

A searing look from Norma Williams.

"—of Miss Williams, and, of course, her uncanny resemblance to Aaliz Heydrich, we would not have been able to commandeer this steamer." Dabrowski held out his hand. "I am Jan Dabrowski, until ten minutes ago captain of the GoldenFolk Regiment attached to the First Division of the ForthRight Army. I have also the honor to be a major in the Warsaw Free Army."

Vanka took Dabrowski's hand. "Pleased to meet you, Major. I am Colonel Vanka Maykov, late of the Fifth Revolutionary Regiment of Foot. And this is my friend and PsyChick, Miss Ella Thomas." The Shade, this Ella Thomas, offered her hand and Trixie was quite amazed to see Dabrowski take it without even the slightest hesitation. Presumably being brought up in the Ghetto deadened a gentleman's sensibilities to matters of racial etiquette, that is if a Pole like Dabrowski could ever be truly regarded as a gentleman.

Indeed, such was her amazement that before she quite knew what she was doing she had also shaken the Shade's hand. She masked a shudder.

Dabrowski looked at the Shade cautiously. "If you don't mind me asking, Miss Thomas, just what part of the Demi-Monde are you from? I don't seem to recognize your accent. It doesn't sound NoirVillian."

Without turning away from her study of the nightscape flashing by outside the steamer's windows, Norma gave a sardonic laugh. "Yeah, Miss Ella Thomas, why don't you tell them where you're really from? That should raise a laugh."

With a despairing sigh the Shade answered. "Like Norma, I'm from the Real World, from what you call the Spirit World."

"You're a Daemon!" gasped an astonished Vanka. "So *that's* why you're such a good medium. Why didn't you tell me?"

"I'm sorry, Vanka, but it's hardly something I could drop lightly into the conversation, now, is it? If you'd known I was a Daemon, you'd never have hired me."

Trixie was astonished. A few days ago she had been firmly of the RaTionalist belief that there were no such things as Daemons and now she seemed to be surrounded by the bloody things.

"So let me get this straight," said an equally bemused-looking Dabrowski, as his eyes danced back and forth between the Shade and Norma Williams, "you two are *both* Daemons."

"Correct," said Norma, "although I'm not big on being called a 'Daemon.'"

"Then what are you doing here in the Demi-Monde?"

The Daemons looked at one another, and reluctantly Norma gave an answer. "Ella's here to help me get back home, to get back to the Real World. I was lured here by Aleister Crowley and Aaliz Heydrich."

"Why?" asked Vanka, who still seemed to be reeling from the revelation of his PsyChick's Daemonhood.

Norma sighed. "It's a long and difficult story. Let's just say that I'm the daughter of someone very important in the Real World and Heydrich believed that by having me brought here to the Demi-

Monde, he could exert some control over my father. It's a simple blackmail scam."

"It would appear from what I heard this afternoon," added Dabrowski, "that there was some danger of the Daemons 'pulling the plug,' as Miss Williams called it, on the Demi-Monde, of destroying our world. Heydrich had Miss Williams brought here as a hostage to prevent this happening."

Norma shook her head vigorously and looked imploringly around the little group. "Look . . . guys . . . there's no chance of that. I can guarantee that no one is pulling the plug on this little holiday haven of yours. No one in the Real World wants to harm the Demi-Monde . . . no one wants to shut it down . . ."

Dabrowski wasn't so easily convinced. "I think it might be better to keep you close, Miss Williams, until we establish the truth of that last statement."

"Guys . . . it's imperative I get out of the Demi-Monde. Heydrich wants my place in the Real World to be taken by his daughter."

Now it was the Shade's turn to be shocked. "Heydrich's going to substitute his daughter for you in the Real World? But why?"

Norma gave a rueful smile. "Heydrich's sentient. He knows all about his previous existence in the Real World. He wants to get back there, to finish what the Nazis started eighty or so years ago."

"Jesus, I *thought* that bastard looked at me sideways when he saw me dancing tonight. He must have recognized me."

For a minute or two everyone in the steamer's cabin fell quiet, each of them lost in their own thoughts. It was Vanka who broke the silence. "Okay," he said wearily, "I'm getting a little confused here, but I have a suspicion that we might be missing the point. Surely the important thing, right now, is for us to avoid being captured by the Checkya. Call me a man of limited ambition but all I'm currently interested in is making sure Beria doesn't have the opportunity to play Billy the Butcher on my body. So can we forget about all this nonsense about 'Portals' and 'Dupes' and suchlike, and just concentrate on getting safely to the Ghetto?"

"But I've *got* to get to NoirVille," persisted Norma.

"You should listen to Vanka, Norma," the Shade said. "As of now we don't have a prayer of getting to NoirVille on our own. I figure our only hope of surviving will be to haul ass to the Warsaw Ghetto and then make a move to NoirVille when the heat has died down."

Norma appeared less than happy with what her fellow Daemon was saying, but any further protests were silenced when Wysochi turned around and addressed Dabrowski. "Looks like the Checkya have barricaded the road 'bout a half-mile ahead, sir. It might be a good time to start walking."

THE JOURNEY TO THE WARSAW GHETTO WAS ONE THAT ELLA WOULD rather forget. It was snowing heavily and without Vanka's coat she would have frozen to death long before they got to the Rhine. As it was, the series of heart-stopping dodges and scuttles out of London and through the backstreets of Berlin that Vanka deemed necessary to throw off the Checkya was enough to leave her tired, cold and very, very frightened.

All the euphoria of actually pulling off the rescue had long since dissipated; now all she wanted was to get somewhere warm and preferably away from the ungrateful bitch limping and whining along behind her. Norma Williams had turned out to be a world-class complainer.

As Dabrowski had suspected, semaphore messages had already alerted the Checkya to be on the lookout for the escapees so when they finally got to the Oberbaum Bridge—the bridge that spanned the Rhine and linked Warsaw and Berlin—they found that it had been sealed off by the SS. No one was leaving the Berlin Sector for Warsaw without their papers being *very* carefully scrutinized. And Vanka pronounced the SS–Ordo Templi Aryanis to be "unbribable."

They made it across the river in a boat rowed by a man who valued money more than his life. It was a scary, nerve-racking twenty minutes spent edging across the Rhine shrouded in the shadows cast by the bridge, sneaking in and out of the lumps of ice drifting along the near-frozen river and thanking the Spirits that the snowstorm that was blanketing the Demi-Monde had become even heavier. It was an unpleasant boat ride but, thankfully, they made it.

Once on the Warsaw side of the river, Dabrowski led his small band through the narrow, crowded streets to an inn standing close to the docks. Dabrowski seemed to be well-known there and his appearance, with his bedraggled companions in tow, warranted not even a raised eyebrow from the landlord. Without a word of inquiry he led the six of them to a table by the fire, then bustled around organizing the serving of a very palatable soup whilst simultaneously sending his maids scurrying off to make rooms ready.

Supper over, Ella sat warming herself by the fire and trying to make sense of what was happening. Considering that only a few days before all she had had to worry about had been paying the rent and scratching up enough money to put herself through college, the change was startling. Startling . . . but surprisingly stimulating.

Oh, it might have been uncomfortable and dangerous in the Demi-Monde but for the first time her life could be described as exciting. Loath as Ella was to admit it, she was actually enjoying the adventure of it all. Okay, so Norma Williams was a pain in the ass, but other than that . . .

She caught sight of Vanka as he strode across the bar, three large tankards of Solution in his hands. Yes, there were things that more than compensated for Norma Williams's incessant moaning, Vanka

Maykov being the best of them. The odd thing about Vanka was that though she knew he was a rogue and a rascal, she *liked* him. He made her laugh and there hadn't been many men in Ella's drab little life who had done that.

But he *was* just a Dupe. And a Dupe who since he had found out that she was a Daemon had become just a little distant, though he had at least muttered to her that Daemon or no, she was still the best-looking girl in all of the ForthRight.

She gave a rueful smile. Wasn't life a bitch: Vanka wasn't nervous about her because of her color but because she was *real*. She laughed to herself; maybe that made him not so much a racist as a realist.

Her ruminations on Vanka were interrupted by Norma. The girl slid herself down into the empty chair next to Ella and began trying to massage some of the fire's warmth into her right knee. To judge by the amount of moaning the girl had done en route to Warsaw, the knee was giving her a great deal of trouble, but if she had come looking for sympathy she would be disappointed. Norma Williams was, in Ella's opinion, a spoiled, arrogant snob.

"Hi," Norma said with a smile.

"Hi."

"Look . . . Ella, truth is we got off to a bad start. Maybe I was a little hyper, a bit uptight after the session with Heydrich. Maybe this whole escape thing freaked me out. Anyway, I was hoping that we might start over." The girl thrust out her hand. "I'm Norma Williams, but you can call me Norma."

Ella took the hand. "Okay. Forget it, Norma."

"So you're the rescue party, right?" she asked in a low conspiratorial voice. "You're the cavalry sent by my father to get me out of this hellhole?"

Ella shook her head. "I wasn't sent by your father. I'm here at the request of the U.S. military."

This evoked a frown. "I thought they'd have sent an army unit to pull me out." Norma laughed wryly. "Don't think I'm not appreciative of your efforts but—"

"They couldn't; they only managed to infiltrate me into the Demi-Monde by using a dormant Dupe jig. All but one of the Portals have been closed and even the last functioning Portal—the one in NoirVille—only works going *from* the Demi-Monde and not vice versa. I'm to get you to NoirVille and to escape using that."

Norma gave a nod of understanding. "Then we'd better get moving as soon as we can. If I don't get out pronto that bastard Heydrich is going to steal my body in the Real World and I'll be stuck here."

"Steal?"

"Aleister Crowley has perfected some piece of black magic called the Rite of Transference. Using that he'll have Aaliz Heydrich take over my body and then . . . well, it's curtains for yours truly."

"Jesus." All Ella could do was shake her head. "That's terrible. You know, this place gets freakier with every passing minute." She took another comforting sip of coffee.

Norma Williams glanced over her shoulder to make sure no one was listening. "Yeah, the quicker we're out of the Demi-Monde and this place is shut down the better. When my father gets to hear just what a fucked-up hellhole the U.S. military has been spending tax dollars constructing, he's gonna go ape."

The words "shut down" gave Ella pause. She looked around the room at Captain Dabrowski and that dangerous sergeant of his sitting in a corner chatting over their flagons of Solution; at the rather subdued girl, Lady Trixie Dashwood, who was slumped in a fitful slumber against the chimney breast; and at Vanka as he paced impatiently up and down the floor of the inn, and she thought it would be a shame if these wonderfully real personalities were to be destroyed. Especially Vanka . . .

Norma seemed to read her mind. "Don't worry about them, Ella.

They're just Dupes. They're not real. It doesn't matter what happens to them, all that's important is what happens to *us*. We're the only real people in this screwed-up shit-heap of a world. We've got to keep our eye on the ball. The only thing we should be worrying about is getting to NoirVille and clearing out of Dodge."

Ella nodded. The girl might be a little cold-blooded but there was no denying her logic. The Demi-Monde was, after all was said and done, just a computer game and the characters in it just figments of ABBA's overfertile cyber-imagination. And there were five million dollars waiting for her at home.

Norma edged closer. "Somehow we've got to persuade one of these Dupes to help us. Maybe that Vanka person; he seems to have a thing for you, Ella."

"Oh, don't be ridiculous, he's just a Dupe."

"Well, Dupe or not, he's got the hots for you. I've seen the way he looks at you and the way he tries to look after you. You've gotten yourself a cyber-beau, Ella."

Ella chuckled derisively to mask her disquiet. She gave Vanka a quick glance: he really was a good-looking man . . . Dupe. *That* was the problem: Vanka wasn't real flesh and blood. If he were . . .

TRIXIE WAS BROUGHT OUT OF HER SLEEP BY A LOUD KNOCKING ON THE inn's door followed by a draft of cold wind whipping around her legs. She batted open her eyes in time to witness the arrival of six large and formidably well-dressed men surrounded by a company of green-jacketed soldiers. From the expression on their faces the new arrivals weren't happy to be out so late on such a dismal night.

Unhappy or not, Trixie judged them to be important—that is, if the way Captain Dabrowski leapt to his feet and went across to greet them was any indication.

"Why have you called us here, Dabrowski?" demanded a large, rotund man of about fifty wearing a huge, all-enveloping fur coat and an aura of pompous authority. "Who are these people?"

As the man drew nearer to the fire Trixie recognized him. She had seen his picture in *The Stormer*: he was Chief Delegate Olbracht, the man the newspaper called "Warsaw's Savior" but whom everybody else called "Heydrich's Puppet Polack." He was the man who, as head of the Warsaw Administration, was charged by the Party with ensuring that law and order prevailed in the Ghetto and that any dissidents or protesters were summarily dealt with. Trixie shivered; he was revolting and looked just as slimy and duplicitous as she had always imagined one of the GoldenFolk—one of the ersatz Aryans—would look.

Dabrowski crossed the floor to shake Olbracht's hand. His usual poise and confidence seemed to have deserted him. As he stood nervously shifting his weight from one foot to the other, his cheeks red and his voice high and uncertain, he gave the impression of an overexcited schoolboy. His demeanor did not inspire confidence and neither, it seemed, did his reply to the plump man's question.

"We have just escaped from the Rookeries, Chief Delegate, and I bring urgent and shocking intelligence. I have heard from Heydrich's own lips that the elimination of all those living in the Ghetto—what Heydrich calls his 'Final Solution'—is to begin within the next three days. The SS–Ordo Templi Aryanis under the command of Archie Clement has been given the task of razing Warsaw—and everyone in it—to the ground."

"Twaddle," sneered the Chief Delegate as he levered himself down into a chair by the fire and took a long gulp from the glass of Solution the landlord handed him. He gave an appreciative smack of his lips and raised the glass vaguely in Dabrowski's direction in an ironic toast. "To Warsaw's foremost Cassandra," he said, and drained his glass. "So tell me, Dabrowski, is this the poppycock I've been dragged out of my bed to listen to?"

"I'm telling the truth."

The chief delegate waved Dabrowski's objections away and signaled the landlord to serve drinks to the other delegates. "You and the other hotheads in your so-called Warsaw Free Army have cried wolf before and yet here we are, still safe, sound and unmolested by Archie Clement's thugs. It is the considered opinion of the Administration Committee"—here he nodded to the men who had accompanied him to the inn—"that it would be ridiculous for the Anglos to attack the Ghetto. Why would they squander men and matériel on destroying Warsaw and the Poles when we pose no threat to the ForthRight?" He shook his head. "It won't do, Dabrowski: Heydrich might not like us Poles much, but he isn't stupid."

"But I have heard—"

"What have you heard? Admit it, Dabrowski, Heydrich might rant and rave, he might bluster and threaten, but he knows as well as we do that to launch an attack on Warsaw would be a waste of time and energy. No, the ForthRight's real enemy are those damned HerEtical witches. That's where the next war will be fought: in the Coven."

There were mutterings of agreement from the other members of the Administration Committee.

The chief delegate waved Dabrowski into a chair. "You look ill, Dabrowski, worn out. Maybe you've started to hear things. I'm told that soldiers who spend too long in the field start to ill-ucinate, start to become a little crazed. Maybe you should take a holiday?"

Dabrowski reacted badly. Perhaps if he had remained calm he might have had a chance of convincing the delegates, but instead he became angry. "Damn it all, Chief Delegate, I have a witness." He pointed to Trixie. "Lady Dashwood was with me, she heard Heydrich—"

"Dashwood? The daughter of Comrade Commissar Algernon Dashwood?" The chief delegate began to laugh. "You really wish us to take the word of the daughter of the man who's working thousands of our young men to death building his railway? Are you seriously suggesting that this committee should accept the corroborating statement of a *Dashwood?*"

Trixie bridled. "I will have you know, sir—" she began, but Olbracht shouted her down.

"You will have me know nothing, young lady," he snapped. "You will remain silent as all women should when men are talking. I have not come here to be harangued by a hysterical child."

For a moment Trixie's temper flared but she knew arguing would be a waste of energy when faced by such idiocy. She kept quiet, sitting cross-armed in her chair, shuddering with suppressed fury. Her time would come.

Dabrowski took a long, calming breath. "What I am telling you is the truth, Chief Delegate. In three days the SS will seal the Ghetto and then begin a systematic annihilation of all the Poles and nuJus in Warsaw. It is time to begin our battle for survival. It is time to mount our uprising. It is time for Operation Storm."

The chief delegate gave a scoffing laugh. "How melodramatic you young people are! Operation Storm indeed. And what will this 'storm' of yours entail?"

"You must issue the order for the mobilization of the Warsaw Free Army. We must evacuate the civilian population to the center of the city. We must barricade the streets around the entrances to the Ghetto and move to defend the Blood Bank. We must send out emissaries to the Coven and to the Quartier Chaud asking for support. We must prepare to fight for our freedom."

"Fight?" said the chief delegate as he jumped to his feet and wagged a finger at Dabrowski. "What are we to fight with? Sticks and stones? According to you, we will be facing the SS, the most ferocious and battle-hardened troops in the whole of the Demi-Monde. What you are suggesting is suicide."

"I have information that there are two barges packed with rifles and ammunition moored on the Berlin bank of the Rhine. Give me a hundred good men and I will lead a raiding party to seize these weapons and use them to arm our soldiers."

"Absolutely not!" shouted the chief delegate. "Such an act of piracy will provoke just the sort of attack you are predicting. Stealing weapons from the Anglos would bring the most severe reprisals down on our heads. Is it your intention to goad them to attack us?" Dramatically, he raised a hand and pointed a finger at Dabrowski. "Is that what you are, Dabrowski, an agent provocateur? Maybe you are a crypto in the pay of the Coven, sent to stir up trouble within the ForthRight? Is this a piece of malicious agitprop sponsored by that witch Jeanne Dark?"

Now it was Dabrowski's turn to leap to his feet. "I am a loyal and patriotic Pole!" he shouted angrily. "I beg you to listen to me. The SS will attack us in days."

"They will not!"

For several long seconds the two men stood, scarlet with rage, glowering at each other in the middle of the sawdust-strewn floor of the inn. It was then a man moved out from the group of delegates to stand beside Dabrowski. Unlike his colleagues, this man wore a beard, a broad-brimmed black hat and a long black coat on whose sleeve was a white armband decorated with a five-pointed star, the sign of the nuJus.

For Trixie this was truly a night when she met all of the Forth-Right's bogeymen: first a Shade and now a nuJu. The peculiar thing was that this nuJu wasn't the beak-nosed, crook-backed creature nuJus were characterized as in *The Stormer*. He looked like a diffi-dent and dusty academic, but though he was a little old and careworn there was a distinct sparkle of intelligence twinkling in his eyes.

"Perhaps I might be allowed to make an observation, Chief Del-egate, on behalf of the nuJu citizens of Warsaw. My people do, after all, make up almost half of the population." Olbracht gave a nod of consent but Trixie could see that he wasn't happy about the old nuJu's interference. "Reluctant as I am," the nuJu began, "ever to demur when one as erudite as yourself has pronounced judgment, Chief Delegate Olbracht, I would counsel against dismissing Captain Dabrowski's warnings out of hand. After all, our Cichociemni cryptos have been sending us warning messages of unusual activity in the Anglo Sector for several weeks now. We know, for example, that all SS leave has been canceled. This would support the captain's contention that they are mobilizing for an attack."

"Irrelevant," Olbracht scoffed. "Tell me, Delegate Trotsky, has your spying told you anything that isn't just gossip and innuendo?"

Trotsky gave a half-smile and delved into a pocket of his battered coat to retrieve a folded piece of paper. "We intercepted and deciphered the following semaphore message not more than an hour ago. It reads: '*To Major T. Hartley, Officer Commanding Death's Head Detachment of SS–Ordo Templi Aryanis: Warsaw District. Implement Case White with immediate effect. Demand to be made of Warsaw Administration for surrender of Daemon known as Norma Williams thought to be in the company of the renegade Captain Jan Dabrowski. Dawn-to-dusk curfew to be imposed. Civilians violating curfew to be shot. By Order Clement.*'"

Trotsky carefully refolded the piece of paper and returned it to his pocket. "I think, Chief Delegate, your optimism regarding the safety of Warsaw and the rationality of Reinhard Heydrich is somewhat misplaced."

Olbracht gave a scornful laugh. "Not so, Trotsky! All Comrade Leader Heydrich is concerned about is capturing a Daemon. He has no arguments with the people of Warsaw per se." He turned to Captain Dabrowski. "Which one is it, Dabrowski, which one of these delinquents is the Daemon? We will give it up to the SS and the Leader will call off his dogs. Who among them is Norma Williams?"

"I refuse to tell you," said Dabrowski.

"Then we'll hand the whole pack of you over to the SS. That'll settle this nonsense."

Trixie saw Vanka edge protectively nearer to the Shade, unbuttoning his jacket. It was a sensible maneuver, one she imitated by nestling a hand around the butt of her Mauser.

"It will settle nothing," said Dabrowski firmly. "Case White is the code name for the ForthRight's plan to destroy Warsaw and all its inhabitants."

"You are wrong, Dabrowski," said Olbracht scornfully. "If we give up this Daemon—"

Trotsky laughed. "Oh, then they'll just find another excuse. This onslaught has been coming for quite a while, Chief Delegate. All Poles—apart from the GoldenFolk, of course—have now been classified as UnderMentionable and denied ForthRight citizenship. Polish nuJus, such as myself, are already confined to the Ghetto by the decree Clement issued a month ago, the so-called *non tolerandis nuJuis*. Our young men are being shipped off to work camps in the Hub in ever greater numbers and we never hear of them again. The Blood Tax is so high and the food rations so low that our people hardly have the strength to live, let alone fight." He gave a rueful shrug. "All it seems to me is that Heydrich has tired of subjecting us to a lingering death and has decided to administer the coup de grâce. Whether we give up the Daemon or refuse, the result will be the same."

Olbracht ignored him. "This mess is your fault, Dabrowski: by associating with Daemons you have brought the Leader's wrath down on Warsaw. You must give this creature up. We must show ourselves to be loyal and obedient members of the ForthRight. We must surrender the Daemon and apologize."

He whirled around and addressed the officer who was commanding the company of soldiers that had accompanied the delegates. "Lieutenant Adamczyk, arrest Captain Dabrowski and all of his companions."

The lieutenant made a move toward Dabrowski then stopped in midstride as the sound of a rifle bolt being worked echoed through the room. All eyes turned toward Sergeant Wysochi, who was pointing his rifle rather casually toward Olbracht. "I don't think the captain has a mind to be arrested tonight, Chief Delegate," he growled.

"Are you mad, Sergeant?" Olbracht gasped. "I could have you shot for this. Don't you know that I'm the leader of the Warsaw Administration, that I'm—"

"You're a dead man unless you and all your pals turn around and get going." There was something in Wysochi's tone that indicated he was in deadly earnest; Olbracht turned pale.

"Captain Dabrowski, order this lunatic of yours to put down his rifle. This is mutiny!"

Dabrowski stood speechless, unable to choose between his sergeant and the man who was, at the very least, his titular commander. Trixie had seen the phenomenon before in young men in the ForthRight: they had been conditioned from birth to obey orders and this made it difficult for them to know how to disobey them.

Sergeant Wysochi took the decision out of his hands. "Don't matter what the captain says, Chief Delegate, after what's happened tonight I'm a dead man anyway, so whether the Checkya arrest me for one murder or two don't make no difference." He raised the rifle to his shoulder and took careful aim at Olbracht's forehead. "Now, sir, are you going alive or are you staying dead?" He clicked off the rifle's safety, the sound ominous in the silence.

Olbracht and the rest of the administration retreated out of the inn muttering threats about "mutiny" and "court-martials."

When the last had gone, Wysochi lowered the rifle. "I think if we're going after those barges, Major Dabrowski," said the sergeant, pointedly using Dabrowski's Warsaw Free Army rank, "we'd better get a move on. I've got a feeling that that prick Adamczyk will be back with more men and then he won't be taking no for an answer. If we move on the barges tonight—"

"Tonight?" muttered Dabrowski. "But we're not ready."

"We've got to take them tonight, Major. Strike while the iron is hot. We've got to present the delegates with a fait accompli."

Fait accompli? wondered Trixie. Now that wasn't a phrase you often heard coming from the lips of a Polack sergeant. There was more to this Wysochi than met the eye.

"Taking those barges will be an act of war that even those cowards and renegades in the administration won't be able to apologize for. Anyway, if we wait Olbracht will alert his SS pals about what we've got planned: by tomorrow those barges will be so heavily guarded we'll need an army to take them."

Dabrowski shook his head. "We don't have enough men."

Wysochi looked over to the young second lieutenant who had been left at the inn when the delegates had scurried off. "You the officer here?" he demanded.

The tall, thin boy stepped forward. "I am, sir . . . er . . . Sergeant." He saluted. "I'm Second Lieutenant Gorski." The lieutenant was utterly unprepossessing. He looked about fifteen years old and was wearing an army greatcoat at least two sizes too big for him. The soldiers in his command were equally ragtag; they did not inspire confidence.

"How many men in your company, Gorski?" asked Wysochi.

"Twelve . . . no, fifteen."

"Are they armed and ready to fight?"

Gorski swallowed, his overlarge Adam's apple bobbing nervously. "Fight who . . . er, whom?"

"The ForthRight, of course! We are going to seize a pair of barges moored in the Berlin docks and confiscate the rifles they're carrying on behalf of the Warsaw Free Army."

The boy's eyes popped. "But my orders are—"

"Do as you're fucking well told!" barked Wysochi. "Major Dabrowski is the ranking officer here."

Dabrowski sighed. "It's no good, Sergeant, even with Gorski's men there are only seventeen of us and that isn't enough to take the barges. *And* we need a man who can operate a steam-barge. My idea was to sail the barges up the Rhine and unload them at the Gdańsk docks but without a barge captain we're stymied. Operating a steam-barge is a tricky business; it's not a job for amateurs."

"I can manage your steam-barge for you." The words were out of Trixie's mouth before she had even realized she was going to say them. Everyone in the room turned to look at her in stunned disbelief. "I worked for two months on a barge with my father last summer," she hurriedly explained. "That was when he was remodeling the traffic-flow system for the Rhine. I spent those months standing alongside the best bargemen in the ForthRight. I can work your steam-barge."

She felt Dabrowski's eyes boring into hers. "Are you certain, Miss Dashwood? Men's lives will turn on your skill. This is no place for schoolgirl bravado."

Trixie bristled. "Major Dabrowski, believe me, I hold my life precious. I would not say this if I had any doubts in my ability."

"It's an ebb tide," observed Sergeant Wysochi. He clearly knew that the ebb tide was the fiercest and the fastest—the one that challenged bargemen's skills to the utmost.

Trixie nodded. "It is also the tide which will get us to Gdańsk docks quickest." She looked from Major Dabrowski to Sergeant Wysochi and back again. "So . . . are we going to take these barges or just stand here all night discussing it?"

26

The Demi-Monde: 56th Day of Winter, 1004

There are six rivers in the Demi-Monde®. The five Spoke Rivers which rise in the central Hub lake—Mare Incognitum—flow Boundarywise and define the borders of the Sectors. These Spoke Rivers—the Thames, the Rhine, the Volga, the Yangtze and the Nile—each have an average current speed of 1 mph, though in the rainy season this can increase substantially. An ebb tide runs for 4 hours each night, when river currents reach a speed of 10 mph. The sixth river (the Wheel) is a Hub river which connects all five of the Spoke Rivers and defines the boundary of Terror Incognita.

—THE DEMI-MONDE® PRODUCT DESCRIPTION MANUAL, JUNE 14, 2013

Fate—ABBA—had granted Comrade Commissar Dashwood a reprieve.

The confusion and panic that enveloped the manor following the escape of the Daemon had been such that Beria seemed to have quite forgotten the order to arrest him. All the fat man had been intent on doing was bustling the Leader out of the house and moving him "somewhere safer" and he had done it so quickly that the baron hadn't had an opportunity to get a decent shot at him. Within fifteen minutes of the explosions rocking the house none of the members of the PolitBuro remained. Dashwood—a little bewildered by the turn of events—had found himself alone in the manor. No one was worried about the safety of a lowly commissar of transport.

But he knew his reprieve would be a temporary one, that once the furor had died down he would be purged. Sooner or later they would come for him. And by his estimation it would be sooner: Beria would probably arrest him at dawn tomorrow, which meant that he had only the rest of the night to prepare.

Yes . . . fate had given him a chance to fight Heydrich. For too long he had been docile. Now was the time to show that there were those in the ForthRight who were ready to fight the evil that was Heydrich's Party. Now was the time to rally the Royalists who had gone underground and lead them in defense of freedom.

As the last SS steamer puffed its way through the manor's broken gates, Dashwood strode up the staircase to his room, where he packed the field uniform he had worn as a colonel in the Royal Guards into a small knapsack. To this he added his Sam Browne belt and his Mauser revolver. He was ready.

There was a knock on the door and a moment later his butler, Crockett, appeared in the room. But rather than wearing his usual outfit of morning suit and spats, the butler now presented in a rather more functional getup comprising a tweed suit and a pair of heavy-duty hiking boots. It was the pistol he had thrust in his jacket pocket that Dashwood found most incongruous. He had never felt it necessary for his servants to be armed.

"I have taken the liberty of packing a few mementos, sir." Crockett indicated the suitcase he was carrying. "The miniatures of your wife and of Miss Trixiebell and suchlike."

"Why?"

"I believe that after tonight it will be difficult for us to return to the manor."

"*Us*, Crockett? I don't need a servant to accompany me; I'm just going away for a couple of days on business."

"My understanding is that this business will necessitate your going into hiding, sir, whilst you organize the Royalist resistance to the Party."

"How?"

"How did I know, sir? Because a good butler knows *everything* about his master; it is impossible to anticipate his requirements otherwise. I have also packed some sandwiches and a bottle of Solution; I have an inkling that it will be a long night. And, if I might be so bold, sir, I would recommend the Webley rather than the Mauser; it is in my opinion a much more effective firearm."

"Crockett, if we're captured they'll execute you."

"Then I will have to rely on your good offices, sir, to ensure that we are not captured."

"Are you sure you want to do this?"

"My family has served the Dashwoods for seven generations, sir; it is unthinkable that a Crockett would not be on hand to assist you in this, your greatest adventure. It is time, sir, to rid the Demi-Monde of these bastard UnFunDaMentalists."

"If you're determined."

"I am, sir. Shall I have Cassidy bring the steamer to the front of the house?"

"Cassidy? Is he coming too?"

A frown from Crockett. "Of course. You are a *baron*, after all, sir, and a man of your rank cannot be expected to *walk* to war. Simmons the gardener will accompany us as well; he is especially disgruntled regarding the mess the UnFunnies made of his front garden. Vandalism, he calls it. I have given him command of the rest of the male staff; they just await your word and then they will rendezvous with us at your convenience. I dissuaded the female staff from accompanying us, but only, I might add, with the greatest difficulty. Cook was especially obstreperous."

"But there might be a Checkya crypto amongst the staff." Dashwood had long suspected that Beria had a spy in his household.

"There *was*, sir, but I took the liberty of burying Chesterton under the rose bed. He will, in my opinion, contribute more to the Dashwood estate in the capacity of fertilizer than he ever did as a footman."

Dashwood nodded solemnly; it was obviously useless to argue. "Very well, Crockett, you'd better tell Cassidy to get the steamer fired up."

As he moved to the door, Dashwood wondered if Trixie was safe. He prayed that she was.

GRIM-FACED, TRIXIE DASHWOOD MARCHED TO WAR THROUGH THE docklands of Warsaw.

She marched to avenge her father, to punish the bastards who had killed him. By the Spirits, she would make them suffer. She would have her revenge. She would build her father a monument out of SS dead. And one day she would kill Heydrich.

That she swore.

"To the left, Major," she heard Wysochi call out, directing their little army.

She would stay close to Wysochi. He was a killer and she wanted to learn how to kill. She wanted to be the best killer of SS there had ever been. Instinctively she dropped her hand onto the butt of her Mauser pistol and checked her watch as they passed under one of the few gaslights still functioning in the Ghetto. She was shocked to see that it was only a couple of hours before dawn. "How far are we from the river?" she asked Wysochi.

"Just a couple of hundred yards." He obviously understood her concern. "Don't worry, we've got enough time. Once we get there we'll find a boatman and bribe him to take us across to Berlin."

"There'll be boatmen about at this time of night?" Trixie asked, dubious that anyone would be mad enough to still be working at four o'clock in the morning, especially on a bitterly cold night like this.

"Lots of them," the sergeant confirmed. "Quite a few comrades like to frequent some of the more accommodating establishments found in the Ghetto's red-light district. Polish women are famous for how friendly they are toward visitors from the ForthRight."

A few hours ago Trixie would have been shocked to her core by the thought that citizens of the ForthRight would despoil themselves by consorting with Polish whores. Not now. Now she knew the ForthRight for the rotten, stinking, hypocritical place it was. Now she knew that the Party leaders had feet of clay.

Bastards.

Wysochi saw the look on her face and misinterpreted it as one of disbelief. He laughed. "You will find, Miss Trixie, that a great many *Party* members like to while away a few hours sampling the flesh-pots of Warsaw. They seem to prefer Polish women to the more frosty UnFunny charms of ForthRightist ladies."

Trixie didn't have the energy to rise to the insult. She didn't care what Wysochi and these other Polish pigs thought of her; all that mattered was that they helped her kill SS.

A burst of cold wind circled her. Trixie pulled up the hood of her cloak and pushed herself forward through the snow. Although the streets leading to the Warsaw docks were made almost invisible by the blizzard, Trixie knew they were getting closer to the river. The smell that was wafting toward them from the Rhine was simply horrendous.

"That's the Gas House, they clean all the filters at night," Wysochi explained when he saw her wrinkle her nose. "The Warsaw Sector produces all the gas used in the Demi-Monde. Not terribly glamorous and not terribly lucrative but without us Poles everybody in the ForthRight would be walking around in the dark."

It might be worth it, thought Trixie, wishing she'd brought her pomander with her; the smell was so bad it made her stomach heave.

Wysochi was as good as his word: it took him only five minutes to find a boatman willing to take the "gentlemen revelers" across the Rhine to Berlin. The eighteen of them boarded the Whitehall Gig and after a whispered plea from the boatman for them to "keep their fucking noise down" they were off. Despite the blinding snow, the boatman seemed to have an unerring sense of where he was—probably, decided Trixie, he just knew to keep the smell of the Gas House at his back—and was able to guide his four oarsmen to a quay a few hundred yards upriver from the Oberbaum Bridge. Even as the boatman struggled to moor the boat against the surging ebb tide, Major Dabrowski jumped ashore and led his company cautiously up the snow-slick steps leading to the dockside.

The attack had begun.

UNFORTUNATELY THE INTELLIGENCE PROVIDED BY TRIXIE'S FATHER was wrong. His file had advised Dabrowski that the munitions would be carried on two barges: a Crowley-class steam-propelled barge towing a Beria-class unpowered drifter barge. What they saw when they had pushed their way through the snowstorm to the quayside were *three* barges; there was a second drifter barge on tow. Trixie's heart sank; whilst she was confident—well, fairly confident—of being able to manage two barges in an ebb tide, three was a different proposition altogether. Only the most proficient of Rhine watermen were capable of running a trio of barges, and then only if the ruddermen managing the drifters were able men who knew their business.

The Rhine was too unforgiving a river for beginners like Trixie.

"It's a trio, Major," Trixie whispered. "I don't know if I can handle a trio."

Dabrowski shot her a look. "What can we do? We've come too far to go back."

"Decouple the third barge. Cut it loose."

"But the rifles . . ."

Fear and rising panic made Trixie's reply sharper than she intended. "Damn it all, Major, do as I tell you or we might lose the whole cargo."

Dabrowski didn't have time to answer. Sergeant Wysochi and two other men, knives in hand, were already up and over the side of the steam-barge, hunting for sentries. Trixie heard the sound of a scuffle, a strangled scream and then a splash as, presumably, a body was heaved overboard. A few seconds later the sergeant reappeared, a savage grin decorating his face. The man was an animal, an animal who was good at killing SS. "Secure, Major," he said sotto voce.

"Right, Gorski," Dabrowski snarled at the young second lieutenant, "get your men on board, half on each of the first two barges arranged along the port side. I want them ready to repel boarders. Things are going to get hot." He turned to Wysochi. "Sergeant, secure Miss Dashwood in the wheelhouse and then get two men into the boiler room and fire it up."

"It's already fired up," commented Wysochi, pointing toward the wisps of smoke coming from the funnel. Dabrowski blushed, embarrassed by his ignorance.

"Shall I cast off, Major?" Gorski asked, barely able to keep the tremble of excitement out of his voice.

Trixie stiffened. The most important lesson she had learned during her time on the Rhine was that on board a steam-barge there could be only one master. More than one person giving orders was a recipe for disaster.

"I give orders on this barge, Major," she snapped. "Whilst on board you will do what I tell you to do, when I tell you to do it. Do you understand?"

Dabrowski looked as though he had been slapped. "How dare—"

"I dare because I am responsible for the management of these barges."

"I will not take orders from a woman."

For Trixie it was an epiphany. That sneering comment from Dabrowski brought home to her that her future—her destiny—was now wholly her responsibility. Her fate was in her hands. The ForthRight had destroyed her old life so now she wasn't obliged to follow its creeds and its social etiquette. To survive in this new, hostile world she would have to be her own woman: strong and independent. Her father had always said that intellectually she was the match of any man, now she had to prove that she had a will to match any man's.

"If my being a woman upsets you then I suggest that you stay ashore or find another to work these barges."

The ultimatum had its effect: Dabrowski took a deep, deep breath and then gave a curt nod. "So be it. But believe me, Miss Dashwood, I will not forget this slight."

Trixie brushed off his threat with a negligent wave of her hand. "It's best if we let the barges drift out into midstream before we get under way, that way we'll have more room to maneuver. Major, have your men free the mooring ropes and cast off the three barges, and you, Lieutenant, find an axe and have somebody cut the hawser tethering us to the second drifter." Orders given, she followed Dabrowski on board the steam-barge. Now there was no going back.

Despite this outward show of confidence, her inexperience nearly did them in. Although Dabrowski managed to free the hawsers tethering the barges to the dock, in her excitement Trixie had forgotten that there was always a security line connecting the steam-barge to an alarm bell. As the unshackled barges, caught by the pull of the tide, began to slide ponderously away from the dock, so the security line tightened until, when they had gone less than twenty feet, the alarm bell began to toll. The response was immediate: lanterns were illuminated, orders were shouted, the sound of hobnailed boots echoed along the quay and then out of the snow-thick darkness raced a detachment of Checkya militia.

"Fire, you useless fuckers," screamed Sergeant Wysochi. A tattered salvo of rifle fire crackled along the barge. It was difficult for Trixie from her position in the wheelhouse to see through the swirling snow how effective the fusillade was, but the screams suggested some of the shots had found their mark.

There was some desultory return fire from the Checkya and a bullet smacked into the side of the wheelhouse, making her flinch away as splinters flew. Instinctively she crouched down, trying to make herself as small a target as possible, then, cursing herself for being such a coward, she stood back up straight. This was no time for cowards. A soot-blackened face appeared around the doorjamb. "Steam's up, miss," the boy yelled, and gave her a thumbs-up. Immediately she hauled back on the drive lever. There was a bellow from behind as the engine powered up and the steam-barge began to shudder and shake as the pistons pounded. The deck beneath her feet trembled. She felt the jerk as the propeller of the steam-barge was engaged and then a shove in the back as the craft began to move under its own power. The noise in the wheelhouse was deafening; she could barely hear herself think.

"You, soldier, get forward to the bow," she screamed at the top of her voice. She saw the look of incomprehension on his face. "Get to the front of the barge and shout when you see the Oberbaum Bridge. I can't see a thing in this snow. You've got to help me aim for the central span." The boy disappeared into the snow.

Maneuvering the heavy barges was a nightmare. Heaving and straining, Trixie had to use all her strength to manage the wheel as the barges, caught by the current, bucked and squirmed along the river. Her muscles ached from the struggle to keep them straight.

Two more bullets smacked into the wheelhouse, but Trixie was so intent on hauling on the wheel, sawing it desperately back and forth, trying to bring the drifters in line directly astern, that she hardly noticed. A wild-eyed Wysochi joined her. "Help me," she gasped. "I need to bring this barge around."

It was only thanks to Wysochi's enormous strength that they managed to wrestle the barges into line. It wasn't a moment too soon. There was a shout from the bow. "I can see the bridge, maybe a hundred—"

The sentence was terminated by the crack of a rifle and a splash as the man toppled over into the river. "Get forward, Sergeant!" Trixie shouted. "I need you at the bow, directing me."

Wysochi hesitated for a moment and then was gone. Without his strength to help her, controlling the barge was almost impossible. She could feel the wheel twisting and squirming ever more violently under her hands as the barges came closer and closer to the eddies that rippled so powerfully around the piers of the bridge. The stern of the steam-barge began to pull out of line, dragged by the drifters as they were caught in the current. Frantically Trixie signaled for more power, doing everything she could to compensate for the yawing of the drifters, terrified that the barges would run out of control, that they would meet the bridge beam-on, that the drifters would be trapped lengthways against the bridge by the ebb tide.

Lieutenant Gorski's head appeared around the door.

"What about the second drifter?" she shouted over the pummeling of the steam engine as it struggled to provide the extra power she demanded. "Have you cut it loose yet?"

"Major Dabrowski is still trying to cut the hawser. The Checkya are making it hot for him. He's lost two men already."

"Get rid of the fucking thing," Trixie screamed, aghast that a girl of her breeding should swear in such a foul manner, then ducked down as a salvo of shots smashed into the barge. Whoever was in charge of the Checkya had obviously worked out that she was intent on taking the barges upstream and that to do so she would have to sail them under the Oberbaum Bridge. The steam-barge was now so close to the bridge that she could see the muzzle flashes from the rifles of the Checkya who had already positioned themselves on the bridge and were firing down on the barges.

"Get under cover," she heard Wysochi yell at his men as he emptied his revolver at the bridge that was now looming over them through the darkness and the snow.

Two pillars of the bridge passed on either side of the steam-barge's bow. Now the turbulence was stronger and it took all of Trixie's strength and all the engine's power to bully the steam-barge, banging and scraping, under the bridge. Then, like a cork popping out of a bottle, the steam-barge was in open water, but her elation was short-lived. Although, miraculously, the first drifter got under the bridge without fouling or capsizing, the second drifter didn't. It twisted, beam-on, jamming itself immovably along the length of the bridge, between the two central spans. Now, no matter how hard Trixie forced the propeller, no matter how urgently she sawed at the wheel, the trio of barges was stuck fast, anchored by the third, the soldiers on board sitting ducks for the shots raining down from the bridge above. The only option Dabrowski's men had was to cower away under the bridge itself and in consequence the Checkya concentrated their fire on the steam-barge's wheelhouse. It was fortunate for Trixie that she had a steel roof over her head, otherwise she would have been killed for certain. As she struggled and strained, twisting the wheel this way and that, furiously trying to edge the barges free, breathing prayers to the Spirits that they would come to her aid, there was an incessant banging and slapping of bullets above her head.

Fate intervened. The commander of the Checkya on the bridge

had the bright idea of throwing grenades down on the barges and their first target was the trapped drifter. As luck would have it, the third grenade blew the hawser that connected the two drifters apart. Freed of the trapped drifter, Trixie felt the steam-barge leap forward, powering away from the bridge, dragging the remaining drifter with it.

Then the second drifter exploded.

THE BLAST WAS ENORMOUS. IT WAS AS THOUGH THE STEAM-BARGE was lifted into the air by a huge hand and then hurled back down onto the river. Trixie was thrown across the wheelhouse, her head smashing against a bulkhead, bashing her into unconsciousness. She came to, her head throbbing, excruciating pain lancing across her left shoulder and her ears ringing from the crash of the explosion. With labored difficulty she hauled herself back up onto her feet. All the glass in the wheelhouse windows had been blown in and now the thick snow and the ice-cold wind were swirling around, slashing into her face and eyes. The steam-barge seemed to be alight; burning debris and cinders from the destroyed drifter covered the decking and this, coupled with the black smoke that enveloped the river, made for a Helish scene. The stench of cordite in the air was suffocating, and she retched, spitting dust and bile from her mouth.

Fortunately the compass had survived the explosion. She tore a strip of cotton from her blouse, used it to wipe the glass clean, and checked her heading. Satisfied that she now knew where they should be going, ignoring the pain in her shoulder, she hauled on the wheel and dragged the barge back to a northerly direction.

As the steam-barge settled on its course, Trixie took a quick look around. At first she thought that she was the only survivor, but then, slowly, painfully, figures began to rise up and after brushing burning cinders from their coats, staggered about as though drunk.

Thankfully Wysochi was one of the survivors, though he had suffered in the explosion. His cap was gone and part of his hair seemed to have been burned away; his face was soot-black and flecked with a myriad of tiny cuts and scratches. Peculiarly, it also appeared that he was steaming: as snow landed on his savaged jacket it dissolved into white steam.

"Are you hurt?" he shouted, and that was when Trixie discovered she was deaf in one ear. She touched it with her fingers; part of her right ear seemed to have been sheared away.

"I've hurt my shoulder, but nothing too serious," she shouted back; a ruined ear hardly seemed to be worth commenting on. She barely recognized her voice; torn ragged by all the screaming she had been doing, it seemed to have dropped an octave. "But don't worry I'll still be able to get us to Gdańsk."

Wysochi gave a curt nod and then disappeared into the darkness. He returned a minute or so later. "Better than I feared, worse than I hoped. Ten survivors. Some are a bit knocked around but they'll live."

"Major Dabrowski?"

"Took a bad knock on the head from a piece of flying spar. He'll make it all right." He staggered as the steam-barge bucked against the tide. "By my reckoning, Gdańsk docks are over there, maybe a half-mile distant. You've got us there. Well done, Miss Trixie . . . and thanks."

Trixie had to admire Wysochi's energy. Despite his wounds, despite the rough bandage that swathed his left hand, despite the savage burns on the side of his face, he still drove the men on. No sooner had they docked the barges than he was all business, dividing what was left of the little army into two groups, braying orders at them to round up men and steamer-trucks and to get them back to the barges as quickly as possible. He wanted the barges unloaded before dawn.

In stark contrast to Wysochi's energy, Dabrowski sat slumped against the side of the barge. The bang he'd taken to the head had been a bad one and he was only semiconscious, not quite understanding what was going on around him.

"I need someone to rouse Dock Captain Kowal," Wysochi said to his major. "I need someone to get the winches and cranes working."

Dabrowski slowly raised his head and stared at the sergeant through glassy eyes. As best Trixie could judge, his mind was concussed and he would be no further help that night.

"I'll go. Let the major rest," she said, and before the sergeant could object she was off striding in the direction of the dock captain's house a hundred yards along the quay from where they had moored the steam-barge. The house was in darkness when she got there, but it didn't remain so for long, not after Trixie pummeled on the front door with the butt of her pistol.

When the dock captain finally opened his front door, he seemed less than impressed by the soot-covered apparition disturbing his sleep. Dressed in just his nightshirt, Dock Captain Kowal studied Trixie as she stood in the doorway, lantern in hand.

"Who the Hel are you?"

"I am . . ."

Trixie paused for a moment, trying to decide just *who* she really was.

" . . . *Lieutenant* Dashwood of the Warsaw Free Army. We have captured two barges from the ForthRight and need you to round up every docker, yard worker and winch operator you can and assemble them to offload the barges now tethered at Number Two Dock."

"Fuck off," he said, and made to shut the door. Trixie's boot prevented it from closing. She would, she decided, have to be firm with him.

"It is imperative that—"

"I said fuck off and I meant fuck off. I'm head of the Guild of Bargees and in that capacity I must tell you that, as we are not at war with the ForthRight, taking those barges by force is an act of piracy. I will not permit my members to risk imprisonment or their lives."

His oration was interrupted by the cocking of a Mauser pistol. Trixie held the weapon to the side of the man's head. "Unless you follow my orders, Dock Captain, I will have no hesitation to blow your fucking mind out."

Kowal looked at Trixie, took a moment to assess just how serious she was and then nodded.

The unloading of ten thousand Martini-Henry rifles and five million rounds of ammunition and the transporting of the same to a secure warehouse was completed an hour after dawn. Exhausted and emotionally drained, the men slumped down and gratefully accepted the bottles of Solution that were handed around.

For her part Trixie sat on a crate of ammunition, trying to ignore the pain radiating out from her left shoulder and the throbbing of her ear, and doing her best not to fall asleep. Never had she felt so tired, so completely wrung out. She closed her eyes for a moment and when she opened them she found the bulk of Sergeant Wysochi standing in front of her with his hand extended.

"Would you do me the honor, Miss Dashwood, of shaking my hand? I would like to thank you for what you did tonight, to thank you on behalf of my major, my men and the Polish people. You are the bravest person with whom I have ever had the honor of serving. If he were alive to see you, Miss Dashwood, your father would be a very proud man."

Trixie took the hand. It was the most moving moment of her life.

27

The Demi-Monde:
56th to 58th Days
of Winter, 1004

The principles of Eugenics may be applied not only to matters of racial management but also to the interpretation as to why certain city-states within the Demi-Monde are more successful than others. This form of macroEugenics has been named "Political Eugenics" (Reinhard Heydrich, Race, Eugenics and the Survival of the Fittest City-States, Party Rules Publications). Using the principles enunciated by the Quartier Chaudian naturalist Jean-Baptiste Lamarck—that all organisms strive toward perfection and that this struggle is stimulated by competition within the bio-system—and applying them in the political arena, the Great Leader has concluded that the success of the ForthRight is a demonstration of the maxim "the survival of the fittest" writ large. In sum the Demi-Monde is a battlefield wherein the races fight for supremacy and it is the ForthRight—and the Aryan people—that has emerged supreme.

—THE PRINCIPLES OF UNFUNDAMENTALISM,

HIS HOLINESS ALEISTER CROWLEY,

MINISTRY OF PSYCHIC AFFAIRS PUBLICATIONS

Trixie couldn't sleep. She was too excited to sleep. Too much had happened, too much was going to happen. Her mind was a whirl of plans and possibilities as she reveled in the thrill of revolution. And, after last night, she *was* a real revolutionary.

According to Heydrich, revolutions were a natural manifestation of the frustrated will of the People. But as Trixie sat sipping her coffee she was determined that it would not be *her* will that was frustrated. She might have been bone-tired, her arm and her ear might have been aching like the very devil and her body might have been covered in bruises, but this wasn't a time to rest. Revolution, as she was discovering, was hard work.

There was the sound of boots clumping across the warehouse and she looked up to see Lieutenant Gorski marching toward her. From the expression on his face he seemed to be even more frightened and confused than ever.

"They've taken the major," he gasped.

"Calm down, Gorski," snapped Trixie. "Who's taken the major?"

"Lieutenant Adamczyk came to the inn where the major was resting ten minutes ago. He had orders from Chief Delegate Olbracht to arrest the major for treason and crimes against the Forth-Right."

"What about the Daemon—Miss Williams—did Adamczyk take her as well?"

Gorski shook his head. "No, that long-haired bloke nipped out of the back door with the Daemon and the Shade before Adamczyk had a chance to nab 'em."

Trixie nodded. She might have guessed that Vanka Maykov

would be too fly to be captured; he had the look of a man who was light on his feet. By now he would have Norma Williams and the Shade hidden away somewhere waiting to see how things panned out.

"Well, Lieutenant Gorski, you'd better get your men on their feet. We've got work to do." She looked at the bodies of the soldiers sleeping on the ground around her, spotted the snoring Wysochi and woke him with a prod of her boot. "Time to get up, Sergeant, time to get revolting."

Wysochi blinked his eyes open and then checked his watch. "Fuck off. It's only eight o'clock. I've only been asleep for an hour." With that he rolled away from Trixie and pulled his *dublonka* over his head.

Trixie kicked him again. "Major Dabrowski has been arrested. Young Gorski here's seen Adamczyk take him away."

"Taken him where?"

"Over to the city hall," spluttered Gorski. "Chief Delegate Ol-bracht's spitting teeth about the raid last night. He's talking of ex-ecuting the major for treason. He wants to put him in front of a firing squad."

The mention of a firing squad at least persuaded a sour-faced Wysochi to sit up and stretch.

Gorski gabbled on. "A message has been received from the Leader himself saying that the ForthRight views the raid on the barges as an act of treason. But the message also says that if we give up the weap-ons and the Daemon, then the city of Warsaw will be pardoned. Only those directly involved with the taking of the barges will be arrested . . ." He trailed off, obviously realizing for the first time that as he had taken part in the raid on the barges then he would be one of those destined to be put up against a wall and shot.

"Should I take my men to go over and free the major?" asked Wysochi as he lumbered to his feet.

"No. Let's take an army." And with a nonchalant wave Trixie signaled to the crowds of people packed into the warehouse.

Wysochi looked where she was pointing: there, sitting on crates, standing around chatting or just generally idling away time, were crowds and crowds of people. "Who the fuck are all these people?"

"Volunteers," said Trixie. "Word of what happened last night has got around. They've come to volunteer to fight the ForthRight."

"So many."

"There are over a thousand kids here."

Kids like me.

"Most of them are useless but they're willing."

"What are they waiting for?"

"Rifles . . . orders . . . and for you and your men to get up off your arses and help organize them."

"But what about Olbracht?" asked Gorski. "He's ordered that the rifles be surrendered."

Trixie laughed. "Fuck Olbracht"—*By ABBA, being a revolutionary is having a terrible effect on my language*—"we're revolutionaries, Lieutenant, and we're dead even if we give up the rifles. And as revolutionaries we take orders from nobody."

In fact, as both Gorski and Wysochi quickly found out, revolutionaries did take orders, but only those issued by Trixie Dashwood. She knew exactly what had to be done and had no hesitation in telling people how to do it. They spent the morning dealing with the seemingly never-ending line of young men and women—that there were so many women amongst them came as a pleasant surprise to Trixie—volunteering to fight for Warsaw. Each of them had to be assessed and issued with a white armband on which were scrawled the letters "WFA"—the initials of the Warsaw Free Army—then they were divided into pairs, each pair issued with a Martini-Henry rifle and one hundred rounds of ammunition. This done, the volunteers were clustered into groups of twenty to be shown how to load and fire the rifles.

When Wysochi inquired why only one rifle was being issued per two volunteers her answer had surprised even him with its callous pragmatism. "We don't have enough rifles to go around, Sergeant; remember we've still got to arm the WFA. So for now one of the pair will have the use of the rifle during the day and the other will have it during the night. Anyway," she added quietly, "a week after the first SS attack only half of the buggers will still be alive. Then they'll have a rifle each."

Trixie relished the bureaucracy of revolution and as the hours ticked by, the mob of overexcited, ill-disciplined volunteers was gradually formed into something approximating to an army. But the one thing that Trixie hadn't anticipated was how the news of *her* involvement in the Battle of Oberbaum Bridge had spread. On numerous occasions volunteers came up to her and thanked her for what she had done for the people of Warsaw, insisted on shaking her hand, inquired if she would be leading a regiment, asked if they could have the honor of serving under her command . . .

It had been heady stuff and perhaps if she hadn't had the stoic presence of Sergeant Wysochi at her side, it might have embarrassed her. Wysochi, though, encouraged this hero worship. "It's important, Miss Dashwood, for soldiers to have a hero. They see you, a girl, a noncombatant, fighting and beating the best the ForthRight can throw at us and they begin to believe."

"Believe what, Sergeant?"

"That all this might not be as utterly bloody hopeless as I think it is."

"IT'S NOON, SERGEANT," SAID TRIXIE QUIETLY. "TIME, I THINK, TO march to rescue the major. Now that we've got an army we've got to make sure that those bastard delegates don't do something silly."

It took a while for Wysochi to cajole the volunteers into ranks but finally, after an hour of screaming, swearing, shoving and kicking, he pronounced himself happy. At a shouted command of "Advance" from Trixie the ragtag army lurched forward. The Uprising had begun.

It was an amazing sensation for Trixie to be marching at the head of her amateur army through the streets of Warsaw.

My army. Ridiculous.

Only a day ago she had been a seventeen-year-old schoolgirl and today she was in command of an army of revolution. "Command"; now that was a word that gave her pause. Since the time she had taken command of the barge no one had once questioned her authority, no one had once protested that they weren't prepared to take orders from a woman. She had assumed command and everyone had assumed her right to do just that. Certainly, she had the formidable Wysochi as her shadow, but it was still remarkable that men and women should so readily do as she told them. Maybe she had a talent for war; after all she loved leading, she loved giving orders and loved taking responsibility.

And now she was finding that she loved adulation.

It was a fine sunny Winter's day and as they marched, the people of Warsaw came out to watch and cheer them along. Somewhere along the line the volunteers had found a drum and an accordion so now as they marched they sang and the people lining the streets joined in with gusto. Soon the avenues of Warsaw echoed with the words of patriotic songs and the crash of boots on cobbles. Before Trixie had led her army half a mile the march had turned into a parade, into a celebration. Children began to dance along beside the marching fighters, old men stepped out of the crowd to shake Trixie's hand, flowers were thrown . . .

The singing stopped when they wheeled into Pilsudski Square.

There, facing them, was a long line of resolute-looking, green-coated infantry. The six delegates stood immediately in front of the soldiers with Major Dabrowski, head heavily bandaged, guarded by two more soldiers, a little to the side. Trixie raised her arm and behind her, her army came to a stuttering halt. Immediately a deathly hush fell across the square.

Trixie swallowed hard and brought her fluttering heart under control. This wasn't a time to falter; this was a time to be resolute. "Bring the Warsaw Free Army into line, Sergeant," she ordered in a loud voice, clearly audible to her army, "and then let's go and hear what these traitorous bastards have to say for themselves."

Together she and Wysochi walked across the cobbled square, with only the snap of their boot heels on the stones invading the heavy silence. In truth she felt a little awkward, as though she, little Trixie Dashwood, had no right to be performing as a leading actor in this revolutionary pantomime. But the look on the face of Chief Delegate Olbracht told her that he, at least, took her very seriously indeed.

"It's Lady Dashwood, is it not?"

"It is."

"You are aware, my Lady, that it is an act of sedition to parade within the ForthRight carrying unlicensed weapons."

Keep it simple, Trixie, but keep it decisive. Make sure the crowd can hear. Make sure the crowd can understand.

"I do not recognize the jurisdiction of the ForthRight within the territory of Warsaw."

Chief Delegate Olbracht gave a snort of derision. "Who the Hel are you to decide what is or is not recognized by Warsaw?"

Trixie laughed and waved her good arm behind her, indicating her makeshift army. "I have a thousand reasons giving me that right. I have a thousand fighters at my back and all of them are proud, free Varsovians. I am acting commander of the Warsaw Free Army."

"Ridiculous. You're just a girl. How can a girl be commander of an army?" laughed Olbracht. "You have no rank. You are not authorized to speak before the Administrative Committee."

"I have assumed command in the absence of Major Dabrowski"— she nodded toward the major—"who, I understand, is being held under arrest by Enemies of the People."

If this revolutionary cant is good enough for Heydrich, it's good enough for me.

"You can't do that."

"The Hel I can't." Trixie raised her voice so that it carried throughout the square. "I fought with some brave men last night to arm the Warsaw Free Army. I watched some of those brave men die to capture the rifles that will prevent that swine Heydrich butchering the people of Warsaw. Their deaths give me the right to speak."

Olbracht shook his head. "Then answer me this: why would you fight for us Varsovians? You're not even a Pole."

There was a murmur through the ranks of Trixie's army; her Russian was so good that obviously a lot of them hadn't realized that Trixie was an Anglo.

"I stand here ready to fight for Warsaw because this is not a fight between the Varsovians and the ForthRight; this is a fight between all free Demi-Mondians and the forces of evil. This is a war of survival, a war where all those who have the temerity to be different from Anglo-Slavs—from Aryans—be they Poles or nuJus or Chinks, must stand and fight or be swept away."

Trixie could hardly believe she was saying this. For her to be actually standing up for the UnderMentionables was simply astonishing.

By ABBA, I have changed.

"I have heard from Heydrich's own mouth the plans he has for the non-Aryan races of the Demi-Monde and those plans will lead to the annihilation of the Polish people. I have heard from Heydrich's own mouth that the Final Solution will mean the death of every Pole, every nuJu and every man, woman and child living in the Ghetto." Trixie raised her voice until she was almost shouting. "I tell you straight, today we must make a decision. Today we must decide whether we fight together or we die together." She was rewarded with cheers from the ranks of the WFA fighters.

The chief delegate stepped forward and, raising his voice above the hubbub of the crowd, addressed the thousands of volunteers standing in the square. "The Administrative Committee of Warsaw has received a communication from the Great Leader: if we will surrender the Daemon known as Norma Williams and the weapons stolen yesterday then the Party will only punish those directly involved with the abduction of the Daemon and those who committed the act of piracy. You are ordered by your legally appointed administration to lay down your weapons." Not one of the WFA fighters moved but the ripple of unease amongst their ranks was palpable. "A handful of lives to save millions!" shouted Olbracht.

"You trust Heydrich?" retorted Trixie, and immediately cursed herself. This wasn't some debating society. This wasn't a time for discussion. Debate and discussion implied doubt, and a revolutionary couldn't afford doubt. Doubt implied weakness and a lack of will.

The chief delegate leapt at the chance given him by Trixie. "We *must* trust Comrade Leader Heydrich!" Olbracht shouted. "Our Leader is a man of honor. He has generously offered us a way of settling this nonsense so that the people of Warsaw are not punished for this girl's recklessness." He turned to Dabrowski. "Major Dabrowski, you are the real commander of the Warsaw Free Army, and as an officer and a gentleman you are duty-bound to put the welfare and the well-being of the people before your own interests. I am ordering you, as the chief delegate of the Administration Committee of Warsaw, to instruct these people to lay down their weapons, to disband this ridiculous Free Army and to surrender the miscreants and the Daemon to the custody of the Checkya."

Every eye in the square turned toward Dabrowski, who flinched back as though physically struck. He looked awful: pale and weak, he had to lean on a stick to stay upright.

Dabrowski seemed to crumble into uncertainty. He looked a different man from the rakish and confident soldier Trixie had known only a day or so ago. Could it be, she wondered, that the injuries he had suffered in the raid on the barges had broken him both physically and mentally? Maybe he was ill? Maybe all his training, all his conditioning as an officer to obey orders given by a superior, was confusing him?

At Dabrowski's silence, the chief delegate smiled an obnoxious little smile. "I think that is all the answer we need."

Around her Trixie felt the volunteers begin to shuffle and to murmur. She was aghast at how a crowd could be so easily manipulated, how easily an army that only a few moments ago had been full of patriotic ardor could be cowed by bluster and braggadocio. She could not—would not—stand by and watch this foul man take control of the situation.

A determined set to her mouth, Trixie turned toward her army and addressed them directly. "The Warsaw Free Army is not prepared to surrender." She paused, unnerved by how the large crowd was listening so attentively. "Yesterday my father was murdered, laying down his life for mine. Today, it is my turn to make a stand for those who have the audacity to be different from the Aryan ideal of Heydrich. I am not a soldier, but I will fight. I am not a man, but I will fight. I am not a Varsovian, but I will fight." She paused for a moment to calm the tremor of emotion that had infected her voice. "And if none choose to follow me . . . then, as ABBA is my witness, I will fight alone."

The square was totally hushed, those gathered in it silenced by their uncertainty.

Trixie was aware of movement to her left as Sergeant Wysochi came to stand next to her. "While I breathe," he announced in a stentorian voice that echoed around the square, "I swear by ABBA that you will never stand alone." He stabbed his fist into the air. "Better to die on our feet than live on our knees!"

Even as the last word left his lips, the Warsaw Free Army erupted in a storm of cheering.

"WHAT DID YOU MAKE OF THAT?" ASKED ELLA AS SHE SAT BY THE window of her hotel room looking down at the scene unfolding in the square below her.

"They're all mad," was Vanka's conclusion.

"They seem determined enough and that Trixiebell Dashwood has been a revelation. I never took her for a revolutionary."

"War does strange things to people and it's often the unlikeliest of individuals who prove themselves the most capable." He sighed and pulled the curtain back over the window. "Trixie Dashwood is a natural leader but that's not enough. The Poles haven't got a prayer."

"Why? There's an awful lot of them."

As he patted the room's scabrous couch—raising a cloud of dust as he did so—and sat down, Vanka shook his head. "I don't think the Poles realize what's coming at them. Clement's SS are the best, the most ruthless and the most formidably equipped troops in the whole of the Demi-Monde. It's going to take more than some stirring words, a mob of ill-armed irregulars and a few jerry-built barricades to keep them out. The SS will crush them before the end of the week."

"They've got weapons now."

"They've got a few out-of-date rifles. The SS have got superior weaponry, they've got discipline, and they've got armored steamers and artillery. This rabble hasn't a prayer."

"I understand that in street-fighting the advantage is always with the defenders."

Vanka shrugged and took a moment to light a cigarette. "We'll see. If they're brave enough and they've got enough of these firebombs

I hear their womenfolk have been cooking up, then they could give the SS a headache, but the key problem the Varsovians have is that there is no way for them to win. They can't defeat the SS. They can't defeat the ForthRight. And if you can't win, the only alternative is to lose."

Ella nodded toward the crudely painted banner that was being paraded around the square by a band of dancing WFA fighters. It read OUR VICTORY IS NEVER TO SURRENDER. "They seem to think that they can fight the SS to a standstill."

"Humbug," snorted Vanka. "Heydrich will never allow himself to be defeated by a bunch of street fighters; he'll put as many troops into the Ghetto as is necessary to get the job done. That's the problem with people like Trixie Dashwood; she's a romantic. That escapade with the barges has gone to her head: she's stopped thinking about the consequences of what she's doing. Romantics are the most dangerous of all soldiers; they're the ones who want to die."

"But, as Sergeant Wysochi said, maybe it *is* better to die on your feet than to live on your knees."

"Heroic tosh," snapped Vanka. "Once you're dead you have no chance of victory. Better to be a live coward than a dead hero."

"That's a very cynical attitude, Vanka."

"Pragmatic rather than cynical, I think. And believe me, Ella, I have absolutely no intention of dying. I think it a better philosophy to let other people do the dying for me. Anyway, these kids seem so enthusiastic to journey to the Spirit World that it would be churlish to deny them my place in the queue." He took a thoughtful puff on his cigarette. "No, our objective is to stay comfortably hidden away here for the time being, to keep out of that bastard Olbracht's way—he's too loyal to the Party for my liking—and wait until they forget what a good idea it would be to give up your pal Miss Norma Williams to Heydrich. Then when the time is right we'll make a run for it. Maybe we'll head for the Coven and board a barge to take you and

Little Miss Misery"—he nodded toward the adjoining room where Norma was sleeping—"to NoirVille. Once we're there you can pay me the million guineas you promised me."

"And then?" prompted Ella, somewhat hurt by the rather mercenary way Vanka was discussing their escaping to NoirVille. She had hoped he might be motivated to help her by something other than money. She had come to think—to hope—that Vanka Maykov might actually have some feelings for her.

"And then you go back to your world and I'll have a good time spending my million in this one."

Apparently not. Maybe now she was seeing his true side; the man was, after all, a con man. A con man who obviously didn't like the idea of having a Daemon as a lover.

She just wished she didn't care for him so much.

BARELY ABLE TO HIDE A SMILE OF SMUG SATISFACTION, ARCHIE CLEMent scanned the map of the Ghetto one more time and checked his watch. It was five minutes to noon; the Leader had ordered him to begin his assault on the Ghetto by midday on the 59th day of Winter and by dint of a Herculean effort the destruction of Warsaw would begin one full day ahead of schedule. He had been set an impossible task but he had done it. Today the Ghetto would be punished for Dabrowski's abduction of the Daemon and his taking of the barges.

"You got all them steamers fired up, Comrade Major Hartley?" he asked the officer beside him. "Won't do for them to miss the big parade, now, will it?"

"We have four steamers in position to lead the assault along Uyazhdov Boulevard, Comrade Colonel."

"Only four?" Clement turned and spat out a wad of tobacco,

which missed the major's brightly shined boots only by inches. "Just *four* steamers ain't gonna get them Rebs fouling their breeches, now, is it?"

"Unfortunately, Comrade Colonel, such was the speed of the mobilization that we had no time to bring up more. But even so, we anticipate only limited opposition. We will conduct an artillery barrage to eliminate the barricades the rebels have thrown up across the avenue then deploy our very finest shock troops."

"Don't do to count your chickens, Hartley. Them damned Polacks showed a lotta grit during the Troubles, so don't you go thinking they're gonna skedaddle just cos we fart in their direction. And make certain sure you've told your commanders that them Rebs is heeled. There was ten thousand rifles on them barges they hijacked."

Now *that* had come as a surprise. According to Beria's assessment, Dabrowski was the archetypal staff officer: a man built for thinking rather than action. That, after all, was why they had selected him. But the attack on the barges had demonstrated an unexpected determination and ruthlessness. Perhaps he would make a more resolute and effective commander of the WFA than they had anticipated.

"With all due respect, Comrade Colonel, they were only Martini-Henrys, obsolete models that are no match for the M4s our own men carry." The major gave his commander a reassuring smile. "I am confident that we will sweep this rabble before us. By nightfall we will be in the Old Town and have control of the Warsaw Blood Bank, and once we have achieved that objective it is only a matter of time before Warsaw surrenders."

Clement nodded. What the major said made perfect sense, but somehow Clement couldn't shake off a nagging feeling of foreboding. Taking Warsaw might, he decided, be a little more difficult than his major believed.

You could never trust a fucking Reb.

―⚒―

Major Dabrowski...

Trixie stopped herself, remembering that now, as official commander of the Warsaw Free Army, Dabrowski was *Colonel* Dabrowski. And Colonel Dabrowski, Trixie decided, was a jealous man.

There was no other explanation for his shoddy treatment of her during the first meeting of the WFA Emergency Executive. He had barely been able to be courteous, never mind thank her for saving him from Olbracht. During the meeting he had strenuously refused to acknowledge her role in the taking of the barges, in the arming of the WFA, in the overthrowing of the delegates or in his elevation to head of the Emergency Executive. All he had seemed intent on doing was stripping her of any role or influence she might have in the WFA.

Indeed, his first act—browbeaten into it, Trixie had to admit, by the regular army officers—was to decree that women could only hold noncombatant positions in the WFA. For Trixie it had been a slap in the face which, almost a day later, she was still fuming about. There seemed little point in having a revolution if all the old prejudices and hatreds remained intact.

Trixie felt a tug on her sleeve. Turning, she found Sergeant Wysochi holding a large enameled mug of soup out toward her. "Drink this," he said with a smile. "It's going to be a long hard day and I don't think Clement will be inclined to allow us a pause in the fighting to take luncheon." Trixie nodded her appreciation of the sergeant's thoughtfulness and sipped the scaldingly hot potato soup. "Put this in your bag too." He passed her a parcel wrapped in newspaper. "It's a black bread and cheese *kanapka*." He noted the look of bemusement on Trixie's face. "It's a sandwich. It'll keep you going if things turn difficult."

"That's very kind of you, Sergeant."

"Just protecting my officers . . . some of 'em anyway. The ones *worth* protecting."

"I'm not an officer; Colonel Dabrowski made that very clear. My role is simply to provide help and sustenance to our brave, *male* soldiers."

Wysochi chuckled. "Well, you should be. After that little speech of yours in Pilsudski Square they should have made you a general. But then the colonel is a little old-fashioned that way; he doesn't much like the idea of women bossing men about." Wysochi gave Trixie an evil little grin. "Me, on the other hand, I quite like the idea of powerful women."

Trixie decided to ignore the rather tasteless innuendo. It was a sign of the remarkable transformation in her life and attitudes that she could even bring herself to chat with someone of such a low rank in society as Wysochi. War jumbled everything up, made all the old certainties . . . uncertain.

"You don't seem to like officers, Sergeant Wysochi."

"Nah. Most of them are tossers, even the regular army ones. But you . . . you might make a fighter. Not a *good* fighter," Wysochi added impishly, "what with you being a girl, but not a bad one." He pushed at the barricade that stretched across the street with his boot. The barricade was a higgledy-piggledy structure that had been erected in a madcap couple of hours from a mishmash of paving slabs, doors, old bits of furniture, wrought-iron fencing, barrels and several trees that had been chopped down and dragged in from some neighboring gardens. "Solid enough," he decided, "but whether it'll be strong enough to stop an armored steamer is another matter."

"It better be," observed Trixie. "This street leads directly to the Blood Bank, so this is where the main SS assault will come. Apparently the lieutenant"—now it was her turn to nod in the direction of Lieutenant Gorski, who was sitting on top of the barricade gnawing at a fingernail—"has been ordered to hold this street to the last man."

"The Spirits help us then. I don't think Gorski could hold his dick with both hands, never mind a barricade with only two hundred fighters. And without good leadership, once it gets hot this lot are going to cut and run."

"They've got you."

"Yeah, they have, haven't they?" Wysochi lit a cigarette, took a deep suck of smoke and gave Trixie a smile. "And they've got you too, and from that look in your eye, noncombatant or not, I think you're intent on doing more than just offering words of encouragement."

They were interrupted by a shout from a lookout stationed on one of the rooftops along the street.

"Balloon!"

Trixie looked up to where the sentry was pointing. There, hovering a quarter of a mile away and perhaps two hundred feet in the air, was one of the ForthRight's new Speke-class hydrogen balloons, its huge red canopy bright in the afternoon sunshine. It seemed so peaceful, so harmless floating there. She could see two men in the wicker basket studying the barricade through a telescope, the lens glinting in the sun.

Wysochi tossed his cigarette aside. "C'mon, the balloon's gone up. Time to make ourselves scarce." He cupped his hands to his mouth. "Take cover," he bellowed to the WFA soldiers standing around their braziers trying to keep warm, then he grabbed Trixie's arm and hauled her toward one of the cellars that had been commandeered into service as bunkers.

"Ignore that," yelled Lieutenant Gorski. "It's only a balloon."

"They're spotting for the artillery," shouted Wysochi over his shoulder as he hurled Trixie down the steps to the cellar.

The discussion was cut short by a strange whistling sound that cut through the air.

Trixie had read descriptions of artillery barrages in the books in her father's library but she was still stunned—literally—by the reality of being at the receiving end of one of them. The explosions of the shells were deafeningly loud, so loud that she felt her one good ear go *pop*; it was as though she had been smashed about the head by two cymbals. But the noise was as nothing to the shock wave which tore out from the blast. Even shielded underground she was hurled against the wall, her head smashing against the brickwork. A shearing pain lanced through her damaged shoulder and for a moment she lay fetuslike on the ground, deaf, numb and shocked by the ferocity of what she'd experienced. Dust and grime thrown up from the blast began to swirl around her; now every time she took in a breath it was flavored with the taste of brick dust. She coughed, trying to spit the choking powder out of her mouth.

She felt a hand on her shoulder, and turning her head she saw a concerned Wysochi looking down at her. He was covered in a patina of white dust, looking as though he had been dipped in flour ready to be baked in an oven. His uniform had also suffered in the blast; the right sleeve of his jacket was torn and the knees of his trousers were tattered and stiff with mud. He spoke to Trixie, but she couldn't hear a thing. She stabbed a finger into each ear and massaged them.

Wysochi nodded and raised his voice. "Are you hurt?"

Trixie staggered to her feet and took a quick inventory. She had a catalog of bumps and bruises but nothing seemed to be broken. She mouthed an uncertain "I'm fine," and was pleased when she heard her own muffled voice.

"Good, then come with me." Wysochi turned and climbed the basement stairs back up to the road level.

The scene that greeted Trixie was one of horror and carnage. About ten of the men and women who had been putting the finishing touches to the barricade had been caught in the open when the salvo of artillery shells had struck and now they lay bent and busted on the torn cobbles. Lieutenant Gorski was lying amongst them; from the odd tilt of his head it was obvious that his neck was snapped.

Trixie looked around; there seemed to be no officers and no NCOs, just a muddle of winded, bemused and very frightened soldiers. Then, out of nowhere there was another explosion, and Trixie and Wysochi were pelted with debris. When Trixie stood up, she found the sergeant slumped still and unmoving at her feet, hit by a flying brick.

She gawped down at Wysochi. It seemed impossible that such a powerful man could be felled. He was a rock. He was indestructible. Panic washed over her. She looked around, frightened, uncertain what to do . . . alone.

"Steamers . . . SS steamers . . ." someone shouted, the quaver in his voice indicating that he was near to panic.

Trixie's naturally combative spirit reasserted itself. "Corporal! Is there a corporal still alive here?" she screamed at the top of her voice, and almost immediately a boy emerged from behind a low wall that surrounded the front garden of what had once been a very elegant house. It was elegant no longer, having taken a direct hit. "What's your name, Corporal?"

"Karol Michalski."

"Get ten men, Corporal Michalski, and as many firebombs as you can carry and station yourself at the top of that house there." She stabbed a finger toward a tall building standing a hundred yards or so in front of the barricade. "Wait until the steamers arrive, then *burn* them."

The corporal hesitated for a moment, then saluted and without another word did as he was ordered. Trixie looked around and saw a soldier staggering around brushing flames out from his trousers. "You, soldier, round up twenty men and station them on the upper floors of that building." She pointed with her revolver to the house that flanked the barricade.

The young soldier shook his head. "No. We've got to retreat out of artillery range—"

"Pull yourself together, man. What's your name?"

"Josef Zawadzski."

"If we run, Zawadzski, the SS will kill us like rats in a barrel. There's nowhere to retreat to. We must stand or we must die." Other men were slowly emerging from their hiding places and Trixie raised her voice so they could hear her. "Yesterday you swore an oath to defend your city to the last man. Today we will find out whether Poles are men of their word or men of straw." Flushed with embarrassment, Zawadzski saluted and then began rounding up his men.

A sergeant, still bemused and baffled by the barrage, stumbled out from a cellar and made an attempt to exert his authority. "No, stay where you are. I command here. You're not a real officer. I say we retreat."

It was a pivotal moment. The men who had been scurrying off to do Trixie's bidding hesitated. They looked uncertainly from Trixie to the sergeant and back again.

She tried to bluff. "I am Lieutenant Trixie Dashwood."

"We ain't got no women officers in the WFA. I'm in charge here and I say—"

They never got to hear what the sergeant was intent on saying. The pistol in Trixie's hand barked and the sergeant dropped to the ground with a bullet hole in his chest. For a second Trixie stood paralyzed by her own ruthlessness. But then she threw off any doubts; she would ponder the morality of her action later . . . if she lived. "He was an Enemy of the Revolution. I command here," she snarled. "I am Lieutenant Trixie Dashwood, and my orders are to hold this barricade and hold it I shall. You—*Corporal* Zawadzski—get those twenty men into that building and when the Anglos come, fire down on them. Understand?"

A nod from Zawadzski.

"The rest of you, get your rifles and your ammunition and man the barricade."

"What about us?" said a voice to Trixie's left.

Trixie turned to find herself looking at a group of young girls, the eldest of whom couldn't have been more than fourteen. Surely they were too young to be away from their parents? Trixie nearly laughed; she was only three years older than them and she'd just shot a man for disobeying her. "Carry the wounded to the basement. Look after them as best you can. The rest of you grab rifles and help defend the barricade."

"Women can't fight," protested one of the soldiers.

The look on Trixie's face silenced him. "It doesn't matter if a rifle is fired by a man or a woman, to the SS trooper it kills the result is just the same. If the SS win, women will be executed alongside the men, therefore they have the right to fight and die just as surely as men."

It was one of those strange moments when silence descends, when all noise and all talking suddenly ceases. It was as though the world was taking a breath. It was as though the world had been suddenly made mute by the horror it was about to witness. Trixie looked around at the men and women manning the barricade and wondered what they were listening for. She strained her one good ear.

There . . .

Far off she could hear the scrunch of steel on stone, could hear the faint *thud-thud-thud* of a steamer's pistons, could hear shouted commands drifting toward her through the sharp, crystalline cold of the afternoon.

A boy, maybe twelve or thirteen years old, darted around a

corner of a building and shouted a message. "The Anglos are advancing through Southgate. Ten minutes."

"Soldiers of Warsaw, prepare yourselves," Trixie shouted.

Now all they could do was wait and she suddenly came to understand how lonely it was to command. Every one of the men and women lining the barricade was waiting for her to say something. She began to pace up and down, shouting at the pale-faced WFA soldiers as she went. "Hold your fire until the Anglos are within fifty yards. Don't waste your shots. When a man falls, one of you without a rifle will take his place. I will shoot anyone stepping back from the barricade. There will be no retreat, there will be no surrender. This is your time, people of Warsaw. This is your time to kill."

THE FIRST STEAMER LUMBERED AROUND THE CORNER FIVE MINUTES later. The SS had taken the rubber tires off the wheels and screwed in large spikes; now the wheels smashed and crushed the street cobbles as the machine passed. Swathed in steel and steam, the huge steamer huffed and puffed its way, slowly, inexorably, toward the barricade. Once it faced them head-on, it stood poised for a moment crouching like some great fire-breathing dragon that had escaped from the depths of Terror Incognita. Then it began to lurch forward, gradually picking up speed, obviously intent on ramming the barricade. Behind the machine swarmed a mass of black-uniformed SS troopers. There was a rat-tat-tat as two Gatling guns housed in nacelles on the top of the steamer opened fire and instinctively Trixie threw herself to the ground. Bullets smacked into the house to her left. Windows smashed, showering glass down onto the road. Somewhere to her right she heard a scream. The steamer picked up speed. It seemed unstoppable, a huge lumbering force of nature.

"Steady, you useless bastards," shouted Trixie. She blushed. She couldn't believe someone of her rank and her breeding could use such profanities. Sergeant Wysochi had a lot to answer for. But when she saw the effect her words had on her troops—they were actually laughing—she was encouraged to go further. "Look at them . . . there are so many of the fuckers even you useless bastards can't miss."

There was a round of louder laughter.

The SS lumbered forward. Eighty yards . . . seventy yards . . . sixty yards . . . fifty yards.

"Fire!"

The soldiers of the WFA began to fire, working their Martini-Henry rifles for all they were worth, pouring fire into the advancing SS. In an instant the bright Winter's sunshine was shrouded with a cloying, choking cloud of cordite.

"Hold hard," Trixie screamed as the steamer hit the barricade. For a moment she thought the barricade would buckle but the tons of earth and timber that they had labored to pour into its construction withstood the charge. Now Corporal Zawadzski's men began to fire down into the ranks of the SS swarming around the beached steamer. A man fell back from the barricade, his face mashed by a bullet. Instinctively Trixie brought her brute of a pistol up, took aim at the SS advancing toward the barricade and pulled the trigger. The Mauser bucked back in her hand, raking her injured shoulder with pain as she worked the trigger and fired again and again and again. Frantically she fired shot after desperate shot into the black mob of the SS, firing until the hammer of her pistol clicked on an empty chamber.

It looked hopeless; the SS were coming forward like a black wave, hosing the barricade with their automatic weapons. Then little Corporal Michalski and his band struck, hurling their firebombs down, turning the whole of Uyazhdov Boulevard into an inferno. In a moment the fashionable tree-lined avenue was turned into a living, burning Hel.

"Now!" she yelled, and two boys—children really, neither was more than ten—leapt over the top of the barricade in a suicidal attempt to throw firebombs into the cabin of the steamer. One was cut down by machine-gun fire but the second managed to thrust his bomb through the driver's observation port. There was a *wooomph* as the bomb exploded and in that instant the sound of pounding steam pistons and scrabbling wheels was accompanied by the screams of the steamer's crew as they were burned to death.

Then, like the ebbing of a tide, the ferocity of the fighting seemed to suddenly falter and, as she watched, the SS began to retreat.

There was a shout from the barricades. "We've beaten them. They're running for it."

"Keep firing," bellowed Trixie, "for fuck's sake, keep firing. Kill as many of the fuckers as you can. Make them remember. Make them scared. Make them dead."

And as she screamed out her orders, Trixie realized that she had never been happier in the whole of her life.

COMRADE MAJOR HARTLEY STOOD STOCK-STILL IN FRONT OF ARCHIE Clement's desk as the colonel idly played with his pencil, rolling it backward and forward between the fingers of his right hand. Finally Clement stopped his fidgeting and slowly raised his gaze.

"So, waddya gotta say for yourself, Major?"

"We encountered greater resistance than we had anticipated, Comrade Colonel. But I am confident—"

"*Con-fee-dent.* Gracious me, Hartley, that's a real two-guinea word, but ah gotta say iffn ah was standing in your boots ah wouldn't be feeling *con-fee-dent.* No sirree. Iffn ah had seen two hundred of mah men blasted to buggery and the rest being forced to retreat by a pack of no-account Rebs, ah don't think ah'd be using a word like 'con-fee-dent.'"

Hartley swallowed hard. The perks and benefits that came with being a high-ranking member of the SS were one thing, but they were granted only after having taken an oath of death or glory. And as the performance of his men this afternoon could hardly be termed glorious . . .

"The Poles have used tactics which are bestial and violate every code governing civilized conduct in war."

Clement looked at Hartley as though he were mad. "You joshing me?"

"No, sir: the Poles have children hurling incendiaries from rooftops. They have booby-trapped buildings."

"Mah, mah, what ruffians we are fighting. Children . . . booby traps . . . whatever will them Rebs think of next? Cuss words? Obscene gestures? You better quit your bellyaching, Comrade Major, cos ah ain't used to having my SS boys having the shit kicked outta them by Rebel scum."

"They are fanatical, Comrade Colonel, and their commander is a madman . . ." Hartley paused and then corrected himself. "A madwoman."

"Them Rebs are commanded by a woman?" asked Clement, suddenly evincing a little more interest.

"Our Balloon Corps Observers report seeing a woman with long blond hair organizing the defenders and one captured Varsovian has confirmed this under interrogation."

"This woman's gotta name?"

"The prisoner didn't know her name. All he was able to say before he died was that she was the same woman who led the attack on the barges. It is typical of these Polish scum that they would force women to fight like men."

"By mah reckoning, this woman is fighting better than a man, iffn the way she booted your ass this afternoon is any indicator." Clement took a long swig of his glass of Solution. "You better saddle up, Major Hartley, and get your boys ready to toe the line. You gonna attack again but this time ah'm gonna help you out by making sure that there's a heavier artillery barrage before you let rip, a barrage so heavy that it'll pound them Rebs to dog shit. And seeing as you caught me in a forgiving mood, Hartley, ah'm gonna allocate the six newly arrived armored steamers to your assault. But listen real tight 'cos ah don't want there to be any misunderstanding: your objective is to take the barricades which block our advance to the Old Town before nightfall. This is your *minimum* objective and iffn them Rebs give you the turnabout again, Comrade Major . . ." Clement gave Major Hartley an empty, cold smile. "Well, ah don't think it's necessary to explain to an SS officer who uses big words like *'con-fee-dent'* how he should act if he goes and fucks up for a second time, now, is it?"

THE ARTILLERY BARRAGE LASTED FOR TWO INTERMINABLE HOURS. Holed up in a basement, Trixie heard and felt rather than saw the destruction take place outside. She tried to number the explosions but lost count when she reached thirty and the blasts were coming so close together as to merge into one. As she huddled against the basement wall, hands pressed over her ears, all she wanted was for the hammering to stop, to be in a place where she wasn't frightened that she'd be buried alive. For two long hours she cowered in the corner of the basement, hoping, praying that one of the shells the Anglos were raining down on Warsaw wouldn't score a direct hit on where she was hiding.

Finally there was silence.

"Out, out," Trixie ordered as she kicked and pushed her troops out of the bunker. "Get back to the barricade."

Reluctantly, tiredly, the defenders did as they were told. Trixie emerged, blinking into the late afternoon sunlight, to a changed landscape. The picturesque Warsaw of only a few hours before was gone and in its place stood a desolate scene of ruined and burning buildings, the air dank and rank with the scorched smell of smoldering astral ether. Trixie gagged at the smell and threw up at the side of the road.

A runner—a small boy wearing the jacket of a dead SS captain—came racing up. "'Oo is the officer commanding 'ere?" he demanded.

"I am," said Trixie.

The boy looked at her suspiciously. "'Oo are you?"

"She is Lieutenant Trixie Dashwood, commanding Number One Barricade, Uyazhdov Boulevard," said Sergeant Wysochi as he tottered out of a bunker to stand beside Trixie. He looked dreadful but he was alive. Trixie felt her spirits rise.

"Where's Lieutenant Gorski?" asked the runner.

"Dead," said Trixie simply, then held out her hand to take the orders the boy had brought.

> To the Officer Commanding #1 Barricade.
>   Greetings,
>   It is imperative that this barricade is held until nightfall. The defenses behind #1 Barricade have been destroyed by enemy artillery fire. If you yield, Warsaw is doomed: there is no defense between your barricade and the center of Warsaw. I beg you, as a fellow Pole, to spare no effort in your defense of our people.
>   May ABBA guide and protect you.
>   Colonel Jan Dabrowski
>   Officer Commanding the Warsaw Free Army

"There is a message for you from our commander," Trixie announced in her loudest voice to the troops who were laboring to repair the barricade. "We are ordered to hold this street until night-fall. If we fail, Warsaw falls. There will be no retreat, there will be no surrender. I am an officer of the Warsaw Free Army and all soldiers under my command will do their duty."

The fighting that afternoon was, if anything, more ferocious and more intense than the first attack. The SS had obviously learned from experience and moved forward more cautiously, house by house, door by door, and, using flamethrowers and grenades, they cleared each house before the main advance reached it.

They brought up more steamers as well, having protected their vulnerable gun and driving ports with wire to prevent firebombs being thrown inside. There was something implacable, unstoppable about the advance, but for all their care and all their planning, in Trixie the SS met someone equally flexible and inventive in her tactical thinking.

She sent Sergeant Wysochi out to mine the basements of the houses that lined the advance of the SS, detonating them when platoons of StormTroopers were inside. She sent snipers under the command of Corporal Zawadzski to harry and disrupt the tail of the SS advance, telling her men to kill officers and signalers. She had the bodies of the dead SS booby-trapped so that anyone touching them was maimed or killed.

But all she and her fighters could do was slow the onslaught; it was impossible to stop the SS advance. By twilight the six armored steamers spearheading the SS attack force were positioned at the top of Uyazhdov Boulevard ready to begin the final assault on the barricade.

A grimed and cordite-stained Corporal Michalski appeared from the shadows after making a reconnaissance. "We've had it, Lieutenant. There are six steamers up there and maybe a thousand of them SS bastards. They're bringing up field guns too. We're fucked. Best iffn we pull back now."

Trixie looked around at the soldiers defending the barricade.

There were perhaps a hundred and fifty of them left, at least a third of them women and a quarter little more than children. They were exhausted, thirsty and hungry.

Slowly she shook her head. "We can't, Corporal. They're still evacuating all the civilians from the houses around Pilsudski Square. If the Anglos break through now there's nothing to stop them slaughtering the whole lot of them. We have to stand."

The corporal gave a shrug. "Okie-dokie, Lieutenant." And then he stopped, looked Trixie straight in the eyes and gave her a salute. "It has bin an honor an' a privilege serving under you, miss." And with that he signaled to his band of boys and girls, who collected up their armfuls of firebombs and the grenades taken from the SS dead and followed Michalski back into the shadows.

TRIXIE HAD REPLACED HER MAUSER PISTOL WITH A WEBLEY TAKEN from a dead SS trooper. Being double-action it was easier for her to fire and a damned sight more accurate, but after an hour of fighting her palm had been ripped to pieces by the kick of the revolver, her right ear was stone-deaf and her fingers were burned and blistered from loading bullets. By her reckoning she must have accounted for thirty of the SS but for every one she downed two seemed to take their place. The WFA ranks were thinning too; the barricades were littered with busted and twisted bodies.

Trixie checked her watch. It was still only six o'clock. It wouldn't be dark for an hour and with the steamers only a hundred yards away there seemed little chance of their being able to hold the SS. They needed a miracle.

And the miracle was provided by Sergeant Wysochi.

Where he had scrounged up the explosives Trixie had no idea, but it was obvious from the size of the blast that the mines he had built in the basements of the two houses that faced each other across the boulevard had been huge. The sergeant waited until the two front steamers were in line with the houses before he pressed the detonator. There was an ear-splitting explosion, the whole street quivered, the fronts of the two tall buildings blew out and then slowly, majestically, the buildings toppled forward, smashing into one another as they crashed onto the street below, burying the two steamers as they fell.

There was a ragged cheer from the WFA fighters, but the respite afforded by the sergeant's booby trap was short-lived. Immediately after the dust settled Trixie could see SS soldiers begin to clamber over the debris, but without the shield offered by the two steamers they made easy targets. The Poles poured rifle fire into their ranks and children hurled bombs down on them from the windows of overlooking buildings. They died in their dozens but still they came on.

For twenty frantic, ferocious minutes it was nip and tuck. The firing from the SS was incredible. It was so heavy that Trixie was scared to raise her head above the parapet to see what she was firing at; all she could do was hold her pistol up to a hole in the barricade and pull the trigger, hoping that at least some of her rounds found a target.

And then suddenly—miraculously—it was over. As the daylight began to fade, the whistles sounded and the SS began to retreat. Dog-tired and hardly daring to believe what she was witnessing, Trixie slumped to her knees, but even as she knelt she felt a hand on her shoulder.

Looking up, she saw the face of a young green-jacketed lieutenant peering down at her. "Do you command here?" he asked.

All Trixie had the energy to do was nod.

"You and your fighters are ordered to pull back to Jerusalem Avenue. Keep to the side of the street, keep to the doorways. I'll manage the rearguard. Good luck."

She felt Wysochi at her side helping to lever her back to her feet and as she tried to brush the dust from her hair she took a moment to look around. Of the two hundred fighters she had begun the battle with there were barely fifty left standing. It had been a mighty near-run thing.

"Get back to Jerusalem Avenue," she shouted, her voice cracked and parched. She turned to the lieutenant. "Thank you, Lieutenant."

He shook his head. "No. It is the people of Warsaw who must thank you."

MAJOR HARTLEY SAT, STUPEFIED, IN HIS ROOM, IDLY PLAYING WITH the glass of Solution. An almost empty bottle of Blood Heat's Finest 20 Percent Solution sat on his desk in mute testimony to the way Hartley had been punishing himself—and the bottle—for the last hour.

He grabbed at the bottle and attempted to top up his glass, but his hand was so unsteady that most of the red Solution tipped over the desk. With a slurred curse, he pulled a handkerchief from his sleeve and tried to mop up the spill. In the end he gave up and simply lowered his forehead into the refreshingly cool pool of Solution.

Even if he hadn't been quite so blood-drunk he would still have been befuddled by how these Poles—these badly armed, outnumbered and ill-trained Poles—had defeated his beloved SS.

He had never ever seen men—and women!—fight like that, as though they were indifferent to death. He was a veteran of the Troubles, a veteran who thought he had experienced every horror war had to offer, but he had never experienced anything to compare to these Polish fighters. They fought like the very possessed, hurling themselves, careless of their own safety, of their own survival, on his

StormTroopers. He wondered for a moment whether they had been drugged, whether they had been dosed with blood, but this he knew was ridiculous. The only thing that would make a soldier fight like that was desperation . . . that and the Fury who was leading them.

What had his StormTroopers started calling her: Lady Death?

No wonder he had failed. And in the SS there was only one remedy for failure.

Major Hartley checked his watch. It was now nearly eight o'clock. His two young sons would be in bed. He took the envelope addressed to his wife and placed it squarely before him. Then, taking up his Mauser, he blew a hole in his head.

28

The Demi-Monde: 79th Day of Winter, 1004

It was that canny nuJu Abraham Eleazar who secured a homeland for his people in NoirVille, a homeland that became known as the nuJu Autonomous District (the JAD). Eleazar developed a chemical additive—Aqua Benedicta—which prevents blood congealing and enabled the Blood Brothers to store and preserve the blood they traded. It was Aqua Benedicta that made the Blood Brothers the Demi-Monde's preeminent blood brokers. The establishing of the JAD was a deal which both parties were pleased to conclude: Shaka and his Blood Brothers secured a supply of Aqua Benedicta and in exchange they respected the independence of the JAD and the right of the JADniks to follow the WhoDoo religion. The only element of friction in this relationship is that the JAD has become a sanctuary for NoirVillian woeMen fleeing husbands and fathers.

—Include Us Out: A Short History of the JAD,
Schmuel Gelbfisz, JAD Hipster Books and Comics

'**ve got lice!" squealed Norma Williams. She leapt to her feet and began to rake her fingers frantically through her hair.

Vanka laughed. "Everybody's got lice. Why should you be different?"

It was true: in the cramped, crowded and decidedly unhygienic confines of a war-ravaged Ghetto, lice—and rats and mice and fleas—had overrun the place. Everyone had lice, just as everyone was filthy and foul and permanently scared shitless that one of the never-ending procession of SS artillery shells smashing into the city had their name on it.

But seeing the look of real horror on Norma's face, Ella took pity on her. Making a real effort—Norma's moaning was incessant—she tried to be reassuring. "If it bothers you that much the best thing to do, when you turn in tonight, is to hang your clothes outside. The frost will kill the lice."

"I don't mean in my *clothes*." Norma lowered her voice and looked suspiciously around at the other people huddled in the cellar. "I mean in my *hair*," she whispered. "I'm infested."

Vanka decided to rejoin the conversation. "Well, you could take off your head and leave that outside at night . . ."

He was silenced by a glare from Ella. The antagonism between those two was becoming a real pain; what had started out as dislike had rapidly degenerated into loathing.

She tried again. "Most of the women have taken to cropping their hair, Norma; wearing it short makes it easier to delouse."

Norma looked at Ella as though she was mad. "Crop my hair? After I took all these years to grow it? Don't be ridiculous. What I want is some hot water, a clean towel, some anti-nit shampoo and a change of clothes." She paused for a moment. "And to get out of this shithole."

Ella had to admit that Norma was quite right: their home *was* a shithole. The really quite pleasant hotel they had checked into when they had first arrived in the Ghetto was long gone, pummeled flat by the incessant artillery bombardment. Now the three of them had been reduced to scratching out a life in the hotel's forty-foot-square cellar, which they shared with the other refugees. It was a dank, dark, dismal existence and Ella hated it.

Just as the twenty or so people she was sharing her cellar home with hated it. Not that they complained much; they were so dispirited that they'd long ago given up complaining. Now they simply sat in the darkness, mute and blank-eyed. Twenty-odd days into the siege it seemed that her fellow cellarniks had become indifferent to what happened to them; the horror and the terror they had experienced had made them numb to their own suffering and to that of their fellow man.

Ella sighed. She wished that Norma had been rendered numb *and* dumb; she wished the girl would stop her continual carping. She didn't know what was worse, Norma constantly twittering in her ear about how horrible things were or the SS artillery trying to smash her to a pulp. For three weeks she hadn't been able to get away from either of them. She'd hardly been out of the cellar since she'd arrived in the Ghetto, had hardly seen daylight in all that time. Snipers made wandering around during the day a dangerous occupation and she only risked it when hunger forced her to scavenge for food. Ella wasn't sure if she could take much more. And neither, she thought, could the Poles.

Desperately, courageously and tirelessly as the Poles had fought, the SS had made steady and relentless advances into the Ghetto. It seemed that every night the WFA was obliged to abandon one stronghold or another as it was overrun. And, as Ella understood it, there were more of the SS now and they had refined their tactics. No longer were they as arrogant and as careless as they had been in the opening days of the fighting; now there was a deadly, callous professionalism about them.

Archie Clement had learned. He'd learned that the best way to beat the WFA was to grind them down, to exhaust them physically and emotionally, to pound them—day and night—with artillery fire. He had made Warsaw into one vast killing zone. The Warsaw Ghetto had become the apotheosis of Asymmetric Warfare.

The general, Ella decided, back in the comfort and safety of the Real World, must be so proud of his creation.

"Is there a Vanka Maykov in 'ere?"

Ella turned toward the door. There, silhouetted by the uncertain light cast by an oil lamp, stood a scrawny boy dressed in a tattered and torn SS jacket with a mud-splattered *chapka* set lopsidedly on his head.

"I'm Maykov," called out Vanka. "And who might you be?"

The boy saluted. "I am Karol Michalski, senior sergeant in Trixie's Terriers. I've got an order to escort you"—he checked a scruffy piece of paper he had in his hand—"an' a Miss Ella Thomas an' a Miss Norma Williams to headquarters to meet wiv the WFA Emergency Executive."

Ella felt a tug on her sleeve. "Why are we being taken to headquarters?" Norma whispered, genuine terror in her voice. She had never come to terms with the fact that Heydrich had put a reward on her head. The lice hadn't helped her peace of mind either.

"It's all right. Vanka and I have an idea that might get us out of this muddle. Get your jacket. Soon, with a bit of luck, we'll be able to say good-bye to Warsaw."

That is, if Dabrowski buys into Vanka's idea.

It was an idea he'd had while creeping around the ruins of Warsaw trying to hunt down a new source of cigarettes and had seen a poster flapping on the wall of what had once been a theatrical agency. The poster announced that as part of Beria's policy of improving bilateral relations between the ForthRight and NoirVille, the Revue Nègre was to be performing in Berlin.

Ella hadn't needed Vanka to explain to her what the Revue Nègre was; she regarded herself as the world's biggest fan of Josephine Baker, the revue's principal dancer. What *had* surprised her was that ABBA had duplicated her in the Demi-Monde. The professor hadn't said anything about ABBA duplicating *nice* PreLived personalities in the Demi-Monde, only psychopaths and murderers. But that she supposed was a consequence of heuristic programming. ABBA was doing its own thing.

Ella had, however, needed Vanka to explain how the Revue Nègre could help in solving their problems. And when he did, she had to admit it was a clever plan, a plan that would allow them to kill three birds with one perfectly aimed stone: it would get urgently needed blood into Warsaw, it would persuade Dabrowski to help them escape from the Ghetto and it would provide an excellent way of smuggling her and Norma out of the ForthRight and into Noir-Ville. It was this plan that Vanka had pitched to Trixie Dashwood, who had, in turn, pitched it to Dabrowski.

Following the sergeant, Ella, Vanka and Norma crept slowly and cautiously out of the sanctuary of the cellar, to emerge, blinking like moles, in the morning light. Ella was aghast at the change war had wrought to the beautiful city of Warsaw. It looked as though some malevolent giant had trampled through the city stomping every building to rubble and leaving a trail of dead in his wake. Bodies littered the roads like obscene confetti, rats and crows picking at them. The stench of rotting corpses filled the air.

For ten heart-stopping minutes the four of them ducked and dived, scurried and scuttled through the shattered city. Finally, at the corner of what had once been a grand, opulent boulevard, Sergeant Michalski stopped.

"That's it over there," he said, pointing to a burned-out building. "That's WFA headquarters. From 'ere on you've got to keep low. There are a lot of SS snipers around this district just waitin' for a chance to blow yer head off."

TRIXIE TOOK A SIP OF HER BLACK COFFEE AND SCOWLED. SHE HADN'T yet got used to the taste of the chicory they had started using to bulk out the fast-depleting reserves of coffee. But then, she mused, it wasn't just coffee that was in short supply. Looking at Colonel Dabrowski, she had a feeling that hope was being rationed too. He looked a beaten man.

The report she had given him was bad news—that was why she'd insisted that only Delegate Trotsky be present when she made it— but she never imagined that Dabrowski would disintegrate as he had. The man was a nervous wreck.

Trixie took another sip of her coffee and another drag of her cigarette.

It was odd, she mused, how war altered people. Some, like Dabrowski, buckled under the pressure, while others, like herself, reveled in the slaughter and the chaos. In the twenty-one days they had been fighting she had changed. It had been twenty-one days during which she had ordered—demanded—that people die. Lots of people— young people, old people, brave people, frightened people . . . men, women and children. And all the time she had to stand firm and resolute; not for a moment could she seem weak or vulnerable. She had to be the rock to which all of her regiment's hopes were anchored. That was her greatest victory: not the Battle of Oberbaum Bridge, not the Battle of Barricade Number 1. No, her greatest victory had been the conquering of her emotions. Emotions were for the weak.

She looked across to Dabrowski. He was weak, so weak he was coming unraveled before her eyes.

Her fingers itched against the holster of her Webley. The temptation to shoot the bastard was almost overwhelming.

Not now.

Not when she still had a chance to offer them hope. Not when she was still here to inject some steel into Dabrowski's spine. Not now that she was *Captain* Dashwood. By the Spirits, Dabrowski had hated doing that: promoting a *woman* to command a regiment. But after the Battle of Barricade Number 1 it had been impossible for Dabrowski to refuse her; if he had, there would have been a real possibility of mutiny.

Dabrowski must have felt her examining him; he looked up, his blank, unfocused eyes searching her out in the gloom of the cellar. "Are you certain, Captain Dashwood?"

"Yes. The SS will take control of the Warsaw Blood Bank within the next four days."

"But you've held them for so long."

That was the problem. Dabrowski and the rest of them had gotten so used to Trixie's regiment being able to repulse the SS that they'd taken it for granted that the Blood Bank was safe. Now they had to face reality. "We haven't the heavy guns or the explosives to keep the SS at bay. We can hurl bodies at them but it won't make any difference. Our fighters are exhausted and outgunned and we're in danger of being encircled. If I don't pull back I'll lose the regiment."

Dabrowski turned to Delegate Trotsky. "What are our supplies of blood like?"

Although it seemed barely possible, the old nuJu was even skinnier than he had been three weeks ago. Skinnier but still with the same resolute set to his long jaw.

By Trixie's estimation, Trotsky had done a fine job in helping the WFA to fight for as long as it had. Famed for his incorruptibility, he had been unanimously elected as the man to administer Warsaw's blood supply and this he had done fairly, making sure that the demands for a bigger ration made by the rich and the powerful were rebuffed. The other delegates hated him for his parsimony, but by carefully rationing each and every drop of blood Trotsky had kept Warsaw going longer than Trixie had ever thought possible. In a different life the man would have made a perfect RaTionalist.

Trotsky stroked his long beard before answering. "Not good. The warehouse where we held most of our blood reserves was hit by SS artillery a couple of days ago. We salvaged what we could." He gave a disconsolate shrug. "By my calculations we have possibly a week's supply . . . not more. With what we can withdraw from the

Blood Bank before the SS take control, Warsaw has perhaps two weeks before its blood supplies are exhausted."

Dabrowski dropped his head into his hands. For a moment Trixie thought he was crying. It was, she decided, a disgusting spectacle; leaders didn't cry.

Finally Dabrowski raised his head and smiled resignedly. "So, Captain Dashwood, two weeks after the SS take the Warsaw Blood Bank we will all be dying of blood starvation. Not a terribly noble end to our little rebellion."

"I must demur," said Trotsky quietly. "At least by fighting, we have shown that the ForthRight army and the SS aren't unbeatable. At least the rest of the Demi-Monde knows that it's possible to defeat these monsters. If a few thousand ill-trained and badly equipped partisans can fight the SS to a standstill then there must be hope for everybody—"

"A poor reward for the sacrifices made by the people of Warsaw," interrupted Dabrowski. "And unfortunately without blood the conclusion is inescapable: we *must* surrender. We must end this carnage now. We have lost over twenty thousand of our best and our bravest to this war; our people have been pushed back to the Industrial Zone, where they cower in holes barely able to find enough food to survive; and now we all face death by blood starvation." Dabrowski gave a dejected shake of his head. "All our glorious revolution has resulted in is death and misery. We should surrender while at least some of our people are still alive and throw ourselves at the mercy of the Leader."

Trixie and Trotsky exchanged glances; the colonel's defeatism seemed total. Didn't he realize that Heydrich had no mercy?

"Eventually the other Sectors will come to our aid," said the old nuJu. "We must give them time."

Dabrowski smashed a fist onto his table. "We have no time! We cannot wait for help. And we cannot retreat, the Boundary Layer sees to that." With a shaking hand he poured himself a glass of Solution. "No . . . we must surrender."

"I think we might be able to organize a delivery of blood to Warsaw," Trixie announced in a loud voice.

Dabrowski slowly turned his shadowed eyes toward her. "And how will you be able to conjure this miracle, Captain?"

"Not me: Vanka Maykov . . . the psychic." She nodded to Sergeant Michalski, who had been guarding the entrance. He opened the door and Vanka ducked inside, accompanied by the two Daemons.

Trixie darted a look toward Vanka and almost despaired. That Warsaw's hopes should rest in the hands of such a dishonest and disreputable man was truly astonishing. When he had first come to her with his proposition her immediate reaction had been to dismiss it out of hand. It sounded ridiculous. It sounded too much like a cheap trick designed to save his worthless Shade-loving skin.

Shades . . .

Trixie might have come to realize that UnFunDaMentalism's classification of some races as UnderMentionables was evil nonsense but with regard to Shades she didn't think she would ever be able to bring herself to trust them. They weren't human and the Rationalist inside her told her they were just *wrong* . . . Lilithian perversions of nature. And that this Ella Thomas wasn't only a Shade but a Daemon to boot made her—it—all the more threatening. Trixie had a sneaking suspicion that as soon as she escaped back to her own world she would seek to destroy the Demi-Monde. What did the Daemons call it? Pulling the plug? No, Shades couldn't be trusted . . . Daemons couldn't be trusted.

Vanka tipped his battered tile and gave Trixie a jaunty wave. "Good morning, ladies and gentlemen," he said in a merry voice, "Vanka Maykov, procurer of blood, at your service."

— ∭ —

ELLA WAS PROUD OF HIM. SHE WAS AS PROUD OF VANKA AS SHE WAS nervous of Trixie Dashwood. While Ella had been shocked by Dabrowski's appearance—he seemed to have aged alarmingly in the days since she had seen him last—this was as nothing to the transformation that Trixie had undergone during her time in the Ghetto. It wasn't just the obvious changes—her magnificent long blond hair had been hacked crudely back into a boyish bob—that had unnerved Ella but the more subtle ones. The look of spoiled petulance that she remembered had gone; the Trixie who stood in the shadows at the side of the cellar was a distinctly harder and more dangerous woman. It was as though something had died inside the girl.

Now the eyes that Trixie Dashwood fixed on Ella were empty, emotionless . . . just as Heydrich's had been. She wasn't particularly enamored of the way Trixie kept fondling the butt of her revolver, either.

"And how do you propose to perform this miracle?" asked Dabrowski.

Vanka took a long draw on his morning cigarette. Cigarettes were now in such short supply that he was rationing himself to three a day—one in the morning, one in the afternoon and one in the evening. As far as Ella was concerned it was one of the few good things to have come out of the Uprising. "With the help of Miss Thomas here, I am intent on buying blood on the black market. I have some experience in trading illicit blood and I believe, given the correct financial inducements, it will be possible to buy sixty thousand liters of blood from the Blood Brothers and have it shipped to Warsaw. As I understand it there are three million people trapped here in Warsaw so sixty thousand liters is two weeks' supply."

"Two weeks . . ." sneered Dabrowski.

"Much can happen in two weeks," interrupted Trixie. "The other Sectors might have a change of heart . . . anything. We should listen to this man."

Dabrowski scowled. "And how much will this miracle cost?"

"Blood is currently trading for one hundred guineas a liter on the black market," explained Vanka.

"Six million guineas!" gasped Dabrowski. He turned to Ella. "You know, Miss Thomas, I am disappointed in you. I expected something a little more imaginative from a Daemon. Isn't the buying of blood on the black market a little prosaic—a little unDaemonic—for someone like you? I would have thought that you would have come to me to tell me you were planning something utterly fantastical like rolling back the Boundary Layer to let all us poor beleaguered Varsovians escape into the Great Beyond." He started to laugh. He sounded almost hysterical. "But then again, I suppose your purchase of blood is equally far-fetched. We don't have six million guineas. Warsaw is almost bloodrupt."

Vanka gave a careless wave of his hand as though six million guineas was a mere bagatelle. "Miss Thomas here has access to certain funds which will comfortably accommodate such an outlay. She will act as your blood donor." No one laughed at the quip, the subject was far too serious for that.

Ella saw every face in the room turn in her direction. "Yes, I can secure the six million guineas."

"You? But you're just a *girl*," said Dabrowski contemptuously.

Ella refused to be insulted. "Girl or not, Colonel, you better believe me when I say I can raise the money. If the WFA can seize back control of the docks for long enough to unload the blood from the barges, then Vanka and I can organize its delivery."

"How long would you need at the docks?" Trixie asked.

"Five hours," answered Vanka.

"Impossible," retorted Dabrowski.

"Not impossible," corrected Trixie quietly. "It'll be costly in lives but my regiment can do it. We'll give you your five hours."

"This is ridiculous. This is also much too good to be true!" objected Dabrowski. "What, may I ask, will you get out of this transaction, Colonel Maykov? As I understand it you are not a man famed for his charitable works."

"The WFA's help in having myself, Miss Thomas and Miss Williams escape from the Ghetto. I have to get to the Berlin Sector to negotiate the delivery of the blood with one of Shaka's lieutenants."

"And then?"

"Then the three of us will travel to NoirVille."

Dabrowski laughed. "So now I understand. We are being bribed: you promise us blood and we get you out of Warsaw."

"In a nutshell: yes," agreed Vanka as he took another irritatingly casual draw on his cigarette.

"And once you're out of the Ghetto what's to stop you just hightailing it to NoirVille and forgetting about us?"

"Nothing. You'll just have to trust me . . . us."

"Ridiculous!" spluttered Dabrowski. "I cannot allow the Daemon—Miss Williams—to leave the Ghetto. It—she—is the last bargaining chip I have with Heydrich. If I surrender the Daemon I am sure that the Leader will be inclined to be more lenient."

"Loath as I am to contradict you, Colonel Dabrowski," came the calm voice of Trotsky, "my own assessment is that the time for surrender is long gone. No matter what we do now, Heydrich will still destroy the people of Warsaw. We've resisted him and given his SS a hiding. He can't allow us to live, because alive we're a permanent reminder to the rest of the Demi-Monde that once people fought to keep their independence. This young man may be a little . . . raffish, but his idea has merit. If we surrender, Heydrich will shoot us all. If we can hold out for just a few more weeks, then there is a chance."

For over a minute Dabrowski sat in silence as he weighed his decision, then finally, reluctantly, he acquiesced. "Very well, Vanka Maykov, we will give you the opportunity to work your magic."

"Great," muttered Norma, "I'm out of this shithole at last."

Ella wondered how Norma would react when she learned *how* Vanka was proposing they get out of Warsaw. At least it would take her mind off the lice.

"THE SEWERS!" EXCLAIMED NORMA. "YOU WANT ME TO ESCAPE FROM Warsaw by crawling through the sewers?"

Vanka nodded. "It is the only way. The SS are shooting anyone attempting to leave the Ghetto, and as there are twenty thousand of the bastards patrolling the walls, the chances of us slipping out that way are nonexistent. The alternative, Miss Williams, is to stay here."

"Screw that. But what happens when we get to the end of the sewer? Where will we come out?"

"On a scarp of the Rhine. One branch empties into the river just below the Reinhard Heydrich Bridge, the new railway bridge that Comrade Commissar Dashwood built. The SS won't be expecting anyone from Warsaw to pop out in Odessa."

"What do you expect us to do then, swim across the river?" sneered Norma.

"Almost," said Vanka casually. "The WFA have a few sympathizers in Odessa, one of whom has a rowing boat. At night it should be possible to scull across between the river patrols. The Anglos are well organized but that is their weakness: they are predictable."

"But even if they can't see us they'll be able to smell us. After crawling through the sewers we'll be covered from head to toe in—"

Vanka gave a snort of impatience. "The time for debate is over, Miss Williams. If you do not wish to take up my offer then so be it."

For several seconds Norma chewed her bottom lip in indecision. "Okay, okay, but I hope you have someone leading us who knows where they're going. I don't want to end up being lost in a latrine."

"Don't worry on that score," said Trixie, and beckoned to a young girl idly smoking a cigarette on the other side of the room. "This is Róza, the best of all the WFA's sewer rats."

The girl, who couldn't have been more than fourteen years old, tossed the cigarette to the ground and wandered across to stand beside Trixie. "How many?" she asked. It seemed to Ella that Róza wasn't a great respecter of rank.

"The two girls," said Trixie, pointing to Ella and Norma, "and the man." She indicated Vanka. "I'll send Corporal—make that *Sergeant*—Josef Zawadzski with you as escort. He's a reliable man." Zawadzski preened delightedly at this sudden promotion.

"I don't need any escort."

"He's escorting the Daemon, not you."

The girl spat on the floor. "Very well. But before we go, let me spell out the rules. When we are underground I am in charge. Any arguing, especially from you"—Róza gave Norma a hard look—"and I'll leave you down there. And don't think I'm kidding. I'll get out alive no matter what happens; you'll get out alive by doing precisely what I tell you to do, when I tell you to do it. Understood?"

There were nods from everybody in the group, even Norma.

"In the sewers no one will speak except me and you will move as quietly as you can. Sound travels in the sewers and the smallest noise can be heard a long way off. Understand that we're not gonna be by ourselves down there: the Anglos have twigged that we're using the sewers to move around and have started to run patrols of their own. Believe me, you don't wanna be in a firefight in the tubes."

She accepted another cigarette from Vanka, who seemed to have taken a shine to the girl, or maybe, Ella decided, they had their dislike of Norma Williams in common. "Okay, next thing: it's dark down there and people have been known to panic. Anyone who panics and starts shouting or crying will be dealt with." Róza patted the large knife she had scabbarded at her waist. "Understood?"

Everybody nodded.

"There will be no lights used in the sewers."

"How will you know where you're going if you don't have a light?" asked Norma, a definite quaver in her voice.

"I count: so many steps and then left, so many more steps and then right. Final point: it's cold down there. Spring is coming and the snow and ice are thawing. The sewers are running fast and high with meltwater so make sure you're well wrapped up and that you're wearing strong boots." She looked disdainfully at Norma's shoes. "Not ballet slippers: wear those and you'll not get a hundred yards. By the time you get out you'll have lost all of your toes to frostbite."

"How far do we have to walk?" asked Ella.

"If we get lucky with the Anglos, just over a mile; if we get unlucky . . . who knows? It depends on how many diversions we have to make. The danger comes when we go under manholes in areas controlled by the Anglos. They have listening posts there and if they hear us they'll toss down grenades."

"Wonderful," muttered Norma. "Are there any rats down there?" she asked, shuddering at the thought.

"No. The sewers are made of Mantle-ite and are perfectly smooth and perfectly round, so there's nowhere for rats to nest." Róza studied Norma carefully. "You . . . Daemon, I hear you've got a smashed-up knee. Are you going to be able to walk a mile without it giving out? It's tough down there and I ain't carrying you."

"Don't worry, Rambo, I'll manage," answered Norma.

"Okay. Once in the sewer we walk in a crocodile, the person behind hanging on to the belt of the person in front. That way no one gets lost and no one gets to fall. You've ten minutes to get ready. I've got some camphor here to spread under your nose; it won't disguise the smell but it'll give you a few moments to get used to it."

Vanka leaned forward until his mouth was next to Ella's ear. "And I've got a big pot of lard . . ."

WHEN THEY LEVERED THE MANHOLE COVER OFF THERE WAS A SIGH AS the noxious gas escaped from the sewer. It was so bad that Ella was forced to take a step back, which was difficult because of the three pairs of trousers Vanka had persuaded her to wear.

And then there was the lard that he had insisted she smear over her body for insulation. She knew the lard made her smell like an oven-ready chicken but it was as nothing to the rancid stench that came out of the sewer. For a moment Ella thought she was going to hurl. It was a smell she remembered from chemistry class—hydrogen sulfide—but in this case the stench of rotten eggs was garnished by the odor of excrement.

She couldn't believe she was going down there. She must be mad. The general hadn't said anything about having to wade through a river of shit to earn her five million dollars.

Bastard.

Once the entrance to the sewer was open, Róza was all business. "I'll go down first," she instructed as she made a quick final inspection of her charges, making sure that their bootlaces were double-knotted and that they were wearing gloves. It seemed faintly comical for a child to be checking on the preparedness of hulking men like Vanka and the sergeant, but Ella was so frightened that she couldn't bring herself to laugh. "At the bottom of the ladder I'll be turning left, heading in the direction of the river." She pointed toward the Rhine to ensure that there was no misunderstanding. "You, Daemon, will come next and I want to feel your hand gripping my belt all the way. Then you will come down"—she pointed to Sergeant Zawadzski—"then you"—Ella got the nod—"and then you, Colonel Maykov, at the back. And remember: no talking. Our lives depend on it."

Orders given, Róza wriggled down the hole.

Ella watched Norma and Sergeant Zawadzski disappear from sight, then it was her turn. She walked over to the manhole and taking a deep breath—which was a mistake; despite the camphor spread under her nose she nearly gagged on the foul smell—she started to climb down the ladder that had been molded into the side of the tunnel. The sewer seemed to be covered in a layer of slimy, slippery ooze that soaked through the leather of her gauntlets and made it difficult to grip the rungs. She was just thankful that the darkness prevented her seeing what it was that was smearing itself over her hands.

It was *that* dark. Not the darkness of night, not the darkness of a bedroom, but the same total, absolute, unrelenting darkness that she imagined a blind person must experience. Except for the thin light coming from the lantern Trixie Dashwood was holding over the open manhole, the sewer was a Stygian black. Ella looked down and saw the lantern's light flickering and dancing on the water streaming below her feet. It looked like a river of thick, black treacle. For an instant she didn't know if she could do it, didn't know if she had the courage to enter that dark world. Sure she had PINC to guide her if things went wrong, but even that reassurance wasn't enough to quell the feeling of panic rising up inside her. And then her foot was in the swirling water.

Fuck, it's cold! No, not cold; it was absolutely fucking freezing.

Only with a real effort of will was she able to force herself to step off the ladder and into the water, the fast-running stream of filth maybe three feet deep, swirling up around her waist. She stood for a moment in shocked paralysis, letting her body come to terms with the numbness that was invading her legs. It was difficult to stand: the current was unbelievably strong and the curved bottom of the sewer was slick with an inch-thick layer of something indescribably horrible and very, very slippery. To make matters worse there were stones and other flotsam and jetsam washed down from the streets above banging into her legs as the water streamed past. For an instant the buffeting threatened to send her tumbling.

It was the thought of falling into a river of diluted shit that brought Ella to her senses. She fastened her hand onto Sergeant Zawadzski's belt and pressed her other arm against the sewer wall for support.

Splaying her legs against the current, she tried to stand up straight, managing to bash her head painfully against the top of the sewer as she did so. The sewer tube could only have been five foot or so in diameter, so she had to crouch to shuffle forward. How she was going to endure walking cramped and crooked in this hellish place was beyond her.

She heard a splash—and a whispered "fuck"—as Vanka waded into the water. Above her the manhole cover was replaced and in that instant Ella was enveloped by a near-total darkness. It was like being buried alive. And to make things worse it seemed that the walls of the sewer glowed with a faint but very eerie green luminescence.

She felt PINC trying to tell her things, trying to explain about LunarAtion, trying to orientate her, but she was so scared and so fucking cold that she ignored it. She felt dizzy, weak, helpless. Ella had never had any real sympathy for people who claimed they suffered from claustrophobia, but now . . .

A hand grabbed her belt from behind, steadying her. Vanka's mouth was at her ear. "It's okay, Ella. I'm here. Take deep breaths."

Thank God for Vanka.

The crocodile began to edge forward, shuffling and sliding in the fetid blackness.

It was a nightmare. Twice Ella fell—each time stumbling over a brick or a stone lodged on the floor of the sewer—immersing herself in the shit-thick water, desperately struggling to keep her mouth closed, trying not to swallow the effluent that now so liberally coated her hair and face, spitting away the despicable taste on her lips. And both times it was Vanka who hauled her up by her belt and back onto her feet.

She had no idea how long they walked; time had no meaning in that terrible darkness. All she knew was that they had been walking long enough for her to be numb from the waist down and covered in shit and sweat from the waist up. She was tired to the point of exhaustion.

Suddenly she felt Sergeant Zawadzski slither to a halt in front of her and a moment later his voice whispered at her ear. "We've got to cross a junction. Keep very, very quiet. Róza will be lighting a lantern for a moment. Pass this message on to the colonel."

Ella did as she was told and then waited in the darkness. And as she stood she realized that the sound of rushing water that had been the only accompaniment to their progress had been augmented by a low rumbling noise coming from overhead. The SS, she guessed, must be moving steamers around on the surface. She could hear the pounding of the heavy wheels on the cobbles, could feel the thud of their huge pistons as they passed, could imagine the weight of the enormous, heavy vehicles pressing down on her.

A light flared.

Ella flinched, screwing her eyes shut tight before cautiously opening them. By the lantern's flickering light she saw that they were at a crossroads of the sewer system, a junction where two sewers met, the two streams merging to form a heaving rapids, the waters swirling in a turbulent whirlpool. Ella shook her head; no one—well, no one as tired as she was—would be able to pass across that maelstrom without being washed away.

Obviously Róza had anticipated the problem: she delved down

under the water and hauled up a long steel pole that had been pre-positioned there. She lifted the pole until it was resting, banister-like, across the mouth of the sewer set at a right angle to their route, the pole just visible above the surface of the rushing water. "Hold hard to the pole," she whispered. "Put your weight against it, it'll stop you being taken by the current. And for the Spirits' sake, be quiet: the Anglos are right above us and they'll be listening." The girl beckoned Sergeant Zawadzski forward and with him holding tight to the end of the pole, Róza used it to shimmy across the whirl-pool to stand at the opposite side of the crossroads. Once settled she waved to Norma to follow her.

The girl did her best, but even in the lantern's uncertain light Ella could see that she was scared witless. She was about halfway across when disaster struck. Thinking about it later, all Ella could suppose was that one of the bricks skittering about in the churning water had smashed into Norma's damaged knee but whatever it was the girl screamed and her leg buckled. In that instant she lost her footing, was caught by the current and was gone, washed down the sewer to their right. Instinctively Ella made to lunge forward to grab her but Vanka yanked her back.

"She's lost . . ." he shouted, but any further debate was ended when the manhole cover directly above their heads was wrenched back and a lantern on a rope lowered down.

"There!" yelled a voice. "A Polish sewer rat."

There was an ear-splitting explosion as Sergeant Zawadzski fired his revolver: the lantern exploded in a shower of glass and the sewer was plunged back into darkness.

"Retreat," Sergeant Zawadzski snarled, and before Ella quite knew what was happening she was being hauled along the passage they'd just marched down. There were more thunderous blasts of gunfire, yellow and red light flaring in the tunnels, the tang of cordite mingling with the stench of excrement. Suddenly there was a mighty explosion and a shock wave of sound bellowed through the sewer, shoving Ella over, throwing her into the fetid water. She was dragged to her feet by Vanka as Zawadzski loosed off shots, the flashes as the revolver fired blinding her. Ella could barely think as she staggered, gasping and spluttering, after Vanka and Sergeant Zawadzski.

Behind her she could hear shouts of men in pursuit and every now and again a bullet whined overhead, flicking from side to side as it caromed off the impervious Mantle-ite of the sewer wall.

Sergeant Zawadzski, lost in the pitch-black labyrinth, pulled a lantern from his bag and lit it. It was a suicidal thing to do. Without light they were running blind, but so too were the pursuing Anglos. Immediately the lantern was lit there was a fusillade of shots from the SS.

As she desperately tried to duck away from the bullets, Ella realized that thanks to PINC she was a natural sewer rat herself, a sewer rat who didn't need light to know where she was going. "Douse the lantern," she ordered. "I know the way . . . follow me! Keep the current at your back! This branch of the sewer circles around under Odessa. Get there and we'll be able to pick up another route that gives out on the Rhine near the new railway bridge."

"You go on," said Sergeant Zawadzski. "I'll hold them here."

"Don't be fucking stupid, this is no time for heroics," shouted Vanka. "Make a stand and they'll settle you with grenades. Our only hope is to run." He grabbed Ella by the arm and dragged her down the sewer shaft. The current was behind them now, pushing them forward, threatening to topple them over. The frigid water was deeper too; it raced past Ella at chest height, making her gasp with the pain as the cold invaded her body.

Another explosion.

The Anglos were throwing grenades in front of them as they advanced. The noise of the explosions was louder . . . nearer . . .

"To the left, to the left," she shouted. "Move, for the love of the Spirits, move!"

Bullets snarled around them. Suddenly Sergeant Zawadzski pitched forward as though he had been kicked in the back.

Scrabbling around in the darkness, Vanka tried to pull Zawadzski to his feet but it was useless. "Dead . . ." Vanka pronounced, then wrenched the sergeant's pistol from his hand and passed it to Ella. "Fire at them. Make them keep their distance. Don't let them get near enough to lob a grenade."

She grabbed the huge pistol by its barrel. It was so hot that it burned through the leather of her gloves and scalded her hand. She ignored the pain. Just as she'd seen in cop movies she held the revolver two-handed and pointed it back along the sewers. She pulled back the trigger. The bang as the pistol fired was deafening but still Ella kept pulling the trigger until the gun was empty.

Now all there was left to do was run.

It was Ella's PINC-inspired knowledge of the sewers that saved them. She led Vanka in a perplexing and confusing series of turns and backtracks until, finally, she managed to throw off the chasing Anglos. Then . . .

"There!" she heard Vanka shout as he lurched along. It took a moment for Ella to make out what he was talking about. Perhaps a hundred yards ahead was the end of the sewer, illuminated by the unmistakable lights of the city. Spirits lifted by how close to salvation they were, the two of them staggered as fast as they dared toward the sewer mouth.

Then, before she had a chance to realize what was happening, the slope of the sewer pitched forward and Ella found herself being hurled toward the river as though she was riding a water chute.

The only thought she had as she tumbled was *Why didn't PINC warn me?*

29

The Demi-Monde:
79th and 80th Days
of Winter, 1004

What is reBop? That, cats and kittens, is a real killer-diller question. So let me lay it on you straight, no chaser: reBoppers are the beat-daddies toot cool who dig jad music, the music most wigged-out and wonky coming to us from the fly and sly hombres who liveth in the nuJu Autonomous District of NoirVille. But think not that reBop is just about the music. Dig to the maximum that reBop is a way of life and a way of afterlife. ReBoppers are zoned in and mucho de able to diggeth the most secret and strange of Demi-Mondian happenings. In terms of the dark, dark WhoDoo magic they are, like, high, fly and too wet to dry.

—Greetings Gate, Let's Agitate, Cab Calloway,
Bust Your Conk Books

I t took a moment when Ella woke up for her to remember where she was. She remembered being spewed out of the sewer, remembered landing in the icy-cold waters of the Rhine, remembered commandeering a boat to get across the river and remembered Vanka dragging her ashore. After that everything was just a confusion of being bustled through the night-black alleyways of Berlin, and brought, numb and confused, to these rooms that belonged to . . .

She struggled for a moment trying to recall the name. It was a funny name.

Rivets.

That was it: Rivets, the young guy who seemed to be Vanka's friend, who had taken them in and given them a bed for the night. It was Rivets who'd shown her to the bedroom she was now occupying. She remembered taking off her foul and soaking-wet clothes, wrapping herself in a blanket and lying down on the bed, but after that, nothing.

She focused her sleep-heavy eyes toward the clock ticking on the wall. It was two o'clock . . . two o'clock in the afternoon if the sunshine streaming in through the window was any indicator. That meant she'd been asleep for almost ten hours. Using an elbow she levered herself into a sitting position—trying to ignore the protests of her aching body as she did so—and looked around. It was really quite a pleasant bedroom, with a high ceiling and elegant furnishings. It was also very neat and tidy, the only jarring note being the pristine white shirt hanging from the wardrobe door with a sheet of paper pinned to the collar.

Odd.

Grudgingly relinquishing the warmth of her bed, she swung her legs out from under the covers, got to her feet and stretched, arching the pain and the cramps out of her back and reaching high with her arms until her muscles announced that they were recovered from the torment of crouching in the sewers. Then, keeping her blanket wrapped tight around her, she tripped over to see what was written on the message.

> *Good afternoon, Ella,*
> *I've had to pop out for a couple of hours. I'll be back at four o'clock. I suggest that you spend the time ridding yourself of some of the friends you've brought with you from Warsaw and making yourself presentable for a night on the town.*

You'll find some towels and other useful items on the dresser.
I'm sorry but your clothes were beyond salvaging so I've had
them burned. I'll bring you a new wardrobe back with me. In
the interim all I can offer you is the use of one of my shirts.
                                      Your friend,
                                      Vanka Maykov

It took nearly an hour, four big pans of piping-hot water, lots of
scrubbing, savage use of a nit comb and nearly all of a bottle of Mrs.
Murdock's Patented Lice Lotion before Ella began to feel clean and
human again. Spirits revived, she'd put on Vanka's shirt and then set
about brewing herself a mug of coffee.

She was just enjoying a second mug when a very smartly dressed
Vanka arrived back at the rooms, looking freshly barbered and laundered and with his arms laden with boxes.

"Ah, so Sleeping Beauty returns to the land of the living," he announced as he placed the boxes onto the table. "You look marvelous,
Ella, and I have to say that that shirt never looked as good on me as
it does on you. How are you feeling?"

Ella curtsied her appreciation of his compliment. "A little battered and bruised but still in one piece. You were very considerate
regarding the toiletries."

"I trust you found everything you needed. Please, treat my
humble apartment as you would your own home."

"This is *your* apartment?"

"It's a bolt-hole I have in Berlin, but because of fears that it might
be being watched by that swine Skobelev I've steered clear of it of late.
Rivets has been looking after it for me." Vanka must have sensed the
unvoiced question. "Rivets is my partner in crime. He helps me with
some of my more unorthodox business ventures."

As explanations went it explained precisely nothing, which Ella
guessed was exactly what Vanka intended. "What's in the boxes?"
she asked as she settled down on the couch.

"Presents . . . presents for you."

"Oh, good; I adore presents."

"The sad fact is, Ella, that having seen you in that shirt I find myself loath to give them to you. You have very fine legs and it is therefore with some reluctance that I must provide clothes designed to hide them from view." With that he tapped a finger on top of the packages. "But first an apology: I must confess to have taken advantage of you when you were asleep last night."

The sudden concerned look on her face provoked a laugh. "Forgive my clumsy phrasing; I took advantage of you to measure your feet whilst you were asleep. I have taken the liberty of selecting two costumes for you. Louffie Louverture—the man we are to negotiate with regarding the delivery of blood to Warsaw—has a penchant for fine clothes and beautiful women so no expense has been spared! And all this is courtesy of Aleister Crowley and the really quite outrageous fee he paid for us to put on the séance at Dashwood Manor." He opened the first box. "This costume is a tad mundane; it is something a fashionable young lady might wear in the afternoon."

Once the package's contents had been laid out across the back of the couch, Ella found herself astonished by the care that Vanka had lavished on the selection of her outfit. The long skirt was cream colored with deep vents at the back that would, she suspected, give it an elegantly flowing line. There was a contrasting short-cut jacket of the deepest blue with a high collar and gigot sleeves, and a white blouse in the most delicate of lace. The whole ensemble was to be topped off by a straw boater dressed with the inevitable veil.

"Do you like it?" he asked anxiously.

"It's marvelous. Vanka, you have exquisite taste."

"But wait! There is my second selection, an ensemble for you to wear when we visit the Resi tonight."

"The Resi?"

"It's a nightclub here in Berlin."

Ella scrolled through PINC to be told that the Resi in the Berlin District of the ForthRight was a duplicate of the original, Real World nightclub that had been famous—infamous, more like—as a hotbed of immorality and decadence in Weimar Germany.

This should be interesting.

"Strange that there should be a nightclub in the center of the ForthRight. I wouldn't have thought the UnFunnies would have permitted it."

Vanka laughed. "You can thank Beria for the Resi; he wants somewhere where he can let his hair down. He goes there to hunt for girls." Vanka lit a cigarette. "Anyway, as rumor has it, he also keeps it open to piss off Crowley; the pair of them hate each other."

"Why are we going there?"

"It's where we'll find Toussaint Louverture—"Louffie" to his friends. He's one of Shaka's chief lieutenants and he's the chap who can organize the shipment of blood."

"You know him?"

"Yeah, I know him. He owes me for a consignment of blood." He gave Ella a rueful smile. "We'll have to be careful; Louverture's a very dangerous man. He's a Blood Brother so the last thing we want him to know is that you're a Daemon. If he finds out then you'll get to NoirVille all right but you'll find yourself being exsanguinated for your trouble." Vanka took a nervous drag of his cigarette. "Hopefully though he's mellowed a little since I saw him last. Word is that since he's hooked up with Josephine Baker he's a changed man."

"Josephine Baker?"

"Yeah. Louverture isn't just one of the big dukes in the Blood Brothers, he also runs the Revue Nègre—which is currently performing at the Resi—though he only does that so he can keep an eye on his Bronze Venus."

Ella clapped her hands in excitement. "We're going to see Josephine Baker tonight?"

A nod from Vanka.

"Then tonight's going to be one of the most memorable nights of my life."

"I just hope we find Louffie in a good mood, otherwise it might also be the last night of your life. That's why I took so much trouble selecting your evening gown." He opened a second box. "I wanted to find a dress for you which would do more than just adorn your superb figure; it had to be a dress so glamorous, so daring, so risqué that no man seeing you in it—especially Toussaint Louverture—would be able to deny you anything. We're lucky that Louffie's one of the few males in NoirVille who isn't enraptured by men. Therefore . . . voilà!"

From out of the second package he conjured a dress of such sublime elegance that for a moment Ella was lost for words. Made from cream satin, it was long, close fitting, backless and, from what she could make out, nigh on frontless. It was the most beautiful dress she had ever seen.

Vanka seemed unsettled by her silence. "I trust you approve of my selection, Ella, but now having seen you, I think even if you appeared for this evening's rendezvous in that shirt Louverture and every man in the Resi would applaud."

"Oh, Vanka, you've been so very kind to me. It's a wonderful, wonderful dress, but you do realize if I wear it I won't be able to disguise the fact that I'm a Shade."

"The Resi is the one place in the ForthRight where you don't have to hide what you are, Ella. With Josephine Baker's Revue Nègre performing there you'll be just one woman of color amongst many. Tonight you are quite at liberty to flaunt both your color and your beauty."

Before she quite knew what she was doing Ella had skipped up from the couch and kissed Vanka on the cheek.

There was an embarrassed pause, then Vanka raised his hand to the place where she had planted the kiss. "I warned you once before,

Ella, that beautiful young ladies being so free with their affections might find themselves in danger of having their affections reciprocated." And with that he leaned forward and placed the lightest of kisses on her mouth. It was like a dam breaking. Before Ella quite knew what was happening she was in Vanka's arms, her mouth hard against his, their bodies merging.

She'd never felt like this about a man before. She felt dizzy with excitement. It was as though the pair of them *belonged* together.

They broke and spent a breathless moment simply holding one another, simply enjoying the comforting feel of each other's bodies. Then Vanka stood back. "Ella . . . I will help you escape the Demi-Monde, I will guard and protect you, I will never leave you. But you must promise me one thing."

"Anything."

"I know here in this world we can never be together; you've told me that I'm just a copy of a Vanka Maykov living in the Real World. So, when you return there, will you find me?"

"I'll find you, Vanka, I'll find you. Vanka . . . Vanka . . . I love—"

"Gor, bugger me but it's brass monkeys out there," complained Rivets as he barged through the door. Ella and Vanka jumped away from one another and urgently looked for something to occupy their attention. Rivets seemed not to notice the awkwardness of the situation that he'd stumbled into, he simply shrugged and dropped the box he was carrying on the floor. "I got most ov the stuff you wanted, Vanka. The point-two-two was a bit ov a pig to source but I found wun in a 'ockshop."

He dug into the jacket pocket of his overtight and overchecked suit, pulled out a tiny revolver and tossed it to Ella. "'Ere's a 'Welcome to Berlin' present from your pal Rivets, Miss Ella. This 'ere's a lady's gun: small and delicate but good at busting hearts." The boy stretched out a hand. "We didn't 'ave a chance for a proper introduction last night. Me name's Rivets and I'm Vanka's oppo."

They shook hands and immediately Ella knew everything there

was to know about the orphan: how he'd been found wandering the streets by Vanka, who'd taken pity on him; how he'd become a dab hand at helping Vanka with his short cons and how his roguish demeanor hid a penetrating intelligence. Undersized and scrawny he might have been but he'd packed a lifetime of experiences into his fifteen years. In many ways he was a pocket Vanka.

"Rivets; that's an interesting name."

"Got it cos I'm good at nailing birds," answered Rivets with a wink, and then for emphasis made a leering examination of Ella's naked legs. "Nice pins—" he began, and then stopped abruptly when he saw the still weeping cuts on her thigh.

"Crikey, you's bleedin'," he spluttered. "Wot is you, a Daemon?"

"Yes, Rivets, she's a Daemon," said Vanka quickly. "But she's a friendly Daemon."

"A *friendly* Daemon." Rivets chewed the oxymoron around for a moment and then eyed Ella carefully. "I ain't never met a real live Daemon before. You sure she's 'armless, Vanka? I 'ear these Daemons are buggers for villainy."

"Oh, Ella is quite harmless, Rivets, except when she's got her dander up." Vanka took a freshly laundered handkerchief from his pocket and handed it to Ella, who used it to dab away the blood on her leg.

She gave the handkerchief back. "Thanks, Vanka."

"My pleasure." Vanka refolded it and put it back in his pocket. "I'll treasure it."

Cautiously Rivets stepped forward to study Ella's legs more closely. "Well, I've got to say, Vanka, that she don't look much like a Daemon, 'ceptin', ov course, that she's a Shade, but then there are a power of Shades down in NoirVille and they ain't Daemons. Well . . . I don't fink they is." He turned to look at Vanka. "Any'ows, Vanka, wot are yous doing palling up wiv a Daemon?"

"It's a long story, Rivets, but all you need to know is that by helping Ella here we're going to make ourselves very, very rich."

Rivets wasn't convinced. "I don't knows about this malarkey, Vanka. Helpin' a Daemon; that's not natural that ain't."

"It's worth ten thousand guineas to you, if you do," said Vanka quietly.

Rivets paused for a moment, letting his imagination run around with the idea of having so much money to spend. "Well, iffn you puts it like that, unnatural or not, I don't suppose there's any real harm in it."

"No, there's no harm in it, Rivets, but it might be an idea, Ella, if you were to get dressed. We don't want anyone else seeing your legs."

As Ella collected her new clothes she was struck by a thought. "Have you heard anything about Norma Williams?"

Vanka shook his head. "No. She's probably dead, drowned in the sewers. I presume you Daemons *can* drown?"

"Oh yes, we can drown. We Daemons can die in the Demi-Monde just like we can die in the Real World."

"Then it's a penny to a pound that she's a goner. So my advice is that we concentrate on our own problems and stop worrying about the late and very unlamented Norma Williams."

It was harsh advice but, when Ella thought about it, utterly pragmatic. Norma Williams was in all probability dead and if she wasn't the chances of her finding her way in the black labyrinth of the sewers without the help of PINC were virtually zero. She'd done her best to fulfill the mission she'd been given; better now to look after herself and to do everything she could to get home in one piece.

THAT EVENING—CLEANSED, COIFFED AND CLOTHED IN HER REALLY quite outrageous gown—Ella walked with Vanka up to the Resi's grand entrance. She felt giddy with anticipation. She was going to an exciting place with the man she loved.

There . . . she had admitted it to herself. It might have been a ridiculous and stupid and impossible and nonsensical thing to have done but she couldn't deny what she felt. When she was with Vanka she felt alive, more alive than she had ever felt in the Real World. And tonight, no matter what happened with Louverture, she was determined to enjoy herself.

The nightclub was *very* busy. There were crowds bustling around the pavement outside trying to cajole the doormen into allowing them into the place; everyone in Berlin, it seemed, wanted to see Josephine Baker perform. Ella wasn't surprised; in a Sector where everything considered even mildly outré was crushed under the dead hand of UnFunDaMentalism, the chance to witness such a decadent, prurient, yet officially sanctioned event made the Revue Nègre the hottest ticket in town. In fact the competition for tables was so intense that even Vanka, usually so confident in his powers of persuasion, seemed doubtful of his ability to talk his way into the nightclub.

Ella had no such apprehensions. She nodded toward the three doormen guarding the club's entrance. "Which one of those doorstops is the main man?"

Vanka looked and frowned. "Karl. The biggest one, the one with the waxed mustache, but it's no use, he's already turned down a ten-guinea bribe."

Arm in arm with Vanka, Ella strolled—putting a coquettish little wiggle in her walk as she did so—over to Karl. "Miss Ella Baker and her friend Colonel Vanka Maykov, here at the invitation of Mr. Toussaint Louverture," she announced.

Karl spent a few moments running an appreciative eye over Ella's long, slinky, cream-colored gown, and, of necessity, the long, slinky, caramel-colored body the gown was so desperately striving to contain. This done, he checked the guest list. "I'm sorry, Miss Baker, but I don't have you on my list."

"That's because I only decided to take up my big sister's kind invitation to see the show an hour ago."

"Your sister?"

Ella tapped a finger on the poster that decorated the entrance to the nightclub. "My *big* sister, Josie."

"I didn't know Miss Baker had a sister . . . er . . . Miss Baker."

"Well, you do now." If anyone could pull off the trick of playing Josephine Baker's sister, Ella knew it was her; she had the color, she had the same slim figure, she was wearing a suitably elegant and quite risqué gown and she had put a decidedly arrogant lilt in her voice. She had spent so much time trying to sing like Josephine Baker that she was pretty confident she would be able to talk like her.

Ella could tell from Karl's expression that he was faced with something of a dilemma. Probably his manager had told him very forcibly that under no circumstances was he to allow entry to the club to anyone not on the guest list but the scene he could imagine ensuing if he turned Josephine Baker's *sister* away was really too horrible to contemplate. In the end he capitulated.

He unhooked the red rope guarding the club's entrance. "Monsieur Louverture has table number sixty-seven, mademoiselle. It is on the far side of the club. I trust you and Colonel Maykov will have an enjoyable evening."

Together they swept regally into the club, Ella doing her best, as she sashayed through the foyer, to restrain herself from laughing out loud at her triumph. Even the tawdriness of the interior didn't dampen her exuberance.

The Resi's reputation was that it had been the epitome of decadence; instead it seemed decidedly low-rent. The club was built around a large rectangular dance floor surrounded by packed tables themselves bordered by more intimate booths set on two low balconies. It was garishly decorated—to Ella's mind it resembled an old-fashioned cinema that had been tricked out in pink and gilt—and lit by dozens of candelabras. There was nothing subtle about the Resi; it looked just what it was: a huge, brash pickup joint.

Yet when Ella entered the room with Vanka, there was only one couple who grabbed the attention of the crowd. That Vanka was, without a doubt, the best-looking and best-dressed man in the room—with his figure, he was born to wear black tie and tails—contributed to this, but it was probably that he was accompanied by a *Shade* that ensured they would be the center of attention. And Ella, knowing that she looked devastating in her gown and her fur wrap, found being the focus of so much whispered gossip really quite exciting. This, she decided, was what it must be like to be famous, to be a celebrity.

Putting an outrageous sway in her bottom, throwing back her shoulders so her figure was shown to its best advantage, Ella led Vanka in what PINC told her was the direction of table 67, smiling and nodding to the other patrons as she undulated past their tables, acting out every fantasy she'd ever had about being a film star.

There was only one man sitting at the table, a tiny Shade—Ella guessed that when standing he would be a good head shorter than she was—aged about forty, sporting an imperial beard and oddly scarred cheeks (Rite of Passage scars, so PINC told her) and nursing a glass of champagne. Small and ugly he might have been but he was immaculately dressed and his jewelry—his overlarge cravat stud and cuff links—twinkled with diamonds.

"Good evening, Louffie," said Vanka.

Louverture pulled his gaze away from a very appreciative examination of Ella's bosom. A rather unpleasant smile split his face; he didn't seem pleased to see Vanka. "As I live and breathe . . . Vanka Maykov. I heard you were dead, Vanka, I heard they deep-sixed you back in Rodina."

"I decided to stay alive until you had paid me the two thousand guineas you owe me."

Louverture studied Vanka in cold silence for several seconds. "I don't remember any debt . . ."

"I doubt that, Louffie, I doubt that."

"I really hope you haven't come here tonight to cause a disturbance, Vanka, as I'm not in the mood to be leaned on." Louverture made a signal to a large, bearded Shade with a bald head and similarly scarred cheeks who was lurking nearby. "I think Gaston will show you out, Vanka. I think it's time you hit the bricks."

Seizing the moment, Ella leaned across the table, making sure that as she did so she displayed a quite reckless amount of cleavage for Louverture's enjoyment. "Vanka and I aren't here to create waves, Monsieur Louverture. My name is Ella Thomas and I've come here tonight to make you a rich man."

"I am already a rich man, Mademoiselle Thomas," said Louverture in a distracted voice, Ella having no doubt what was distracting him.

"An *obscenely* rich man," she countered.

"This frail of yours shooting straight dice, Vanka?"

He nodded.

"Then you and Vanka may join me, mademoiselle, not because you promise me riches but because you are a Shade with the courage to disport yourself in such a dissolute manner in this den of racism. In the ForthRight such moxie—such foolhardiness—is to be encouraged."

Ella needed no second bidding; she slid into Louverture's booth, closely followed by Vanka.

"May I offer you a drink, mademoiselle . . . Vanka? The champagne provided by the management is quite palatable."

Both Ella and Vanka nodded their agreement and Louverture signaled Gaston to serve his two guests.

"Monsieur Louverture—" began Ella, but her host held up a hand to silence her in mid-sentence.

"I am afraid I must forgo the immediate satisfaction of my curiosity, mademoiselle, and the enjoyment of the no doubt enthralling explanation of your intended philanthropy. The entertainment is about to begin and I have a managerial responsibility to ensure that the Revue performs seamlessly."

Barely were the words out of Louverture's mouth than a line of seven musicians, all painted in blackface and wearing tuxedoes and bowler hats, trooped onto the dance floor playing their instruments as they marched. Ella shuddered in disgust; it was the first time that she had seen real black people sporting this sort of makeup. With their huge white lips and their goofy eyes there was something grotesque about them, something almost golliwog-esque. Ella had to stifle the urge to leap to her feet and harangue them for having no self-respect, for somehow demeaning their race. But then she remembered that she wasn't back in twenty-first-century New York, she was in a pastiche of a time-lost Berlin dropped seemingly at random in the middle of the most racist Sector of a make-believe world.

And as she listened to the band, Ella realized that the combo's one saving grace was that even if their makeup and costuming were comical and degrading, then at least the same couldn't be said of their playing. Each and every one of them seemed to be a master musician and the driving jazz—or rather, jad—they conjured soon had the whole audience swaying.

Happy that his musicians were playing to his satisfaction, Louverture seemed to become bored. He turned back to Ella. "So, mademoiselle, you were about to tell me how you would make me fabulously wealthy."

There was, Ella decided, no point in beating around the bush. "I understand that you are able to secure large quantities of blood."

Louverture leaned back in his seat and gave a doleful shake of his head. "You are a beautiful young woman, mademoiselle, and as such I would recommend that you limit your interests to gowns and to other feminine frivolities. As Vanka has no doubt told you, the trade in blood is a robust occupation, suitable only for men."

Ella smiled. "I take my inspiration from Miss Baker: I do not let the opinion of others deter me from doing what I feel I need to do. And what I need, Monsieur Louverture, is to secure the supply of sixty thousand liters of blood, more if I can get it."

Louverture gawped. "I think you, mademoiselle, are as much the comedienne as Josephine herself. Such a quantity of blood is enormous, simply incredible. The cost—"

"I understand that the black-market rate is one hundred guineas a liter, which makes it a transaction worth six million guineas."

Louverture covered his discomfiture by taking a long gulp of his champagne. "Six million guineas? You got pockets that deep?"

A simple nod from Ella.

"Where would you wish this outrageous quantity of blood to be delivered?"

"To Warsaw."

Louverture gave a loud guffaw. "Impossible! It might have escaped your notice, mademoiselle, but the powers that be in this pestilential place they call the ForthRight have decided to eliminate that part of their population. Warsaw is now a war zone and hence the Rhine is patrolled by ForthRight naval vessels with orders to sink any barge entering those waters without requisite authorization. Even the most courageous of captains would be reluctant to undertake such a mission."

"I will offer two hundred guineas a liter, delivered to Gdańsk dock."

Ella felt the gaze of Louverture settle on her as he tried to assess whether she was on the level. Louverture shook his head. "It is still impossible. To smuggle such a quantity of blood is beyond the wit of man."

"Of course, monsieur," Ella said sweetly, "if such a transaction is too big for you, then I must find a more powerful partner."

As she thought it might, the prospect of letting twelve million guineas slip through his fingers caused Louverture to make a hasty reconsideration. "Twelve million guineas? That's a fortune."

Ella took a sip of her champagne and waited for greed to work its magic. "I promised you I was going to make you an obscenely rich man!"

Louverture laughed. "Beautiful women like you, Miss Thomas, promise men many things. Unfortunately they generally promise much more than they ever deliver."

"Monsieur Louverture, believe me, I never disappoint. I never tease. When I say I will do something, I *always* deliver. I have never left a man unsatisfied." Vanka choked on his champagne and it took both men at the table a few moments to digest Ella's little announcement. "But for twelve million guineas, there is one other service I would ask to be included in this bargain."

This had been Vanka's *real* brainwave. The problem Ella and Vanka had struggled with was how to smuggle Ella out of the Forth-Right; as a Shade she was too easily identified and hence would never be able to get through CheckyaPoints, especially now that her alias of Marie Laveau was known and the passport Vanka had acquired for her useless. But if she traveled as part of the Revue Nègre she would be just one Shade amongst dozens.

Louverture's right eyebrow arched in suspicion at Ella. "And this is?"

"I need to travel to NoirVille, but unfortunately I lack the necessary documents. I want to become a temporary member of the revue."

"That's not a problem; better too many beautiful women than

too few. No, the problem is the blood; *that* I've gotta think about."
Just then the music coming from the dance floor shifted and immediately Louverture turned toward the stage. "But if you will indulge
me for a moment, mademoiselle, this is the climax of the evening.
This is Miss Josephine Baker's pièce de résistance."

Ella recognized the dance immediately. It was the *danse sauvage*,
the dance that had made Josephine Baker into one of Europe's biggest and most controversial stars. As the music mutated into a rippling pattern of African rhythms, Josephine Baker, accompanied by
a tall, muscular male partner, took the stage.

For a moment Ella could barely breathe with excitement: Josephine Baker was her heroine. Josephine Baker was the girl who had
achieved everything that Ella was determined to achieve. She had
been born into poverty in St. Louis at the turn of the twentieth century and had the courage to quit her native America to seek fame
and fortune. She had made a new life for herself in a faraway country
and found stardom as a dancer and singer in the Paris of the 1920s.

Josephine Baker was a girl who had triumphed over adversity,
just like Ella intended to.

Ella was simply thrilled to be seeing Josephine Baker in the
flesh . . . and there was a *lot* of flesh on display. All the dancer was
wearing as she whirled onto the dance floor was a pair of black
satin bikini pants and her iconic skirt made up of a string of artificial bananas. The pants, the skirt and her broad smile—which
seemed to illuminate the Resi—constituted *all* her costume. Her
near-nakedness drew gasps from the audience and there were some
jeers and catcalls from the more UnFunDaMentally inclined customers but these were drowned out by the cheers and the applause
of Josephine Baker's fans.

For Ella it took a moment for the dream and reality to mesh.
Somehow La Baker seemed smaller than she had imagined, younger
too, but when she started to dance there was no mistaking her. No

one could mistake the sheer energy and exuberance the girl brought to her dancing. But there was more than energy and a dancer's panache in her performance . . . there was also an unbridled eroticism.

When she had read about Josephine Baker's *danse sauvage*, Ella had imagined that apart from the nudity, it would be pretty tame. She had been wrong. It was obvious that the authors who had described the decadence that had washed through Continental Europe in the early 1920s hadn't been brave enough to tell the truth about the levels of salacious debauchery plumbed in postwar Berlin and Paris.

Now Ella realized what all the fuss had been about, just why Josephine Baker had shocked European society a century ago. Her dance was earthy, it was animalistic, it was erotic and it was untamed. Shit . . . it was borderline pornographic.

As Josephine Baker spun and twirled across the floor, snaking and slithering her slim and wonderfully toned body around her partner, Ella began to understand why the dance had been labeled "degenerate" by the critics of the day. Josephine Baker connived to include all the moves and gestures in her dance that any "respectable" person would know to be taboo. The one saving grace was that the dancing was performed at such breakneck speed that it was almost impossible to appreciate just how down and dirty it actually was. And it *was* obscene . . . obscenely artistic.

The girl, Ella decided as she watched openmouthed, had to be double-jointed; there was no other way to explain how anyone could leap and cavort as Josephine Baker did. Dressed in her tiny costume, she tore across the stage in a whirlwind of splits and pirouettes, wriggles and shakes. Her arms, rump, head and legs all moved seemingly independently of one another, shaking and snaking to the various rhythms laid down by the band's pulsating jad.

The remarkable thing was that though her audience was liberally flecked with a sizable number of Shade-hating SS officers—the quantity of black uniforms Ella could see attested to that—the vast majority of the audience loved her, clapping and cheering, laughing and shrieking as the black dervish whirled across the dance floor. In two or three breathless minutes the *danse sauvage* was over, leaving the audience stunned . . . agog with astonishment.

She was replaced onstage by a chorus of crooning men, who obviously ranked much lower in Monsieur Louverture's affections than Josephine Baker. "She's amazing, is she not?" breathed Louverture as he mopped his forehead with a handkerchief, gazing all the while in a rapturous manner at the stage where Josephine Baker had just performed. Here, Ella thought, was a man in love.

He was also a man who was no longer in the mood to talk business: for the next ten minutes he resisted all Ella's attempts to get him to commit to supplying blood to Warsaw. Even the prospect of earning twelve million guineas didn't seem enough to overcome his intransigence. She was just on the point of admitting defeat when she became aware of a woman standing next to her clad in a gown of shimmering blue silk, a color that set off her tawny skin to perfection. The huge brown eyes of Josephine Baker gazed down at Louverture and his guests.

Looking at her, Ella realized the photographs she had studied of her heroine didn't do her justice. Sure she was as lissome as she had been pictured, sure her hair was flattened in her trademark slicked-down, Eton-crop hairstyle, and sure her eyes were as expressive and as enticing as Ella had imagined they would be—but no photograph could ever capture the sheer vitality that radiated out of the woman. Just standing there, hip cocked, smiling down at Louverture, Josephine Baker pulsed with energy and unsuppressed joie de vivre.

"Say, Louffie honey, ain't cha gonna introduce me to your new friends?"

Louverture and Vanka leapt to their feet so quickly that they rattled the table. "*Ma cherie,*" crooned Louverture as he kissed the dancer's hand, "may I have the pleasure in introducing Colonel Vanka Maykov and his friend, Mademoiselle Ella Thomas. Colonel, mademoiselle, I have the great honor of introducing the Black Venus . . . the Shade Goddess . . . Mademoiselle Josephine Baker." Josephine Baker held out her hand to Vanka, who bobbed his head to kiss her fingers, then shimmied herself into the seat next to Louverture, rewarding him with a flirtatious little peck on his cheek. As Louverture poured her a glass of champagne, she looked up and smiled at Ella.

"You a dancer, honey?" Josephine Baker asked. "You sure got the chassis for it."

"I was a dancer when I was younger, Miss Baker, now I sing."

"No kidding?" Josephine Baker raised her left eyebrow in surprise. "You looking for a job, honey?"

"Miss Baker, nothing would give me greater pleasure than to sing in a show in which you were starring. And hopefully, if the business proposition Monsieur Louverture and I have been discussing comes to fruition, then I will be able to do just that."

"Business proposition? What kind of business proposition, Louffie baby?"

Ella answered the question for Louverture. "I'm in the market to buy blood."

"A *lot* of blood," added Louverture quickly. "Mademoiselle Thomas wants me to ship sixty thousand liters of blood to Warsaw."

Josephine Baker eyed Ella shrewdly. "And why's a Shade like you getting so het up about all those Blank cats holed up in the Ghetto?"

"Because, Miss Baker, if we don't help the Poles today, then they won't be around tomorrow to help *us*. One day everybody, black and white, is going to have to help defeat Heydrich."

Josephine Baker smiled and then raised her glass in acknowledgment of Ella's reply. "Good answer, Miss Thomas, good answer. You know, I pulled outta the Rookeries two years ago when Heydrich started to get hot and heavy with those cats who weren't of the pale persuasion. This UnFunDaMentalist jive ain't warm and welcoming to us Shades so I hauled ass to Paris, where no one gives a rat's fart whether I'm black, white, green or blue . . . well, they didn't used to until that piece of shit Robespierre started mouthing off. That cat and the rest of the Gang of Three are really screwing the Quartier up. Bastard Dark Charismatics; I hate them all." She took another long pull of her champagne. "This is the first time I've been back to the ForthRight since then and I can tell you, Miss Thomas, it's gonna be the last time. To me what color your skin is don't matter a fig, what matters is the color of your soul, and Heydrich's soul is blacker than my skin will ever be."

Ella nodded her agreement. "I hope the day will come when skin color just means nothing more than the tone of your skin, when your religion is just seen as the way your soul speaks, when the place where a person is born has no more weight than the throw of dice and when we are all born free, when understanding breeds love and brotherhood."

"That's a big piece of mouth for a girl as young as you, Miss Thomas," said Josephine Baker quietly. "Did you write that?"

"No, Miss Baker, *you* did. It's one of the most important things I ever learned."

Josephine Baker stared at her. "I don't remember—"

Ella moved swiftly on. "The problem, Miss Baker, is that Heydrich is making war to ensure the racial purity of the Demi-Monde. Conquest will give him the opportunity to erase all those he perceives to be UnderMentionables—subhumans. And both of us, Miss Baker, and you too, Monsieur Louverture, are included in that category."

That had a salutary impact on the mood around the table.

"So do the cats in Warsaw have a chance?" asked Josephine Baker.

"It all depends on how you define having a chance," said Ella. "The Poles will never be able to defeat the Anglos but the longer they can keep fighting, the more people will come to realize that the ForthRight can be beaten. And that, I think, will be the greatest gift the Poles can give the people of the Demi-Monde: belief that fighting the ForthRight isn't just an exercise in futility."

"Is such a thing possible?" asked Louverture. "Are the Poles really willing to fight on despite the odds?"

"Only if the other Sectors help; the Varsovians can't survive and fight without ammunition, without food and without blood."

The conversation was interrupted by the arrival of a waiter who handed Louverture a note. He unfolded it and read the message. "*Ma cherie*, your no-account count over there on table twenty-five"— he nodded across the floor of the nightclub—"has invited us to join his party."

He gave Ella and Vanka a smile of apology. "Monsieur . . . mademoiselle . . . you must excuse us, but unfortunately Miss Baker has her duties as the foremost star of musical theater in the whole of the Demi-Monde to attend to. If you will excuse us." Both he and Josephine Baker rose from the table, but then Louverture paused. "I will consider your proposal, mademoiselle. Perhaps it might be possible for you to attend me again, say at four o'clock tomorrow afternoon? We are rehearsing a new routine . . ." He left the sentence unfinished as he bowed his au revoir.

30

The Demi-Monde: 81st Day of Winter, 1004

The future of UnFunDaMentalism is inextricably linked with the success of the ForthRight. If and when the ForthRight expands politically and/or geographically so UnFunDaMentalism will expand in lockstep. The decision of the Medi city-states (Paris, Rome and Barcelona) in the Quartier Chaud to make a Unilateral Declaration of Independence from Venice and to reject ImPuritanism in favor of UnFunDaMentalism indicates the attraction of UnFunDaMentalism (and Biological Essentialism) to certain of the more perceptive Leaders active in the Demi-Monde, within whose ranks Senior CitiZen Robespierre is most certainly numbered.

—EDITORIAL COMMENT, THE STORMER, 82ND DAY OF WINTER, 1004

I can have fifty thousand liters of blood on a barge by the second day of Spring . . . in ten days," Louverture confirmed offhandedly, reluctant to take his attention away from the girls rehearsing their routine on the Resi's dance floor. "We can have it shipped up the Rhine accompanied by paperwork that says it's a delivery of palm oil for a broker in Berlin. At the last minute we'll redirect it to the Warsaw docks. And as for your other request, the revue will be departing for Paris tomorrow and you are welcome to accompany us, Mademoiselle Thomas."

"How much?" asked Vanka.

"The price is the one agreed with Mademoiselle Thomas. Two hundred guineas a liter, ten million guineas in total, payable upfront."

"Half now and half on delivery," countered Vanka.

Louverture nodded. "Very well, but the second half is payable as soon as the barges are alongside Gdańsk docks. It's your responsibility to unload the blood."

"Do you have the bank account where the funds are to be transferred?"

Louverture pushed a tightly folded piece of paper across the table, which Ella placed securely in her purse. Then they shook on the deal.

Ella looked at Louverture sternly. "Monsieur, you are unaware that I am a clairvoyant. Just one touch of another person's hand and I know all their secrets. And now, having shaken your hand, I know that you intend to renege on the deal we have just made. When the two barges are at the mouth of the Rhine, it is your plan to demand a further two hundred guineas a liter or you will have the barges turn around and return to NoirVille."

Louverture frowned. "Mademoiselle . . . you are mistaken . . . I would never—"

"Monsieur Louverture, I would strenuously advise you against this sort of duplicity. If you attempt to cheat me I will have no hesitation in advising Lord Shaka of the side deals you have been doing with Victor Lustig that have deprived him of almost a million guineas of profit. I don't think I need to remind you of how unforgiving Lord Shaka and his Blood Brothers are of those who cheat them."

The frown deepened. "How—"

"As she says, Ella is the most proficient clairvoyant in the whole of the Demi-Monde," explained Vanka airily. "She knows everything."

"So? Do we have a deal then, monsieur?" asked Ella. "A deal we are *both* intent on honoring?"

"You have, mademoiselle," said Louverture unhappily.

—☙—

"WE'VE DONE IT, VANKA, WE'VE DONE IT!" EXCLAIMED A JUBILANT Ella as she skipped out of the Resi. "We've organized the blood for the Ghetto *and* by tomorrow we'll be on our way to NoirVille."

"Not 'we,' Ella; it's *you* who will be on *your* way to NoirVille."

Ella stopped dead. "What . . . what do you mean?"

"Oh come on, Ella. You can't really imagine that I'll be able to hide myself away in a troupe of Shade singers and dancers. I'll stick out like a . . . well, like a Blank in a troupe of Shade singers and dancers. No, it's best that you travel to NoirVille alone; it's safer that way."

"Vanka . . ." Up until that moment she had been very happy; she was, after all, a girl in love, a girl who had steadfastly refused to think about leaving him and going back to the Real World. But now the unpleasant reality of how different they were came sweeping over her.

Vanka gave her hand a reassuring squeeze. "It's for the best. Ella, I have to know you're safe. So let's just concentrate on getting to a Blood Bank and sending the money to Louverture. The quicker we're back at my lodgings the better."

The Berlin Blood Bank was just around the corner from the Resi. It was a spectacularly big building, a vast stone temple that dwarfed anything Ella had seen in either the Demi-Monde or the Real World. The white stone it had been constructed from shone bright and pure in the sharp Winter sunlight. Looking at the Bank she thought the Demi-Monde's programmers must have modeled it after one of the great central banks of the Real World: it was all huge columns, magnificent stone steps that climbed up to enormous doors and the whole lot decorated with a confection of majestic sculptures of forgotten dignitaries. Remarkably the walls and the carved columns were perfect; there was not a crack or a scratch to be seen anywhere. It was so perfect as to be unnatural.

"How old is the bank?" she asked, preferring to hear the answer from Vanka rather than PINC.

"We don't know exactly," answered Vanka as he looked anxiously around for Checkya agents. "The Blood Banks are classified as Wonders of the Ancient Demi-Monde. They're built from Mantle-ite, the same stuff the sewers are made out of, hence the green sheen."

"Is that why the building is in such mint condition?"

"Yes, Mantle-ite is impervious to wear or corrosion and invulnerable to attack. They hose the banks down once a week and, hey presto, they're as good as new. So believe it or not, this building"—Vanka waved toward the bank—"is—depending on which learned professor of preHistory you're inclined to believe—somewhere between ten thousand and a hundred thousand years old."

"But who do these historians think built them?"

"Here, in the ForthRight, UnFunDaMentalist dogma has it that Heydrich's super-Aryans, the Pre-Folk, were responsible." Vanka gave Ella a crooked smile. "Apparently we Anglo-Slavs could build edifices like this before we were seduced by people like you."

Ella laughed. "I apologize."

"Don't," said Vanka. "Having seen you in that dress last night I forgive my ancestors all their indiscretions. They would have needed a will of steel to resist women as beautiful as you." He gave her arm another squeeze and Ella almost cried as an odd feeling of both sadness and happiness washed over her.

As they climbed the steps two Checkya officers emerged from the Bank; Vanka immediately pulled Ella to one side. "If you keep your veil tight, Ella, I think it will help avoid any unpleasantness. If you're challenged just tell them you're one of Josephine Baker's troupe."

More than a little worried by how edgy Vanka seemed, Ella did as she was asked. And then she froze. Over at the other side of the steps lounging nonchalantly against the wall of the Bank was Professor Septimus Bole. She was sure it was him. She recognized the long skinny body, the great rudder of a nose and the small shaded spectacles. Instinctively she made to move toward him, but the crowds jostling around the Bank's entrance stopped her and when they cleared the professor had vanished.

She frowned; why was the Dupe of Professor Bole haunting her? She was sure she had seen him when the Checkya had raided her apartment and now he was here. But why didn't he speak to her?

She didn't have a chance to ponder. With another nervous look over his shoulder, Vanka led her through the great doors and into the vastness beyond.

The Banking Hall was enormous, so enormous that though there were thousands of people milling around it still felt empty. The ceiling stretched a good two hundred feet over Ella's head and the hall must have been at least four or five hundred feet wide. How deep it was she couldn't even guess; it just seemed to disappear into the distance.

It was also incredibly noisy, resonating with a strange clacking sound, as though a million rattles were being played simultaneously.

Vanka noticed her confusion. "The noise is coming from the screens in the Transfusion Booths. That's where customers can move both the money and the blood they've got in the bank." He pointed to the stone walkways that coiled up the walls winding from floor to ceiling and along which niches—the Transfusion Booths—were set at ten-foot intervals. "The screens are what you use to view your accounts and to make infusions and transfers. They reckon there are half a million Transfer Screens in every single Bank—one for every four people in a district—and that's why Banks are always so noisy."

Taking Ella by the arm, Vanka led her up along one of the walkways until they came to an unoccupied booth set about twenty feet or so up from the floor of the Bank. Here she found herself staring at what seemed to be a bizarre, clockwork interpretation of an ATM. There was a viewing port, which looked not unlike those employed on old-fashioned mutoscopes—the "What the Butler Saw" machines—that had been the staple of fairgrounds and amusement arcades a hundred years ago, and above this was a large screen similar to the moving-type message boards that she had seen in movies featuring airports of yesteryear. The booth was equipped with a clunky-looking keyboard—an image of a handprint to its left—set on a shelf positioned below the mutoscope viewer. Finally there was a faucet to the right of the keyboard from where she presumed blood was dispensed.

"Let's get going, Ella," urged Vanka. "I hate Banks, they're always crawling with Checkya. You begin by placing your hand on the red handprint. That allows the Bank to identify you."

"How?"

"The Spirits only know," said Vanka impatiently.

Gingerly she placed her hand over the symbol indented into the surface of the shelf. For a second nothing happened, although she had the distinct impression of a tingling along her palm. Then the little squares that made up the screen started to whirl, clacking loudly as they spun. When the letters on the squares eventually stopped rotating Ella saw a message spelled out for her.

THE BANK OF BERLIN WELCOMES
ELLA THOMAS

Wow . . . I'm in!

PLEASE ENTER YOUR PASSWORD

Password? Without thinking she began typing.

LILITH

Now where did I conjure that from?

PASSWORD ACCEPTED

"You've been accepted," breathed a relieved Vanka as the little squares whizzed around again.

CASH OR BLOOD TRANSACTION?

Ella typed "CASH."

WHICH ACCOUNT DO YOU WISH TO ACCESS?

She typed in the account number of the SS–Ordo Templi Aryanis.

PLEASE ENTER THE PASSWORD FOR THIS ACCOUNT

Ella typed in "THELEMA." Even if she hadn't read Crowley's mind she'd have known that was the password he'd have chosen. Thelema was the black magician's occult creed, based on the philosophy of "Do what thou wilt shall be the whole of the law."

PASSWORD ACCEPTED

WHICH SERVICE DO YOU REQUIRE?

1. WITHDRAWALS
2. DEPOSITS
3. TRANSFERS
4. OTHER

Ella hit the "3" button and immediately the letters that made up the screen clattered around.

> ACCOUNT NAME AND NUMBER TO WHICH THE TRANSFER IS
>
> TO BE MADE
>
> AMOUNT
>
> DATE TRANSFER TO BE EXECUTED

Ella dug out the piece of paper that Louverture had given her and, fingers dancing over the keyboard, sent five million guineas winging its way. Next she paid the half-million guineas she'd promised Burlesque Bandstand.

The letters spun again.

"Do you have an account, Vanka, an account that the Forth-Right can't block?"

Vanka had, and again Ella worked the keyboard. "There," she said with an air of triumph, "ten million guineas, all that was left in the Ordo Templi Aryanis account, is now safely resting in the account of Vanka Maykov. When you've paid Louverture the second tranche that'll leave five million guineas for you. How does it feel to be a multimillionaire, Vanka?"

"Great," said Vanka testily. "Can we go now?"

"In a moment," said Ella as the screen churned again.

> ANOTHER SERVICE?

With a shrug, Ella typed in her question.

> WHAT SERVICES AVAILABLE?

The answer that rolled around on the screen left her numb.

ELLA THOMAS YOUR SECURITY CLEARANCE IS SUCH THAT YOU ARE
ABLE TO ACCESS THE DEMI—MONDE® IM MANUAL

"What's an IM Manual?" asked Vanka. "I've never heard of anyone accessing an IM Manual before."

"I'm not sure," said Ella as she worked the keyboard again.

IM MANUAL?

The answer came back immediately.

THE INTERFACE MANIPULATION MANUAL FOR THE DEMI—MONDE®

Ella's fingers danced over the keyboard.

ACCESS DEMI—MONDE IM MANUAL.

The response was instantaneous.

PLEASE BE ADVISED ELLA THOMAS THAT YOU HAVE GRADE 8
(CAPTAIN OR ABOVE) STATUS. IN ACCORDANCE WITH PROTOCOL 57
THIS ALLOWS SUCH INDIVIDUALS, WHEN DEPLOYED IN THE DEMI—
MONDE® AND FACED BY MORTAL DANGER, TO MAKE EMERGENCY
ONE—HOUR CHANGES TO THE DEMI—MONDE'S CYBER—MILIEU. IN
ORDER TO PRESERVE THE DUPES' PERCEPTION OF THE LOGICALITY
OF THE DEMI—MONDE® SUCH CHANGES MAY NOT VIOLATE THE
NATURAL LAWS PREVAILING IN THE DEMI—MONDE. ALSO NOTE THAT
BEFORE SUCH CHANGES ARE MADE PERMANENT THEY MUST BE
RATIFIED BY THE DEMI—MONDE® STEERING COMMITTEE. IF SUCH
RATIFICATION IS NOT RECEIVED BEFORE ONE HOUR HAS ELAPSED
THE AMENDMENT TO THE CYBER—MILIEU WILL BE ANNULLED.

PLEASE ENTER "YES" IF THESE CONDITIONS ARE UNDERSTOOD AND
ACCEPTED.

Ella stood staring at the screen for several indecisive seconds.

She could get into ABBA!

She could alter the Demi-Monde!

Taking a deep breath, she brought her finger over the "Y" button and pressed.

THE DEMI-MONDE® IM MANUAL

OPTIONS:

1.   LOCATE DUPE

2.   ADD DUPE

3.   DELETE DUPE

4.   AMEND DUPE CHARACTERISTICS

5.   AMEND DUPE PERCEPTIONS

6.   AMEND CYBER-MILIEU CHARACTERISTICS

Eureka!

She swallowed hard, her mind buzzing with possibilities. Using the IM Manual she could find out if Norma Williams was still alive and she could help the people of Warsaw. If she could manipulate the Demi-Monde there was no end to the possibilities of what she could do.

"We've got to go, Ella," she heard Vanka whisper urgently in her ear.

"Just a few seconds more."

"No . . . now!" He pulled her around so that she was facing back toward the hall.

What she saw chilled her blood. There on the floor of the Bank were four black-uniformed SS troopers pointing up toward them.

"That bastard Louverture has sold us out," snarled Vanka. "I should have known better than to have trusted a Blood Brother. Come on, we've got to run for it."

Ella barely had time to stab a finger on the keyboard's "CANCEL" button before he dragged her away from the booth and was racing her back along the walkway.

They nearly made it.

That there were only four SS officers and miles of interlinked walkway to run along made escape almost too easy. It was like a life-or-death version of snakes and ladders, with Vanka and Ella running up and down between the levels, dodging among the press of customers, while the SS officers scurried after them shouting and yelling and all the time trying to anticipate which way the fugitives would go.

They were out-thought by Vanka. He managed to get himself and Ella to a walkway only ten feet or so above the floor of the Bank and then, grabbing Ella by the hand, jumped to the floor below. The maneuver was so unexpected that just for an instant the SS were flummoxed, and an instant was all that Vanka needed. He hauled Ella to her feet and together they raced to the Bank's exit.

Vanka's smile of triumph was short-lived: the pair of them ran straight into two large SS troopers who were standing guard at the door. Even as Vanka turned to yell a warning to Ella, he was felled by a savage smack from a blackjack.

"UP YOU GET, COMRADE MAYKOV, AN' YOU AN' THE SHADE MOVE NICE an' easy toward that black steamer parked over there by the pavement. His Holiness Comrade Crowley would like a word."

With a quick look to Ella, Vanka climbed painfully off the floor, rubbed the bump on his head and then the pair of them were pushed and shoved into the steamer. The SS sergeant clambered in after them and shut the door firmly behind him, the black-tinted windows and the heavy steel body of the steamer sealing them away from the outside world.

A sour-faced Crowley was seated waiting for them. He used the revolver he was holding to wave them into the seat opposite his. "Have they been searched?" he asked.

"Yes, Your Holiness, we frisked both of them. They're clean."

And you enjoyed every second you were doing it, you pervert, added Ella silently. *But fortunately you weren't perverted enough.*

Crowley relaxed. "So I finally manage to track down the elusive Vanka Maykov and his mysterious PsyChick, Mademoiselle Laveau. I cannot tell you how happy I am to have found you. At last we have an opportunity to resume the acquaintanceship that was so abruptly interrupted by your disappearance from Dashwood Manor. You should know, Maykov, that your abduction of the Daemon has caused me some considerable embarrassment; I was heavily criticized by the Leader for not recognizing you for the villain you are." He took a long suck on his cheroot and then blew smoke into Vanka's face. "Yes, capturing you and Mademoiselle Laveau will be quite a feather in my cap. The Leader is *very* anxious to meet her again."

"How did you find me?" asked Vanka.

"A little bird whispered in my ear, a little bird who is very anxious that Mademoiselle Laveau stop dabbling in the Dark Arts. But really, Maykov, I'm not here to answer your questions, you're here to answer mine. Firstly: what were you doing conniving with that black wretch Louverture? And please don't dissemble; Karl, the doorman of the Resi, is a loyal Party member."

"I was trying to buy blood."

"I suspected as much. I have had you investigated, Maykov, so I know you are a reprobate with a history of blood trafficking." Crowley flicked ash from his cigarette over Vanka's knees. "Unfortunately for you this is one deal which will remain unconsummated. By to-night Louverture and the rest of the black trash performing at the Resi will have been declared personae non gratae and thrown out of the ForthRight. But a question arises: what were you doing in the Bank?"

Now this, Ella realized, was a bloody difficult question to answer. That the money to pay for the blood had come from the coffers of the Ordo Templi Aryanis was not, she guessed, an answer that would be popular with His Holiness. Vanka seemed to be stumped for an alternative and believable answer and therefore opted to stay silent. It was a silence that provoked Crowley; he slashed the barrel of his revolver across Vanka's face.

"Answer me!" he snarled as he raised his hand for a second strike.

"No . . . !" Ella blurted out.

With a thin smile of triumph dressing his mouth, Crowley turned his attention to Ella. "My, my, a cross-racial show of affection. My cup really does runneth over. This will make my work at Wewelsburg all the more delicious. The Leader has evinced a great deal of enthusiasm to meet you again, Mademoiselle Laveau, but what condition you are in when he meets you . . ." Crowley glanced back to Vanka and gave a sardonic laugh. "I presume you are aware of the punishment for the Race Crime of Miscegenation, Maykov? It's gelding." He shook his head in mock dismay. "I am disappointed in you, Maykov, it's never advisable to mix business with pleasure, though I admit your slattern of a PsyChick has a certain appeal."

"I'm no slattern—" began Ella, but her protest was stymied by a slap across the face.

The pain was worth it. Despite the difficulty she had in reading Crowley, in that instant she knew what he had planned for her and Vanka and it was an insight that made her blood run cold. But she had learned other things too . . . important things.

All she had to do now was get away from this monster.

"Be quiet! I will not be interrupted by a primitive such as you. Remember I have seen you perform! No woman other than a trollop would disport herself in such a lascivious manner. Your kind should know their place, and in your case that is on your back."

It was the gleam in the man's eye that gave Ella an idea. "Dat's right, sir," she said, mumming her NoirVillian accent. "Ah would sure like to perform on mah back for such a fine man like yous."

"Disgusting," muttered Crowley, but his interest in Ella seemed to ratchet up a little.

"An' then maybe you'd get to feel mah fine, long legs around yous." And to the astonishment of the three men crammed in the steamer's cabin she began to slowly draw the hem of her long skirt up over her legs. "Dey says ah's got the prettiest ankles in all ob de JAD." As though to emphasize the point, she wriggled her foot around. "But ah tinks dat it's mah calves dat are de nicest." She pulled the skirt up over her knee and hooked her leg around so that Crowley could get a view of her silk-stocking-encased calf. "Den dere am some gentlemen who am ob de opinion dat it is mah thighs dat am de fings dat makes paying for me to service dem worthwhile."

Ella artfully drew the skirt over her thighs. Three sets of eyes were locked in stunned appreciation of the succulent flesh she was displaying. Then she started giggling. "Ob course it might be de ting hidden *between* mah legs dat dey find most exciting." With an evil little wiggle she delved her hand under her skirt. When it reappeared it was holding the small but very businesslike revolver Rivets had procured for her just the day before, a revolver that she was pointing straight between Crowley's eyes.

"I would be obliged, Your Holiness, if you would lower your weapon . . . the one you're holding in your hand, that is." All trace of the NoirVille accent had vanished; now her tone was much more threatening. "I shall count to three and if you haven't surrendered your weapon by then I will shoot you through the eye."

"My dear young lady, don't you realize that my colleague here has a pistol jammed in the ribs of your friend Vanka Maykov?"

"One!"

Crowley swallowed hard. "This is ridiculous. Shoot me and you won't get ten yards."

"Two!" Ella decided not to count to three.

Screw playing fair.

Instead she shot Crowley in the shoulder, the impact of the bullet causing him to pull the trigger of his own weapon. The gun exploded, the bullet smacking with a wet thud into the SS sergeant's leg. Vanka didn't need a second invitation; he smashed his elbow back into the thug's face.

"Out!" he shouted as he pushed open the steamer's door and jumped into the road, kicking the second SS trooper standing guard there squarely between the legs as he did so.

All Hel broke loose. A steamer that had been trundling along Blumenstrasse swerved to avoid the door that Vanka had thrown open, crashed into a dray cart hauling a shipment of potatoes coming in the opposite direction and demolished two stalls standing by the side of the road. In seconds the street was reduced to a shouting, cursing, fighting chaos and it was a chaos that Vanka, dragging Ella behind him, used to escape Crowley's goons.

THEY REACHED VANKA'S ROOMS A BREATHLESS TEN MINUTES LATER. Once he was sure they hadn't been followed, Vanka sent Rivets off to reconnoiter the Resi and to see what was happening there.

The boy was back in less than an hour. "By the Spirits, Vanka, you've really gorn an' done it now. The streets is swarming wiv Checkya. They say there's bin an assassination attempt on His Holiness Comrade Crowley by some Shade bint who's a WhoDlum crypto. From wot I've bin told they're puttin' guards outside every Blood Bank in the ForthRight and at every mooring point along the Rhine and the Volga, *and* they're searching every cart and steamer leaving the ForthRight." He shook his head. "Yous an' Miss Ella 'ere are a couple of really 'ot potatoes."

"Fuck."

"I fink there's more bad news as well, Vanka. I sees that black item Louverture bin led away for questioning by the SS."

"There goes our chance of smuggling you out of the ForthRight, Ella. Our best bet is to stay hidden until the SS get tired of looking for us."

"I can't do that, Vanka, I've got to save Norma Williams," said Ella quietly. "When Crowley slapped me"—and here she brought her fingers up to the four red welts that decorated her cheek—"I read him . . . not clearly, his mind is too well shielded for that, but well enough. Norma Williams is alive and Crowley has her held in a place called Wewelsburg Castle."

"Then the cow might as well be dead," snorted Vanka. "Lots of people go into Wewelsburg Castle but I've never heard of any of them coming out. It's the headquarters of the SS. We'll never be able to rescue her from there."

"I know," admitted Ella. "But the other thing I learned from Crowley is that he's having her moved soon. They're taking her somewhere to use her in the Rite of Transference. I couldn't read where—Crowley had blocked that piece of information—but I know she'll be moved on the last day of Winter. That'll be our chance to rescue her."

"First you've got to find where Crowley's taking her."

"To do that I need to get into a Blood Bank again. Once I'm there I'll be able to find out about Norma *and* I'll be able to help the people of Warsaw. Working the IM Manual has given me an idea as to how I can have the Varsovians escape Heydrich."

"What? Have you gone crackers? You won't be able to get within half a mile of a Blood Bank without the Checkya spotting you."

"Which is the last Bank that Beria and his crew would think I would use?"

Vanka thought for a moment. "Oh fuck . . . the one in the Ghetto."

31

The Demi-Monde: 82nd Day of Winter, 1004

I regret to inform you, Comrade Leader, that my Ministry has received a communication from Venice, endorsed by Doge Catherine-Sophia, stating that until ForthRight troops have been removed from the Warsaw Ghetto all trades handled by the Rialto Bourse with respect to the ForthRight will be suspended. It should be recognized that a full 90 percent of intra-Demi-Mondian trades are conducted through the Bourse and that almost 70 percent of the ForthRight's blood bonds and promissory notes are held by Venetian financial institutions. Without the loans raised on the Bourse it will be difficult for my Ministry to finance the longer-term ambitions of Operation Barbarossa. The ForthRight Guinea will also, effectively, be off the Blood Standard, which will have major—negative—repercussions in terms of its rate of exchange vis-à-vis other Demi-Mondian currencies.

—LETTER WRITTEN BY COMRADE COMMISSAR HORATIO BOTTOMLEY, FORTHRIGHT CHANCELLOR OF THE EXCHEQUER, TO COMRADE LEADER HEYDRICH, DATED 82ND DAY OF WINTER, 1004

When, six hours later, the three of them—Rivets had insisted on coming along to protect Vanka and the ten thousand guineas he'd been promised—finally emerged, foul and stinking, through the manhole in Zapiecek Square in the center of Warsaw's Old Town, Ella made the silent pledge that that was the very last time she would ever travel by sewer.

This was reinforced by the experience, when she first poked her head out through the manhole, of having a rifle shoved in her face by a ragged boy who looked barely old enough to shave. That the boy had a piece of tattered cloth with the words "Lieutenant: WFA" scrawled on it pinned rather crudely on the sleeve of his filthy jacket only confirmed to Ella just how desperate the plight of the Varsovians was.

"Who goes there?" the boy squeaked.

"My name is Ella Thomas, and I am the girl who, if you prod me with that rifle one more time, is going to jam it up your ass and pull the trigger." The cold fury in Ella's eyes persuaded the boy to back away.

"Gor . . . I'm sorry, Miss Ella. I didn't recognize you, wot wiv yous bin covered in all that shit." He paused as though waiting for some reaction from Ella. "Don't cha know me, Miss Ella? It's me, Lieutenant Michalski." He stepped as close to Ella as the smell coming off her would allow. "You ain't bin down in those sewers for four days, 'ave you? No wonder you smell so ripe."

Ignoring him, Ella eased herself out through the manhole and spent a few minutes trying to massage some warmth back into her hands and her ass. Finally, feeling vaguely human again, she gave Lieutenant Michalski her best effort at a smile. "It's good to see you again, Lieutenant, and congratulations on your promotion. I would appreciate it if you would have someone take us to the headquarters of Colonel Dabrowski. It's vital that we meet with him right away."

DABROWSKI LOOKED UP WHEN THE THREE OF THEM ENTERED AND gave a tired smile. In the few days since she'd last seen him he seemed to have deteriorated terribly: his face was gaunt and his skin the color of old parchment. His voice trembled when he spoke.

"Now, here are some bad pennies. I never thought to see either you, Colonel Maykov, or your friend Miss Thomas again." He peered into the gloom toward Rivets. "And who's he . . . reinforcements?" He laughed at his own weak joke. "So you made it, eh? I thought when I heard that you'd been ambushed in the sewers that that was the end of you. Pull up a seat." He nodded to three oil drums. "Aren't you going to welcome our visitors, Captain Dashwood?"

Trixie stared at Ella with a look of real dislike on her face. "Did you organize the delivery of the blood?"

There was no point in sugarcoating the pill. "We organized it and I paid for it," explained Ella, "but our contact has been arrested by Beria. As we understand it, there's no chance of the blood being delivered."

Trixie gave the door a savage kick. A mist of brick dust drifted down from the ceiling. "I knew we should never have trusted a fucking Shade."

Ella felt Vanka move closer to her; he was obviously as nervous of Trixie as she was. The girl seemed borderline out of control.

"Please . . . Captain . . ." the colonel pleaded. "You must forgive the captain. These have been difficult days." He looked at Ella and gave a wan smile. "You tried, and for that I am grateful. But now it is over. We lost control of the Warsaw Blood Bank to the SS this morning."

"How bad is the situation?"

"We have two weeks . . . possibly less. There are close to three million civilians crowded in the Industrial Zone and without blood we are finished."

"I might have another idea," began Ella. "Another idea about how we can save the people of Warsaw."

"My, my, Miss Thomas, you Daemons are very devils for ideas, aren't you?" The sarcasm in Trixie's voice was palpable. "What will it be this time? Will you use your Daemon's knowledge of the Demi-Monde to fly all of us out of the Ghetto on winged horses?"

No one spoke, but the silence was almost audible. So far as Ella could judge, Trixie seemed to be on the brink of a nervous breakdown. The savage fighting had finally taken its toll.

"You're quite right to be doubtful, Captain Dashwood," Ella began, "and you're equally correct in believing that, as a Daemon, I know things about the way the Demi-Monde works that you don't." She took a deep breath. "It may be possible to alter the Demi-Monde so that your people can escape the Ghetto."

"How?" said Trixie quietly.

"Actually it isn't my idea; it's Colonel Dabrowski's. I think I might be able to open the Boundary Layer."

"Oh, stuff and nonsense," said Trixie scornfully. "No one can do that."

"I think I can," said Ella simply. "Not permanently, but long enough for your people to escape."

There was a stunned silence. Even Vanka seemed shocked by what she had said.

Dabrowski broke it. "How long will you be able to keep the Boundary open?"

"I don't know," admitted Ella, "but certainly for no more than an hour. The Demi-Monde is governed by people—by Spirits, if you prefer—who have granted me the power to make changes to your world, but these changes will only last one hour. That might be long enough to move your people out of Warsaw."

"Move them where?" asked Trixie.

"Into the Great Beyond."

"Absolutely ridiculous," she sneered. "We don't know what the Beyond is like. We might not be able to live there."

"I think you will," answered Ella carefully; she didn't want to complicate matters by mentioning PINC. "My understanding of the Demi-Monde is that its geography and climate are uniform; this means that in the Beyond the air will be breathable, the wood workable, the soil farmable and the water drinkable. You can see for yourself that trees grow happily there and that the Beyond is home for a great many animals: buffalo, ibex, wild pig . . ."

"But what about blood?" said Trixie scornfully. "No Demi-Mondian can live without blood."

"There are Blood Banks in the Beyond," interjected Vanka. "When Speke made his balloon ascent he reported seeing them."

"Look, Captain Dashwood," added Ella, "I'm not saying this is a perfect solution to your problems. In the Beyond your people will have no access to the goods and commodities provided by the Industrial Zone. It'll be a pretty primitive life."

"But it will be life," said Delegate Trotsky quietly. "All my people have here is the certainty of death." The old nuJu shifted his backside on the oil drum he was using as a seat. "It has long been the dream of my people that one day we would journey to the Promised Land, a place where nuJus would have a home and be free of persecution. We nuJus made a Covenant with ABBA that in exchange for our obedience to His laws He would lead us to the Promised Land. It is this Covenant that has sustained us through all our trials and tribulations. Perhaps the Promised Land referred to by the prophets is the Beyond? Many nuJu theologians have speculated that it might be."

Trixie gave the door another kick. "With all due respect, Delegate Trotsky, this isn't the time for religious revelations or mystic prognostications. We need hardheaded RaTionalism. There are almost three million people trapped here in the Ghetto; we must be sure that they are not escaping certain death here in the Demi-Monde for certain death in the Great Beyond."

Ella nodded sympathetically. "I appreciate your frustration, Captain Dashwood, but it's no use me promising something I can't deliver. I'm not even certain I'll be able to open the Boundary at all. But it *is* a possibility and anything must be better than sitting here watching your people being pounded to death by SS artillery. And, as your colonel has said, you have only two weeks' supply of blood left."

"How will you perform this miracle?" asked Trotsky.

"While I was in Berlin I gained access to a thing called the IM Manual—"

"The IM Manual?" he murmured. "A strange coincidence: Immanual is the nuJu prophet our holy writings foretell will lead my people to the Promised Land."

"The IM Manual allows me to make alterations to the Demi-Monde, but to do this I will have to get into the Warsaw Blood Bank. The only way to use the IM Manual is through one of the Bank's Transfusion Booths."

Trixie gave another sneering laugh. "Then doing that will take a second miracle, Miss Thomas: the SS have now occupied the Warsaw Blood Bank."

"Can you retake it?"

Trixie ran a cordite-blackened hand through her cropped hair. "Maybe. Temporarily. It'll take two hundred fighters to take the Bank and to hold it. How long will you need in the Bank to work this magic of yours?"

"Thirty minutes."

"Make that three hundred fighters. The problem isn't so much fighting our way *into* the Bank, it's that there will be no way we can fight our way out of it. It'll be a suicide mission."

"There's no other way," said Vanka quietly. "To give the three million people trapped in the Ghetto a chance to escape, three hundred fighters must sacrifice themselves."

"You're very generous with my fighters' lives, Colonel."

"Oh, I'll be with them, Miss Dashwood, keeping an eye on young Ella here."

Dabrowski drained his glass of Solution. "You're right, of course, Colonel Maykov, but to venture into the Great Beyond is still a huge risk. Despite what Miss Thomas says, no one knows what dangers might be waiting there. It might be as inhospitable as Terror Incognita. And it will need careful planning. The settlers who go must take seeds and livestock with them, they must take tools and enough food to last them until their first harvests are in. There are a thousand and one things which must be thought of." Dabrowski trailed off as though cowed by the enormity of the decision he was being asked to make. He gave his head a mournful shake. "No . . . it's not a decision I am willing to make."

"Then let the people choose," prompted Ella. "Ask them to vote as to whether they stay or go. That's the democratic way."

"Democracy, eh?" chortled Trixie. "Your friend Miss Norma Williams—the other Daemon—spoke of that. It's nonsense. It has no place in the Demi-Monde."

"And what is this 'democracy' of yours, Miss Thomas?" asked Delegate Trotsky.

"It's a system of government where all the adults in a society vote to elect a leader or a government . . . or, as in this case, vote on something that radically changes their way of life."

"It is a ridiculous system," Trixie Dashwood sneered. "All your democracy is, is a fancy name for mob rule. How can common people know who the best leader is? How can common people know how a nation should be governed? The people must be *told* what to do. Your democracy is a recipe for indecision, muddle and anarchy."

Dabrowski had no such doubts. "No, Miss Thomas is right. The people must be told the risks and the dangers they will be facing if they journey into the Great Beyond and the risks and dangers they face if they stay here in the Ghetto. And then they must choose themselves. It is they who must decide whether they stay or go. Yes, it is for the people to decide, not me."

Trixie stared at him with a mixture of astonishment and contempt. "Colonel, I beg you, don't do this. You cannot *ask* the people, you must *command* the people. A strong leader does not debate, he orders."

"Enough," announced Dabrowski. "We will put the facts before the people of Warsaw and they will decide. If they choose to journey into the Great Beyond it will be their decision, not mine." He gave a wry smile. "But the more immediate problem I have is to find a commander mad enough to take and to hold the Blood Bank."

"That, Colonel, is an honor I claim," said Trixie. "But know this, Shade, if you fail again and condemn three hundred of my fighters to an unnecessary death, I swear by the Spirits that my last act in this life will be to kill you with my bare hands."

And looking at her, Ella knew she meant every word of the threat.

EVEN DABROWSKI, WHO SEEMED TO ELLA TO BE INCREASINGLY LOSING touch with reality, recognized it was impractical to have all of the one and a half million adults in Warsaw gather together to hear what needed to be said. So, following the advice of Delegate Trotsky, the word was passed around the Ghetto that each district should elect representatives, and these representatives would in turn attend a meeting where they would be advised of Ella's proposal and have an opportunity to debate it. After this they would return to their electors to explain what they had heard. In this way, Trotsky hoped, the citizens of Warsaw could make their own informed decision as to whether they would stay or leave.

With five hundred representatives to accommodate, it was decided that the meeting would be held in one of the now empty warehouses in the Industrial Zone. And it was here the next afternoon that Dabrowski took the stage before the massed ranks of the representatives. "My friends and fellow citizens," he began, his voice so weak and tremulous that it barely reached those standing at the back of the warehouse. "I have called you here today in order that we may decide upon our future. I will be brutally frank with you: we have lost control of the Blood Bank and our attempts to secure deliveries of blood from outside the Ghetto have failed. We have a little under two weeks' supply of blood left."

That statement shocked the audience into silence; death was staring them in the face.

"Until yesterday I thought I would be standing before you to tell you that it was time for us to surrender and to throw ourselves on the mercy of Reinhard Heydrich. But now there is a new hope, which promises an uncertain—even a dangerous—future. And being dangerous, it is a future which each and every one of you, individually, must decide to accept or to reject. We believe we have a chance to breach the Boundary Layer."

For a moment the crowd in the warehouse was silent and then it exploded in a storm of questions. Only by slamming a wooden mallet hard onto the table he was using as a lectern was Dabrowski able to restore order.

"I repeat: we have the possibility—and I stress that it is only a possibility, not a certainty—of opening the Boundary Layer and passing through to the Great Beyond."

"Is the Great Beyond safe?" someone shouted.

"We believe it to be habitable. We see animals roaming there, we see trees growing there, we see grass flourishing there and, most importantly, we see Blood Banks standing there. Our own legends tell us that our ancestors once inhabited the Great Beyond. So the answer, as best we can judge, is yes, the Great Beyond is safe. But we will only be able to keep the Boundary open for one hour and then it will close forever. Once you have moved into the Beyond there will be no coming back." Dabrowski was silent for a moment. "But, of course, this will also mean that never again will you have to worry about the lunatic ambitions Heydrich has of destroying our people. It will be a new beginning."

"When must we make this decision?" This question was yelled from the back of the warehouse.

"Our intention is to try to open the Boundary Layer in two days. And I remind you, there will be no returning to the Demi-Monde; everything you will need to start a new life in the Beyond must be taken with you. Once in the Beyond there will be no recourse to the Industrial Zone. Life in the Beyond will be hard." Dabrowski leaned against the table as though drained of energy and for a moment Ella, standing at the very back of the warehouse, thought he was going to faint. Then he gathered himself. "I would ask you representatives to provide me with the names of all those wishing to travel to the Beyond within the next twenty-four hours."

Another question was yelled from the opposite side of the room: "And those who choose not to go?"

"The army will fight on. The people of Warsaw will fight on."

"Good old Trixie," someone shouted, and there was a round of cheering. But most of the crowd stayed silent; they had obviously decided that certain death was not for them.

32

The Demi-Monde: 85th Day of Winter, 1004

I am moved to protest the alarmingly dilatory progress the SS has made in subjugating the Warsaw Ghetto. As you will be aware, the Case Red aspect of Operation Barbarossa may not be commenced until Case White has been completed, Warsaw pacified and our rear is secured. As Case Red necessitates the maneuvering of the ForthRight army through the Hub the attack MUST be initiated not later than the 1st day of Spring if the army's advance is to be completed before ThawsDay, the 60th day of Spring. After ThawsDay the Hub nanoBites wake from hibernation and anything penetrating more than six inches below the surface of the HubLand will be immediately devoured. This, of course, makes it impossible for men and matériel to advance or maneuver in the Hub. Be in no doubt, Comrade Colonel, that the inability of your SS to subdue the Ghetto could lead to the failure of Operation Barbarossa.

—Letter written by General Mikhail Dmitrievich Skobelev to SS Colonel Archie Clement, dated 80th day of Winter, 1004

They emerged from the manhole at the edge of the square and, once she was certain that the coast was clear, Trixie Dashwood hustled her troops into position, the soldiers hunkering down behind the walls of a burned-out building whilst she surveyed the Bank through her battered telescope.

Ella kept as far away from the girl as was physically possible. She had seen the way the girl looked at her and there had been real hate in her eyes. The best thing she could do, Ella had decided, was to keep maximum real estate between the two of them until Trixie had cooled down. The way Ella saw it, the quicker she was out of the Ghetto the better.

There was a nudge from Vanka, who handed her his telescope. "Tell me what you think, Ella."

She brought the telescope up to her eye. The Warsaw Blood Bank was as large and imposing as the one in Berlin and had been built from the same invulnerable Mantle-ite. Despite the carnage and the destruction that surrounded it, the Bank stood undamaged and inviolate in the center of the square, shimmering green in the sunlight. From what she could see the only notable difference between this Bank and the one in Berlin was that the Varsovians, for whatever reason, had built a stone extension onto its front, and it was here that the SS garrison was gathered.

Vanka explained. "So many people visit the Banks that some of the Districts have built Commercial Centers that abut onto them. Firms of lawyers and accountants lease office space in them and there are restaurants and restrooms, all the things the Banks lack."

"Is that why the SS guard is concentrated there?"

"Correct. And of course, as the only way into and out of a Bank is through the Center, that makes it an ideal bunker from which to defend the place. Let's see how many of those SS bastards there are waiting for us."

Vanka took the telescope back and spent a good five minutes counting the SS soldiers.

"I make it fifty of them," he announced finally. "So with the ones inside eating and resting, I guess there're around seventy-five of the buggers. But I don't see any artillery, so that's a blessing."

"Only seventy-five?" queried Ella.

"I'm not surprised. Clement is concentrating his men along a line that surrounds the Industrial Zone, ready to make his final assault. The problem here though isn't the size of the garrison; it's the hundred yards of open square between us and the Bank's entrance. It's a killing ground. All I think we can do is run for it and hope we catch the SS napping."

Ella was less than impressed. "You must be joking. Anyone trying that will be cut down in an instant."

"Then let's hope our lunatic captain can think of a better idea."

Fortunately she could. Even as Vanka asked the question Trixie Dashwood shouted orders to her second-in-command, Lieutenant Michalski. "Have the men spread out and search for a roadworthy steamer. Once they've found that, we need sheets of steel capable of resisting M4 fire bolted and chained to its sides. We're going to make our own armored steamer."

It was the first battle that Ella had ever found herself fighting in and the word that best described the experience was "terrifying." Stepping out from the wall she was cowering behind was to enter a cauldron of flying bullets, explosions and screams of the wounded.

For the first forty yards of the advance on the Bank their improvised armored steamer worked perfectly. Protected by the huge steel sheet chained to its front, the WFA fighters walked slowly and steadily across the square while the SS poured hundreds of rounds of rifle fire quite ineffectually in their direction. The noise of the bullets smacking into the steel was horrendous but Ella consoled herself that it was better to be deafened than to be dead.

By the time they had covered fifty yards it was apparent that whoever was commanding the SS had come to the belated realization that they were wasting their time and that they needed something with a bit more grunt to stop the steamer. And it turned out that Vanka had been wrong: the defenders did have artillery. Thankfully the first shot from the six-pounder was wild, whistling six or seven feet above the steamer, the only effect of the near miss being to galvanize the steamer's driver to urge more speed out of the vehicle. Unfortunately he wasn't quick enough: just five yards from the Bank the steamer was hit amidships by the field gun.

As the steamer's boiler exploded in a fury of scalding steam, the WFA fighters made their final, desperate assault on the Bank. It was mayhem, a jump-cut sequence of death and carnage. For an instant it seemed as though the attack would be repulsed; the SS, knowing that if the WFA fighters got inside the Bank they were dead men, fought with ferocious bravery born of desperation. The two sides were reduced to blasting each other from a distance of a few feet.

It was then that Sergeant Wysochi charged forward and blew open the Commercial Center's front door with a shotgun. Now the WFA fighters were able to fight their way into the Bank and the killing could begin in earnest.

The mêlée that ensued was confused and murderous. Not that Ella saw too much of it, Vanka having pulled her back down behind the smoldering remains of the steamer, shouting that she was too important to risk in a firefight. Gradually the superior numbers of the WFA and their sheer bloody-mindedness told. They were in.

"Barricade the doors and windows!" screamed Trixie as she hurdled the debris and the bodies that littered the Bank's entrance. "They'll be on us soon."

Ella felt Vanka's hand on her head. "Keep that lovely head of yours down, Ella, the SS will be doing their damnedest to shoot it off in a moment."

It was timely advice. No sooner had she stooped down below the level of the windows along the front of the Commercial Center than there was a fusillade of automatic fire and the ceiling and back wall behind her exploded, showering plaster and glass everywhere.

"Fire, you bastards!" she heard Trixie command. "Make them keep their distance!" She stabbed a finger toward Ella. "And you, Daemon, get working your magic."

"Where's the Banking Hall?" Ella yelled at Vanka, who nodded and led her crawling to the back of the Commercial Center and through a pair of wide double doors into the huge Banking Hall beyond. It was identical in size and layout to the one in Berlin, the only difference being that this room was silent; all the chattering screens were still. As she scuttled into the vast hall all she could hear was the snap of the hobnails of her boots on the Mantle-ite floor and the rattle and crack of rifle fire coming from the Commercial Center. It was an eerie, desolate place—the green fluorescent glow of the Mantle-ite seemed more intense than she remembered from Berlin.

She strode over to the nearest Transfusion Booth and placed her hand on the indented shape to the left of the keyboard. Immediately the screen came to life, the rotating symbols clattering around.

THE BANK OF WARSAW WELCOMES

ELLA THOMAS

PLEASE ENTER YOUR PASSWORD

There was a tremendous explosion, big enough to send a shock wave shuddering through the hall that almost knocked Ella off her feet. "You'd better get a move on," urged Vanka. "I think the SS are a little annoyed about our taking the Bank. That was heavy artillery. Trixie Dashwood's little band of desperadoes ain't gonna last long against that."

As quick as she was able, Ella typed in her password and accessed ABBA's IM Manual, shuffled through to "AMEND CYBER-MILIEU CHARACTERISTICS," and then pressed "ENTER."

WHICH ASPECT OF THE CYBER–MILIEU DO YOU WISH TO AMEND?

Ella typed "OPTIONS?"

AMENDMENT OF CYBER–MILIEU CHARACTERISTICS

PARAMETERS THAT MAY BE AMENDED INCLUDE:

1.	BLOOD SUPPLY
2.	CLIMATE
3.	COMMODITY SUPPLY
4.	DEMOGRAPHY
5.	ENVIRONMENTAL AND PHYSICAL CONSTRAINTS
6.	FLORA AND FAUNA
7.	GEOGRAPHY
8.	HUB, THE
9.	INDUSTRIAL ZONE, THE
10.	IRRIGATION
11.	PORTALS
12.	RIVERINE CHARACTERISTICS
13.	RUNES
14.	SCALAR CHARACTERISTICS
15.	TERROR INCOGNITA
16.	TOPOGRAPHY
17.	URBAN BAND, THE
18.	WASTE MANAGEMENT AND THE SEWERAGE SYSTEM

Ella looked at the screen dumbfounded. There was no mention of the Boundary Layer. She felt panic well up inside her. What if she couldn't do what she had said she could? What if all these brave WFA fighters were dying for nothing?

Think, Ella, think.

What was the Boundary Layer?

It was the means by which ParaDigm's programmers had confined the population of the Demi-Monde. Therefore it was a "constraint." She typed in "5." Immediately the tiles that made up the screen began to clack around.

ENVIRONMENTAL AND PHYSICAL CONSTRAINTS

PARAMETERS THAT MAY BE AMENDED INCLUDE:

    1.   BOUNDARY LAYER

    2.   DEPTH OF SOIL LAYER

    3.   DISTRIBUTION AND VORACITY OF NANOBITES

    4.   THE MANTLE

Thank the Spirits!

She typed "1."

BOUNDARY LAYER

PARAMETERS THAT MAY BE AMENDED INCLUDE:

    1.   DISTANCE FROM CENTER OF THE DEMI—MONDE[®]

    2.   HEIGHT

    3.   PENETRABILITY

    4.   TACTILITY

    5.   TRANSPARENCY

Desperately trying to keep her hands from shaking, she typed in "3."

BOUNDARY LAYER

YOU HAVE CHOSEN TO AMEND: PENETRABILITY

IS THIS TO BE A LOCAL AMENDMENT? Y ∕ N

Yes, for the love of God, yes!

PLEASE USE THE MUTOSCOPE VIEWER

Ella did as she was asked and saw a map of the Demi-Monde displayed there. At the outer circumference of each District the Boundary was designated with a code, the code for the Warsaw District's Boundary being WBL-1. Ella typed in the reference code.

DO YOU WISH THE BOUNDARY LAYER WBL−1 TO BE MADE
PENETRABLE? Y ⁄ N

Yes, yes, yes . . .

IN WHAT TIME FRAME (DEMI−MONDIAN REFERENCE) DO YOU WISH
THIS AMENDMENT TO BE EXECUTED?

Frantically Ella typed "IMMEDIATE."

CONGRATULATIONS ELLA THOMAS IN ACCORDANCE WITH
PROTOCOL 57 YOU HAVE MADE AN EMERGENCY ONE−HOUR
AMENDMENT TO THE PENETRABILITY OF THE BOUNDARY LAYER
AT WBL−1. THIS AMENDMENT IS SUBJECT TO RATIFICATION BY
THE DEMI−MONDE® STEERING COMMITTEE. IF SUCH RATIFICATION
IS NOT RECEIVED THE AMENDMENT TO THE CYBER−MILIEU WILL
BE ANNULLED IMMEDIATELY AFTER THE ONE−HOUR EMERGENCY
PERIOD HAS ELAPSED.
DO YOU REQUIRE ANY OTHER SERVICES? Y ⁄ N

Ella typed "Y." This was her chance to find out where the SS were going to take Norma Williams after Wewelsburg Castle, to find out where Crowley would conduct his Rite of Transference.

THE DEMI−MONDE® IM MANUAL
OPTIONS:

1. LOCATE DUPE

2. ADD DUPE

3. DELETE DUPE

4. AMEND DUPE CHARACTERISTICS

5. AMEND DUPE PERCEPTIONS

6. AMEND CYBER—MILIEU CHARACTERISTICS

She pressed "1" and immediately she was asked:

NAME OF DUPE TO BE LOCATED?

It was then that she remembered that because she was a renegade Dupe, ABBA wasn't able to track Norma Williams. *Think* . . .

She had a stroke of inspiration.

"AALIZ HEYDRICH," she typed.

The Transfer Screen whirled.

DUPE AALIZ HEYDRICH IS LOCATED AT EXTERSTEINE.

DEMI—MONDIAN COORDINATES SECTOR 1/N5°W/6.5MILES

Ella quizzed PINC regarding ExterSteine but again it let her down: it had no knowledge of the place.

But even as she desperately tried to memorize the coordinates of ExterSteine there was another tremendous explosion from the front of the Bank, and Trixie, followed by her bedraggled fighters, staggered into the Banking Hall. She looked across to Ella. "Have you done it?" she shouted.

"Yes," replied Ella. "Just one more minute."

Trixie shook her head. "There are no more minutes. There's nowhere to go and the SS are advancing. We're trapped here. This is where we die."

"Perhaps not." Ella turned back to the Transfusion Booth.

—◊—

"It appears the rebels have ceased firing, Comrade Colonel."

Archie Clement frowned. That wasn't like the Rebs. As he'd seen over the past few weeks, these bastards fought like madmen, digging into every ruin, every cellar, every pothole and then fighting to the last man. Even his SS had been taken aback by their fanaticism and by how readily they were prepared to sacrifice their lives for their ridiculous cause. And it was all the fault of that bitch Trixie Dashwood.

But who could have thought it would have been a seventeen-year-old girl who would stiffen Dabrowski's spine? Even Beria hadn't seen that one coming. Without her the Poles would have folded in a fortnight, just as they had planned they would. That bitch had a lot to answer for.

"How long?" he asked.

"They haven't fired a shot for ten minutes."

"We got the steamers here yet?"

"Just one, Comrade Colonel, the other was ambushed on Leshno. A couple of kids with firebombs . . ."

Clement nodded grim acknowledgment and spat out a wad of tobacco. These Rebs were fucked more ways that a ten-bob whore but still the diehards fought on. Fucking suicide bombers; it was impossible to defend against Rebs who were prepared to sacrifice their lives to blow up steamers. And the attrition rate had been fearful: more than half the steamers employed in the Ghetto had been lost to booby traps and to incendiaries. The cost was ferocious and Horatio Bottomley was already sending letters of complaint to Crowley. Bottomley would just love it when he heard that the Rebs had retaken the Bank.

Clement lifted his cap and ran a hand through his blond hair.

Why the Rebs had attacked the Bank was beyond him; they must have known that he would never allow them to leave with any blood, they must have known it was all pointless. All they had succeeded in doing was making him look foolish.

He kicked at a shell case, sending it skittering over the cobbles; that bastard Bottomley should get his fat arse down here to the Ghetto and help fight these lunatics, then he'd stop moaning about what the war was doing to his budget.

He just hoped Beria's ruse worked.

"Get a squad together to advance under cover of the steamer."

"Shall I make sure they've got a flamer with them, Comrade Colonel? Might be best to burn the buggers out. They could just be lying doggo in there, waiting for a chance to ambush us. You know how sneaky these Polacks are. They've no honor. They're just fucking animals."

What the SS captain was saying made sense. It was standard operating procedure that once a Ghetto building was taken it should be packed full of straw, the straw doused with lamp oil and the whole lot set alight, burning up the building and any Rebs hiding in it. But not the Bank; incinerate a Blood Bank and Bottomley would really lose his rag.

"No, Comrade Captain, no burning. This has gotta be done real delicate. Damage the Transfusion Booths in the Bank and you'll be busted down to private quicker than a goose shits beans."

The captain shouted his orders and ten minutes later the steamer rumbled up. After weeks of fighting, the steamers were unrecognizable as the sleek machines that had begun the campaign: extra armor had been bolted around the vulnerable boiler, the driver's cabin had been swathed in mesh to stop firebombs and the body was covered in barbed wire to deter suicide bombers from leaping aboard. Now they looked like what they were: ugly and brutal killing machines.

"Number Five Troop: get ready to let it rip," yelled the captain.

"Stay to the left side of the steamer. That's the side furthest away from the Reb bastards who will be trying to blow your damn fool heads off." He signaled the driver and with a lurch the steamer began to crunch toward the Bank.

Clement clicked his fingers and his aide handed him his telescope. He made a careful study of the Bank but apart from the tattered curtains drifting aimlessly in the breeze and a broken front door flapping backward and forward there was no movement and certainly no sign of Rebs waiting to open fire. An uneasy feeling drifted down his spine. Could the bastards have escaped? He dismissed the idea; it was still two hours to dusk, there were no sewers running under the Bank and his forces had a complete view of the whole circumference of the building. It was impossible for the Rebs to escape without being seen.

Maybe they'd simply decided they'd had enough. Maybe they'd committed suicide. Death before dishonor and all that.

The steamer was already halfway to the Bank and nary a shot had been fired.

Where were they? Maybe they were holed up in the Banking Hall. They'd know that the SS would be reluctant to fire in there.

The steamer smashed into the side of the Commercial Center and as it scrabbled for grip its huge studded wheels gouged ruts into the granite pavement. For a minute or so it bucked and shoved in a futile demonstration of brute ignorance, then the drive shaft was disengaged and it stood huffing and puffing in disgruntled impotence.

Clement turned his telescope toward the crouching figure of the captain, watched him make a signal and his SS StormTroopers race around the stalled steamer firing as they went. There were no answering shots and after a few seconds the shooting petered out in an embarrassed sort of way.

Silence.

They couldn't all be dead, could they? Maybe the place was booby-trapped. The Rebs were experts at that; every bloody door, every staircase, every body of a dead SS trooper was wired to a grenade. He'd lost hundreds of men that way. And the ones who survived knew to be cautious. He just hoped the captain was one of them.

Apparently he was. The captain emerged from the Bank and signaled the all-clear.

Clement frowned; it had been too easy. He gestured to his bodyguards, and once they had flanked him he began to walk across the square. He didn't normally risk himself at the front line but in the case of a Bank he was prepared to make an exception. When he got to the Bank he saw that the front of it was a mess, with six bodies of Reb fighters lying on the ground amidst all the other detritus of war. The captain was standing sheepishly in the corner of the Commercial Center. "How many bodies, Comrade Captain?"

"Just the six, Comrade Colonel."

"Six? So how many Rebs you reckon were holding this bombproof?"

"I'm not sure, Comrade Colonel. They lost a hundred during their assault."

Clement used the toe of his boot to nudge the arm of one of the dead rebels. The red lettering on the white armband tied around it read "WFA-D." The "WFA" Clement knew stood for "Warsaw Free Army" so the "D" presumably stood for "Dashwood." Little Trixie Dashwood appeared to be becoming very full of herself.

"The WFA-D is the Polacks' best regiment, Comrade Colonel. We believe they were responsible for the seizure of the two barges that precipitated the attack on the Ghetto."

Clement nodded. "Any bodies in the Banking Hall?"

The captain ushered Clement through to the huge hall, which, apart from a couple of shattered candelabra and the haze of cordite that had drifted through from the front of the building, was undamaged. And there wasn't a soul—dead or alive—to be seen. "So where are all the Rebs, Comrade Captain?"

"They're not here, Comrade Colonel."

"Ah can fucking see that!" snarled Clement. "You trying to tell me that six Rebs held off five hundred SS StormTroopers for the most part of half an hour?"

"Er . . . yes, Comrade Colonel."

"That's real hard mouthing, Comrade Captain. You go around saying that one Reb is worth ninety-odd SS StormTroopers and you're gonna earn yourself an invitation to a necktie party. That's heresy."

The unfortunate thing from Clement's point of view was that though it was heresy it was also the only logical explanation, unless of course the Rebs had a witch working for them, a witch who was very adept at making fighters disappear into thin air.

EVEN ELLA WAS ASTONISHED WHEN SHE MANAGED TO CONJURE—literally—a manhole in the middle of the floor of the Transfer Hall. Everyone in the Demi-Monde knew that Mantle-ite was impenetrable.

"How?" Vanka asked as he stood openmouthed, staring at the manhole.

"I've altered the configuration of the Demi-Monde's sewer system so that one comes up here under the floor of the Bank. But we've got to be quick; I programmed the amendment to last just twenty minutes. That's enough time for us to get out, but hopefully not enough time for the SS to get here and discover how we escaped." Ella addressed the surviving members of Trixie Dashwood's WFA-D regiment. "If we go now, there's a chance we can get out of here with our lives."

They didn't need a second telling. The manhole cover was off in an instant and the hundred and ninety-odd survivors followed her through the sewers back to the Industrial Zone. It took twenty minutes of wading through shit and slime before they emerged and then, ever cautious, Ella insisted that it be she who was the first to climb the steps of the sewer pipe and push open the cover. When she poked her head out she was relieved to find that PINC hadn't let her down: she was slap-bang in the middle of Warsaw's Industrial Zone amid a very boisterous crowd of Varsovians. There were shouts of greeting and then Delegate Trotsky bustled over to meet the returning troops.

"Ah, the great thaumaturgist herself," he chortled as he helped haul Ella out from the sewer. "You have performed an amazing feat of magic, young lady."

"Is the Boundary Layer open?" asked Ella as she tried to brush some of the worst of the sewer's muck from her overalls.

"It opened just as you said it would."

"When?"

"Twenty . . . thirty minutes ago."

"Have you gotten everybody through? The opening in the Boundary Layer will close after one hour."

"All those Pilgrims . . ."

Pilgrims?

" . . . who wish to go are now on the other side of the Boundary. But please come and see for yourself; there are those who would like to thank their savior personally before the Boundary closes."

Exhausted and filthy though she was, Ella allowed herself to be led through the streets of the Industrial Zone toward the Boundary, and an amazing sight awaited her there. It was as though a five-mile-long curtain of the sheerest blue chiffon had been pulled back to reveal the vast, seemingly endless plains of the Great Beyond, and there, standing silent and uncertain in that great sea of grass and woodland, were the people of Warsaw. There were millions of them: men and women laden with their bundles and their cases, children sitting on carts holding their dolls and their toys, families surrounded by their horses and by baskets full of squawking chickens. Certainly they looked worried—many of them looked just plain terrified—but there was a resolve about them that Ella found strangely uplifting. Gazing out on this huge exodus, Ella had never imagined that people could be possessed of such an indomitable spirit that they could endure and survive all the hate and fury that the ForthRight had thrown at them and still have the strength and resolve to take on a new adventure.

Colonel Dabrowski was there with the migrants, leaning on the shoulder of a young woman. He saluted Ella as she passed. He looked spent but happy enough; perhaps, she thought, that was what Dabrowski needed, a fresh start away from all the killing and the violence.

As she walked toward the open Boundary, the crowd parted before her, the men and women of the WFA following Dabrowski's lead and saluting her. It was a surreal moment and not one she particularly enjoyed; it was too embarrassing for that.

Trotsky brought Ella to a halt at the very edge of the Boundary and then in a loud voice addressed the people of Warsaw. "Lady IMmanual . . ."

Lady IMmanual? Where did that come from?

" . . . you have revealed yourself to be our most Revered Messiah, sent by ABBA to lead the people of Warsaw from the jaws of death to a new life in a new world. For that we give thanks and the assurance that you will never be forgotten." With that he knelt before her and kissed her hand. As one, everyone else knelt.

All Ella could do was stand and shuffle her feet uncomfortably.

"Will you say something before we leave this world of strife for-ever?" asked Trotsky.

Now they want me to start making speeches. What do you say to people who are about to venture into the unknown?

She turned toward the kneeling crowd, looking out over the millions of people. Suddenly she remembered a long, long time ago standing in this very spot with her people bowed before her. But she hadn't been Ella Thomas, she'd been . . .

Who?

Then she had stood before her kneeling worshippers naked, shaven, her skin dyed a deep crimson and black snakes tattooed over her body. She could *see* herself; it was a revelation so real that it transcended déjà vu. It was so real that it was déjà vécu: the feeling that she had already *lived* . . . already lived as some type of pagan goddess.

Lilith . . .

And then in an instant the vision was gone, but the memory brought a change in her. Now the words simply flowed out. "We are very different," she said in her loudest voice. "The Demi-Monde is not my home and I came here reluctantly. But in the Demi-Monde, living alongside the people of Warsaw, I have learned many lessons. And the most important of these is that every man, woman and child, no matter how they are created and no matter how they look or think, deserves an opportunity to live without fear of persecution. My heart goes out to all those of you who have lost loved ones . . ." She had to stop for a moment as the memory of all those poor men and women being murdered by the SS flashed before her eyes. "But now, thanks to ABBA and the IM Manual, you have all been offered a new start in a new world. I beg you, make this world one where there is no hatred and no animosity. Make it a world of tolerance and understanding, a world where differences unite men and women rather than divide them, where everyone, no matter what their color or their gender, is treated equally. You have an opportunity to make a new world and I call on you to make it not only a new world but also a just and a peaceful world. May ABBA be with you all."

Trotsky stood up and bowed. "We will always give thanks to the Lord ABBA and his most Holy Daughter, the one He sent to save us and to lead us to the Promised Land, our Messiah: the Lady IMmanual. Henceforward we will keep this day holy. Henceforth this will be the PassOver, the day when the people blessed by the Lady IMmanual passed over from the Demi-Monde into the Promised Land."

Sermon over, her congregation had got back to its feet and its members busied themselves making their final preparations for what they were calling the Great Pilgrimage. Ella sidled up to Trotsky.

"Delegate Trotsky," she said quietly, "before you go I would like your advice."

"Yes, my Lady."

"You are a very knowledgeable man, so tell me why someone as important as Aaliz Heydrich should have been taken to a place called ExterSteine."

"ExterSteine is a place of immense occult significance, my Lady; it is UnFunDaMentalism's holiest of holies. For Aaliz Heydrich to have been taken there means she is to be involved in one of Aleister Crowley's despicable rites, and as it is so close to Spring Eve—"

"Spring Eve?"

"Freyja's Night: the last night of Winter. It is, after Walpurgisnacht, the most magical night in the UnFunDaMentalist calendar. It is the night when Crowley performs his most profound magic. It must be that Aaliz Heydrich is to participate in this year's Freyja's Night rituals; these always take place at ExterSteine and must always be completed before dawn. Does this answer your question, my Lady?"

"Yes . . . thank you. And may I wish you and your people every good fortune and every happiness in the Great Beyond." She looked up and frowned. "I think this is when we say good-bye, Delegate Trotsky. If I am not mistaken, the Boundary Layer is beginning to close."

TRIXIE STOOD WATCHING AS THE CROWDS THAT MADE UP THE EXODUS trudged deeper and deeper into the Great Beyond. She understood that Trotsky was intent on setting up the first settlement around the Blood Bank situated five miles from the Boundary but there were other, more adventurous spirits who had decided that they wouldn't settle until they had explored all of the Beyond. These brave souls had already marched over the horizon; the colonization of the Great Beyond had begun.

She felt the looming presence of Wysochi at her side and gave him a wry smile. "I thought you would have gone with the pilgrims, Sergeant. I always had you marked down as the pioneer type, the sort of man who could tame a wilderness."

A sheepish Wysochi shook his head. "Nah, Colonel, I couldn't go."

It took a moment for Trixie to remember who the "colonel" was that Wysochi was referring to. She'd only been given command of the remnants of the WFA half an hour ago. "Now, that does surprise me, Sergeant. There isn't some girl here in Warsaw who has stolen the heart of the brave and resolute Feliks Wysochi, is there?"

"No . . . of course not." He shuffled his feet awkwardly. "What about you, Colonel? Weren't you tempted?"

It was a disturbing question. In fact when she thought about it she realized that she had never for an instant contemplated going, which was odd because up until a few weeks ago the RaTionalist that had been Lady Trixiebell Dashwood would have leapt at the chance to explore the Great

Beyond. How things—how *she*—had changed. "No, my place is here in the Demi-Monde. I've got things to do here."

"Like what?"

"Avenge my father," she answered automatically, and then realized that she hadn't actually thought about her father for days . . . for weeks. All she ever seemed to think about was killing SS Storm-Troopers. "I've got to defeat Heydrich and the ForthRight. I've got to smash UnFunDaMentalism; I've had a bellyful of religion."

"Good," said Wysochi. He kicked the ground in an absent-minded sort of way. "And what do you make of Ella Thomas?" he asked casually.

Trixie moved nearer to Wysochi so that there would be no danger of their conversation being overheard. "I am never comfortable with religious types, Sergeant, especially those who have performed miracles. It gets the men confused: they don't know whether they should obey their officers or their god."

"Still, it's good for the men to believe that ABBA is on their side."

"ABBA is one thing, live saints are quite another, especially live saints who go around preaching democracy. And I still have a suspicion that when—if—she gets back to the Spirit World then it will go badly for the Demi-Monde. That Shade Daemon is bad news."

Wysochi frowned as he pondered on what Trixie was saying. "I see what you mean. So what do you think we should do? She's very popular with the men; they're calling her the Messiah."

"And that's what makes her so dangerous, Sergeant. We can't allow her to infect the men with her stupid Daemonic ideas. Things like this democracy of hers . . ." Trixie gave a dismissive laugh. "The last thing I want is for the men to start believing that they have some ABBA-given right to elect their leader. The election of a leader is a fatuous idea and will only result in anarchy and disorder. If the WFA is to survive and the ForthRight is to be defeated we have to unite behind one strong leader." The way she said this meant there was absolutely no doubt as to whom she saw that strong leader being.

"Then it would be better if Ella Thomas was to . . ." Wysochi left the suggestion hanging.

Trixie smiled. "Death solves all problems, Sergeant: no Messiah, no problem. And I suppose on a battlefield it's very easy for a live saint to become a much-mourned martyr."

Wysochi nodded. "Very easy."

"How many of the WFA are left?" Trixie asked.

"Maybe four thousand, give or take. We've lost a thousand holding the Industrial Zone and about a thousand opted to go with Trotsky and the other Pilgrims into the Beyond."

"From acorns, Sergeant, great oaks do grow. One day people will say that from these four thousand grew the army that defeated the ForthRight and smashed UnFunDaMentalism. But now, Sergeant, we have to make some hard decisions. There are too few of us to hold the Industrial Zone, so the only option is to break out of the Ghetto. That, though, raises the question as to where we go once we do that."

"The Coven," Wysochi answered. "Delegate Trotsky received a message by pigeon post from the Empress Wu saying that the Coven will grant all members of the WFA sanctuary. It seems Wu has finally come to understand that it's impossible to trust Heydrich. The Coven is preparing for war."

Trixie nodded. "Then that's where we must go. I guess Clement will take a few days to bring up his reserves before he attacks. In five days' time, on the first day of Spring, that's when I reckon he'll try to take us. And that's when we'll break out, on Spring Eve. Clement will never expect that, and maybe with surprise on our side . . ."

The pair of them began to walk toward the building where the rest of the WFA officers were waiting, but ten yards or so before the entrance Trixie stopped, turned to Wysochi and held out her hand. "There may not be time later, Sergeant. I would like to thank you for everything. Without you—"

"There's no need to thank me, Colonel."

"Trixie."

"Trixie." Wysochi shook the offered hand. "I would do it all again, Trixie, and gladly."

"You should have gone to the Beyond, Feliks."

"Not without you, Trixie," said Wysochi, "not without you." And as he turned away, Trixie was sure he was blushing.

VANKA TOSSED HIS CIGARETTE DOWN, GROUND THE BUTT UNDER HIS heel and pushed himself away from the pile of crates he had been hiding behind for the past five minutes. He watched as Trixie Dashwood and Sergeant Wysochi disappeared into the building and then gave his head a philosophical shake. Why was it that people always disappointed him?

33

The Demi-Monde: 90th Day of Winter, 1004—Spring Eve

I am pleased to announce that following much diligent and painstaking work my team at the Reinhard Heydrich Institute has successfully uncovered the secrets of galvanicEnergy, the solution of which has eluded us for so many years. Although our experimentation regarding the harnessing of this remarkable new energy source is in its infancy, we will be pleased to demonstrate our galvanicEnergy generator—the Faraday Thermopile—to you at your earliest convenience. The Thermopile, which converts heat energy into galvanicEnergy, is now fully tested and has been proven to be both safe and reliable. I trust that after said demonstration you will be moved to release the long-overdue tranche of funds owed to the Institute in order that I might pay my loyal and long-suffering staff.

—Letter written by Professor Michael Faraday to Comrade
Vice-Leader Beria, dated 17th day of Autumn, 1004

Tonight he would reclaim his title. No longer would he be Comrade Commissar Dashwood. From tonight he would, once again, be *Baron* Dashwood, Royalist nobleman and officer. The waiting was over.

Tonight he would disrupt Operation Barbarossa by destroying the railway line he had built *and* bring help to Trixie—hadn't she been a revelation!—and her beleaguered WFA.

"Are all the men in position, Captain?" the baron asked.

"Yes, sir," said a beaming Crockett, who delighted in his new rank. "Sergeant Cassidy has seven of our best men—all veterans of the Troubles—stationed on the Odessa side of the Reinhard Heydrich Bridge. He has orders to derail the train before it picks up speed after crossing the bridge."

"How many men do we have to take the internment camp?"

"Twenty, sir. I've included a number of Poles, sir, officers cashiered out of the army in the purge that followed the Dabrowski debacle."

"Good thinking, Crockett." And it *was* good thinking; the baron had been more than a little concerned about the reception he would get from the Polish slave workers when he came to free them. To have a few Poles on his side wouldn't be a bad thing. He took a deep breath. "And so, let's get to it. And may ABBA be with you . . . with all of us."

AFTER AN UNEVENTFUL JOURNEY THROUGH THE ROOKERIES—WITH it being Spring Eve, even the most dutiful of soldiers relaxed their watch a little—Cassidy brought the stolen steamer carrying the baron and his party to the Reinhard Heydrich Railway Bridge a little after seven in the evening.

Spring Eve: the Time of Brotherhood and Goodwill Toward Men, but Sergeant Bob Cassidy and his men showed precious little of either toward the poor drunken unfortunates who were guarding the railway bridge. Even as the guards raised their glasses in a festive toast, so they were dispensed with in a flurry of shots.

Once the bridge was secure, Cassidy was about his business. He waved his band of ruffians out of the shadows where they had been lurking and into position to await the arrival of the military transport train scheduled to cross the bridge in just an hour's time.

The operation had gone so smoothly that all that was left for the baron to do was to shake Cassidy's hand, to wish him luck, and to remind him—for at least the fifth time—that he shouldn't use more than two hundred pounds of explosives to derail the train. It was difficult for the baron to establish whether Cassidy took his instructions seriously as all the man's attention was directed to the rifling of a dead guard's pockets.

With a shrug the baron marched his ragtag crew off toward the internment camp. It took them fifteen minutes to get to the camp and, just as he had promised, Crockett's little army was there waiting for them.

The baron thought it indicative of how a totalitarian regime like the ForthRight so ruthlessly eliminated any spark of initiative in its soldiers that when he strode up to the camp's gatehouse no one questioned his demand to see the camp commandant. Men in uniform presenting themselves at strange hours and issuing nonsensical orders were part and parcel of military life in the ForthRight; it was better to obey orders than to question them.

The commandant, his mind doused with Spring Eve goodwill and Solution, attended the baron five minutes later, his eyes heavy and his shirt hanging out of his trousers. "Comrade Commissar?" began the bewildered man. "I had heard—"

The camp commandant stopped in mid-sentence. By the baron's reckoning he was so befuddled by booze and blood that he probably couldn't quite remember what he had heard. The last thing he wanted to do was insult a senior member of the Party by repeating the slanderous rumor that the comrade commissar had been pronounced a nonNix and an Enemy of the People.

"All a misunderstanding," said the baron, waving away the commandant's suspicions. "I have been reappointed by the Leader as the man responsible for the operation of the rail line. There has been a subsidence on one of the embankments and we desperately need men to help shore it up before the arrival of the first of the military expresses."

"How many men do you need, Comrade Commissar?"

"I would be grateful if you would parade all the Polish workers," ordered the baron.

"*All* of them?" There was real concern in the camp commandant's voice. "There're almost five thousand of the bastards, Comrade Commissar, and it being Spring Eve I've only got twenty men on duty. These Poles are desperate men and twenty guards aren't nearly enough to control them. Perhaps it would be best to parade them in chains?"

"That won't be necessary." The baron gave the commandant a reassuring smile. "Don't worry, Comrade Commandant, I have brought twenty of my own men with me to supplement your guards."

The baron nodded toward Crockett, who came to attention and saluted smartly when the commandant's gaze alighted on him. "Comrade Captain Crockett at your service, sir, late of Wellington's Wranglers. My men are able soldiers, sir; they won't let you down."

The Poles—grumbling and bad-tempered—were paraded just twenty minutes later. Running an eye over the shuffling, complaining ranks, the baron decided that the commandant had a right to be worried; they certainly looked a mutinous mob. The Militia guards eyed them warily and kept their M4s pointed in their direction.

"I would like to address the workers," announced the baron.

The commandant looked at the baron with surprise. Nobody *addressed* the Polacks; you screamed at them and you kicked them, but you didn't *address* them.

Even as the commandant was turning this oddity over in his

Solution-muddled mind, the baron moved to stand directly in front of the bedraggled and decidedly unhappy workers. "Polish men," he shouted at the top of his voice, "as I speak to you, the forces of the ForthRight are moving to crush the last of the Warsaw Free Army."

There were growls of anger from the ranks. The camp commandant drew his Mauser and cocked it. It was obvious from the look on his face that in his opinion the sooner all Poles were crushed the better.

"Only a few thousand brave soldiers of the Warsaw Free Army stand against the thugs of the SS and the evil of Reinhard Heydrich," the baron continued. "I have pledged myself to help Warsaw to survive."

There was stunned silence around the parade ground as everybody tried to work out what the baron was saying. The commandant's hazy thought processes struggled with the conundrum of how the baron came to be using words like "thugs" and "evil" when describing the SS and the Great Leader.

"Now is the time to throw off the shackles of slavery!" shouted the baron.

With a look of bemusement on his face the camp commandant turned to the baron; his bamboozled mind had at last managed to make two and two equal four. Unfortunately this mathematical insight came too late to save him. The baron smiled at him and put a bullet through his head, and as Crockett's men dispatched the other guards in similar fashion, the Polish prisoners just stood immobile on the parade ground, stunned by the turn of events.

"Polish soldiers," began the baron in a loud voice, "as I speak to you, men of the Royalist Defense League are seizing a train laden with guns and ammunition—enough to arm every one of you." The baron looked up and down the ranks of the dirty and bemused Poles. "I ask you to join me in attacking the SS in Warsaw and helping our brave WFA comrades in their fight against tyranny."

And to the baron's astonishment, the men started cheering.

—∾—

THE TRAIN WAS EARLY. CASSIDY HAD ONLY JUST SET THE BOMB—HE
hadn't been able to remember whether the baron had told him he
needed two hundred kilos of explosive or four hundred kilos, so
to be on the safe side, he'd opted for the latter—and run the fuse
behind the shed they were using as protection from the blast when
he heard the whistle announcing the train's imminent arrival. Of
course, the baron had also got him confused about the direction the
train was to come at him from, but, thankfully, once he'd realized
it was arriving from the Rodina side of the bridge, he'd managed to
nip out and relay the bomb in time. A minute later, when he saw the
train's lanterns, he scratched a match on the side of the shed, lit the
fuse and prayed that he hadn't cut it too long. If the bomb exploded
after the train had passed, the baron would be mighty ticked off.

The bomb exploded exactly where Cassidy had intended: under
the engine, directly beneath the boiler. Unfortunately, as he decided later, he should have used only two hundred kilos—maybe
that should have been two hundred *pounds*—of explosive. At four
hundred kilos the bomb didn't so much derail the train as pick it
up and toss it disdainfully aside. There was a huge, ear-shredding
scream of steel on steel, the train seemed to pause for a moment
as though gathering its breath and then it jumped the tracks and
plunged down the earth embankment, dragging the line of seven
carriages it was hauling with it.

Fuck!

For a moment the train lay huffing and puffing on its side like
some great wounded beast. Then all Hel broke loose. The boiler
exploded and if the sound of Cassidy's bomb detonating had been
loud, this was positively earth-shaking. Shards of metal flew like so
much shrapnel through the air, wrecking the wooden shed Cassidy
was using for cover, a flying rivet almost taking his head off. This he

decided was a damned sight more exciting—and dangerous—than tending to the gardens of Dashwood Manor.

He waited a few moments until he was reasonably confident that nothing else was going to go bang and then peeked out from behind the smoking ruin of the shed. The train's firebox had been split open by the explosion, spewing burning coals all around, and by the light from the fires the coals had started he saw that the cargo carried by the trucks had been spilled along the line. Cassidy set off at a trot to see what the spoils of war were. Initially he was disappointed—all there seemed to be were boxes upon boxes of tinned meat—but at the third wagon he struck lucky, almost tripping over long wooden boxes containing automatic rifles.

With a whoop of triumph he waved to the boy who had command of the signal rocket and a second later a red flare was arching across the night sky.

Cassidy gave a satisfied smile; he had just pulled off the first robbery of a railway train in the history of the Demi-Monde. He would be famous. It might even be the first step on a very lucrative career. All he needed was more trains.

THE BARON HADN'T APPRECIATED HOW DIFFICULT IT WOULD BE TO FASH-ion the Polish prisoners into an army. Once they had broken out of the camp, once they had got to the wrecked train, once they were armed, then all discipline seemed to desert them. All they were intent on was revenge; all they wanted to do was to kill people . . . any people. But the baron knew they didn't have time for revenge. Once day dawned there would be no hiding from the SS and they would be hunted down like dogs. By the baron's calculations they had, at most, ten hours, ten hours to decide the fate of what was left of the WFA and of Trixie.

It was Crockett and his gang who, by dint of much cursing and haranguing, managed to bring about half of the Poles into some semblance of order. It was this motley crew that marched to relieve Warsaw. They came within an ace of failing.

If the commander of the ForthRight forces stationed in Odessa had been more resolute and more decisive he could have moved to block the advance of the baron's improvised army. But he was a man of little initiative and, confused and perplexed by the strange messages he was receiving about a breakout by Polish prisoners, he kept most of his men safely in barracks and allowed the baron's army to pass through Odessa largely unopposed.

If there had been fewer veterans of the Troubles in the ranks of the Polish escapees—men used to action and to taking orders—then Crockett wouldn't have been able to keep control and the army would have quickly disintegrated into a mob.

If their attack had taken place during the day, the baron's army would soon have become lost in the jumble of Odessa's unfamiliar backstreets. But at night they had the glow of the fires sweeping through Warsaw to guide them and they could follow the trails of fairy lights formed as artillery shells arched through the sky to fall with a crump on the Industrial Zone.

But most of all they were lucky that it was Spring Eve and half the ForthRight Army was drunk.

They attacked the Southgate entrance to the Ghetto. It wasn't a coordinated or a well-managed assault but it was effective. The last thing the SS guards were expecting was to be attacked from outside of the Ghetto, and certainly not by thousands of well-armed and vengeful Poles. Resistance crumpled and in a matter of minutes the Poles were in Warsaw, but there was no time for them to rest on their laurels. The baron and Crockett drove their men on, screaming at any who paused to pillage wagons or became involved in firefights, reminding them that the bigger prize had yet to be won.

The odd thing was that as they advanced through the ruined streets of Warsaw they met surprisingly little resistance. All the baron could assume was that Clement had received word of their impending attack and, determined not to find himself fighting an enemy to the front and to the rear, had pulled his forces into a defensive line to the east of the Ghetto. With disturbing ease the baron's army smashed through the SS and made it to the barricades that marked the final line of the WFA's defense.

Baron Dashwood barely recognized his daughter; he had to convince himself that this dirty, ragged girl with the hacked crop of hair was indeed his beloved Trixiebell. But it wasn't just the change in her appearance that the baron found difficult to accept; she had, in just a few weeks, metamorphosed into someone completely different from the skittish and unworldly Trixiebell he had known and loved. She had become harder and colder. Even the embrace she had given him seemed reluctant . . . almost embarrassed.

But he had to admit to being mightily impressed by the way she managed her army and her officers. She was decisive and she was respected and all of the battle-hardened WFA officers who made up her command team unquestioningly acknowledged her authority.

Maybe, the baron decided, when all the fighting and the mayhem was over, he would see his Trixiebell again. But looking at the huge sergeant who loitered so protectively behind his daughter, the baron had the feeling, as all fathers have at some point in their lives, that Trixiebell wasn't *his* anymore. He had been superseded in his daughter's life by this brutal sergeant Wysochi.

It was the sergeant whom his daughter turned to now. "Divide the fighters brought in by my father between our four regiments. The newcomers are to be integrated into the WFA."

"It might be better to allow my men a chance to rest for a moment, to get something to eat. They've been living on scraps . . ."

Trixie looked at her father with something approaching shock on her face. She was obviously not used to her orders being questioned.

"Father," she said in a voice so low that only the baron and Wysochi could hear her, "*I* command here. When I give an order it is to be carried out. This is not a debating chamber and I do not run my army as a democracy. Do you understand?"

The baron was thunderstruck. "But all I was suggesting, Trixie—"

"Father, please. When we are with others you will address me as 'Colonel' or 'sir.'" Trixie turned back to Wysochi. "Disperse the newcomers between the four regiments. It's eleven o'clock now; I want the army ready to break out of the Ghetto at midnight. I want to attack while the SS is still off balance."

"There is a problem, Colonel," said Wysochi. "A number of the newcomers are—were—officers in the ForthRight army and have expressed a reluctance to take orders from WFA commanders."

"Is there a focus of this protest?" Trixie said quietly.

"A man named Wozniak. He was a colonel before he was purged."

"Have former colonel Wozniak join me."

The man who was ushered into Trixie's presence was tall and dirty and the labor camp had left him with a twitch in his left eye and a heavy limp. But although he had been physically bashed about by his time doing hard labor on behalf of the ForthRight, his arrogance remained undiminished.

"Where is this Colonel Dashwood I have been brought to see?" he demanded.

"I am Colonel Dashwood," said Trixie quietly, "and I generally expect my soldiers to salute me when they are brought into my presence."

Wozniak gawped at Trixie. "You're the commander of the WFA? No . . . this must be a joke. You're just a girl. This is ridiculous. I'm not taking orders from a girl."

If Trixie was disturbed by Wozniak's disdain she didn't show it. "I have four thousand men under my command, Wozniak, and I think you will find that they all accept my orders because they have confidence in my abilities as a military leader. The thing that matters isn't my gender but my ability to lead and to kill SS."

The grim implacability of what Trixie said gave even the bumptious Wozniak pause. He looked at her a little more carefully. "I am sorry, young lady, but war is a field of endeavor only trained *men* have any business being involved in. Girls like you should confine themselves to nursing the wounded and cleaning."

"I presume from this that you will be disinclined to obey my orders?"

"Correct, and I will instruct my men to do likewise." He shook his head. "No, to have a woman leading an army is quite unacceptable."

Trixie was quiet for a moment. And though Wozniak took this as a sign of the girl's indecision, the baron knew otherwise: Trixie was always quiet when she was struggling to control her temper.

No one said a word; a deathly silence fell on the room. Then slowly and deliberately Trixie took her pistol from its holster and placed it on the table in front of her. This done, she began speaking again as though Wozniak hadn't said a word.

"The one thing I have learned during my time fighting the SS is that there is no place for ambiguity or debate in an army. So, I ask you just one more time, Wozniak: for the sake of the Polish people, will you take my orders?"

Wozniak looked about, trying to gauge the mood of the other men gathered there. Then his eyes settled on the pistol resting in front of Trixie. He obviously came to the conclusion that this was just a show of bravado on her part. She was, after all, just a girl.

"No," he said finally.

Trixie raised her pistol and shot him through the forehead.

The baron was rendered speechless by the implacability of his daughter. He had never believed Trixie—or any woman for that matter—would be capable of such a barbarous act. It was unthinkable ... unbelievable ...

Trixie continued giving orders as though nothing untoward had happened, as though she routinely shot her officers. A chilling thought occurred to the baron: maybe she did.

Part IV

SPRING EVE

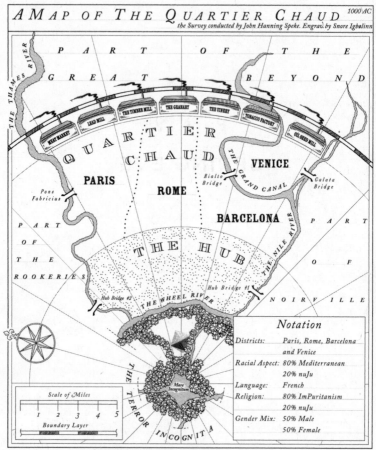

A MAP OF THE QUARTIER CHAUD

1000 AC

the Survey conducted by John Hanning Speke. Engrav'd by Snore Igbolinn

PART OF THE GREAT BEYOND

THE THAMES RIVER

QUARTIER CHAUD

MEAT MARKET · LEAD MILL · THE TIMBER MILL · THE GRANARY · THE VINERY · TOBACCO FACTORY · OIL SEED MILL

PARIS

ROME

VENICE

BARCELONA

Pons Fabricius

Rialto Bridge

THE GRAND CANAL

Galata Bridge

PART OF THE ROOKERIES

THE HUB

THE NILE RIVER

PART OF

Hub Bridge #1

Hub Bridge #2

THE WHEEL RIVER

NOIRVILLE

Mare Incognitum

THE TERROR INCOGNITA

Notation

Districts:	Paris, Rome, Barcelona and Venice
Racial Aspect:	80% Mediterranean 20% nuJu
Language:	French
Religion:	80% ImPuritanism 20% nuJu
Gender Mix:	50% Male 50% Female

Scale of Miles

1 2 3 4 5

Boundary Layer

Reproduced by kind permission of Snore Igbolinn, Cartographer–General to the Court of His HimPerial Majesty, Shaka Zulu

MAP OF THE QUARTIER CHAUD.

PLATE 4

The Demi-Monde:
90th Day of Winter,
1004—Spring Eve

Operation Hoodwink: *The ultimate success of Operation Barbarossa and of the Final Solution turns on the usurping of the nuJu-controlled financial power of the Rialto Bourse.* **Item One:** *Vice-Leader Comrade Beria is to undertake a black propaganda program designed to deceive Doge Catherine-Sophia into believing that the objective of Operation Barbarossa is the invasion and subjugation of the Coven rather than the Quartier Chaud.* **Item Two:** *Efforts will be made to sponsor and promote the work of Robespierre and others in the Quartier Chaud sympathetic to the ForthRight to sever ties with Venice and to make political and religious alignment with the ForthRight.* **Item Three:** *Royalist cryptos within the ForthRight will be fed disinformation to be communicated to Venice.* **Item Four:** *Efforts will be made to ensure only weak/incompetent leaders take control of Rebel forces within the Warsaw Ghetto, this to minimize potential obstacles to the successful execution of Case White.* **Item Five:** *An Export License for the delivery of M4s to the Coven to be issued, the weapons to recompense for services rendered to the ForthRight by Empress Wu.*

—Minutes of the ExtraOrdinary PolitBuro
meeting held under the guidance of the Great
Leader on the 39th day of Winter, 1004 (copy to be
withheld from Comrade Commissar Dashwood)

Norma had no idea how long she had been held in the cell. There were no windows so it was impossible for her to distinguish night from day. In fact, the only way she could mark the passage of time was by the trays of food that were periodically pushed under her cell door, but as all she was fed was fruit and water the meals soon merged into one. There was no breakfast, lunch or dinner in Wewelsburg Castle, there was only feeding time.

Now she was really stuck in the Demi-Monde. Now she was really one of the Kept.

By her best estimate, it was maybe a week since she and Ella Thomas had entered the sewers. She remembered going down into that stinking blackness, she remembered the brick smashing into her knee, she remembered being swept away, fighting for her life in those putrid rapids, but after that . . . nothing. The next memory she had was lying—cold, wet and exhausted—washed up on a mud bank at the side of the Rhine.

A couple of children had found her and then two burly men had carried her to a mean little hut and dumped her on a cot beside a potbellied stove to dry out. The Witchfinder had come the next day. She remembered him examining her—she still had the bruises where the bastard had poked and prodded her—and then he'd had her loaded into a closed steamer to transport her to Wewelsburg Castle. She knew the name of the place because the Witchfinder had taunted her for the whole of the hour-long drive, taunted her about the impossibility of being rescued from Wewelsburg Castle.

For days all she had to do was sleep, eat and listen to the rats scratching around in the darkness. Only once had her captors visited her, to strip her of all her studs and her earrings and make sketches of her tattoos, but even this they had done in total silence.

But today, she sensed, was going to be different. Today there seemed to be a frisson of excitement in the air. From what Norma guessed to be early morning she had heard people scurrying to and fro along the corridor outside her cell and the barking of orders.

Now, as she lay on her hard cot, she heard boot heels snapping on the flagstones as someone marched down the corridor toward her cell. The footsteps came to a halt at her door. She heard a key turn in the lock and then the creak of the door as it reluctantly opened on oil-hungry hinges. Her visitor entered the cell holding a lantern before him and Norma had to flinch away, shielding her eyes from the glare.

"On your feet, Daemon." It was the Witchfinder, his voice hard and angry.

It took a real effort of will for Norma to sit up. She had given up hope of being saved, she had given up hope of ever getting back to the Real World.

"Take her," the Witchfinder ordered. "I want her cleaned up and her hair dyed—and I mean *all* her hair—within two hours. She must be made presentable for His Holiness."

Two women SS warders grabbed Norma, pulling her to her feet, then dragged her out of her cell and along the corridor to a small, cold bathroom decorated in surgically white tiles. There they tore off all her soiled clothes, forced her to stand under a scalding hot shower whilst she was washed and scrubbed and her hair bleached a platinum-blond color.

When they had finished, the Witchfinder came to inspect the naked Norma. "She has no tail," he observed in a disappointed voice.

"Daemons of her rank are subtle creatures, Witchfinder Major," answered one of the female guards, "able to ape the form of humans perfectly."

A disappointed grunt from the Witchfinder. "She is very gaunt," he observed. "Perhaps a little *too* gaunt."

"Not gaunt, Witchfinder Major, healthily slim," replied the guard. "Her diet has been in full accordance with the principles of Living&More laid down by His Holiness Comrade Crowley. Since she came to Wewelsburg, she has been fed just fruit and filtered water. All bad humors and harmful toxins have been purged from her body. She is purified just as the Other, in ExterSteine, has been purified."

The Other? ExterSteine?

"Very well," said the Witchfinder. "Bring her to the steamer."

From somewhere Norma conjured the strength to protest. "Look, pal, I ain't going—"

She was silenced by a savage slap across her face. "Be quiet, Daemon, you are not to speak. If you utter one further word I will have you gagged. Remember, I know you for the trickster you are. You should understand that all have been forewarned to be on their guard lest you seek to subvert them with your unholy wiles and your silver tongue."

Norma almost cried; she was so tired, so dispirited, so helpless that she was only a moment away from being broken. She was just so fed up with being in pain, being cold and being abused. All she wanted was to get out of the Demi-Monde and to go home.

But at least they let her retain her modesty, handing her an ankle-length sheath made of rough white cotton, which she gratefully slipped over her body. Then they manacled her wrists behind her back and led her to a steamer standing puffing in the courtyard of the castle. Well, not just *a* steamer but a veritable convoy of steamers. Crowley, it seemed, was taking no chances: he didn't want there to be any risk of Norma being rescued again.

The Witchfinder called over the SS-major in command of the convoy. "You understand your orders, Comrade Major? Your men will provide an escort to the Hub and will then establish a cordon sanitaire around ExterSteine at a distance of one mile. Under no circumstances are you or any of your men to come closer than that, otherwise your somewhat uncouth psychic vibrations will interfere with the ritual to be conducted by His Holiness Comrade Crowley. Understand?"

The major snapped a salute.

So she was going to have the pleasure of Crowley's company again, presumably so that he could enact his Rite of Transference. The chances were in a few hours she would be dead. A strange calm descended on Norma; she determined to meet whatever fate had in store for her philosophically.

It was her first sight of daylight since she had entered the sewers an eternity ago and she was surprised by the glorious feeling of sunshine on her face. The last time she had been outside, the Demi-Monde had been in the grip of Winter, but now there was a definite feeling of Spring in the air. Unfortunately her enjoyment of the sunshine was short-lived. The Witchfinder gave her a hefty shove in the back to bundle her into the rear passenger cabin of the steamer and once she was seated he blindfolded her.

They drove for perhaps twenty minutes until finally, after bumping along what was obviously an unmade road, the steamer came to a halt and Norma was pushed outside. By the smell of her surroundings she knew that she was no longer in the city: the air smelled almost fresh; there wasn't even a hint of the foul tang of overcrowded humanity that perfumed the Rookeries. She was in the countryside, which meant she was in the Hub. It was a suspicion reinforced when she heard birds singing. Birds didn't sing in the Rookeries, they coughed.

As she was pushed roughly forward, she felt the cold of snow beneath her naked feet, but after a walk of ten minutes or so this was replaced by rough stone.

"Climb," ordered the Witchfinder in her ear, and Norma found herself stumbling up a long, steep stone staircase, so long that by the end of it her damaged knee ached like the devil and her breath was coming in pants. Then, with the wind cutting through the thin cotton of her dress, she was led across what she imagined to be a narrow wooden bridge.

With a touch on her goose-pimpled arm the Witchfinder brought her to a halt and removed the manacles from her wrists. "Welcome to ExterSteine, Daemon," boomed out a familiar voice.

It was Spring Eve: Freyja's Night.

Tonight was the night upon which Crowley would perform his magic, when he would perform the Rite of Transference. And from what Ella had learned from Trotsky and the IM Manual, the rite would be held at this mysterious place ExterSteine. If Ella was to save Norma Williams, then she had to do it before dawn; once the Rite of Transference was complete Ella wasn't even sure there would be a Norma Williams left to rescue.

But getting to ExterSteine seemed an impossible task. Here she was stuck in the chaos of the Ghetto's Industrial Zone with less than eight hours of the last night of Winter remaining. Just eight hours to save Norma Williams. There was however one ray of hope: the word was out that once Baron Dashwood's mishmash of an army had been brought into some semblance of order then the attempted breakout of the Ghetto would go ahead. Presumably with the SS still confused by the baron's attack, there was a better chance of success, but having seen how weak and tired the WFA soldiers were it was difficult for Ella to be optimistic.

"Tea?"

Ella looked up to find Vanka, an enamel mug of steaming tea in his hand, standing in front of her. "Our glorious leader Colonel Dashwood has decided, as it's Spring Eve, to distribute the last of the tea rations. I had been hoping for Solution but Trixie Dashwood is a very austere commander who doesn't want any of her soldiers drunk before the breakout." Vanka looked around at all the fighters crowded into the warehouse and shrugged. "Fuck knows why; I'd have thought that it was best we all died pissed."

She took the scalding-hot mug carefully in both hands. "Thanks, Vanka. I don't know what I'd do without you."

"My pleasure." He sat down beside her. "Penny for them. You've been sitting lost in thought for nigh on ten minutes."

"I'm just wondering how I can get to ExterSteine."

"Oh, not again. I thought—"

"Please, Vanka, I've got to rescue Norma; it's what I was sent to the Demi-Monde to do."

He held up his hands in mock surrender. "Okay, but I think you're getting a little ahead of yourself; the first thing we've got to do is get out of the Ghetto alive. Do that and *then* we can start worrying about rescuing Norma I'm-a-shrew Williams."

"What do you think are our chances?"

"Of getting out of the Ghetto? The same chance we've got of rescuing Norma Williams: piss-poor. With the reinforcements the baron's brought in there're about six or seven thousand WFA stuck here in the Industrial Zone and Clement has about five times that number of SS StormTroopers surrounding us. My guess is that in the confusion a couple of hundred of us might slip through, but no more. But then as long as you and I are numbered amongst the living, who gives a damn?"

Ella looked around the warehouse where she was sitting, casting an eye over all the young WFA fighters clustered there going through their final preparations in advance of the breakout: cleaning their rifles, checking their ammunition, doing the thousand and one things that soldiers do to take their minds off the slaughter to come.

They all looked so young.

"They've asked me to perform a blessing before the fighting starts," she said quietly.

Vanka laughed. "Why not? You're the one who performs miracles, Ella, you're the one who opens impenetrable Boundary Layers and suchlike. Maybe they should ask you to perform another miracle. Maybe you could make them all bulletproof?"

"Don't be silly, Vanka," Ella protested, but as always she found his refusal to take anything seriously hugely comforting. "I just find all this blessing business odd."

"Odd for Ella Thomas perhaps, but you're not Ella Thomas anymore, are you? Now you're the Lady IMmanual, ABBA's right-hand woman."

The unfortunate thing was that what he said was true. Since the Miracle of the Beyond people *had* been treating her differently. Everywhere she went in the cramped enclave of the WFA's final redoubt the fighters saluted her as she passed; when she walked into a room the conversation immediately ceased and everybody stood and bowed reverently.

Ella was no longer "the Shade" or "the Daemon." Now she had a new name, one that was whispered in worshipful tones. Now she was the Lady IMmanual. Now she was the Spirit who had led the people of Warsaw to the Promised Land, the Holy Woman who had parted the Boundary, the Divine Savior sent by ABBA to save His children.

Now she was the Messiah.

Those who believed in her and her ability to perform miracles had a new sign, one that she saw daubed on walls everywhere in the Ghetto, the same sign that a great many of the fighters had embroidered after the letters "WFA" on their armbands. It was the sign of the inverted "V"—a lambda sign, supposedly signifying the drawing back of the veil that cloaked the Beyond. And those who wore the symbol called themselves IMmanualists.

It was an indication of how rapidly IMmanualism had swept through the ranks of the WFA that of the three hundred fighters gathered in the warehouse almost all wore the sign. For Ella all this attention and reverence was at best mildly amusing and at worst hugely embarrassing, but, she mused, if it brought comfort to people what was the harm in it?

"So you think I should bless them, Vanka?"

Another uncaring shrug. He took out his watch to check the time. "There's only an hour to midnight, so I don't think we've got enough time for you to play Lady IMmanual and piss about blessing people, which is just as well because I don't think Colonel Dashwood would approve. And anyway, what I'm more worried about is who's going to bless *you*? I think you're in more danger than any of these kids."

"How so?"

Vanka edged a little closer. "Because these kids will only have the SS trying to kill them; you're going to have the SS *and* Trixie Dashwood trying to off you."

She could not hide her surprise. "What?"

"The trouble with you, Ella," he said quietly, "is that you always want to see the good in people. With me it's different: I see them for the shitbags they really are. I eavesdropped on a conversation between Trixie and that tame gorilla of hers, Wysochi. They're planning to kill you during the breakout."

"Kill me? Are you sure?"

He nodded. "Believe me, that's what they're plotting. People like Trixie Dashwood don't like rivals."

"Rival? I'm not Trixie Dashwood's rival!"

"Shh!" He put a finger to his lips. "Keep it quiet. And for your information, yes, you *are* a rival—for her fighters' allegiance. When half the WFA is wearing the Sign of the Lady IMmanual on their sleeve then Trixie knows she's got competition, and believe me, the last thing the commander of an army wants is to be second-guessed by a religious icon."

"Come on, Vanka, Trixie Dashwood and I have been through a lot together; she knows I'd do nothing to undermine her authority."

"Oh yeah? That's not how she sees all this business about democracy you were spouting. And now that you're the Lady IMmanual—the Messiah—people are starting to listen to you. I've heard mutterings in the ranks that the fighters think it should be you who's leading them, not her, and *that* must have gone down like a lead balloon with Trixie the Terrible. And she's a devil when it comes to purging opposition; there's something of a Heydrich about that young lady."

"Now you're going too far, Vanka. Trixie's fighting Heydrich."

"Yeah, and she's fighting fire with fire. She hates the SS and the UnFunDaMentalists almost as much as Heydrich hates Poles and nuJus, and that sort of hatred distorts the soul. I thought when her father returned from the grave that it might have had a calming effect on little Trixie but from what I hear she's as hate-filled as ever. Shooting that poor sod Wozniak . . ." He shook his head. "She enjoys killing a tad too much for my liking."

"Oh, come on, Vanka."

"Don't 'oh, come on, Vanka' me. You didn't see her reaction when she read one of the pamphlets young Penn over there produced." He glanced in the direction of a tall, thin fighter who was sitting in a corner of the warehouse scribbling in a notebook. "That twerp is the worst of *all* the bloody IMmanualists. You know he's writing down every word you say as though it's the word of the Spirits."

"Oh, William's harmless enough."

"Harmless!" Vanka nearly gagged. "His little pamphlet giving an account of the Miracle of the Beyond and recording your Sermon on the Boundary nearly caused Trixie Dashwood to bust her stays. She hates you, Ella."

Much as Ella wanted to deny it, she knew deep down that Vanka was right: Trixie *did* hate her . . . hated her enough to kill her. And that was why, since the parting of the Boundary Layer, Trixie had been avoiding her, instinctively staying far enough away from Ella so she couldn't be read.

"So what do we do, Vanka?"

"The WFA is going to try to break out of the Ghetto at midnight. I've a feeling in my water that during the fighting it's planned that you succumb to lead poisoning." He pulled out his Colt revolver and checked that it was fully loaded. "So it's probably time we made ourselves scarce. We need to keep a very low profile until the fighting starts and then head for the long grass."

"But what about the Twelve? They won't leave me."

"Oh, those idiots." Vanka stole a look at the twelve men and women who had elected themselves as Ella's personal bodyguard—the Twelve, they called themselves—and who were now seated in a phalanx around her, just out of earshot. "Let's take them with us. They may be following you around like a bunch of lovesick puppy dogs but they're good fighters."

"But then how will we get to ExterSteine?"

"Bloody ExterSteine. Bloody Norma Williams. I wish you'd forget about saving that bitch. But if you must, I've got an idea—"

He was interrupted as Rivets scuttled up and began to speak breathlessly. "Someone's coming, Vanka. I think it's that big bastard Wysochi you told me to keep an eye out for."

Vanka took Ella by the arm and led her toward the rear exit of the warehouse. "Time to go. I think Trixiebell Dashwood is intent on doing some early Spring cleaning."

"She's gone," Wysochi whispered in Trixie's ear when he reported back. "I should have known that fly bastard Maykov would have anticipated what was going to happen. Shall I send out men to look for her?"

Trixie shook her head. "No, we'll deal with this matter later." She smiled guilelessly at the five officers who now made up her Military Council. It didn't do for commanders to discuss the assassination of rivals in front of their officers; it was bad for morale. "We have learned that the SS have infiltrated cryptos into the WFA charged with the assassination of the Lady IMmanual." The use of the Shade's ridiculous honorific caught in her craw. "We believe that the most vicious and dangerous of these cryptos is the Russian who calls himself Vanka Maykov. Maykov has persuaded the Lady IMmanual that she is in danger and that only he can help her escape the Ghetto. In reality he is intent on leading her to a trap set by the SS. Sergeant Wysochi was to have taken the Lady IMmanual into protective custody but that slippery rascal was too quick for us."

"Then we must send out search parties."

This comment came from the newly promoted Captain Michalski, who was, much to Trixie's disgust, the most fervently IMmanualistic of all of Trixie's officers. This was a shame; she and Michalski might have been through some tough times together but unfortunately his religious conversion rendered him untrustworthy. When push came to shove, she wanted officers around her who knew only one commander: her. Michalski wouldn't make it through to the morning; Wysochi would see to that.

"We have no time, Captain Michalski, the breakout commences in less than thirty minutes. All our attention must be directed toward the preservation of the WFA as a fighting force." She looked sternly around the table. "We will concentrate our attack on Westgate. That's where we'll make our breakout. Once through there, we'll head for the Anichkov Bridge, then over to the Coven. The Coven has confirmed that all WFA fighters will be given sanctuary in their Sector."

"If I might make an observation." Everyone in the room turned toward Baron Dashwood. "I have been thinking over the attack I made on the Reinhard Heydrich Railway Bridge—"

"We have precious little time for idle discussions, Major."

"What I have to say will only take a moment, Colonel." There was a definite edge in her father's voice and Trixie felt her hackles rise.

She hated it when he used that tone; she wasn't a child anymore. *She* was the senior officer here, not him. No one told her what to do anymore. She took a deep breath, trying not to let her annoyance show. It had been a mistake to have put her father in command of a regiment; he presumed on his relationship with her too much. No other officer would have had the temerity to interrupt her like this.

"Very well, Major, what is this *observation* of yours?"

"I didn't realize it at the time, but the train was heading in the wrong direction. It was traveling *from* Rodina *to* the Rookeries."

"So what?"

"If the train was bringing munitions to support an attack on the Coven it should have been going the other way. I think Heydrich has hoodwinked us . . . has hoodwinked me, rather. Operation Barbarossa isn't a plan to invade the Coven, it's a plan to invade the Quartier Chaud. Heydrich must have known I was a Royalist all along; he was using me as part of his black propaganda campaign to confuse the Medis and Doge Catherine-Sophia. He didn't want Venice getting wind of an impending attack so he's been pretending that the Coven was his objective. All that nonsense in *The Stormer* about the ForthRight invading the Coven was just that: nonsense. Maybe that whole eavesdropping episode in the manor was stage-managed. Maybe Beria *knew* that Dabrowski was a crypto."

Trixie shook her head. "What difference does it make? So the ForthRight is making war on the Quartier Chaud rather than the Coven. The fact remains I've got seven thousand fighters who need to break out of the Ghetto and find sanctuary."

"Find sanctuary where?"

"I told you. The Covenites have offered us—"

"The Coven has signed a nonaggression pact with the Forth-Right. I think we're being led into a trap. That's why our patrols have told us the SS are weakest toward Westgate. We're being funneled toward the Coven—"

"Nonsense! Clement has made a tactical error, one that I am determined to exploit. Your supposition, Major, is based on the flimsiest of evidence, a single train going in the wrong direction. There might be a hundred reasons why that happened."

"But I am sure—"

"Enough!" Trixie spat out the word. "There is no more time for debate. You have your orders, Major Dashwood, I expect them to be carried out. Do you understand?"

For a moment their eyes locked. It was the baron who lowered his gaze. "Yes, Colonel."

Her hand still trembling with anger, Trixie raised her glass of Solution from the table. "Then all that remains, gentlemen, is to make a toast: to a free Warsaw and a free Demi-Monde. May the blessings of ABBA and of the Lady IMmanual be on you and your soldiers."

NORMA RECOGNIZED THE VOICE. IT WAS ALEISTER CROWLEY, though the way his voice echoed and reverberated suggested they were standing in some sort of hall or cave.

"I am so pleased, Daemon, that you could join us in our celebration of Freyja's Night, to help us in the performing of the ritual that proclaims the coming of Spring."

Norma's blindfold was untied. Standing there, blinking in the gloom, she saw she was in a huge, pitch-dark cavern with burning tapers dotted around the wall for illumination. She shivered, but not through cold; the cavern was a terrifying place. It must, she decided, be made from Mantle-ite, which was why eerie green shadows skittered like specters around the bare walls.

Norma had the impression that she had walked into the gullet of some huge serpent: the walls were decorated with murals of the most bestial kind, concocted from screaming reds and tormented yellows with huge snakes and dragons twirling and twisting in demented patterns. And as her eyes got used to the gloom, she saw that deeper into the cave the murals became increasingly frenzied, brighter and bolder colors depicting events from some forgotten mythology, the artwork primitive and savage, a primeval kaleidoscope.

It looked for all the world like a set from a horror movie, and the players were as loathsome as the set.

There were, as best she could judge, thirteen people gathered in the cavern and all of them—with the exception of Crowley—were dressed in deep purple robes with their faces hidden by quite hideous masks depicting various mythological animals. Well, she hoped they were mythological: the beasts that inhabited Terror Incognita were rumored to be pretty monstrous.

Crowley took a step forward, allowing Norma to get a better look at him. In contrast to his adepts, the magician was unmasked and wore a long flowing robe colored the darkest red and embroidered in gold with a myriad of runic symbols. Around his head was an inch-thick golden band with a gleaming red ruby at its center.

"Where am I?" asked Norma, desperately trying to mask the quaver in her voice.

"You are at ExterSteine, Daemon, perhaps the most magical of all places in the Demi-Monde. ExterSteine is a group of five tall pillars of Mantle-ite created when the Demi-Monde was young, before the Confinement. We are now atop Lilith's Tower, the tallest of all the columns, where the Pre-Folk formed this cavern. It was here, or so mythology would have us believe, that Lilith performed her most vile and debased magic. But that was long ago; where you are standing, Daemon, is now UnFunDaMentalism's holiest place."

"Why have you brought me here?" She asked the question despite the fact that she had a pretty good idea already. Still, better to hear it from the horse's mouth, as it were.

"Every Quarter's Eve I gather my innermost circle of adepts here to give thanks to the Spirits for the changing seasons. In the UnFunDaMentalist calendar the most important Quarter Eve is this one, the one which celebrates the movement of our world from the barren cold of Winter to the lush fertility of Spring." He pointed to a shuttered hole high up in the roof of the cavern. "The rays of the rising sun will pour through that opening tomorrow morning to signal the death of Winter and the birth of Spring."

Totally non compos fucking mentis.

Crowley began to prowl around the floor of the cavern, pontificating as he went. "But tonight we do more than merely celebrate Spring Eve. Tonight we will push back the very boundaries of magic. Tonight, Daemon, we will perform the Rite of Transference, a rite never attempted before. The Lady Aaliz Heydrich will take possession of your body in the Real World and for the first time, a Demi-Mondian will manifest themselves *physically* and not just spiritually in the Real World. Tonight, we in the ForthRight will take our first step along the path that will lead to the Unification of the Two Worlds and the triumph of UnFunDaMentalism throughout the Kosmos."

A twenty-four-karat screwball.

"Well, if it's all the same to you, I think I might pass."

Crowley chuckled. "I am afraid that is not possible, Daemon; you have a leading role to play in the little drama we will be enacting tonight. Your cooperation is essential."

"Go screw yourself. I'm not cooperating while a prick like you tries to steal my body."

He moved toward her. "The options you have, Daemon, are stark. You either cooperate in the performing of the Rite of Transference or you will be disposed of. If you refuse I will ensure that you die in the most painful and prolonged manner." His lips were so close to Norma's ear that she could feel his sweet breath on her cheek. "I will have you drained of blood, drip by drip by drip. Do you understand?"

Out of the corner of her eye Norma caught a glimpse of the Witchfinder running his tongue over his fleshy lips.

Yeah, I understand, you mad bastard, and I've got a sneaking idea who would volunteer to do it.

Norma reluctantly acquiesced; anything was better than that piece of shit being given the free run of her body.

With a self-satisfied smirk of triumph, Crowley gestured to one of his adepts. "If you would ask the Lady Aaliz to join us."

Aaliz, when she entered the cavern, looked entirely different in appearance from the clean-cut RightNix girl whom Norma had met at Dashwood Manor. Her blond hair had been dyed a raven black. Her ears were circled with piercings, which, as far as Norma could see, were decorated with the studs taken from her own ears. And she now had a Celtic cross tattooed on her shoulder, the design copied from the one Norma sported.

To all intents and purposes, Aaliz Heydrich was now Norma Williams. And Norma realized that with her hair dyed blond and her studs removed, *she* was now Aaliz Heydrich.

As she watched Aaliz Heydrich strut across the floor of the cavern, Norma experienced a weird out-of-body sensation. It was as though she were watching herself walk toward her. And that was when she noticed the weird difference between herself and Aaliz: Aaliz was her mirror image. Everything about her was reversed: they had inscribed the Celtic cross tattoo on Aaliz's right shoulder rather than on the left. She could tell by the way Aaliz used her left hand to brush back an errant trail of hair that she favored that hand;

Norma would have used her right. Even the parting in her hair was to the right, while Norma's was to the left.

Freaky.

And when Norma thought about it, she realized that the majority of Demi-Mondians were left-handed.

Crowley's voice cut through her reverie. "Tomorrow, at dawn, the power of the Goddess of Fertility, Freyja, will claim the world from the frosted grip of Goddess Skadi. The blossoming of dawn's light will signal the Goddess Freyja's rise to dominance in the Demi-Monde and the rebirth of the world. And when this light falls on the Lady Aaliz it will also signal her rebirth in the Spirit World." He turned to his gathered disciples. "Let us prepare."

The Witchfinder stood behind Norma. She felt his scuffed fingers fidgeting at the bows that tied the straps of her dress, felt a tug as the bows were undone and felt the dress slipping from her shoulders, sighing to the ground to leave her standing naked.

Crowley eyed her slim, naked body hungrily.

She had read about the prurient, vile things Crowley—when he had been a black magician in the Real World—had persuaded his disciples to do to conjure Spirits, had read about the degenerate and bestial antics he and his supplicants got up to in the place he called the Abbey of Thelema. Her flesh crawled when she thought about the bastard so much as touching her.

She saw that Aaliz Heydrich had been similarly stripped. Now the two girls stood stark naked facing each other across the cavern. The Witchfinder didn't know where to look first.

"You, Daemon," announced Crowley, "will be adorned with the Runes of Power and the incantations that will demand the Spirits manifest themselves."

For the next half-hour Norma was obliged to stand stock-still as Crowley's adepts daubed designs and emblems over her naked body, culminating in the drafting of the sign of the Valknut on her forehead. When she looked up, she found that Aaliz Heydrich's body had been similarly decorated.

Crowley circled the two naked girls, examining his disciples' handiwork. "You should know, Daemon, that all magic is about harnessing man's natural power through the application of the magician's will. Willpower is the essence of all magic. Through the sublimation of your natural powers to my will, I will be able to direct and order the Spirits. But where is this natural power of man most evident? The answer lies in the sexual appetites of men and women. Sexual lust is the natural companion of magic; wed sex and magic and a psychic engine of vast occult potency is created."

Crowley must have seen the look of mounting horror that dressed Norma's face. He chuckled. "Do not be alarmed, Daemon, I am not suggesting that you participate in a sexual ritual. Far from it; with both you and the Lady Aaliz being pure in body you exert a huge attraction to the Spirit World. Your beauty, your purity and your latent, unexpressed sexual appetites, Daemon, will stimulate my adepts to heights of sexual desire, and thus stimulated they will generate all the sexual energy necessary to bind the Demi-Monde with the Spirit World." He clapped his hands in triumph. "But first we must have the Sacrifice of Blood."

CROCKETT PUFFED CONTENTEDLY ON HIS CLAY PIPE. "DID MISS TRIX-iebell listen, Major?" he asked from his perch on a crate in the warehouse that Baron Dashwood's regiment had made its home.

"No."

"So what are we going to do, sir?"

Baron Dashwood was torn. He was an officer and a gentleman so his first instinct was to do what he was ordered to do by his commanding officer. That his commanding officer was also his daughter made the prospect of ignoring those orders even more difficult. But he was certain that the WFA were being led into a trap and whilst he had a responsibility to Trixie and the WFA he also had a responsibility to the two hundred men under his command.

It was a difficult, an impossible decision, and unfortunately it was one he had to make quickly: there were only fifteen minutes left until the breakout began. He looked around at the men huddled in the warehouse—many of them the Poles he had freed from the work camp. He couldn't betray these men; he couldn't allow them to be needlessly killed or captured by the SS.

He loved Trixie but . . .

The irritating thing was that it was his own arrogance that had brought him to this: if he hadn't assumed that Heydrich was just a vicious idiot then he would have realized that it was he who was being played for a fool, that it was he who was being played as a patsy. How Heydrich and his cronies must have laughed when he swallowed their charade about the ForthRight attacking the Coven. How they must have howled when they allowed him to escape from Dashwood Manor knowing that he would warn his Royalist friends in the Coven and in this way reinforce Heydrich's little pantomime. How could he have been so stupid as to have underestimated them? How could he have forgotten how cunning these bastards were? But the game wasn't over yet. Maybe *they* had underestimated *him*.

"We're not going to Westgate with the rest of the army," he said finally. "That's what the SS want us to do. We're going to get out through Southgate and then head east to the river and down into the Hub. Assemble the regiment, Captain Crockett. If we're challenged by the SS we'll tell them we're an Anglo regiment being reassigned to the attack on the Quartier Chaud. Tell the men they're only to fire as a last resort. We'll escape the Ghetto using guile, not muscle."

Crockett gave the baron a salute. "Sounds like an excellent idea to me, Major, I always had a strange aversion to fighting to the last man."

—᷒ᨆ᷒—

For Trixie the final battle of the Warsaw Uprising was the worst experience of her short military career. It was the one she came closest to losing.

Despite the reinforcements, despite the confusion caused in the SS ranks when her father had smashed his way into the Ghetto, despite the best efforts of her fighters, the breakout soon degenerated into chaos.

As the first of them vaulted the barricades shortly before twelve, Trixie knew that it would be a murderous night. Within seconds the battle had become a fire-racked confusion, and the fighters of the WFA were cut down in swaths as they desperately fought their way through the ruins of the city toward Westgate. The carnage was terrible and Trixie sensed that outnumbered and outgunned, they were doomed.

The weather saved them from complete annihilation. It was the last night of Winter and the season had obviously determined to go out with a flourish. The blizzard that swept through the Ghetto was as bad as any she had ever experienced, so bad that it was impossible to see more than a few yards ahead, to distinguish snow-covered friend from snow-covered foe. These last savage snows of Winter churned with the smoke from burning steamers and smoldering buildings to make the Ghetto a scene from Hel.

But even shrouded by the blizzard, the losses were terrible. After an hour of the bitterest fighting of the whole Uprising, only a battered remnant of the WFA smashed its way to Westgate. And there in the smoke- and snow-drenched darkness, the Poles and the SS grappled with each other in hate-filled fury, their firefight enveloping the gateway.

But in the end the sheer bloody-mindedness of the Poles triumphed and Trixie led her fighters out of the Ghetto.

—◌◌◌—

The FIGHTING PROVIDED THE PERFECT COVER OF CHAOS AND MAYHEM for Ella, Vanka and Rivets—together, of course, with Ella's twelve dutiful disciples—to make their escape.

But rather than going toward the river as Ella had expected, Vanka headed for Middlegate and what with the weather and the darkness, and the fighting being concentrated towards the Boundary side of the Ghetto, they were able to evade the few SS patrols there were and come safe into Odessa. The reason Vanka had led them there was made clear when they were crouched by a barbed-wire fence that surrounded what looked like a flat, treeless playing field.

"Where are we?" whispered Ella as she scrolled through PINC.

Vanka was quicker with his answer. "Welcome to the John Hanning Speke Balloon-O-Drome, home to the First Aerial Detachment of the ForthRight Observation Corps."

Ella peered out into the darkness that shrouded the Balloon-O-Drome. There, gently swaying in the breeze, she could just make out the bulbous form of a balloon. The penny dropped. "You mean us to *fly* to ExterSteine?"

Vanka nodded enthusiastically. "It's the only way. Anyway, I've always wanted to go up in a balloon. We're fifteen miles from ExterSteine and it's only"—he checked his watch—"five hours to dawn and as the wind shifts to the east between midnight and six in the morning it's a perfect time. By my reckoning ExterSteine is almost due east, so all we'll do is let the wind carry us in that direction until we see the standing stones and then let out the hydrogen from the balloon and—"

"Crash?"

"Sink gracefully to the ground," he corrected. "Look, Ella, I know it's a pretty madcap sort of scheme but unless you can think of a better way of us getting to ExterSteine before dawn, this is all that's on offer."

"It's madness."

"You're not frightened of heights, are you?"

"It's not the heights that frighten me, it's the depths that come rushing up to greet you when you crash that I've always found discouraging."

"Don't worry, Ella, flying can't be *that* difficult."

"You're not suggesting *you're* going to fly it!"

"Of course," answered Vanka casually. "Who else? Anyway, it'll be fun!"

"Fun? That's a hydrogen balloon you're talking about; one bullet and we'll be toast."

"It's night; no one will see us."

"What about the guards? They're not just gonna let us waltz in and steal one of their balloons."

"Most of them will be drunk by now. It's Spring Eve and everybody gets drunk on Spring Eve. And if there are any guards who aren't drunk then your Disciples will settle them."

Before Ella quite knew what was happening Vanka flourished a pair of wire-cutters, cut a hole in the fence and she was running behind him toward the balloon. All the guards protecting the Balloon-O-Drome must have been drunk as no one challenged them, or maybe none of them believed that anyone would be mad enough to steal a balloon. Closer to, the balloon looked enormous but very fragile. The canvas of the cover was stretched over a thin bamboo frame, and the basket that hung beneath was woven from what looked to be wholly inadequate wicker.

"There isn't room for more than two or three people in that basket. What are the rest of us going to do?"

"Don't worry about them," answered Vanka. "Rivets will come

with us—he's only little. The rest will be all right. They're tough guys and they'll make their way to the Quartier somehow. But I think they'd appreciate it if you said a few words of thanks before we go."

"How about a prayer?" suggested Ella, only partly in jest.

ONCE OUT OF THE GHETTO, IT WAS EVERY MAN AND WOMAN FOR themselves. It was impossible for Trixie to control or to command the survivors of the WFA. So far as she could judge, the chance of their being able to fight through Odessa and St. Petersburg to the Anichkov Bridge was very slim.

But the peculiar thing was that now, when they were at their most vulnerable, the SS threat had receded. There were still fire-fights going on all around the perimeter of the Ghetto, but not with quite the intensity of before. It seemed that—despite her father's misgivings—their plan to escape through Westgate had worked: there were hardly any regular ForthRight Army soldiers defending the route south through Rodina to the Coven. But there was still a march of almost fifteen miles ahead of them and by the look of her soldiers that would be fifteen miles too far.

Wysochi provided the solution. Using a sharp tongue and a blunt boot, he drove the fighters up onto their feet and off searching for steamers. These he commandeered at the point of a rifle, and soon a veritable motorized regiment was puffing through the streets of Rodina, each steamer crammed full of fighters. It took them an hour to get to the Anichkov Bridge, and as the convoy wheezed to a halt by the side of the Volga River, she could see that now just the half-mile span of the bridge separated the WFA from the safety of Rangoon.

But as Trixie studied the bridge, her father's observation began to trouble her. She had expected the whole length of the St. Petersburg bank of the Volga to be alive with ForthRight assault troops as they prepared to attack the Coven, but it was virtually empty. Certainly, there was a sizable force of SS defending the bridge, but that's all they were doing: defending it. One thing for sure was they weren't attacking the Coven.

"Have you seen my father?" she asked Wysochi.

"No, though I've heard that he took his men east."

East?

For a moment Trixie felt hurt . . . betrayed. How could her father have deserted her on tonight of all nights?

"There's no ForthRight Army waiting to attack, Sergeant."

Wysochi shrugged. "The ForthRight have probably delayed the attack because of the weather. No one wants to advance into the teeth of a blizzard."

Trixie nodded. It was a sensible explanation and better than her father's idea that Heydrich had changed his mind and abandoned the attack on the Coven. Leaders like Heydrich didn't change their mind; that smacked of weakness.

"How many men do we have left?" she asked.

"Maybe a couple of thousand," Wysochi guessed. "It was hot work." He cocked an ear back toward St. Petersburg. "And the SS aren't far behind us." He was right; even with only one good ear she could hear SS steamers advancing toward them through the chilled silence of the night.

"Can we force the bridge?" she asked.

"I don't think we have any other choice, Colonel. And if we're going to do it we should do it soon, otherwise we're going to end up as meat in an SS sandwich."

At a signal from Trixie, the remaining WFA fighters attacked the bridge and it was an attack that soon degenerated into mayhem.

Later, all she could remember was ordering their steamers to smash through the barricades defending the bridge; the rest was just a blur of firing, fighting, yelling and cursing. The SS detachment stationed on the St. Petersburg end of the bridge had obviously not expected to be attacked from the rear but they fought bravely and the cost of the victory was appalling.

When Trixie eventually arrived on the Coven side of the bridge, she was flanked by only a tattered and battered rump of the army of seven thousand men and women she'd led over the barricades just two hours before.

"The Sacrifice of Blood?"

Crowley laughed at her concern. "Oh, don't fret yourself, Daemon, your life isn't to be forfeit. I just need a little of your blood to seal the psychic union between you and Lady Aaliz."

He gestured to the Witchfinder, who moved forward with an evil-looking knife clasped in his hand.

"Hold out the Daemon's forearm," commanded Crowley.

"No way!"

But there were too many of them to resist. They forced her right arm out and the Witchfinder ran the tip of his knife along it, slicing a six-inch cut in her pale flesh. Immediately blood began to run, collected in a gold goblet by an adept.

Face flushed with excitement, Crowley pointed to a small stage set in the center of the cavern. "Bring the Daemon to the altar," he boomed, "and, Lady Aaliz, if you would approach through the unformed part of the pentagon, being careful not to step on the rest of the design." He pointed to the pentagon painted on the floor of the cavern that surrounded the altar, indicating the one missing side.

"Now, my Lady," said Crowley, "if you would please kneel in the direction from which the dawn light will enter our temple."

The Lady Aaliz did as she was bade.

"Have the Daemon kneel facing the Lady Aaliz."

None too gently the Witchfinder forced Norma into the pentagon and pushed her down so that she was face-to-face with Aaliz, the girls forming human bookends to the altar. "Ah, the perfect yin and yang," mused Crowley. "The perfect antipodes: one blond, the other dark."

A trio of musicians seated at the very rear of the temple began to play, the music they conjured from their instruments cacophonous, disturbing and somehow alien.

In the corners of the cavern incense burners were lit and acrid red smoke began to drift through the temple. The smell that tugged at Norma's nostrils made her head swim, and she began to feel strangely divorced from reality.

A priestess set a golden tray bearing two goblets—one containing Norma's blood—on a stand to the side of the altar. Once the woman had retreated from the pentagon, Crowley turned to address his small audience. "The altar has been encased in this pentagon for two reasons: it seals the altar from the Demi-Monde, which makes it a more . . . comfortable place for the Spirits to occupy, and secondly, it forms a magical barrier that safeguards onlookers from the occult forces our spells will release." He stooped down and with two swift swishes of a piece of chalk and a few muttered incantations closed the pentagon.

Satisfied, he moved to stand behind the altar, then spread his arms and called out, "I command ABBA, the deity that rules this, the Demi-Monde, to send the soul of Aaliz Heydrich to the Spirit World, there to inhabit the body of Norma Williams." Crowley walked around the altar nine times waving an incense burner to and fro, wafting thick, acrid smoke over the two kneeling girls.

"First, the Lady Aaliz must drink the blood of the Daemon and by doing so subjugate its will and its astral power." He offered the golden chalice to Aaliz, who, with obvious relish, drank down the thick, red liquid.

"Now, Daemon, drink this." Crowley noted the look of revulsion on Norma's face. "Do not worry, it is not blood. This is *zelie*, a potion made from the hallucinogenic plant called ayahuasca that grows in the Hubland; its use was much favored by the shamans of Old Rodina. To this I have added the juice of boiled fly agaric mushrooms, to make a cocktail to unlock your mind from the hegemony of your will." Norma reluctantly downed the draft. The tart red liquid made her head spin.

"Join hands," commanded Crowley, and Norma unthinkingly stretched out her hands toward Aaliz, who intertwined her fingers around hers.

"Let the Rite of Transference commence."

THE SEVEN MEN AND FIVE WOMEN WHO MADE UP ELLA'S BODYGUARD gathered expectantly around the basket. She found the way they looked at her vaguely disconcerting; they really did believe they were in the presence of someone truly holy. The problem was she didn't have a clue what to say to them. As she gazed into those trusting, imploring eyes, she wondered what she, little Ella Thomas from New York City, could say that would inspire these people, that would give them hope. She turned to the greatest speechwriters in history for inspiration.

Thank you, Mrs. Little and your English lit class.

"Friends, Demi-Mondians, countrymen, lend me your ears."

Now a little from the greatest speechifier of them all, Winston Churchill.

"We have seen joined the greatest battle in the history of the Demi-Monde. It is a battle between good and evil; between those who wish to be free and those who wish to enslave them; between those who would embrace understanding and tolerance and those whose philosophy is infused by hate. But it is a battle that must be won. It will not be an easy victory. We see stretching before us an ordeal of the most grievous kind. We have before us many, many months of struggle and suffering. But we must be victorious. We *must* have victory. Victory at all costs—victory in spite of all terrors—victory, however long and hard the road may be, for without victory there is no survival. And make no mistake, my friends, we now fight for our very survival."

Though JFK wasn't bad either.

"Let the ForthRight know we shall pay any price, bear any burden, meet any hardship, support any friend, oppose any foe, to assure this victory and the success of liberty and equality within the Demi-Monde. Let the ForthRight know we wish a new world order, one where the strong are just and the weak secure and the peace is preserved."

Not forgetting the inimitable Martin Luther King.

"My friends: I have a dream that one day this world will live out the truth in the creed that all men and all women are created equal. I have a dream that even the ForthRight, with its vicious racists and a Leader whose lips drip with the bile of detestation and subjugation, will be transformed into an oasis of freedom and justice. I have a dream that one day people will be judged not by the color of their skin but by the content of their souls."

A little touch more of Churchillian rhetoric.

"So I ask you to go forth and spread the message that all of the Demi-Monde must unite against the plague that is UnFunDaMentalism. Tell the people of the Demi-Monde that we must unite to wage war by land and by river. We must wage war with all our might and with all the strength ABBA has given us. We must wage war against a monstrous tyranny never surpassed in the dark and lamentable catalog of human crime. Tell them we must fight and we must be victorious."

And round it off with a dash more Martin Luther King.

"But be assured that one day the chimes of freedom will ring out through the Demi-Monde proclaiming the coming of a world where men and women, black and white, HerEtical and HimPerialist, will join hands as equals and as friends. That is my message. I pray to the Spirits to keep you safe and to give you the courage and the strength to face the trials to come."

After she had finished speaking an unnatural silence descended on her audience. Then one of the twelve—the long beanpole William Penn, who had been so assiduously scribbling in his notebook as she had been talking—stood up. There were tears trickling down his cheeks. "We pledge, Lady IMmanual, that we will take your message to the Demi-Monde. We pledge that your message of democracy and the defiance of tyranny and injustice will be spread to all the Sectors. We pledge to work night and day to rally the Demi-Monde to defy the evil of the ForthRight and of UnFunDaMentalism. We pledge our undying loyalty and allegiance to our Savior, the Lady IMmanual and the creed of IMmanualism."

Bloody hell.

Then the twelve knelt before Ella, who, remembering what she had seen the televangelists do on TV, went around placing her hand on each of the bowed heads whilst intoning, "May ABBA be with you."

At last Vanka intervened. "Well, thank you very much, ladies and gentlemen. Thanks for everything. Best of luck with your preaching. Go forth with the blessing of the Lady IMmanual and all that. Yeah, go forth and multiply. Now we've got to be going." He hopped into the basket and held out a hand to Ella. "C'mon, then, time to go flying."

Once his two passengers were safely in the balloon's basket, Vanka nodded to William Penn. "If you would cast off the mooring ropes."

There was a judder, a lurch, and slowly the balloon began to rise.

"What did you think, Vanka," she gasped as she watched the ground begin to slowly recede, "about what I said down there?"

"I think if you carry on making speeches like that the IMmanual-ites will never let you leave the Demi-Monde." He beamed at her. "And if that's the case, I might even be persuaded to become one myself."

As Trixie walked to the Rangoon side of the Anichkov Bridge she saw a deputation standing waiting to greet her. Unconsciously she ran a hand through her sweat-drenched hair, trying to make herself just a little more presentable. She almost laughed; after what she had been through it was a ridiculous thing to worry about.

Two of the deputation stepped forward. The leading woman was tall and well made, and despite the rather severe cut of the trouser suit she was wearing appeared elegant and quite feminine, thanks to the wonderful cascade of blond hair that tumbled down to her waist.

"I am Lady Lucrezia Borgia," she announced in a voice so refined that it bordered on the haughty, "first deputy to Her Imperial Highness Wu, empress of all the lands known as the Demi-Monde."

Another megalomaniac.

Trixie set her face to bland and saluted. "I am Colonel Trixiebell Dashwood, commander of the Warsaw Free Army."

"Empress Wu sends her greetings to such a courageous soldier and offers you and your troops sanctuary in the Coven."

"I am very grateful, Madam First Deputy."

"Where is the one called the Lady IMmanual?" The question came from the girl standing behind First Deputy Borgia, and in contrast to the first deputy's serenity, the second woman radiated impatience and petulance. She was clad from head to toe in combat gear and carried a repeating rifle slung over her shoulder. Trixie knew her instantly, knew her by her cropped brown hair, by her gleaming eyes that seemed to flash and sparkle as she spoke, and by Loki's symbol, the large wooden cross hanging from her neck. This was the infamous Jeanne Dark, leader of the Suffer-O-Gettes, the scourge of HimPerialism, the enemy of UnFunDaMentalism, the chief witch of HerEticalism.

A few weeks ago Trixie would have made the sign of the Valknut to ward off the evil that Jeanne Dark represented for the natural order of things, but not now. Now all she saw was a rival, and rivals weren't something to be afraid of. Rivals were something to be eliminated.

"I asked you a question."

The sharpness in Jeanne Dark's voice brought Trixie out of her reverie. No one—*no one*—spoke to her like that.

"When you address me you will use my rank. I am Colonel Dashwood."

"Very well, *Colonel* Dashwood: where is the Lady IMmanual?"

"The Lady IMmanual? She was lost. We believe she has been tricked by a man named Vanka Maykov into surrendering herself to the SS."

"Fuck," snarled the girl. "Now that, Colonel Dashwood, was a careless, costly mistake." With a snort of disgust she spun on her heel and marched back toward the end of the bridge. The look the first deputy directed toward the witch's retreating figure suggested there was little love lost between the two Covenites.

"You must forgive my colleague Reverend Deputy Dark," said First Deputy Borgia, "she is apt to be a little temperamental." She smiled diplomatically. "We have prepared accommodation for your fighters in a nearby barracks, but while they are resting the empress Wu has commanded an audience with you."

"Now?" Trixie looked down at her soiled and tattered combat overalls. "Perhaps I might be given a few minutes to—"

"Empress Wu is very insistent that she meet you immediately. She is aware that you are a soldier and apt to be somewhat careless regarding your appearance. But your army's presence on Coven soil has the most profound political implications, implications which must be urgently resolved."

Trixie nodded; the Coven giving the WFA sanctuary must have sent Heydrich into a paroxysm of fury. "I wish Major Wysochi to accompany me."

Wysochi grinned when he heard his instant promotion, but Trixie knew eyebrows would be raised if she insisted on having a mere sergeant as her second-in-command.

"Is he your Preferred Male?"

"Preferred Male?"

The first deputy gave a condescending smile. "It is a Covenite term for the male a Femme allows to accompany her and provide her with certain physical comforts."

She glanced at Wysochi, whose grin broadened. "Yes, Major Wysochi is my Preferred Male."

"Very well, but Preferred Male Wysochi should understand that he is to walk behind you and never address a Femme without being addressed first."

The first deputy turned and led Trixie and Wysochi from the bridge.

As the night floated past, Norma felt the air in the temple become heavier, almost syrupy. Sounds were muffled, as though they were coming to her from far, far away. She felt distanced not just from the music but from reality. With every passing moment her world contracted. She seemed to be falling into herself.

As she and Aaliz Heydrich knelt face-to-face and hand in hand through the long night, she experienced a growing sensation that she was merging with the girl. It was almost as though she and Aaliz were beginning to inhabit the same body . . . the same consciousness . . . the same soul.

She saw a bead of sweat trickle from Aaliz's brow and felt the identical one course over her own forehead.

In an apathetic sort of way Norma sensed the tempo of the ritual become more frenzied. The rhythm of the unrelenting music was becoming faster, the stench wafting from the incense burners more pungent, and the ululations and the cavortings of Crowley and his adepts more fervent. The cavern was heavy with magic, and inside the pentagon strange and nebulous forms manifested themselves.

Ghosts and specters . . . the Intangible . . . floated . . . through the thickening air, their gossamer fingers drifting over . . . through Norma and Aaliz. The Spirits had come, and their coming announced that the moment of Transference was imminent. There would be no time for anyone to rescue her now.

FROM WHAT SHE HAD SEEN OF BALLOON RIDES ON TELEVISION, ELLA had thought them to be tranquil, calm, almost beatific experiences, with the balloonists drifting high and silent in a sun-kissed sky. But as she quickly discovered, balloons were in fact noisy affairs, with the wicker basket and the cordage creaking and groaning, and the fabric of the balloon rippling and flapping in the wind.

The balloon stank too: the dubbin that waterproofed the canvas canopy had a rancid smell. And all the while the Winter blizzard that swooped around the basket pushed and pummeled the balloon, making it slip and slide through the air in an unsettling way, as though she were riding a pendulum. It was also bitterly cold floating around in the night sky, so cold that she was forced to duck down beneath the side of the basket to get away from the freezing wind.

She didn't stay there long. The noise, the smell, the cold and the continual swaying of the basket in the air currents meant that they had barely floated a couple of miles from the Balloon-O-Drome before she was obliged to get back to her feet to retch over the side of the basket.

"Good shot," observed Rivets. "There's a coupla thousand of them ForthRight soldiers below us an' now one of 'em's got a faceful of vomit."

Ella wiped her mouth and then—cautiously; she hated the way the basket tipped when she shifted her weight—peered down to the ground below. In the darkness it was easy to see the lanterns the Forth-Right Army had placed to light their way along the newly opened Hub spur of the Trans-ForthRight Railway. The flickering snake of trains coiled and twisted along the railway line that connected the Forth-Right with Hub Bridge Number 4.

No . . . not Hub Bridge Number 4. They were advancing toward Hub Bridge *Number 2!*

A frown creased her brow; the ForthRight Army was going the wrong way. All the trains and the steamers and the marching soldiers were advancing in the direction of the Quartier Chaud.

"The ForthRight's attacking the Medis," she gasped, and even as the words tumbled out of her mouth she realized that that was what she hadn't been able to read in Crowley's mind the last time they'd met. Somehow Crowley's—Heydrich's—duplicity had been hidden from her and PINC.

But how? And why?

Vanka shrugged. "Doesn't surprise me; Heydrich's a crafty sod. All that stuff he fed Baron Dashwood and Dabrowski was obviously moonshine. Probably just playing silly buggers to keep everybody off balance." He laughed. "The funny thing is that the nonaggression pact he signed with the Coven was probably genuine; it'll go down in history as the only pact Heydrich ever honored in his whole rotten life."

"But what about the WFA? They've been offered sanctuary by the Coven."

"I don't think you need worry too much about them; by the look of things there's been some hard fighting in the Ghetto." He pointed to the smudge of flames that lit up the night in the direction of the Boundary. "No, I don't think too many of the WFA are going to get out of that Helhole."

Vanka was right; even from a height of—Ella guessed—two thousand feet and a distance of two or three miles, the sound of the armies fighting it out in the Ghetto was plainly audible.

Despite Vanka's confidence that the east wind would drive them toward ExterSteine, progress was agonizingly slow. The balloon seemed caught in a vortex of wind, spinning indecisively over the Rhine where the Reinhard Heydrich Railway Bridge crossed the river, giving the three passengers a marvelous view of the frantic efforts of the railway engineers who were trying to clear the carcass of the train derailed by Baron Dashwood's men.

At first their sedate progress didn't trouble Ella, but as time slipped by and the balloon refused to move at anything more than the aeronautical equivalent of a snail's pace she became increasingly anxious. Vanka was obviously as worried as she was; he began to drum his fingers on the side of the wicker basket.

"What's wrong?" she asked.

"There's so much snow on the top of the balloon that it's slowing us down. I'm worried that if we aren't on the ground by dawn the wind will shift to the south, and that will take us toward the center of the Demi-Monde." He passed Ella his telescope. "If you look to your right, you can just see Mare Incognitum."

Ella peered through the snow-drenched night, and sure enough, glinting in the moonlight was a large lake—at least two miles across, by her estimation—set slap-bang in the middle of the Demi-Monde. She checked PINC, but all the information it had was that the center of the Hub was an undeveloped area off-limits to Demi-Mondians and allocated to ABBA for future cyber-development. Rather disturbingly PINC named this area Terror Incognita.

"Is that a problem?"

"I don't know how long this balloon is going to stay airborne; I think we've got a leak. And the last thing I want to do is come down in Terror Incognita."

"Why's it called *Terror* Incognita? What's there to be terrified of?"

"The Terror's full ov monsters an' lots ov ovver horrible fings—" began Rivets.

"No one knows," Vanka interrupted. "Explorers have crossed the Wheel River but none of them has ever come back. And this Winter the ForthRight sent in a regiment of SS to have a look around and they were lost too. All we really know about the place comes from the drawings Speke made during his balloon ascent last year."

"And that is?"

"Not much. We know that it's heavily forested and that it's home for one of the Wonders of the Ancient Demi-Monde. You can just see the Great Pyramid now, it's almost directly south."

Ella swung the telescope around and examined the horizon. PINC had made no mention of any pyramid but there, nevertheless, illuminated by the moonlight, was a structure that looked for all the world like Khufu's Great Pyramid. But it wasn't the eroded and corroded monument Ella remembered from her history books; this one was white, sharp sided and pristine. She didn't remember Khufu's pyramid having a hexagonal platform at its very summit either.

How odd.

"It's glowing!"

"Everything made out of Mantle-ite glows in the dark. In the dark it emits green stuff scientists called LunarAtion. It's the same effect you saw in the sewers."

As she moved the telescope around the central area of the Demi-Monde, she saw several huge pictures drawn on the ground around Mare Incognitum. From what she could make out there was a spider, a snake, a shark and what looked like a man; each of them was a good two or three miles in length and, just like the pyramid, they glowed under the moonlight. "Wow! Those pictures are like the Nazca geoglyphs."

"Oh, you mean the Speke Etchings. Yeah, we didn't even know they existed until a year ago. As they're invisible from ground level they were undiscovered until Speke went up in his balloon."

"Who made them?" She had to ask because according to PINC they didn't exist.

"No one knows."

"They're amazing. I'd really love to see them up close."

There was a ripping sound from above Ella's head. She looked up to see that part of the balloon's canvas had torn away.

"It looks, Ella, as though you're going to get your wish."

THAT THE BARON AND HIS MEN GOT AS FAR AS THEY DID WITHOUT any trouble was down to the Poles; the baron had never realized just how much cheek, how much chutzpah, Poles had. They were the ones who shouted the ribald replies to the SS guards when they were challenged and the ones who laughed and joked as they marched along, deluding the SS into believing they were just reinforcements on their way to the front. By dint of the Poles' impertinence and by not firing at anyone the baron's regiment made it safely through the Ghetto, out through Southgate, along Odessa's Deribasovskaya

Street, and across the new railway track. And that's when things had gone wrong. Obviously the ForthRight military had been shaken by Cassidy's train attack and their reaction had been to dramatically increase the number of soldiers guarding the railway line.

Unfortunately the sentry whom Cassidy tripped over was young, overeager and one of the few men in his company who wasn't drunk. The boy had been cowering away from the blizzard in the lee of a water tower when Cassidy, frozen and not in a very accommodating mood, fell over him. The conversation that ensued was brief and noisy.

"Who goes there?" said the boy through chattering teeth.

"Someone who's not as stupid as you are, that's for sure," snarled Cassidy as he hauled himself out of the snowdrift he'd been tumbled into. "Spirits damn it, boy, what are you doing hiding away like that?"

The boy, with a terrified look on his face, did his best to face Cassidy down. "I-I-I s-s-said who goes there?"

"Why-why-why," Cassidy mimicked a little unkindly, "should I tell a f-f-fucking idiot like you anything?"

"Be-be-because I'm guarding this water tower."

"Well, P-P-Private, I'm Sergeant B-B-Bob Cassidy of the First Anglo Rangers and me and my f-f-friends have been ordered to get our a-a-asses over to Hub Bridge Number Two to help with the attack there."

Cassidy was betrayed by the want of a button. If his ragged greatcoat still had had some of its buttons it wouldn't have flapped open in the wind to display his blue jacket, the one he had worn when he had been fighting on the Royalist side during the Troubles. The boy saw the jacket, his eyes boggled and then he made what would prove to be a fatal mistake.

"Royalists!" he screamed. "We're under attack by Royalists!" And then to compound his mistake, he fired his rifle. By the time Cassidy had smashed his rifle butt into the boy's head the damage had been done. The alert rippled around the ForthRight troops stationed along the railway line.

"Royalists to me," screamed the baron. "Captain Crockett, we're to advance at the double, due south."

The look he got from Crockett was very articulate. He knew as well as the baron what lay to the south.

"That's the direction where there are the fewest enemy," the baron shouted by way of explanation. "We'll get to the Wheel River and then—"

It was lucky for the baron that the shooting began when it did, otherwise he would have been forced to explain to Crockett just what he did plan to do. And if he *had* explained he doubted that Crockett or indeed any of his regiment would have followed him. But by his estimation a probable death was preferable to a certain one and, after all, someone, sometime had to survive Terror Incognita. He just hoped it would be him.

FORTUNATELY FOR THE BALLOONISTS, THE BLIZZARD EASED AND THE wind shifted back, driving them to the east and blowing them— unnoticed in the snow-filled darkness—a hundred feet over the campfires that marked the SS cordon around ExterSteine. When the wounded balloon finally expired, they came to rest, by Vanka's estimation, about a half-mile to the west of ExterSteine. The landing was what Ella described as a "soft crash": the basket hit the ground with a considerable bump but as the ground was covered with a thick layer of snow the impact was cushioned. The three of them emerged from the tangle of ropes and wreckage and pronounced themselves grateful that none had any broken limbs. Barely pausing for breath, they set off toward the five stone columns that made up ExterSteine and which could be seen glinting ahead of them in the dawn's half-light.

Dawn.

As Ella looked to the east, she could see the unmistakable smudge of red light on the horizon signaling that dawn was imminent.

"How long before sunup, Vanka?" she whispered—sound traveled easily in the Hub—as she slid and slipped over the pristine snow of the Hubland.

"Half an hour at the most."

"Not enough time."

"Maybe not to rescue Norma but maybe enough to stop the Rite of Transference."

"How do you figure that?"

"I remember an article in *The Stormer* that described the rites Crowley performed to welcome the beginning of Spring. It said something about there being a window cut in the roof of the cavern set at the top of the tallest ExterSteine column and that it was through this window that the first light of the first day of Spring was directed. According to Crowley, this first light of Spring had great occult significance. Maybe if we can block the window we can stop the rite."

They ran as hard as they could through the swirling snow and the faltering darkness, guided by the shimmering Mantle-ite columns, and as they came closer the otherworldliness of the structure became more apparent. ExterSteine was made up of five gigantic columns that stabbed like rigid fingers out from the middle of the flat, snow-dressed grassland that was the Hub, the Mantle-ite columns luminous in the darkness. Ella guessed the tallest column of the five—Lilith's Column—stood over two hundred feet tall and was about a hundred feet in girth. Lights flickered at the summit.

A strange, eerie feeling washed over her.

She'd been here before.

"That's where the Rite of Transference must be taking place," she called out. "That must be where Crowley conducts his rituals."

Vanka pointed to a staircase that wound around the column. "And that's the way up."

Ella could only think that the rite being performed by Crowley was so secret that he wanted as few people to witness it as possible and that was why there were no SS StormTroopers guarding the staircase. Indeed, all the Hubland stretching out around Exter-Steine seemed deserted, the snow untarnished by footprints or steamer tracks.

Climbing the column was tough; the stairs were steep, the steps slippery with ice and snow, and the savage wind buffeted them every step of the way, but there was no time to pause for breath. As she climbed she couldn't resist the temptation to drift her fingers over the runic inscriptions etched over the surface of the Mantle-ite column. And though the runes were written in the untranslatable Pre-Folk A and though even PINC couldn't provide her with an interpretation of what the inscriptions said, *she* knew what was written there . . . knew that once she had spoken this strange language.

IN LILITH | I, LOKI, WAS REBORN.
AND REBORN | LILITH SCORNED
ABBA'S HARMONY. THROUGH LILITH'S
SORCERY | THE HARMONY
WAS DESTROYED.
HARMONY SHE SAID | IS THE ICED TOUCH
OF THE IDEAL. | THE DEAD HAND
THE FROZEN SOUL | THE UNVOICED IDEA
THE UNFURLING | OF THE FLOWER
NEVER BLOSSOMING.
TO BUILD | ANEW
LILITH | IN HER QUIET FURY

RAZED. | THIS IS THE FIRST TRUTH.
TO BUILD | YOU MUST FIRST DESTROY.
THE RUINED PERFECTION OF THE VANIR ERASED.

She had no time to ponder on what was written; the dawn light that with every passing minute advanced over the eastern horizon urged her on. Time was short. Desperately she pushed her protesting body up the stairs until she arrived, breathless, panting and dizzy from her exertions, at the flat, circular top of the column that tilted toward the rising sun. She found herself standing on the summit of the world.

Ella hated heights and she had never been in a situation where her feeling of vertigo was so intense. The Demi-Monde stretching out below her seemed a very long way down and she was made to feel even more vulnerable by the way the wind whistled around her as she struggled to keep her footing on the slick Mantle-ite.

"Over there," Vanka shouted over the howling gusts. "To the east. The shutters must be over there."

Leaning into the wind, they pushed their way to the eastern side of the column. Vanka was right: a pair of great wooden shutters covered that side, facing toward the rapidly rising sun. There was a huge wooden lever next to them that presumably operated the shutters.

Why aren't they guarded?

Vanka whipped his belt from around his waist. "If we tie this around the handles of the shutters that'll stop them being opened!"

His explanation was interrupted by the unmistakable sound of a revolver being cocked. They looked up to see Burlesque Bandstand—a much thinner-faced Burlesque Bandstand, it had to be said—wrapped in a *dublonka*, sitting with his legs dangling carelessly over the side of the column and brandishing a purposeful-looking Webley pistol in their direction. By the light of the rising sun Ella could see there was a body of a dead SS StormTrooper beside him.

He raised the pistol and took careful aim at Vanka's forehead.

"'Appy First ov Spring, Wanker, you bastard."

EMPRESS WU WAS HOLDING COURT IN THE SHWEDAGON PALACE, which dominated East Rangoon. After the cramped hustle and bustle of the Rookeries the huge gardens that surrounded the palace came as a surprise to Trixie; she found it difficult to believe there could be anywhere in the Demi-Monde so profligate with space. It was as though she were walking through a place that was in the Demi-Monde but not of the Demi-Monde.

Once inside the palace she was ushered briskly along the brilliantly decorated corridors until she was brought to a halt before two vast and richly embossed doors. First Deputy Borgia turned to her. "This is the Hall of the Great Dragon. Beyond these doors is seated the Sacred Presence of the Great Empress Wu. You will address the Great Empress as 'Your Imperial Majesty.' You will approach the Great Empress Wu with your eyes averted; under no circumstances are you to gaze on her Divine Form directly. When you reach the black line inscribed across the floor of the hall you are to genuflect—"

"Kneel? Colonels in the WFA don't kneel to anyone."

"Please, Colonel, try to understand. This is Coven protocol, it cannot be changed."

Oh yes it can, decided Trixie as she gave the first deputy a nod of acceptance.

"Under no circumstances are your knees, your hands or any other parts of your body to cross that line. You may answer the questions posed to you by Her Imperial Majesty but whilst you may answer her questions—"

"Under no circumstances am I to address her directly," suggested Trixie peevishly. She was too tired for this nonsense.

"Indeed. You may use your inferior Anglo tongue when making your replies; the Empress Wu is familiar and fluent in all of the primitive languages of the Demi-Monde." The first deputy glanced disdainfully at Wysochi. "Your Preferred Male is not permitted to enter the Hall of the Great Dragon. Only Femmes and NoNs may gaze upon the Divine Form of the empress."

Instructions completed, the First Deputy made a sign to the two sentries guarding the entrance to the hall—both the guards were women, and both, Trixie noticed, were armed with brand-new M4s—who hauled the doors open to reveal the vast hall beyond.

M4s . . .

Why would Heydrich have provided the Coven with M4s if he was about to make war on it?

Still pondering this, Trixie strode off across the beautifully inlaid teak floor toward the small woman she could see seated on a throne at the far side of the room.

By repute the Empress Wu was the most beautiful woman in the Demi-Monde, but as she was protected from any indiscreet peeking by drapes of sheer silk wafting in front of her Trixie was unable to confirm or deny the rumor.

She came to the black line the first deputy had warned her about and with just a moment's hesitation dropped to her knees and bowed to the shadowed form of the empress.

"You are very young," observed a lilting, almost singsong voice.

Trixie remained silent. In truth she didn't quite know how to reply; she *was* young.

"And very dirty."

This too was correct. Looking down at her knees, Trixie could see that her filthy, matted trousers were leaving streaks of dirt on the immaculately polished floor.

"But this, I suppose, is to be expected when one is confronted by a Femme so given to martial pursuits. I understand that you are a remarkably able soldier, Colonel Dashwood; is this true?"

There seemed to be little point in being modest. "Yes, Your Imperial Majesty, I have enjoyed some success in fighting the Anglos."

"But you are an Anglo yourself, are you not?"

"I am, Your Majesty, but I have sworn to fight with the people of Warsaw against the tyranny of Reinhard Heydrich and UnFunDa-Mentalism."

"You have decidedly unForthRight views for one so young."

"My age does not, I believe, detract from the correctness of my opinions."

"Nor from the arrogance of your attitude, it would seem," came the testy response. "You should be aware that the Coven and the ForthRight are allies . . . friends."

So her father had been right. Heydrich had deceived them.

Heydrich had deceived them so comprehensively that he had persuaded Trixie to lead her army into the hands of his "friend and ally." She and the WFA were now at the mercy of the Coven.

A heavy silence fell on the hall. Finally the empress spoke again. "I have consulted the iChing, which advises that I should avoid war with the ForthRight, that I should not seek to tweak the tiger's tail. This I believe is good advice; violence, in my opinion, is a poor substitute for the delicate deceits of diplomacy. But the price of peace is often a heavy one in that it involves the betrayal of those who trusted us." Again a silence and then a soft laugh. "Unfortunately betrayal and duplicity are indispensable parts of statecraft, and when one rules a nation or leads an army one quickly grows calluses on the soul, calluses that deaden finer feelings and dampen the pain engendered by betrayal. It is the express wish of Leader Heydrich that, as a token of the Coven's friendship toward the ForthRight, we execute all members of the army you brought with you to the Coven and that we deliver you, in chains, into the custody of the ForthRight."

No, you won't.

As surreptitiously as she could, Trixie unbuttoned her tunic. The fools hadn't searched her thoroughly enough—she had a small Colt holstered under her armpit. "That, Your Imperial Majesty, will only demonstrate to Heydrich that the Coven is weak, and weakness is not a trait he admires."

More silence. Trixie's hand closed around the butt of the Colt.

"An interesting point, but not persuasive." There was the tinkling of a small bell and immediately the doors to the hall swung open.

Resplendent in the immaculate black uniform of the SS–Ordo Templi Aryanis, Colonel Archie Clement strode into the hall.

Trixie knew that she was a dead woman.

How long they knelt there Norma didn't—couldn't—know; she'd spent the night encased in a magical bubble. Everything that happened outside the pentagon seemed distant, almost dreamlike. Even when Crowley and his adepts tore their gowns from one another and pranced around the cavern in a frenzied orgy of sexual indulgence it hardly touched on Norma's consciousness. But now the music was louder and even more frenzied, the screams of Crowley and his adepts as they shouted out their spells and incantations more impassioned. She sensed the ritual was coming to its climax.

Suddenly the shutters set high in the roof crashed open, allowing a shaft of sunlight to stream through, down into the cavern. In that instant, Aaliz Heydrich was bathed in a halo of golden light and the runes painted on her body seemed to writhe and twist like living things. Her body began to tremble. A low moan escaped her lips. And then, with a terrible scream, she arched back and collapsed unconscious to the floor of the altar.

Norma felt herself tumbling into a dark nothingness, but just before she slid into unconsciousness she saw Crowley's face, his mouth drawn back in the rictus of a smile.

The Rite of Transference was complete.

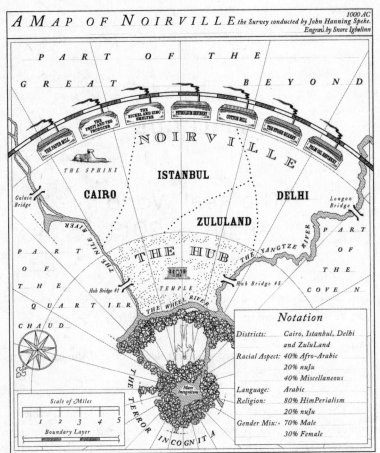

MAP OF NOIRVILLE.

PLATE 5

EPILOGUE

The Real World:
August 1, 2018

She awoke slowly . . . cautiously, taking long careful moments to ori-entate herself toward the challenges to come, settling her nerves for what would be the performance of a lifetime . . . of two lifetimes.

She kept her eyes closed, feigning sleep, but still she gathered information using her other senses.

Smell . . .

The professor was close by; his cologne was unmistakable, almost overpowering. That was a comforting realization; it was good to have a friend and ally in the room. But despite the competition of the professor's cologne she still detected the brush of a very femi-nine perfume on her nose. This presumably signaled that the First Lady—her mother—was in the room; she was touched by her solici-tude. And as a background fragrance there was that signature aroma of disinfectant and urine that was inescapably "hospital."

Touch . . .

She could feel the stiff, clean bedsheets under her fingertips—

my, how long her nails were!—could feel the press of the regimented arrangement of the blankets that confined her as she lay on the bed.

Taste . . .

Ughhh . . . yes, the bilious taste in her mouth, presumably a result of weeks of being fed intravenously.

Hearing . . .

She could hear them whispering, so concerned, so considerate, so desperate not to disturb her. There was the president's gruff, mahogany voice as he dealt brusquely with an aide who was reminding him of a "prior engagement." The First Lady was sobbing quietly to her left. And providing a 70 b.p.m. backbeat to the room's whole bated cacophony was the *beep, beep, beep* of her heart monitor.

She took a surreptitious breath, preparing herself. She opened her eyes.

"She's awake!"

"Oh, thank you, God!"

"Please, she'll be very weak."

"Please don't crowd around her. Please don't overexcite her."

"Oh, Norma, darling, it's Mommy."

She gave a weak smile, thankful that the plastic tube masked any element of theatricality.

"Weak . . ." she gasped in a ragged voice.

The doctor—white coat, stethoscope, worried expression, must be a doctor—pushed closer and lifted her wrist, presumably checking her pulse. "Probably a little anemic, young lady; we'll organize a blood transfusion if that's okay by you."

She couldn't suppress a big smile; that would be very, very okay!

THE DEMI-MONDE

Glossary of Terms
and Slang

4Telling: Predicting the future. From the declension 1Telling = silence; 2Telling = speaking of the past; 3Telling = speaking of the present; 4Telling = speaking of the future.

ABBA: The chief deity of all religions in the Demi-Monde. God. Referred to as "Him" in the ForthRight and NoirVille, as "Her" in the Coven and as "Him/Her" in the Quartier Chaud.

AC: After Confinement (see also Confinement).

Aryan: The bedrock of UnFunDaMentalism. The Aryan ideal is to be blond, blue eyed and fair skinned, that is, the same physical profile as the Pre-Folk from whom the Aryan people are supposedly descended. The UnFunDaMentalist Eugenical Policy espoused by the ForthRight propounds the belief that by careful identification of those citizens of pure Aryan stock and the ensuring—through legislation, propaganda and education—that these Aryans only mate with their own kind, over ten generations all racial contaminants can be bred out of the ForthRight.

Awful Tower, the: The 1,150-foot-tall geodetic iron structure built in the heart of the Paris District to commemorate the signing of the Hub

Treaty of 517, which marked the end of the Great War. Always contentious because of its phallic shape, the tower divided aesthetic opinion, leading to its being generally referred to as the Awful Tower. Following the Great Schism it became a symbol of UnFunDaMentalism and masculine supremacy within the Medi districts of the Quartier Chaud. A corrupted remembrance of the Real World name "Eiffel Tower."

b&t: Blood and tonic: a cocktail of blood, gin and tonic water favored by the more sophisticated set in Rodina.

BC: Before Confinement (see also Confinement).

Beyond, the: See Great Beyond.

Biological Essentialism: Biological Essentialism is a cornerstone of the UnFunDaMentalist doctrine. It is predicated on the principle that the sexes occupy Separate Spheres of intellectual, economic and social functionality within the Demi-Monde, and that these Separate Spheres are ordained by ABBA and are thus natural, fixed and immutable. ABBA, by making the sexes biologically, psychologically and intellectually different, has equipped them for different tasks in life. UnFunDaMentalism teaches that the preservation of these distinctive Spheres of Activity is vital if social harmony is to be preserved, and for women this means adherence to the mantra of "Feeding, Breeding and MenFolk Heeding" given to them by ABBA.

Blanks: Derogatory NoirVillian slang term for Anglo-Slavs and all others of a pale persuasion.

Blood Banner: The flag that the Party's SS regiments carried before them when they fought their first battle during the Troubles and seized control of Berlin's Blood Bank. A sacred relic of UnFunDaMentalism.

Blood Brothers: The NoirVillian gangsta sect responsible for the black-market trading of blood. The leader of the Blood Brothers is Shaka Zulu.

Blood Hounder: A half-human, half-animal creature developed by the SS specifically to track down Daemons. Blood Hounders have an enhanced sense of smell and are able to detect one drop of blood at a distance of one hundred yards.

Blood Standard: The monetary system adopted on a Demi-Monde-wide basis by which the paper currencies issued by a Sector are convertible into preset and fixed quantities of blood.

Boundary Layer, the: The impenetrable, transparent "wall" that prevents Demi-Mondians leaving the Demi-Monde and entering the Great Beyond. UnFunDaMentalism officially defines the Boundary Layer as a Selectively Permeable Magical Membrane.

Censure: Slang term for the Political ReEducation experienced by ForthRight citizens who are obliged to attend a Compulsory Corrective Counseling Clinic. Such attendance is mandatory for those citizens found guilty of displaying deviant, degenerate religious/political/sexual beliefs.

Checkya, the: The secret police of the ForthRight, administered by Vice-Leader Lavrentii Beria. A corrupted remembrance of the Real World word "Cheka."

CheckyaPoints: Border, road and river check-posts operated by the Checkya.

CitiZen: The official term for a citizen of the Quartier Chaud.

Cleansing, the: The purging of Royalists and other Enemies of the People conducted in the ForthRight at the end of the Troubles.

Confinement, the: The mythical event leading to the sealing of the Demi-Monde behind the Boundary Layer. As a consequence of the Fall of the Pre-Folk from grace with ABBA (see also Lilith), ABBA punished the peoples of the Demi-Monde by confining them behind the impenetrable Boundary Layer in order that they should not corrupt the rest of His/Her Creation with their Sin. Only when they have repented all their Sins, have come to Rapture and returned to Purity will ABBA, once again, smile upon them and allow them to be reunited with the rest of the Kosmos.

crypto: Originally coined to describe a Suffer-O-Gette terrorist who had infiltrated the ForthRight, but now commonly used to refer to all spies and fifth-columnists active in the Demi-Monde.

Daemons: Mischievous and occasionally malignant (when in league with Loki) Spirits who manifest themselves in the Demi-Monde. They may be identified by their ability to bleed.

Dark Charismatics: The coterie of men (and only men have been recorded as Dark Charismatics) who exhibit the most extreme and malicious form of MALEvolence. Dark Charismatics, though physically indistinguishable from the host population, are extremely potent, possessing a perverted and grossly amoral nature. As such, Dark Charismatics present a morbid and extreme threat to the instinctive goodness of Demi-Mondians. The only reliable means of identifying Dark Charismatics is by the examination of their auras by Visual Virgins.

Declaration of Ancestry: The proof of racial purity necessary in the ForthRight to claim status as an Aryan. The authenticated and apostilled genealogical chart that confirms an Aryan's ancestry is uncontaminated by UnderMentionables for ten generations.

Dialectic ImMaterialism: A wholly pessimistic philosophy— developed by Karl Marx—that proposes that it is the unending and irresolvable Antagonistic Contradictions between the Sectors that have led to the state of Permanent Revolution in the Demi-Monde. Not only are these Antagonistic Contradictions—themselves a product of differing race, ethnicity, language and religion—incapable of being settled by compromise but they will inevitably lead to the destruction of the Demi-Monde. Everything mankind might do to avert this destruction is immaterial, or in the famous words of Lord Marx himself: "In the end we're all borscht."

ExCreatures: The nanoBites which inhabit the rivers of the Demi-Monde and which are responsible for the consuming of sewage pumped into the rivers, rendering it harmless and capable of being washed through the Boundary Layer. A.k.a. MicroFish, ShitSprats.

Femme: Covenite term for "woman."

ForthRight: The Demi-Mondian state created by the union of the Rookeries and Rodina. A corrupted remembrance of the Real World term "Fourth Reich."

Future History: The mathematically based science that has empiricalized 4Telling.

galvanicEnergy: Electricity. Discovered by the ForthRight scientist Michael Faraday.

Ghetto, the: The Warsaw District of the Rodina Sector, where the Checkya have confined all ForthRight UnderMentionables.

GoldenFolk, the: Certain classes of UnderMentionables—especially the Polish—who, after careful consideration by ForthRight genealogists, are deemed worthy to be classified as Aryan. A corrupted memory of the Real World word "Goralenvolk."

Great Beyond, the: The vast and heavily forested area of the Demi-Monde that lies outside the Boundary Layer.

Hel: The Demi-Mondian term for the underworld. A remembrance of the Norse word "Hel."

HerEticalism: The official religion of the Coven. Developed by the Empress Wu, HerEticalism is a religion based on female supremacy and the belief that if the Demi-Monde is to survive and flourish it must be protected from MisMANagement, which, in turn, will require the subjugation and ultimate elimination of nonFemmes (a.k.a. Men). HerEticalism rejects heterosexual sex, believing it to be an artificial sociopolitical patriarchal construct by which nonFemmes have oppressed Femmes. Instead, HerEticals practice Femme2Femme sex, known as MoreBienism. HerEticalism teaches that the utopian condition of MostBien—the achieving by Femmes of political, religious, economic, intellectual and sexual supremacy in the Demi-Monde—will only be secured when the male of the species has been eliminated from the breeding cycle. More radical HerEticals—notably the Suffer-O-Gettes—are of the opinion that the ultimate expression and apotheosis of MostBien will require the total extermination of all nonFemmes.

HimPerialism: The official religion of NoirVille, based on an unwavering belief in male supremacy and the subjugation of women (or, as they are known in NoirVille, woeMen). HimPerialism teaches that Men have been ordained by ABBA to Lead and to Control the Demi-Monde and that woeMen's role is to be Mute, Invisible, Supine and Subservient (subMISSiveness). Further, HimPerialism states that an individual's Machismo may be enhanced by the exchange of bodily essences, a practice known as Man^{2}naM. HimPerialism has a more aggressive brother religion known as HimPeril, which espouses violence as the only means of securing the triumph of HimPerialism in the Demi-Monde.

HimPeril: The militant/terrorist wing of HimPerialism, HimPeril is dedicated to the use of violence and intimidation to achieve male supremacy and the subjugation of woeMen. The leader of the HimPeril movement is Mohammed Ahmed, a.k.a. the Mahdiman.

Hub, the: The grass and swampland area situated between the urban area of the Demi-Monde and Terror Incognita.

iChing: The Covenite method of divination and 4Telling.

ill-ucination: The illness manifested by those who are unable to distinguish between real and imaginary worlds. nuJu psychiatrists also refer to it as "schizophrenia."

ImPuritanism: The official religion of the Quartier Chaud. ImPuritanism is a staunchly hedonistic philosophy based on the belief that the pursuit of pleasure is the primary duty of mankind and that communion with the Spirits can only be achieved during orgasm. The ultimate aim of all those practicing ImPuritanism is the securing of JuiceSense: the experiencing of the extreme pleasure that comes from an unbridled sexual orgasm. To achieve JuiceSense requires that men and women are spiritually equal and that man's proclivity toward MALEvolence is controlled and muted.

jad: The swing music that came out of the JAD. A corrupted remembrance of the Real World word "jazz."

JAD: nuJu Autonomous District. The area of NoirVille settled by the nuJus and granted independence by His HimPerial Majesty Shaka Zulu.

JuiceSense: The ultimate orgasm. A corrupted remembrance of the Real World word "jouissance."

Kept, the: Those Daemons captured in the Demi-Monde and denied a return to the Spirit World.

LessBien: Derogatory slang term for a woman who finds sexual enjoyment/comfort/satisfaction with another woman. A play on the word "MostBien." A corrupted remembrance of the Real World word "lesbian."

Lilith: The semi-mythical Shade witch—adept in the esoteric knowledge of Seidr magic—who corrupted the Demi-Monde and brought down the Pre-Folk. The Dark Temptress who initiated the Fall.

Lilithian: ForthRight adjective describing the lascivious and sexually corrupting inclination of women.

Living&More: The dietary and lifestyle regime of UnFunDaMentalism designed to detoxify the body and to render it safe from possession by Dabs and Backers, the evil Spirits and sprites that torment Demi-Mondians. Living&More also promotes sexual modesty and restraint (especially in women) in order that women do not fall prey to their dormant Lilithian tendencies. Living&More has declared that sexual relations—except for the purposes of procreation and the birthing of Aryan children—are unnatural and an affront to ABBA. A corrupted remembrance of the Real World word "Lebensreform."

LunarAtion: The green light emitted by Mantle-ite in darkness and, most notably, when it is struck by moonlight.

MALEvolence: The theory developed by the Quartier Chaudian thinker Mary Wollstonecraft that postulates that war is caused by men but suffered by women. In her Theory of MALEvolence, Wollstonecraft identified that men, by their natural and undeniable inclination to obey orders given to them by superiors—no matter how nonsensical or barbaric such orders are—are susceptible to disproportionate influence by their more unbalanced peers and hence are inevitably and inexorably drawn toward violence as a solution to disputes. The muting of MALEvolence is the ambition that led to the creation of ImPuritanism. Consideration of MALEvolence was also instrumental in prompting Professeur Michel de Nostredame to identify the malignant Dark Charismatics lurking within the Quartier Chaudian population. A corrupted remembrance of the Real World word "malevolence."

Man²naM: The practice of NoirVillian men exchanging bodily essences in order to enhance their Machismo.

Mantle, the: The impenetrable crust of the Demi-Monde situated below the topsoil.

Mantle-ite: The indestructible and invulnerable material used by the Pre-Folk to construct sewers, water pipes, Blood Banks and the Mantle.

Medi, the: The area of the Quartier Chaud comprising the Districts of Paris, Rome and Barcelona.

mixling: The slang name for mixed-race Demi-Mondians. A corrupted remembrance of the Real World word "Mischling."

MoreBien: The Covenite name for Femme/Femme lovemaking.

MostBien: The more extreme HerEtical belief that the utopian state of MostBien—the achieving by Femmes of political, religious, economic, intellectual and sexual supremacy in the Demi-Monde—will only be secured when the male of the species has been removed from the breeding cycle, or simply removed, full stop.

nanoBites: The submicroscopic creatures that inhabit the soil layer of the Demi-Monde. In the Hub they occupy all but the top six inches of soil, in the Urban Band all but the top five feet of soil and in the Great Beyond all but the top twenty feet of soil. They consume everything—except Mantleite—they come into contact with, converting it to soil. A.k.a. Nibblers.

NoirVile: The derogatory slang term for NoirVille.

NoN: The official term in the Coven for a eunuch, now adopted Demi-Monde-wide. A corruption/contraction of the phrase "he ain't got none."

nonFemme: Covenite term for "man."

nonNix: The ForthRight term for an individual who has—because of racial, social, political or sexual deviancy—relinquished all rights and protection they enjoyed as a citizen of the ForthRight.

nuCommandments, the: The nine precepts of UnFunDaMentalism.

nuJuism: The religion of the nuJu diaspora, this is an unrelentingly pessimistic religion that teaches that suffering and hardship are life-affirming and are endured to prepare the followers for the coming of the Messiah who will lead them through Tribulation to the Promised Land.

Ordo Templi Aryanis: The most zealous and uncompromising of all UnFunDaMentalist sects. Their belief is that the Anglo-Slavic people will not reclaim its oneness with the Spirits—lost after the Fall—until it is racially cleansed and all contaminating racial elements (the Under-Mentionables) have been eradicated. The OTA's military wing, the SS–Ordo Templi Aryanis, is responsible for the protection of the head of the Church of the Doctrine of UnFunDaMentalism, His Holiness Comrade Aleister Crowley.

pawnography: A term coined by HerEticals to disparage the ImPure Material produced and distributed in the Quartier Chaud. HerEticals deem all such material to be a violation of Femme rights as it degrades Femmes and encourages violence against them. The HerEtical term for ImPure Material is pawnography as it is said to lead to Femmes selling (or pawning) their bodies to satisfy the crazed lusts of nonFemmes. Such pawnography encourages a belief in nonFemme superiority as it celebrates the power of the penis. A corrupted remembrance of the Real World word "pornography."

Portals: Places where Daemons can move into and out of the Demi-Monde.

Preferred Male: A Coven term for the nonFemme a Femme allows to accompany her and to provide her with physical services and comforts.

Pre-Folk: The semi-mythical race of godlings who ruled over the Demi-Monde before the Confinement and who were brought low by the sexual connivings of the Seidr-witch Lilith. The demise of the Pre-Folk is known in Demi-Mondian mythology as "the Fall." UnFunDaMentalism teaches that the Pre-Folk were the purest expression of the Aryan race.

PreScience: A Venetian school of philosophy dedicated to the study of (and the making of) prophecies and 4Tellings, especially in the areas of economics and finance. The greatest of all PreScientists are Professeur Michel de Nostredame and Docteur Nikolai Dmitriyevich Kondratieff of the Future History Institute, Venice. A corrupted remembrance of the Real World word "prescience."

PsyChick: A female assistant to a medium or other psychic.

RaTionalism: An avowedly and uncompromisingly atheistic creed developed by the renegade Rodina thinker and ardent Royalist Karl Marx, which strives by a process of Dialectic ImMaterialism to secure logical explanations regarding the Three Great Dilemmas. RaTionalism denies all supernatural interpretations with respect to the Three Great Dilemmas and does not acknowledge any input that cannot be verified by the five senses.

Ratties: The slang name for RaTionalists.

reBop: The argot prevalent within NoirVille, most widely used by enthusiasts of jad music.

Red Gold: A slang name for blood.

RightNix: The youth wing of the ForthRight.

Royalism: The belief that leaders of Sectors are chosen/anointed by ABBA through the principle of the Divine Right of Kings.

Seidr: The ancient magic of the Vanir and of Lilith.

Shades: The slang term for NoirVillians.

SisterHood: The women who dedicate themselves body and soul to the creed of UnFunDaMentalism.

Solidified Astral Ether: The substance which makes up the soft tissue of all Demi-Mondians.

Solution: A cocktail of vodka and soda with one or more shots of blood. Usually available in 5 percent, 10 percent and 20 percent strengths of blood.

SS: Soldiers of Spiritualism, the military wing of the Church of the Doctrine of UnFunDaMentalism.

steamers: Steam-powered vehicles popular in the Demi-Monde.

Suffer-O-Gettism: A contraction of Make-Men-Suffer-O-Gettism. The militant/terrorist wing of the HerEticalism movement, Suffer-O-Gettism is dedicated to the use of violence and intimidation to achieve Femme supremacy and the subjugation/extermination of nonFemmes and the ushering in of MostBien. The leader of the Suffer-O-Gette movement is Jeanne Dark.

Terror Incognita: The area extending in a radius of four miles around Mare Incognitum and bounded by the Wheel River. A totally unexplored region of the Demi-Monde. No explorer venturing into Terror Incognita has ever returned. A corrupted remembrance of the Real World phrase "terra incognita."

ThawsDay: The 60th day of Spring when the nanoBites wake from their

Winter hibernation. After ThawsDay only the most desperate or the most stupid of Demi-Mondians venture into the Hub.

Three Great Dilemmas, the: The philosophical and religious arguments relating to the Creation, the Confinement and the Purpose of the Demi-Monde.

Troubles, the: The two-year-long civil war in Rodina and the Rookeries during which Reinhard Heydrich (aided and abetted by Lavrentii Beria) overthrew Henry Tudor and Ivan Grozny. Heydrich subsequently merged the two Sectors as the ForthRight, uniting them under the single religion of UnFunDaMentalism.

UnderMentionables: A catchall term for all those considered by UnFunDaMentalism to be racially inferior and hence subhuman (including, inter alia, nuJus, Poles, Shades, HerEticals, Suffer-O-Gettes, HimPerialists, RaTionalists, those of a sexually deviant disposition and those deemed to be genetically flawed). A corrupted remembrance of the Real World word "Untermensch."

UnFunDaMentalism: UnFunDaMentalism is an array of political, racial, metaPhysical, sexual and social ideas and philosophies relating to the purification of the Demi-Mondian race, the triumph of the Aryan people and the rehabilitation of the semi-mythological Pre-Folk. Adopted as the state religion of the ForthRight, the ultimate aim of UnFunDaMentalism is, by a process of selective breeding and measured culling, to eliminate the contamination of the UnderMentionable races from the Demi-Monde's Aryan stock (Aryans are generally considered to be the Anglo-Slavic races) and by doing so to return the Aryan people to the racial perfection they possessed before their ancestors—the Pre-Folk—fell from ABBA's Grace. UnFunDaMentalism preaches that its followers espouse Living&More, or life reform, which involves clean living, vegetarianism and homeopathy and an abstention from alcohol, excessive blood consumption, tobacco and recreational sex.

UnFunnies: The slang name for UnFunDaMentalists.

Valknut: The emblem of the ForthRight, comprising three interlocking triangles.

Vanir: The WhoDoo name for the Pre-Folk.

WhoDlum: The terrorist wing of the WhoDoo sect dedicated to the use of violence and intimidation to achieve the chaos and anarchy necessary for the WhoDoo devils—the *baka*—to thrive in the Demi-Monde.

WhoDoo: The cult religion of NoirVille based on a distorted remembrance of Seidr.

woeMen: The NoirVillian term for women.

zadnik: Demi-Mondian slang for a male homosexual and, more generally, for a NoirVillian male. The word is derived from the Russian "zad," meaning "arse."

COMING SOON
the Second Book in the
Demi-Monde Saga

The
Shadow Wars

The second chapter in Rod Rees's gripping,
brilliantly imagined series about a virtual
world dominated by history's most
terrifying villains and the young woman
lured inside, who must risk everything if
she is to save the world . . . and herself.

"Explosively creative barely defines Rod Rees's
The Demi-Monde. It blew me away as the novel
skated on the razor's edge between where we
are today and where we're headed tomorrow. . . ."

—James Rollins, *New York Times*
bestselling author of *The Devil Colony*

ISBN: 978-0-06-207037-1

wm
WILLIAM MORROW
An Imprint of HarperCollinsPublishers

**Available wherever books are sold,
or call 1-800-331-3761 to order.**